GEN

EDEN VOL. 1

© 2015 GEN MANGA ENTERTAINMENT, INC. ALL RIGHTS RESERVED.

EDEN™, GEN™ & GEN MANGA™ ARE TRADEMARKS OF GEN MANGA ENTERTAINMENT, INC./

NO PART OF THIS BOOK MAY BE REPRODUCED OR TRANSMITTED IN ANY FORM OR BY ANY MEANS, ELECTRONIC OR MECHANICAL, INCLUDING PHOTOCOPYING, RECORDING, OR BY ANY INFORMATION STORAGE AND RETRIEVAL SYSTEM, WITHOUT THE WRITTEN PERMISSION OF THE PUBLISHER

FOR INFORMATION, CONTACT GEN MANGA ENTERTAINMENT, INC.

COVER ART............................BASH
COVER DESIGN...............RICHARD RODRIGUEZ
ANOMAL..............................BASH

PUBLISHED BY
GEN MANGA ENTERTAINMENT, INC.
250 PARK AVENUE, SUITE 7002
NEW YORK, NY 10117 USA
WWW.GENMANGA.COM

PRINTED IN CANADA

EVERY EFFORT HAS BEEN MADE TO ACCURATELY PRESENT THE INFORMATION PRESENTED HEREIN. THE PUBLISHER AND AUTHORS REGRET ANY UNINTENTIONAL INACCURACIES OR OMISSIONS, AND DO NOT ASSUME RESPONSIBILITY FOR THE ACCURACY OF THE INFORMATION IN THIS BOOK. NEITHER THE PUBLISHER NOR THE ARTISTS AND AUTHOR OF THE INFORMATION PRESENTED HEREIN SHALL BE LIABLE FOR ANY LOSS OF PROFIT OR ANY OTHER COMMERCIAL DAMAGES, INCLUDING BUT NOT LIMITED TO SPECIAL, INCIDENTAL, CONSEQUENTIAL, OR OTHER DAMAGES. CORRECTIONS TO THIS WORK SHOULD BE FORWARDED TO THE PUBLISHER FOR CONSIDERATION UPON THE NEXT PRINTING.

GEN
MANGA

EDEN

Vol. 1

Bash

I WANT YOU TO SEVER THESE CHAINS.

SOMEDAY,

EVEN IF
I FORGET
EVERYTHING,
I WANT
YOU TO
REMEMBER.

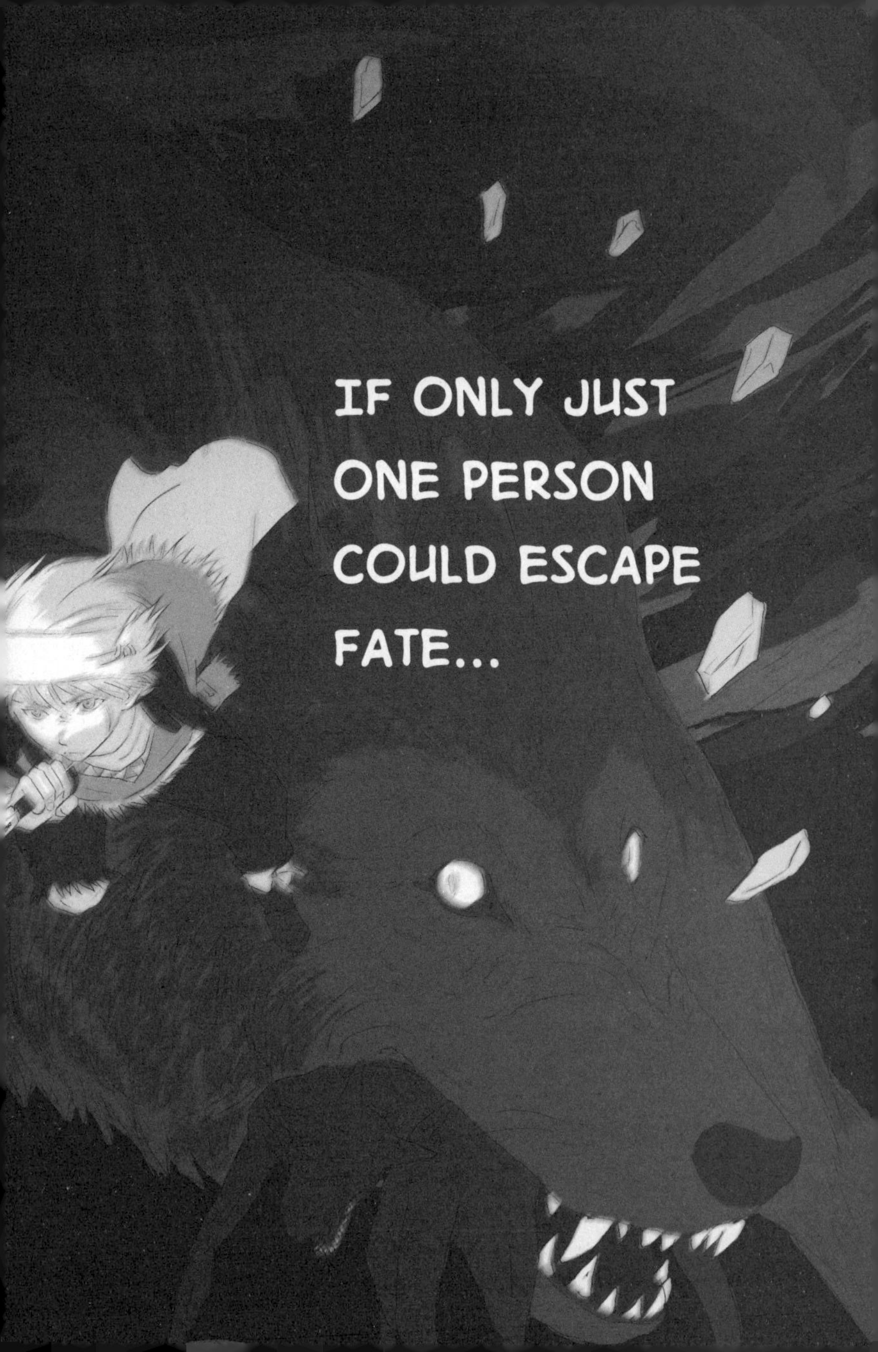
IF ONLY JUST ONE PERSON COULD ESCAPE FATE...

THEN THAT WOULD
BE ENOUGH.

**STAGE 1
POISON OF AN ANGEL**

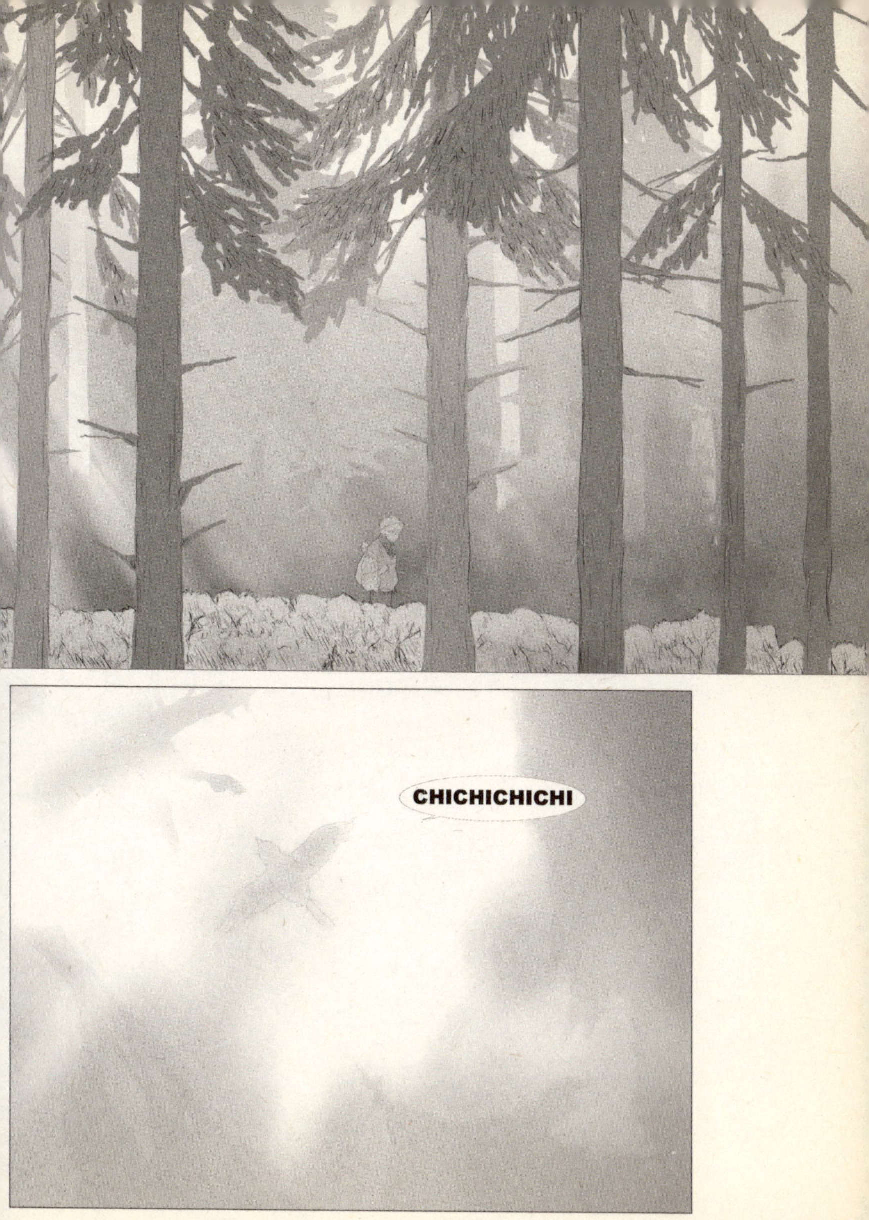
CHICHICHICHI

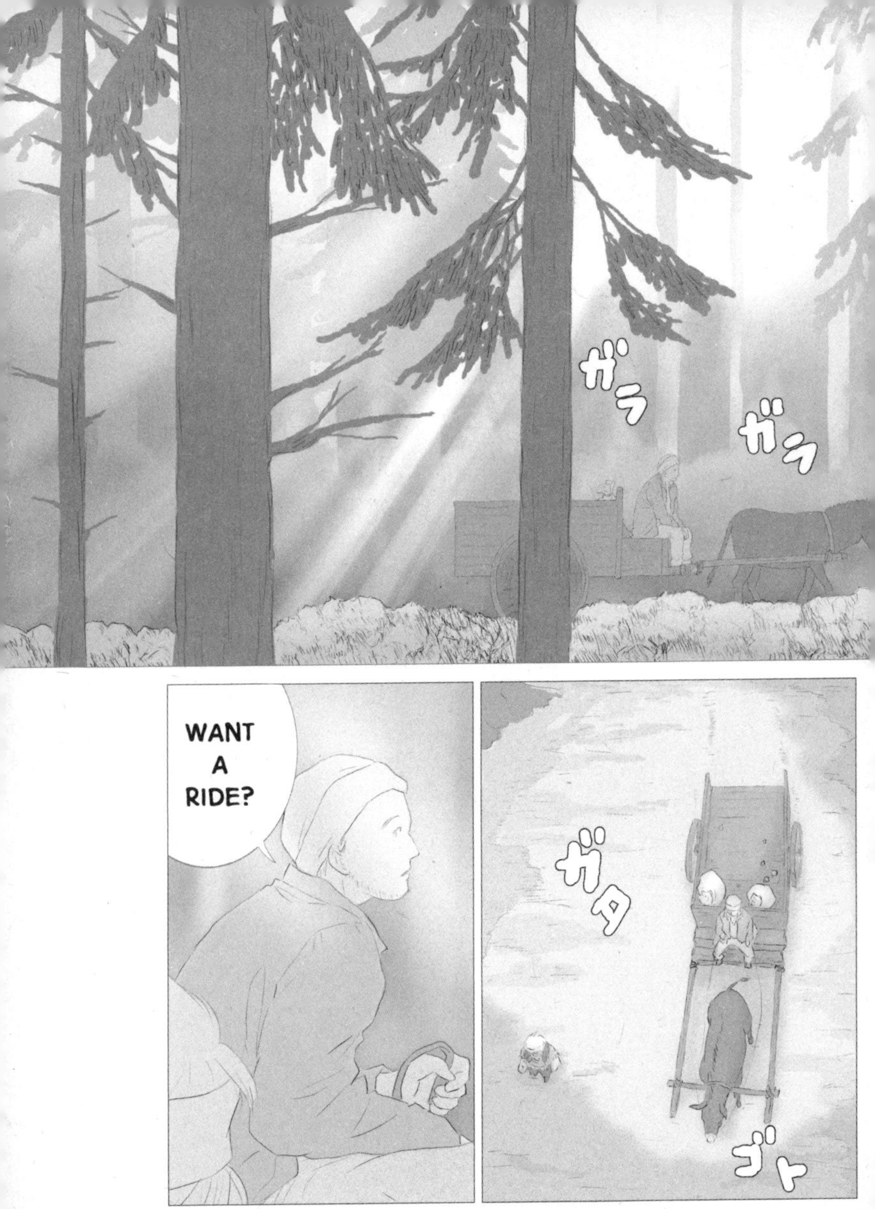
ガラ
ガラ
ガタ
ゴト
WANT A RIDE?

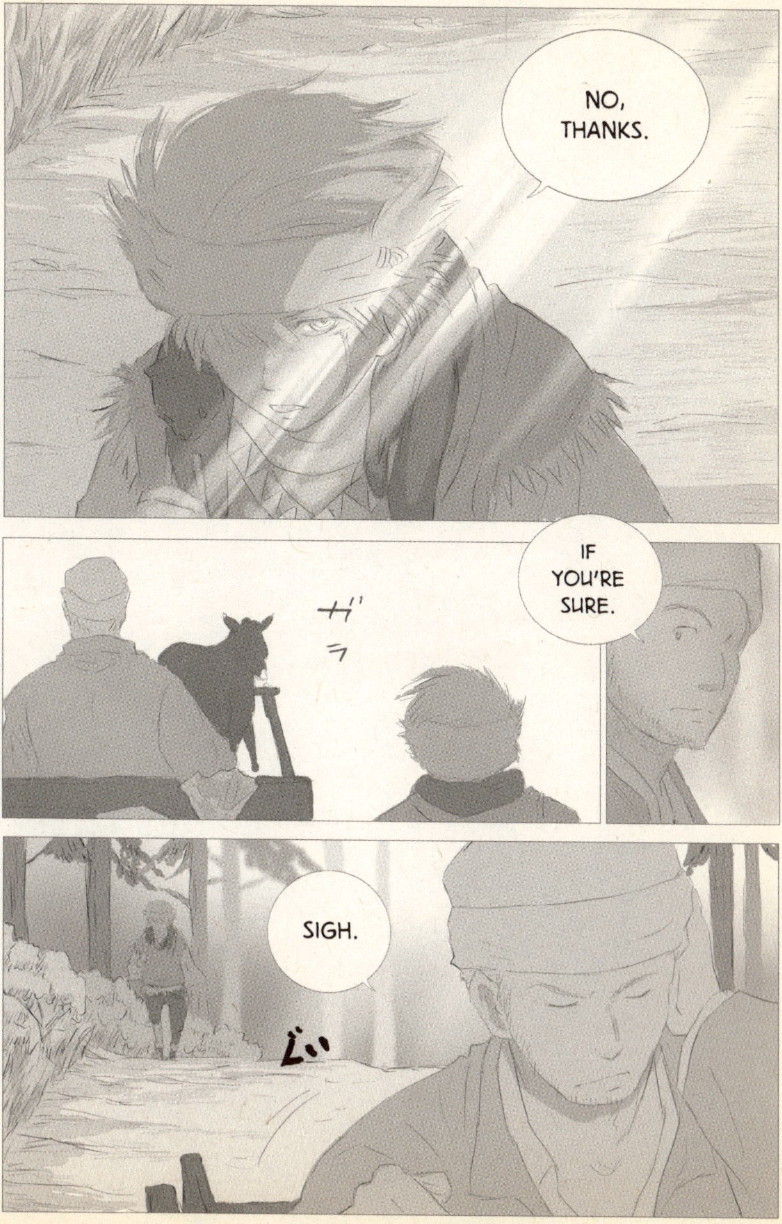
NO, THANKS.
IF YOU'RE SURE.
ガラ
SIGH.
じい

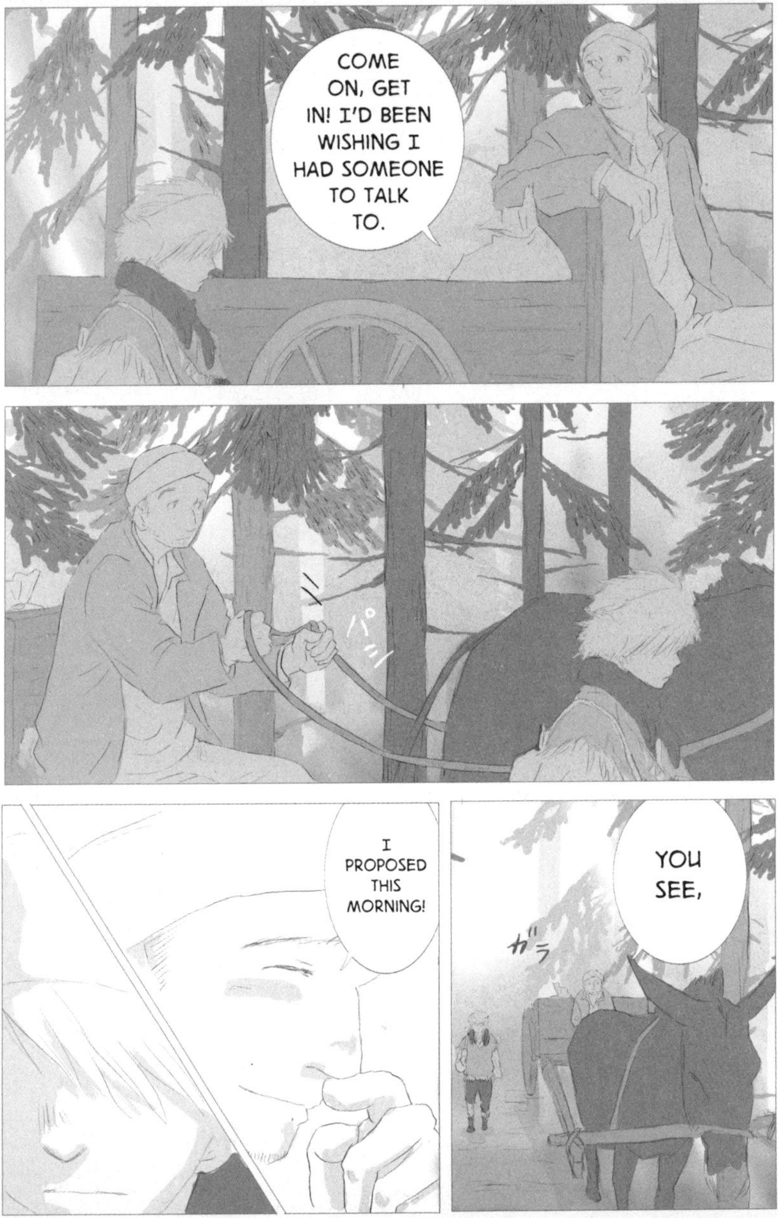
COME ON, GET IN! I'D BEEN WISHING I HAD SOMEONE TO TALK TO.
YOU SEE,
ガラ
I PROPOSED THIS MORNING!

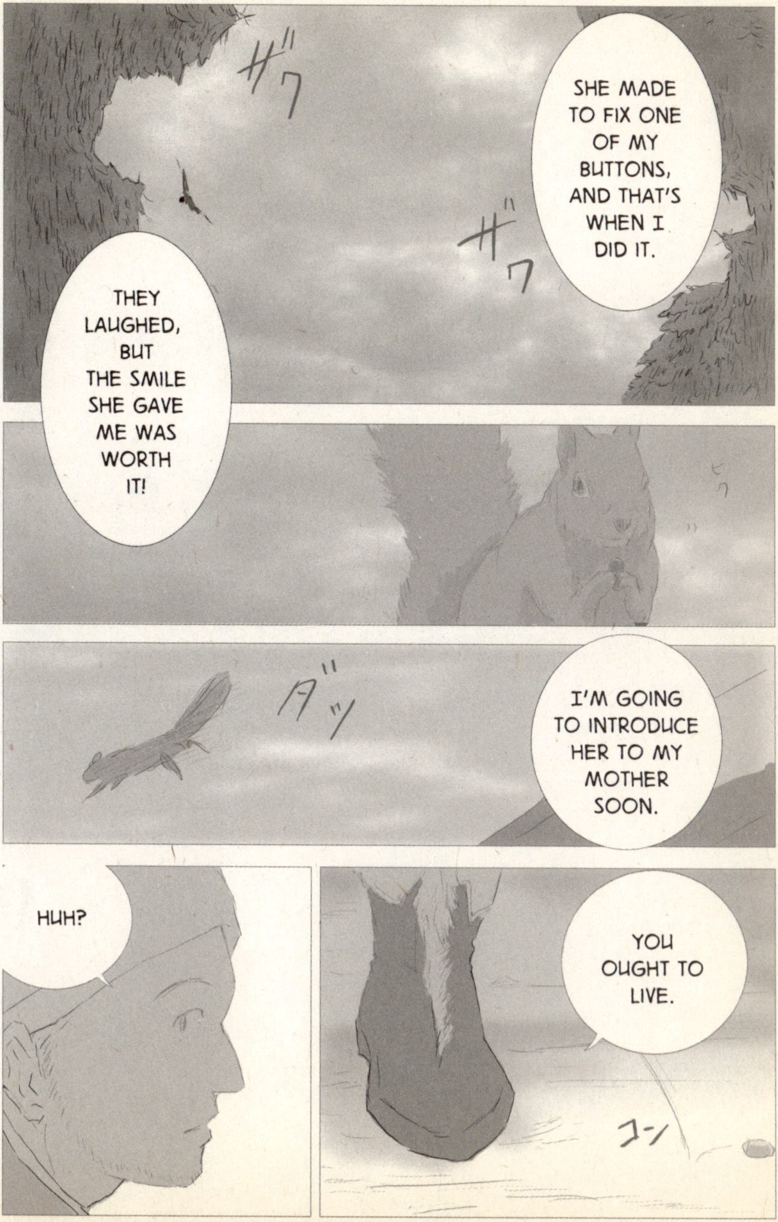
SHE MADE TO FIX ONE OF MY BUTTONS, AND THAT'S WHEN I DID IT.
ザワ
ザワ
THEY LAUGHED, BUT THE SMILE SHE GAVE ME WAS WORTH IT!
I'M GOING TO INTRODUCE HER TO MY MOTHER SOON.
ダッ
YOU OUGHT TO LIVE.
コン
HUH?

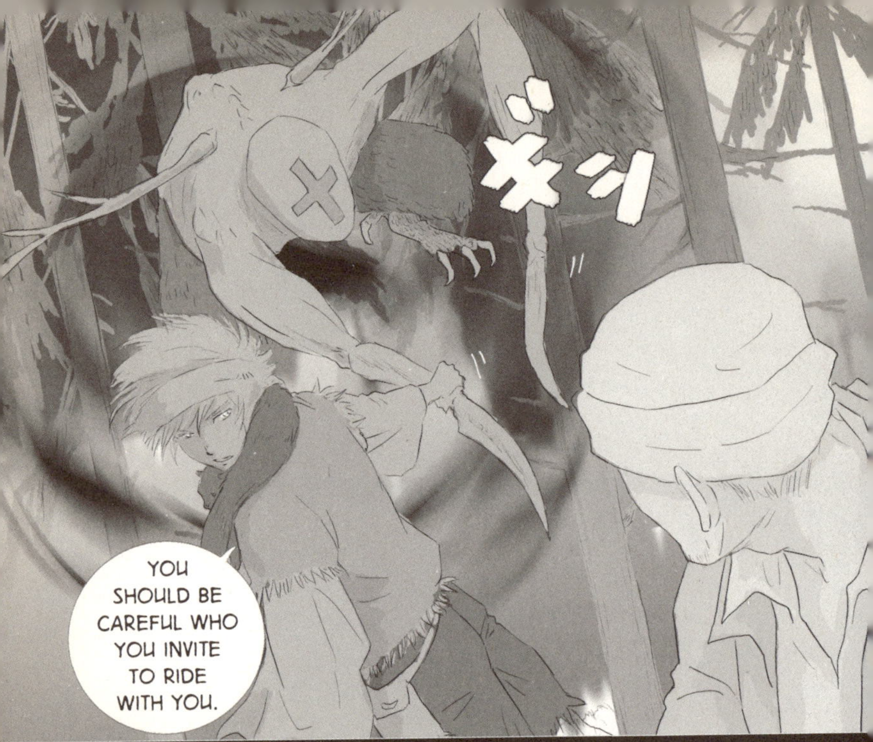
ズッ
YOU SHOULD BE CAREFUL WHO YOU INVITE TO RIDE WITH YOU.
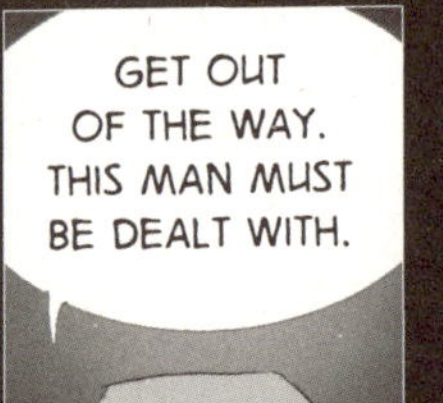
GET OUT OF THE WAY. THIS MAN MUST BE DEALT WITH.
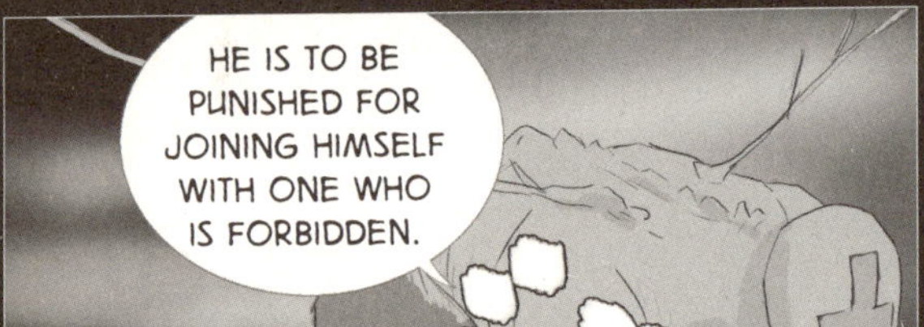
HE IS TO BE PUNISHED FOR JOINING HIMSELF WITH ONE WHO IS FORBIDDEN.
バキッ

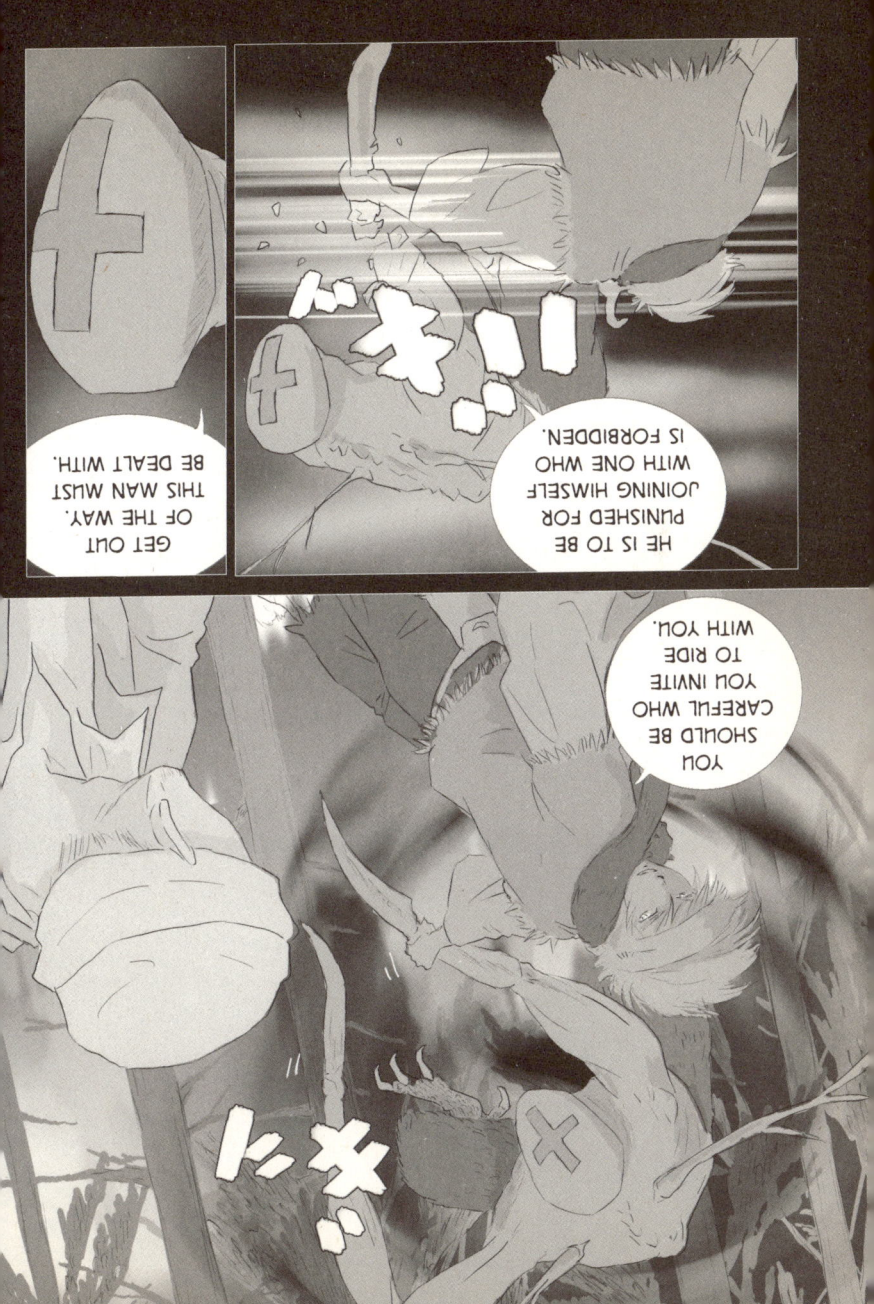

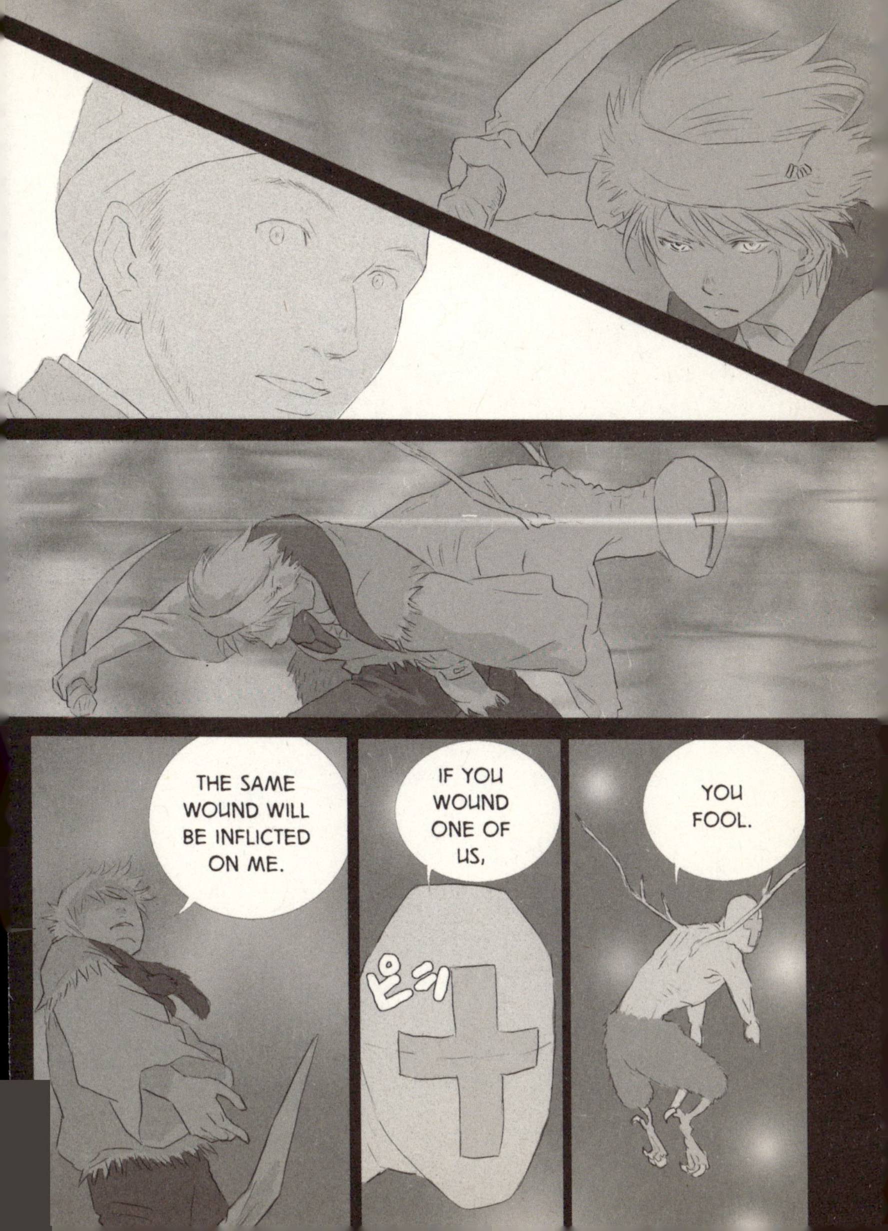
YOU FOOL.
IF YOU WOUND ONE OF US,
THE SAME WOUND WILL BE INFLICTED ON ME.

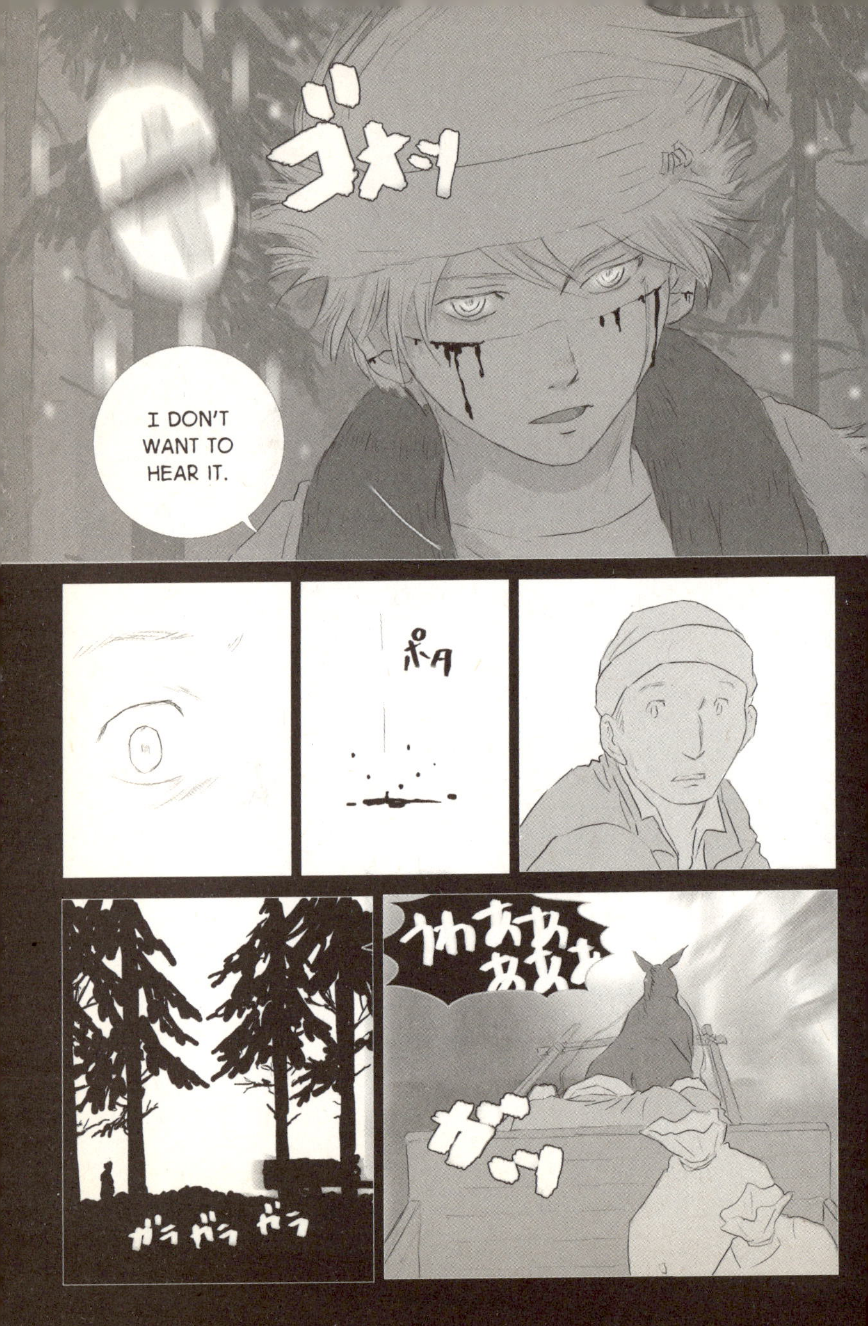
ゴメーッ
I DON'T WANT TO HEAR IT.
ポタ
うわあああああ
ガッ
ガラガラガラ

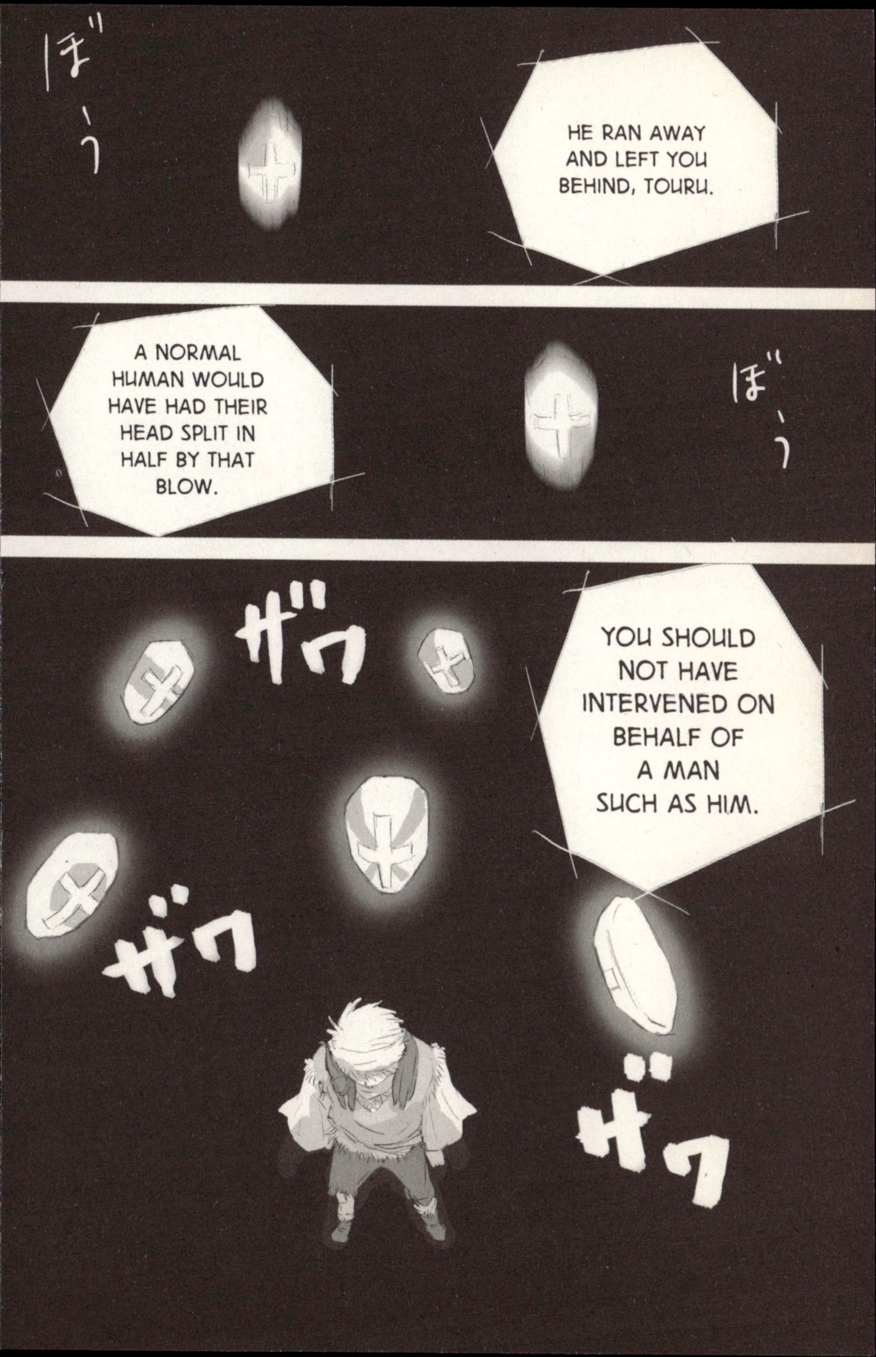
HE RAN AWAY AND LEFT YOU BEHIND, TOURU.
ぼ〜っ
ぼ〜っ
A NORMAL HUMAN WOULD HAVE HAD THEIR HEAD SPLIT IN HALF BY THAT BLOW.
YOU SHOULD NOT HAVE INTERVENED ON BEHALF OF A MAN SUCH AS HIM.
ザワ
ザワ
ザワ

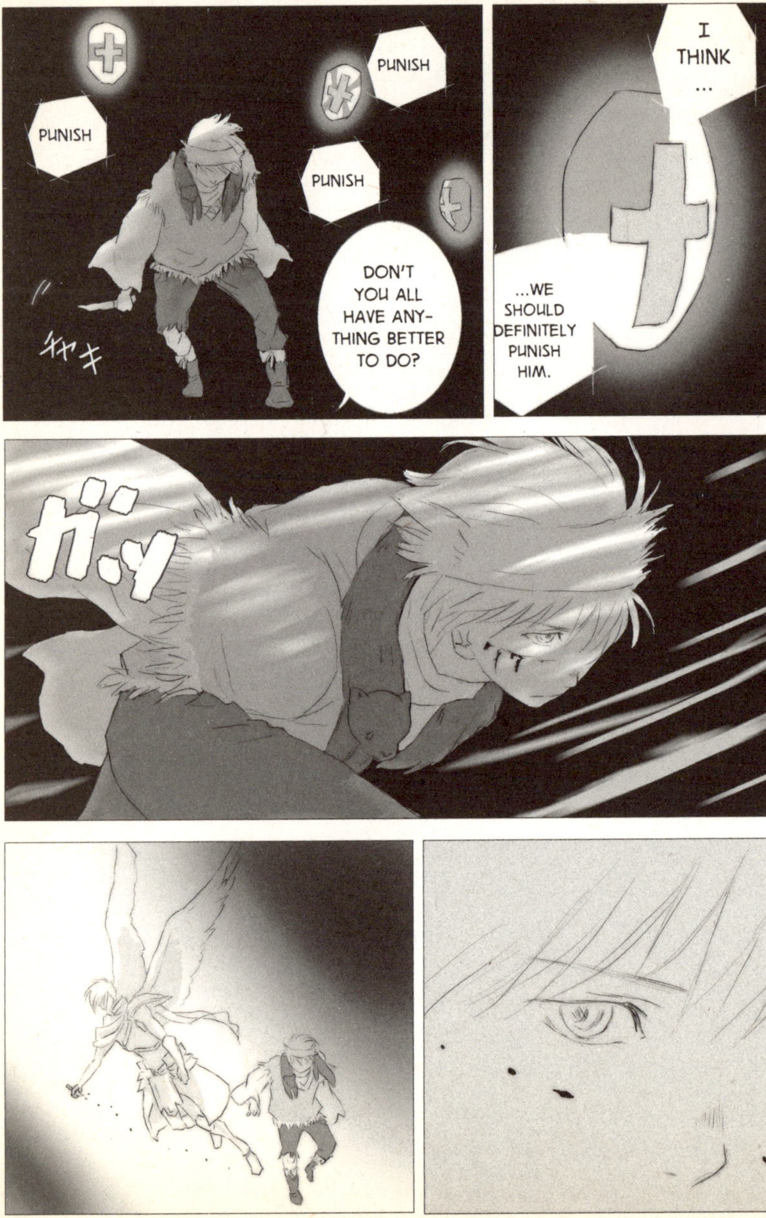
I THINK ...
...WE SHOULD DEFINITELY PUNISH HIM.
PUNISH
PUNISH
PUNISH
DON'T YOU ALL HAVE ANY-THING BETTER TO DO?
チャキ
ガッ

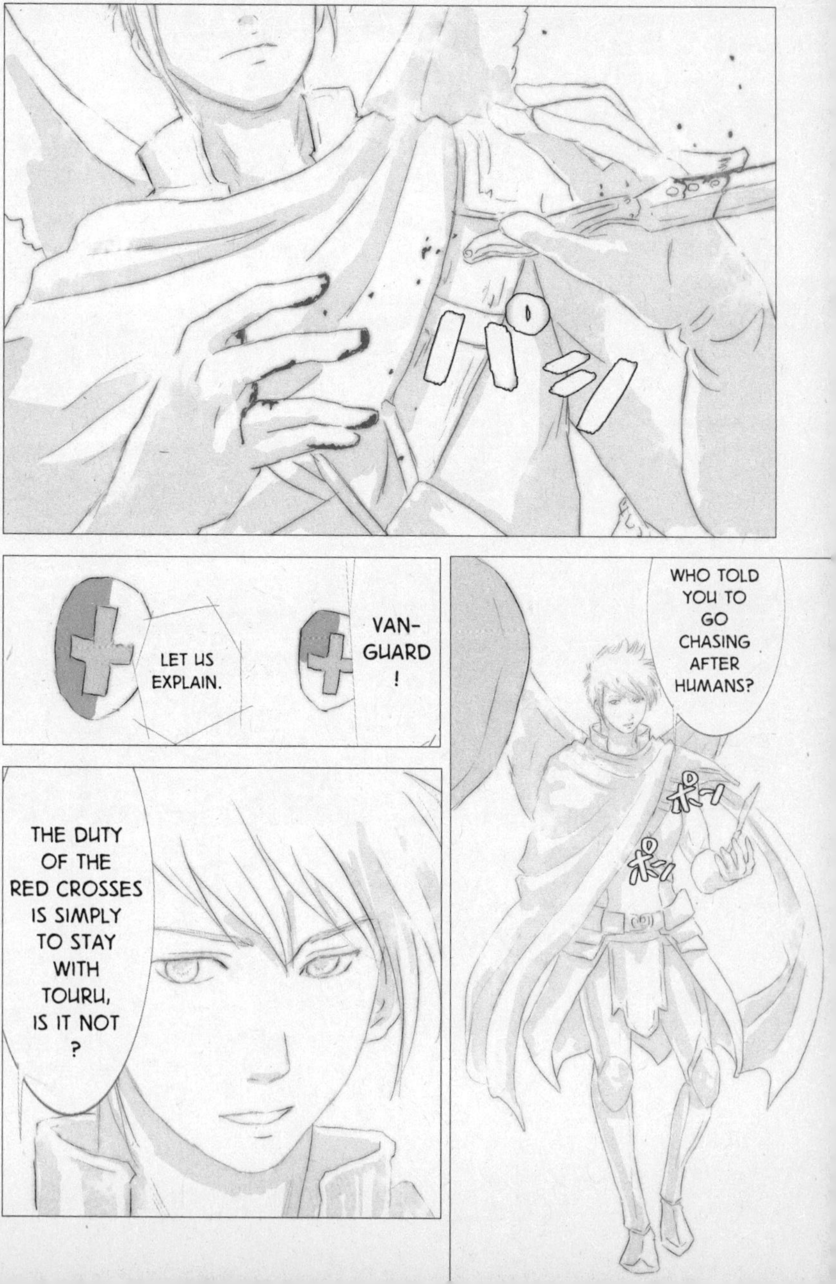
WHO TOLD YOU TO GO CHASING AFTER HUMANS?
VAN-GUARD !
LET US EXPLAIN.
THE DUTY OF THE RED CROSSES IS SIMPLY TO STAY WITH TOURU, IS IT NOT ?

パシ
THIS KNIFE...
...SHOULD PROVE A MUCH MORE RELIABLE SERVANT.
ドン
!!
HOW DO YOU LIKE IT, TOURU?
ボA
ボA
グラ
ドン

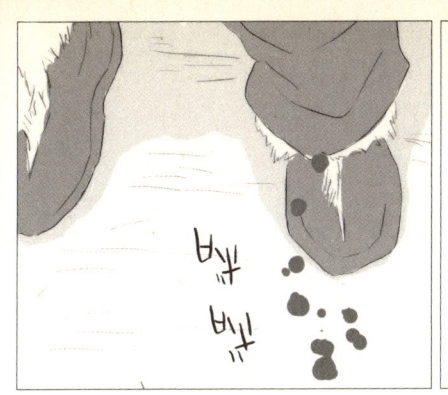

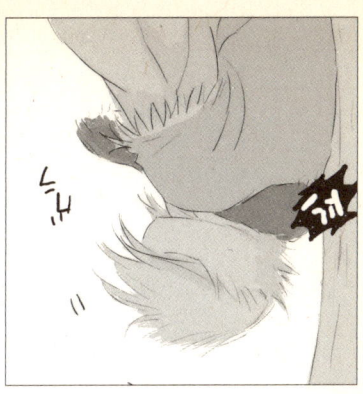

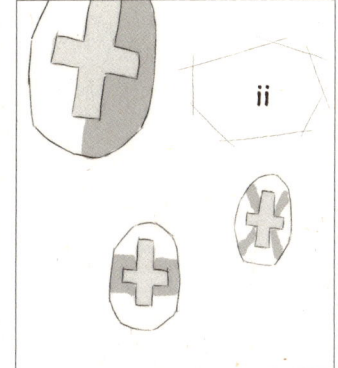

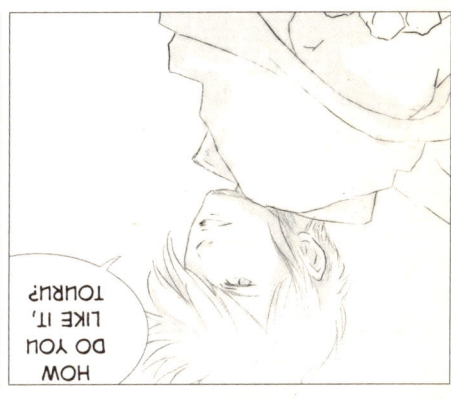

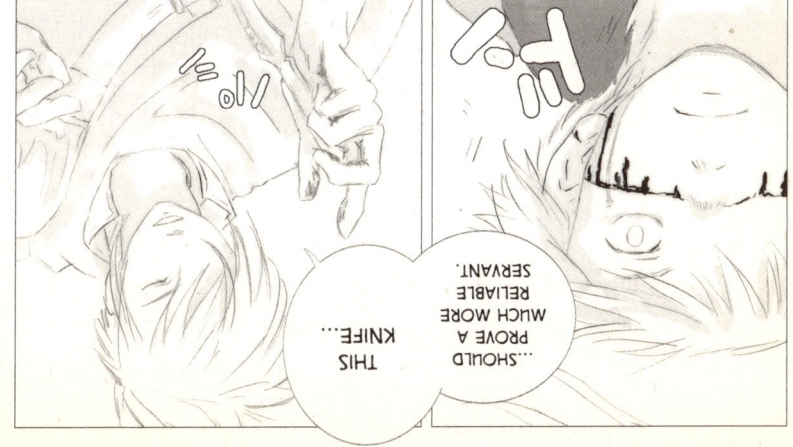

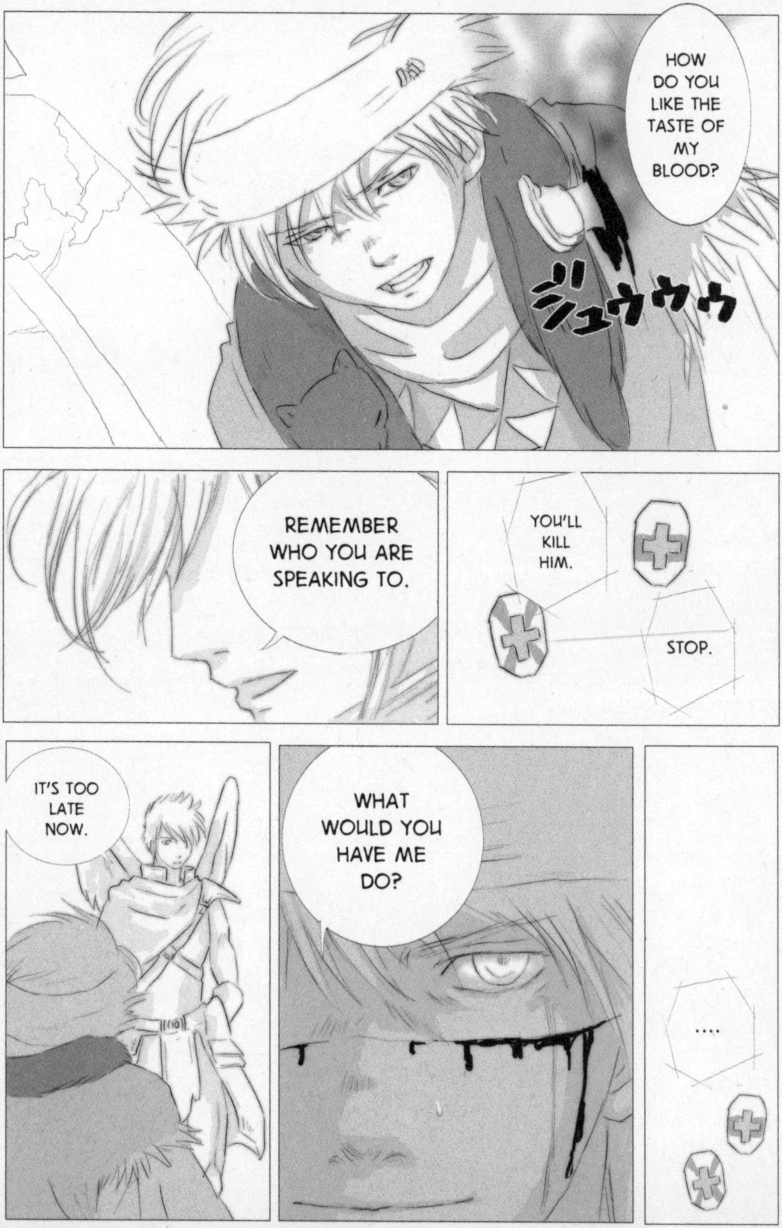
HOW DO YOU LIKE THE TASTE OF MY BLOOD?
ジュウウウ
YOU'LL KILL HIM.
STOP.
REMEMBER WHO YOU ARE SPEAKING TO.
....
WHAT WOULD YOU HAVE ME DO?
IT'S TOO LATE NOW.

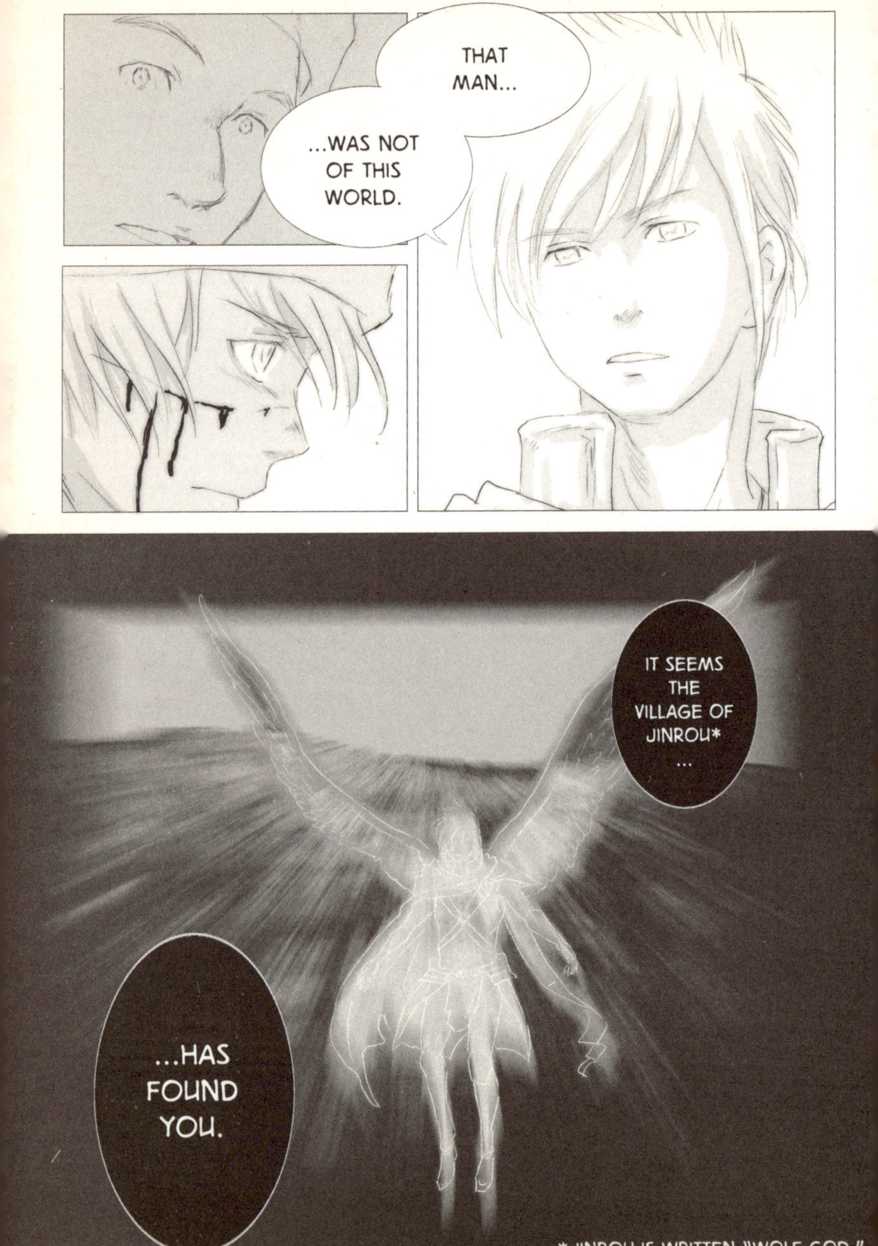
THAT MAN...
...WAS NOT OF THIS WORLD.
IT SEEMS THE VILLAGE OF JINROU* ...
...HAS FOUND YOU.

*JINROU IS WRITTEN "WOLF GOD."

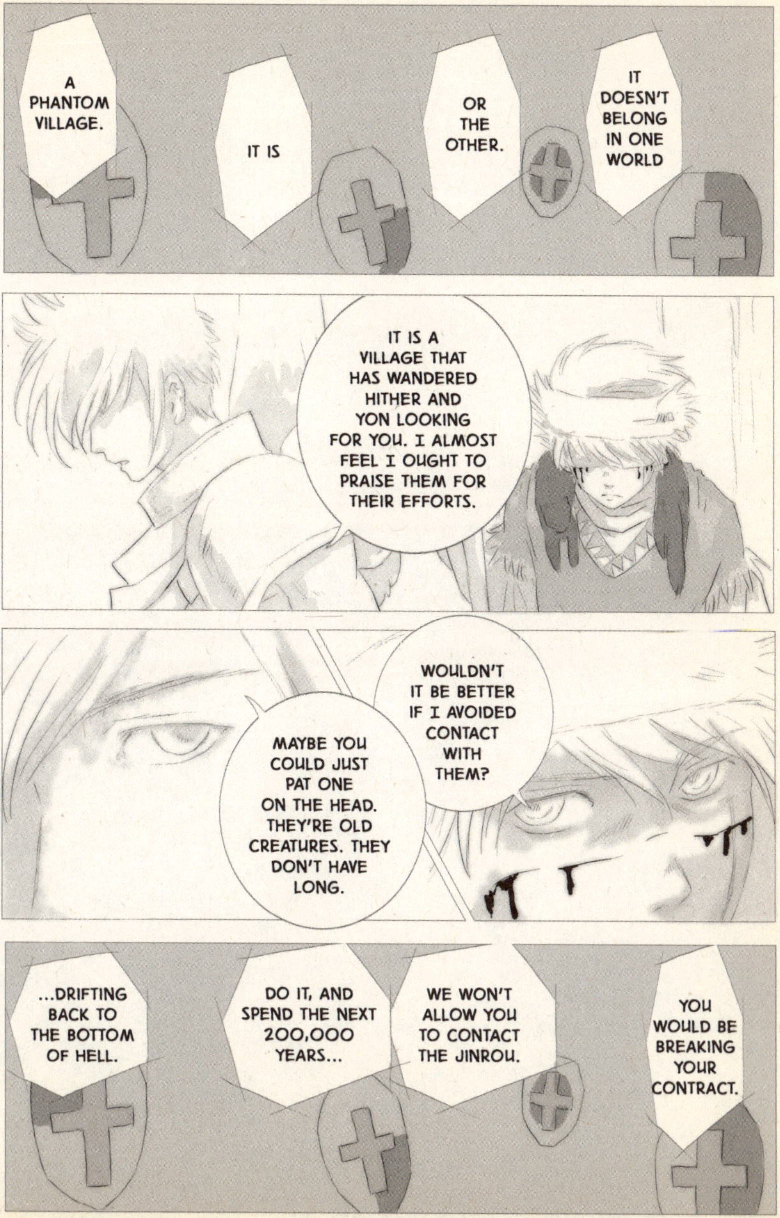
IT DOESN'T BELONG IN ONE WORLD
OR THE OTHER.
IT IS
A PHANTOM VILLAGE.
IT IS A VILLAGE THAT HAS WANDERED HITHER AND YON LOOKING FOR YOU. I ALMOST FEEL I OUGHT TO PRAISE THEM FOR THEIR EFFORTS.
WOULDN'T IT BE BETTER IF I AVOIDED CONTACT WITH THEM?
MAYBE YOU COULD JUST PAT ONE ON THE HEAD. THEY'RE OLD CREATURES. THEY DON'T HAVE LONG.
YOU WOULD BE BREAKING YOUR CONTRACT.
WE WON'T ALLOW YOU TO CONTACT THE JINROU.
DO IT, AND SPEND THE NEXT 200,000 YEARS...
...DRIFTING BACK TO THE BOTTOM OF HELL.

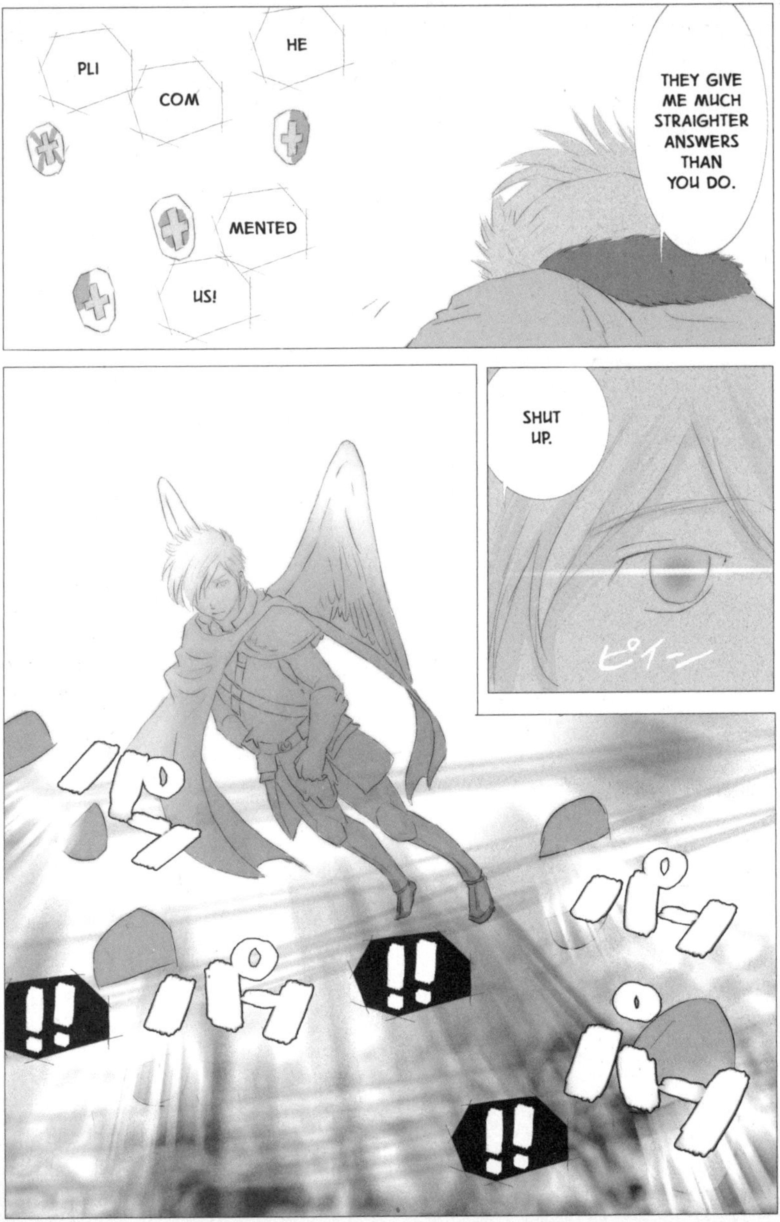
THEY GIVE ME MUCH STRAIGHTER ANSWERS THAN YOU DO.
HE
COM
PLI
MENTED
US!
SHUT UP.
ピイーン
パーン!!
パーン!!
パーン!!

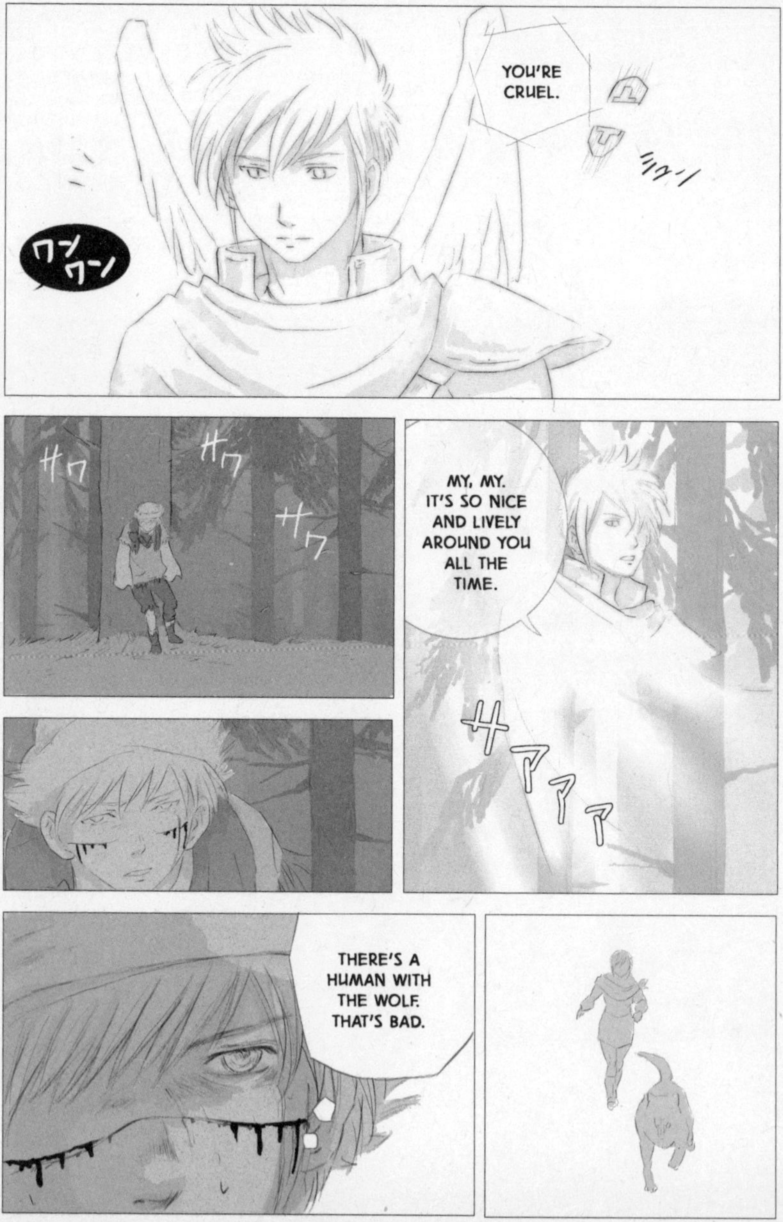
YOU'RE CRUEL.
シクン
ワンワン
MY, MY. IT'S SO NICE AND LIVELY AROUND YOU ALL THE TIME.
サアァァ
サワ
サワ
サワ
THERE'S A HUMAN WITH THE WOLF. THAT'S BAD.

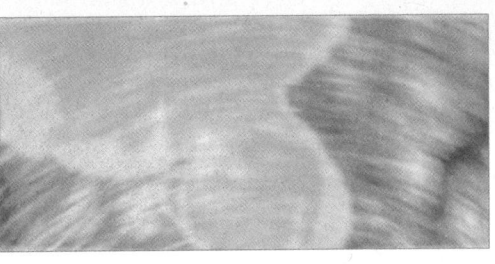
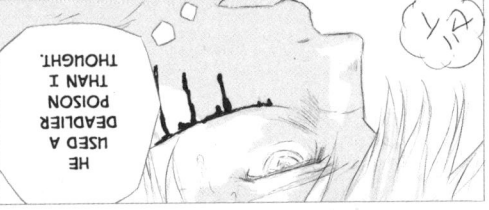

HE USED A DEADLIER POISON THAN I THOUGHT.

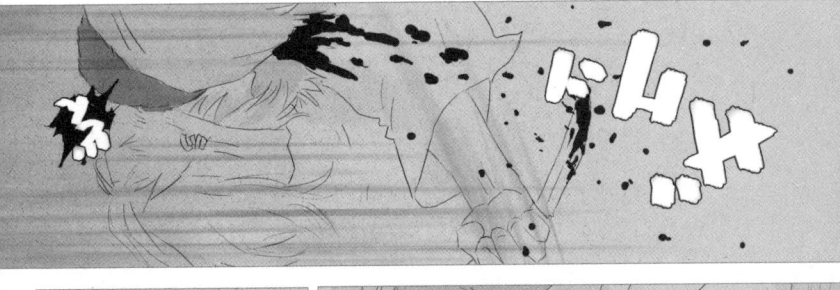
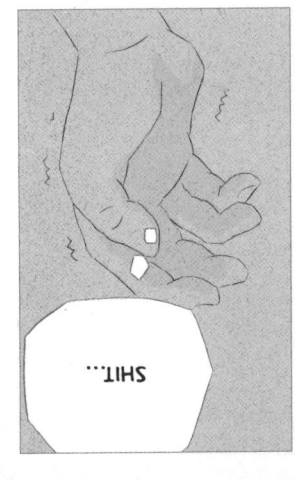

...SHIT.

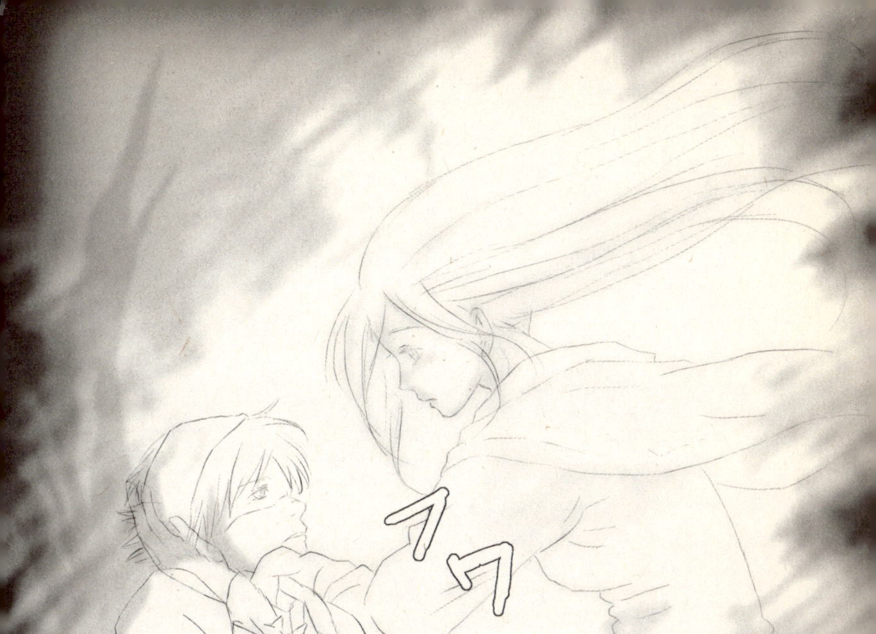
フワ

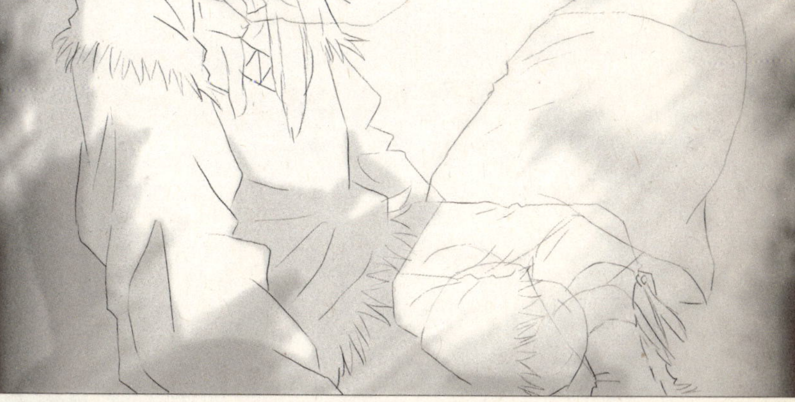
I CAN'T HEAR ANYTHING. I SMELL FLOWERS, AND I SEE... A WOMAN?

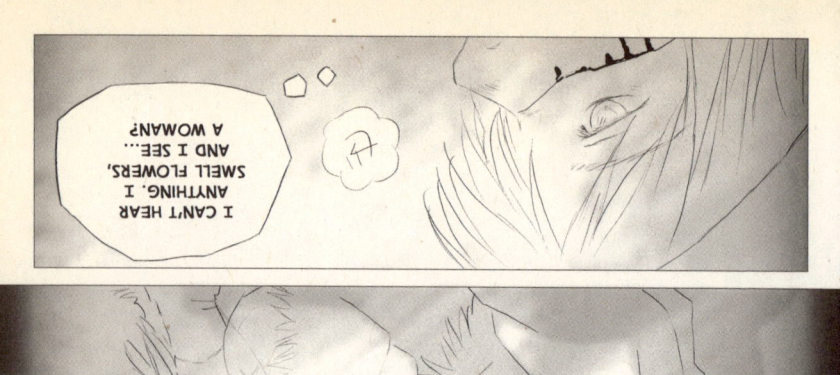

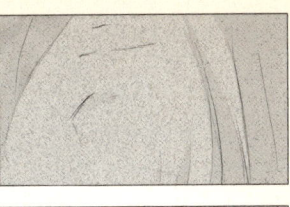

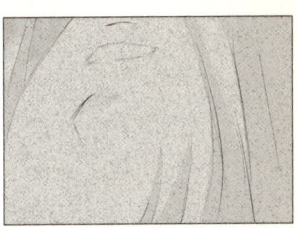

TOURU.
サワ
サワ
WHINE ?
I'M FINE.
WE'VE GOT TO HELP HIM.
YOU NEED TO GET AWAY FROM HERE.

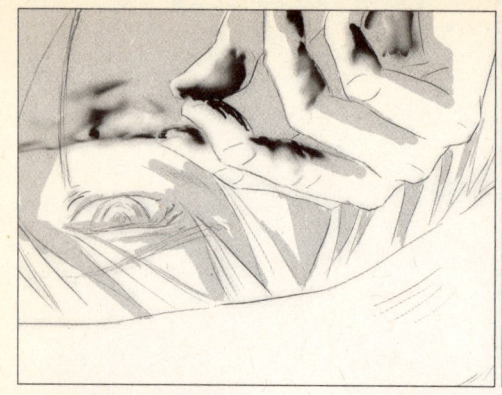

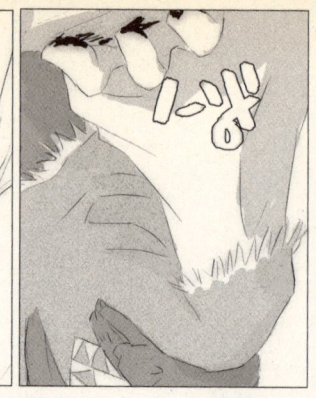

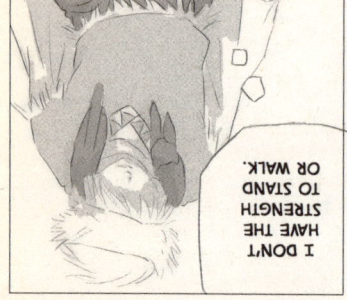

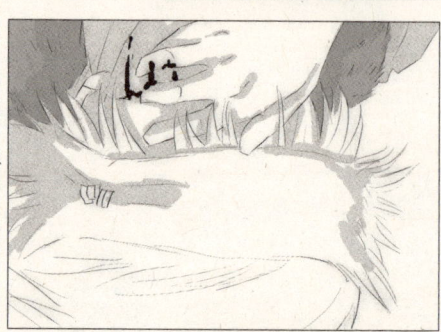

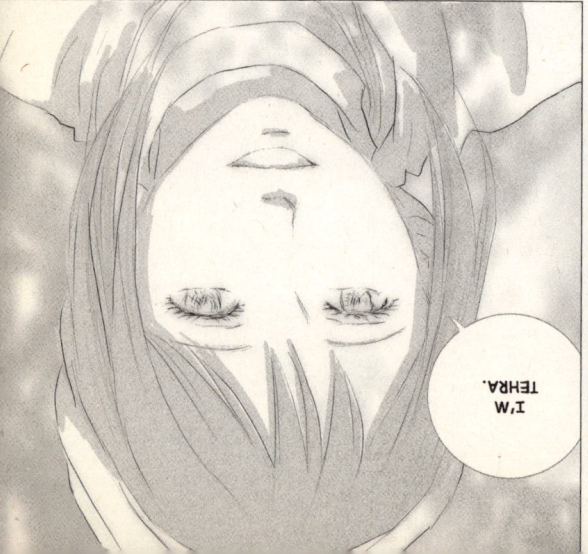

I'M TEHRA.
RELAX. I'M JUST PACKING HEALING HERBS AROUND THE WOUND.
I DON'T HAVE THE STRENGTH TO STAND OR WALK.
ぱーー

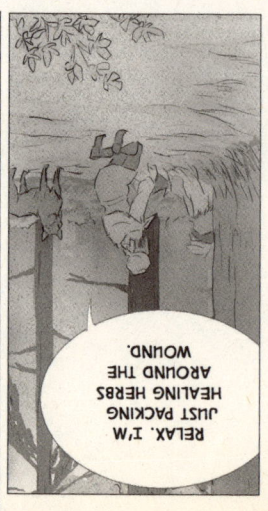

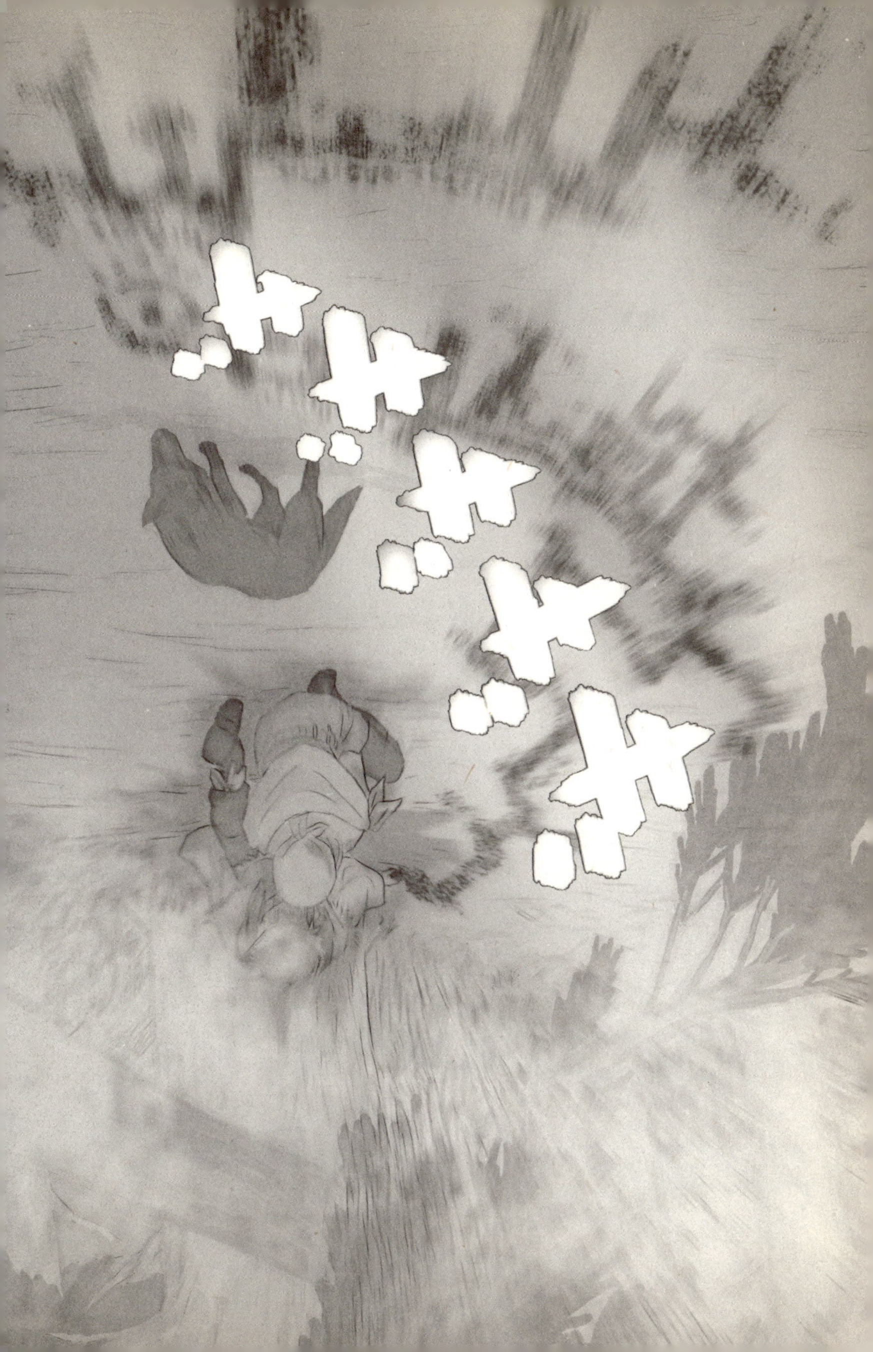

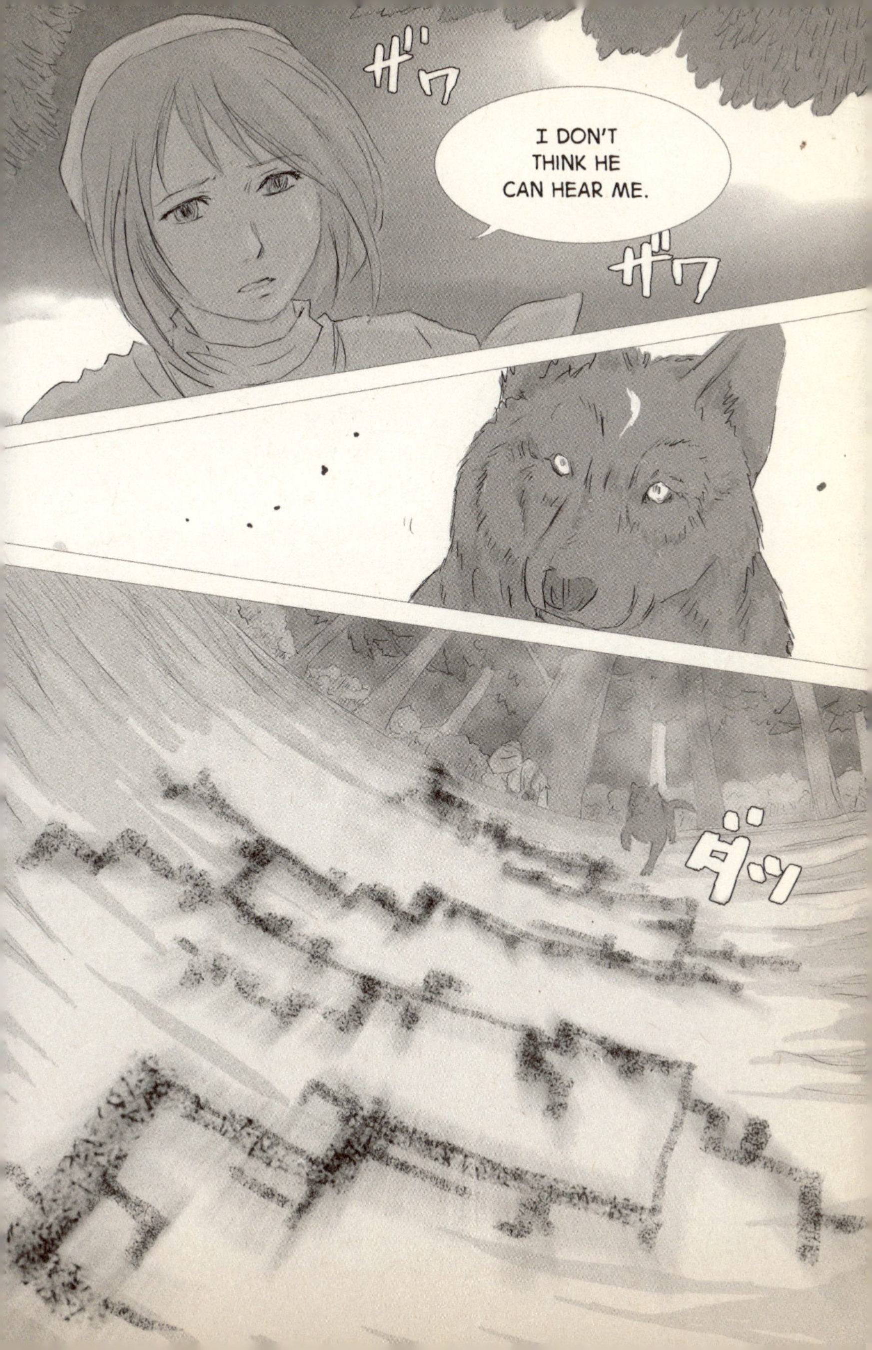
ザワ
I DON'T THINK HE CAN HEAR ME.
ザワ
ダッ

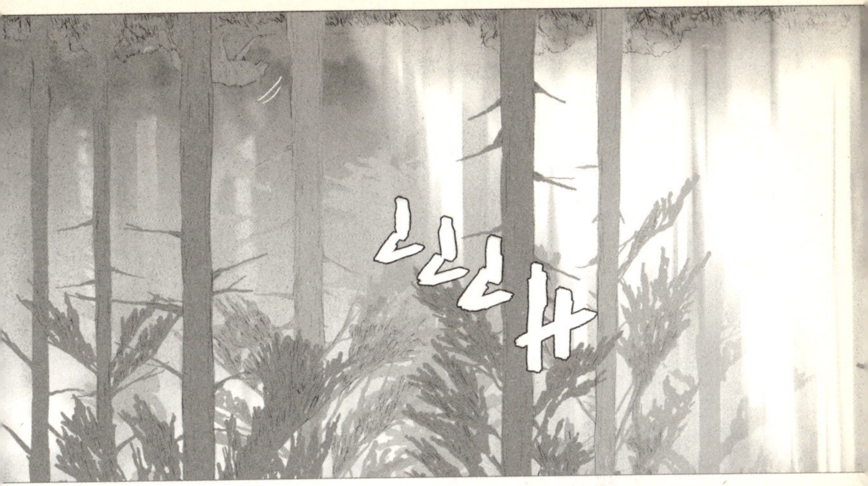

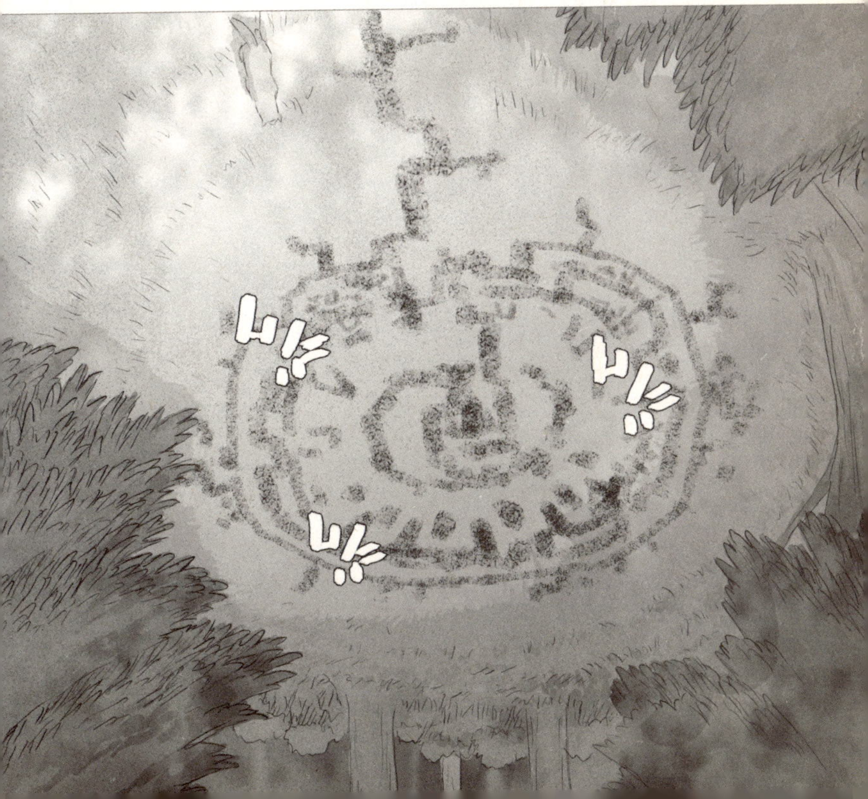

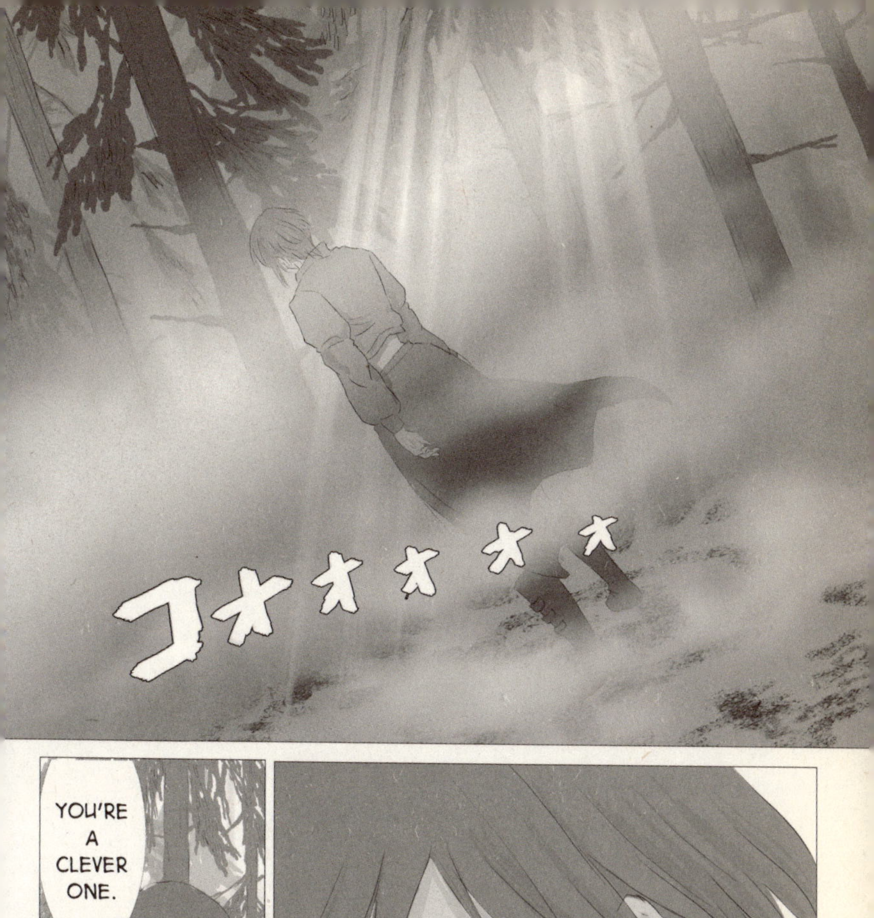
コオオオオ

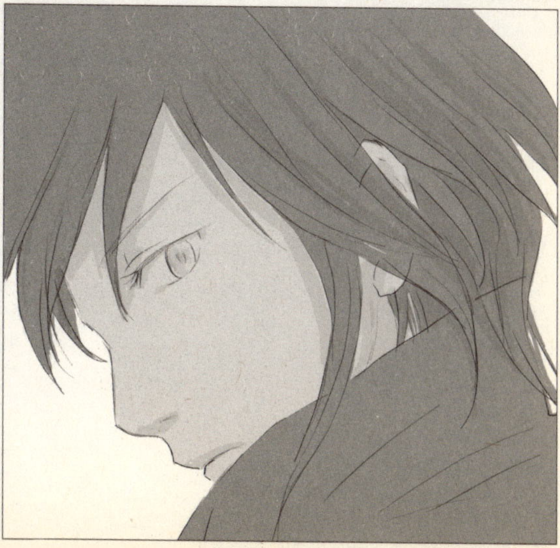

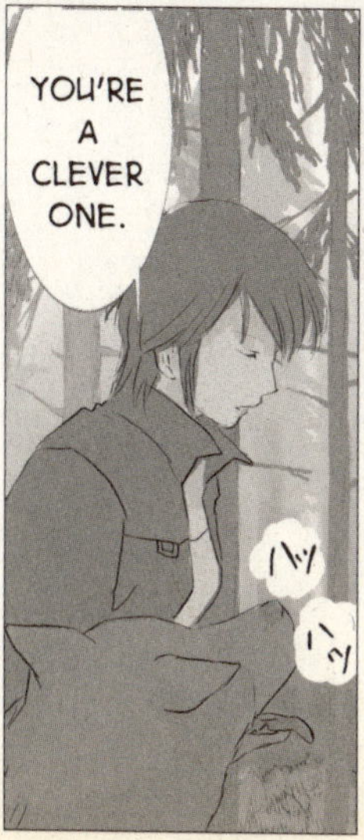
YOU'RE A CLEVER ONE.
ハッ
ハッ

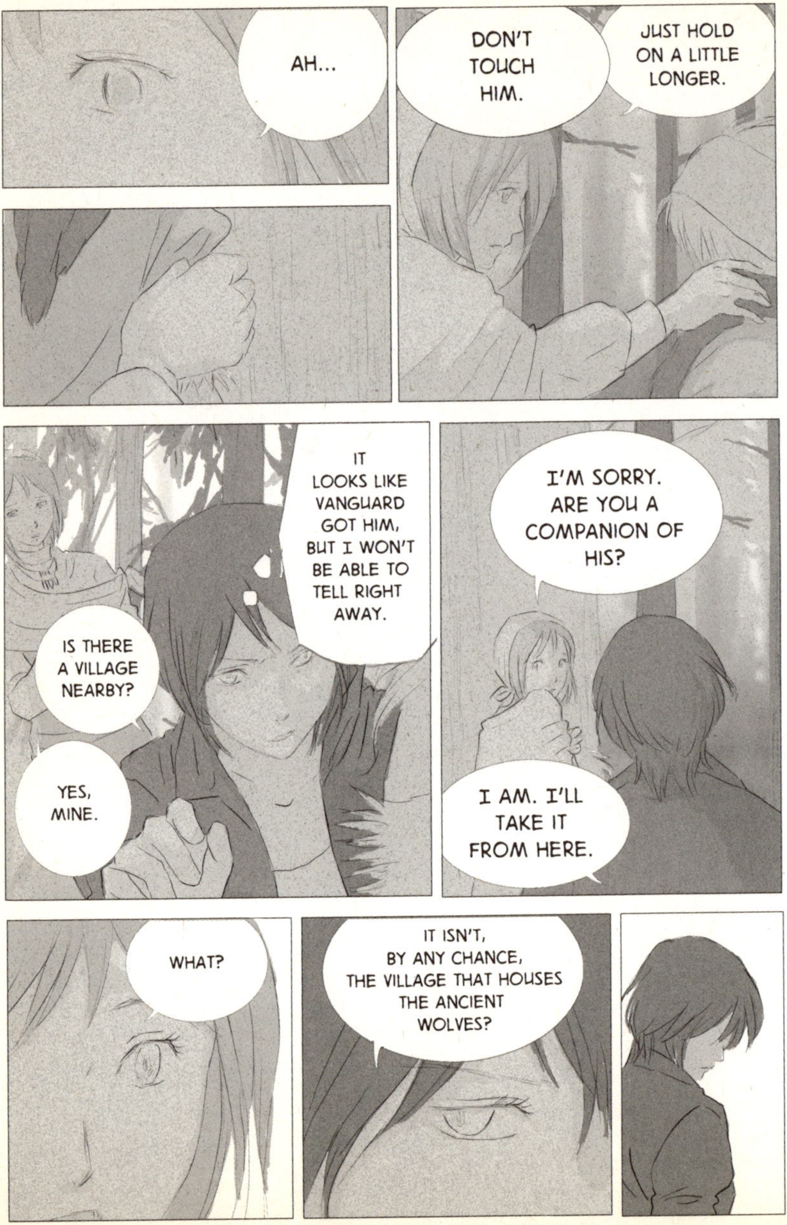
JUST HOLD ON A LITTLE LONGER.
DON'T TOUCH HIM.
AH...
I'M SORRY. ARE YOU A COMPANION OF HIS?
I AM. I'LL TAKE IT FROM HERE.
IT LOOKS LIKE VANGUARD GOT HIM, BUT I WON'T BE ABLE TO TELL RIGHT AWAY.
IS THERE A VILLAGE NEARBY?
YES, MINE.
IT ISN'T, BY ANY CHANCE, THE VILLAGE THAT HOUSES THE ANCIENT WOLVES?
WHAT?

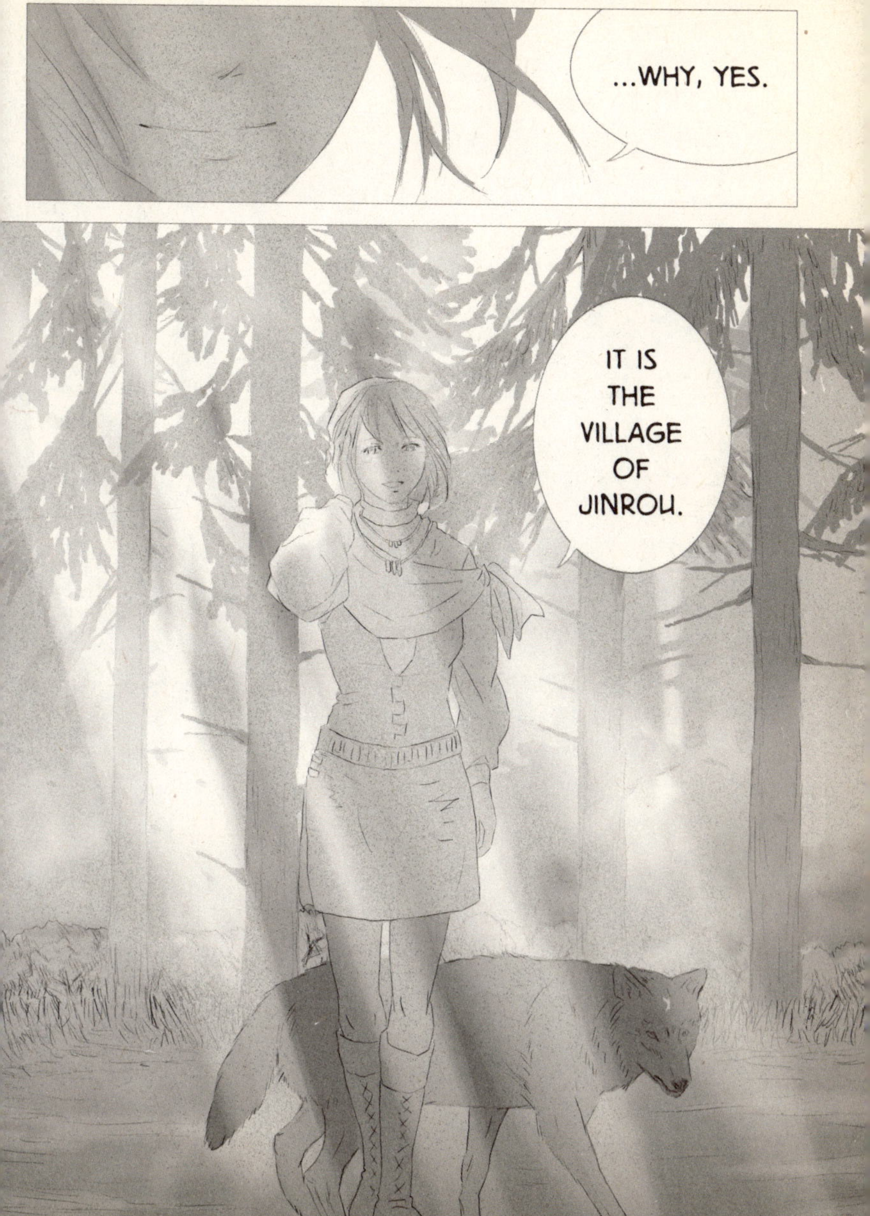
...WHY, YES.
IT IS THE VILLAGE OF JINROU.

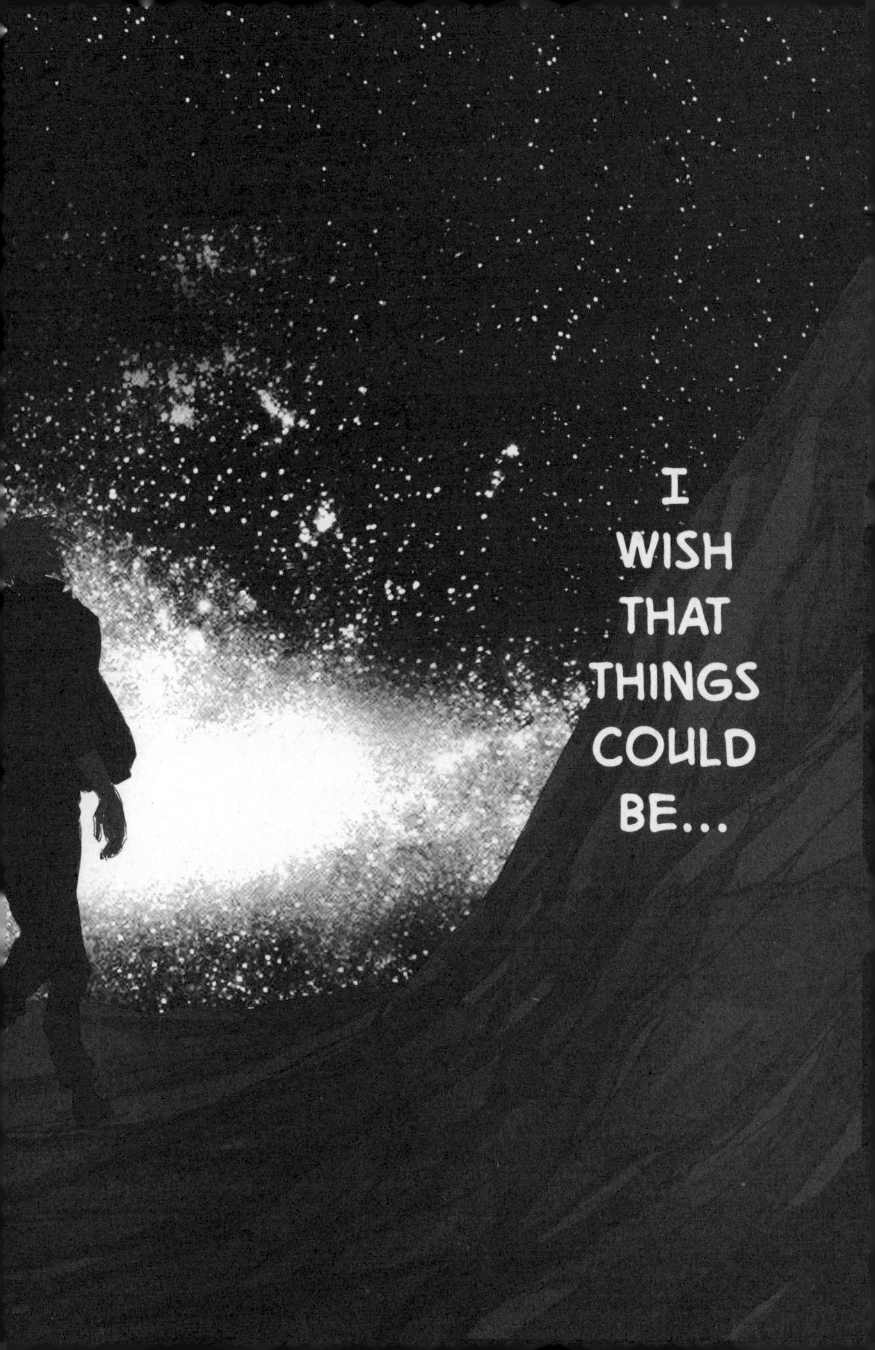
I WISH THAT THINGS COULD BE...

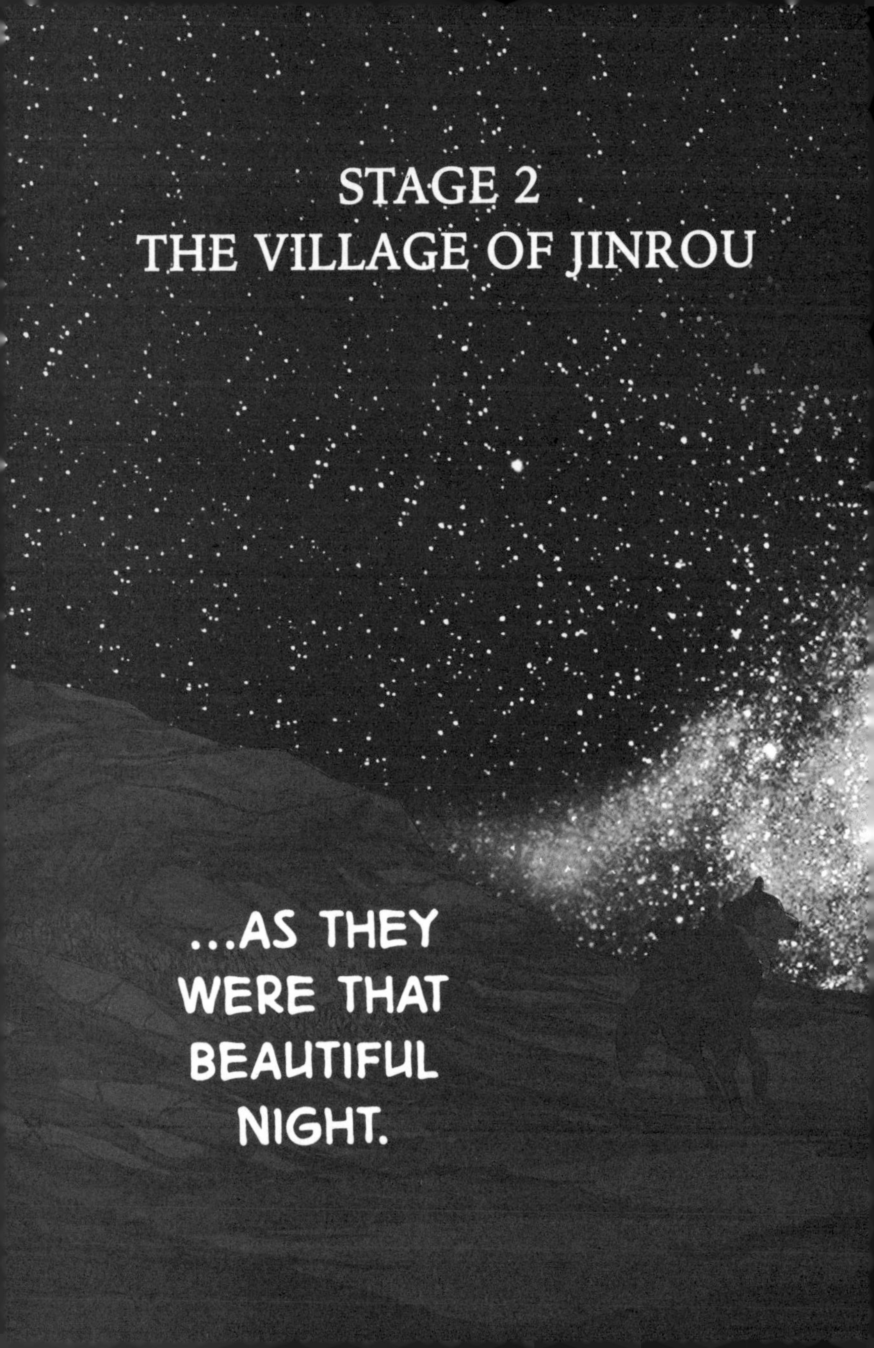
STAGE 2
THE VILLAGE OF JINROU
...AS THEY WERE THAT BEAUTIFUL NIGHT.

カリ
カリ

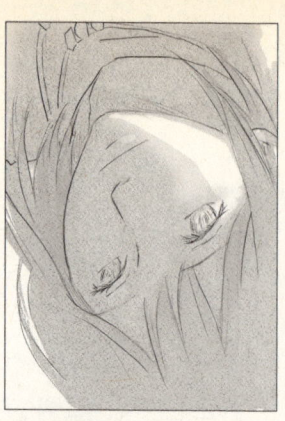

NOTHING OUT THERE?

WOOF!

I SEE. GOOD JOB.

HEH HEH.

WELCOME BACK.

KNGAH!

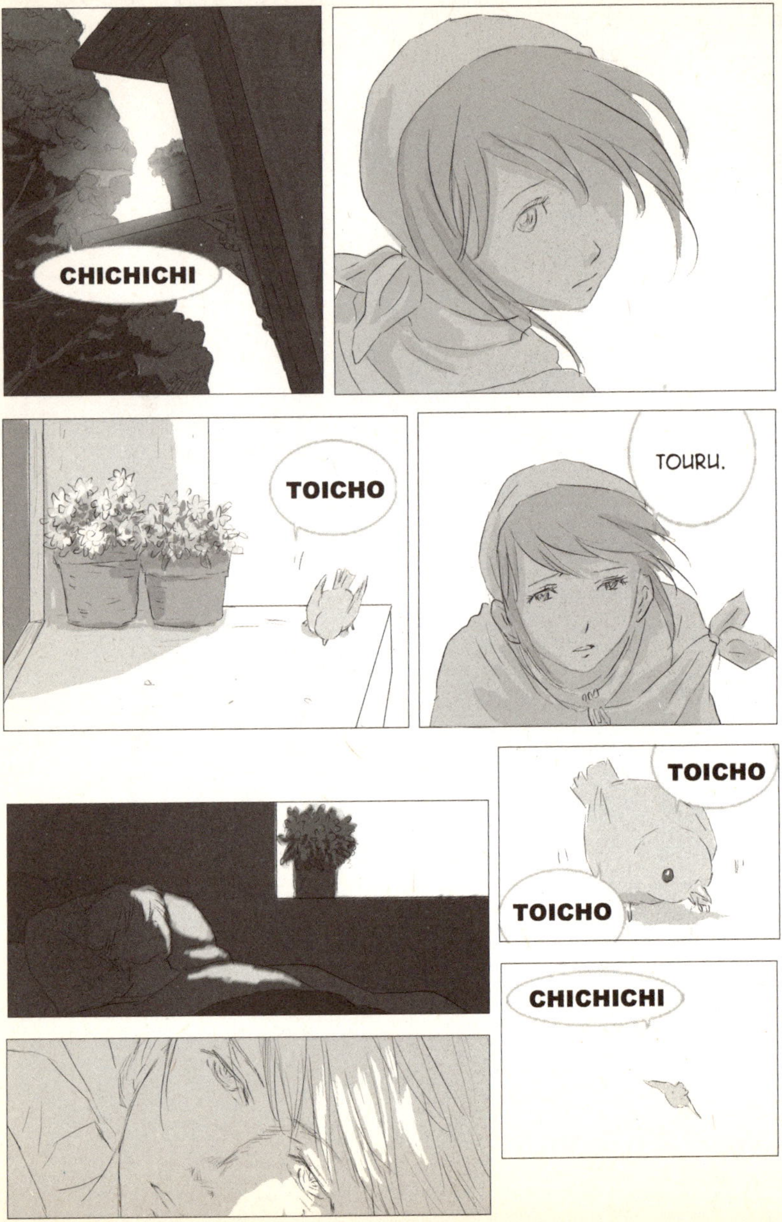
CHICHICHI
TOURU.
TOICHO
TOICHO
TOICHO
CHICHICHI

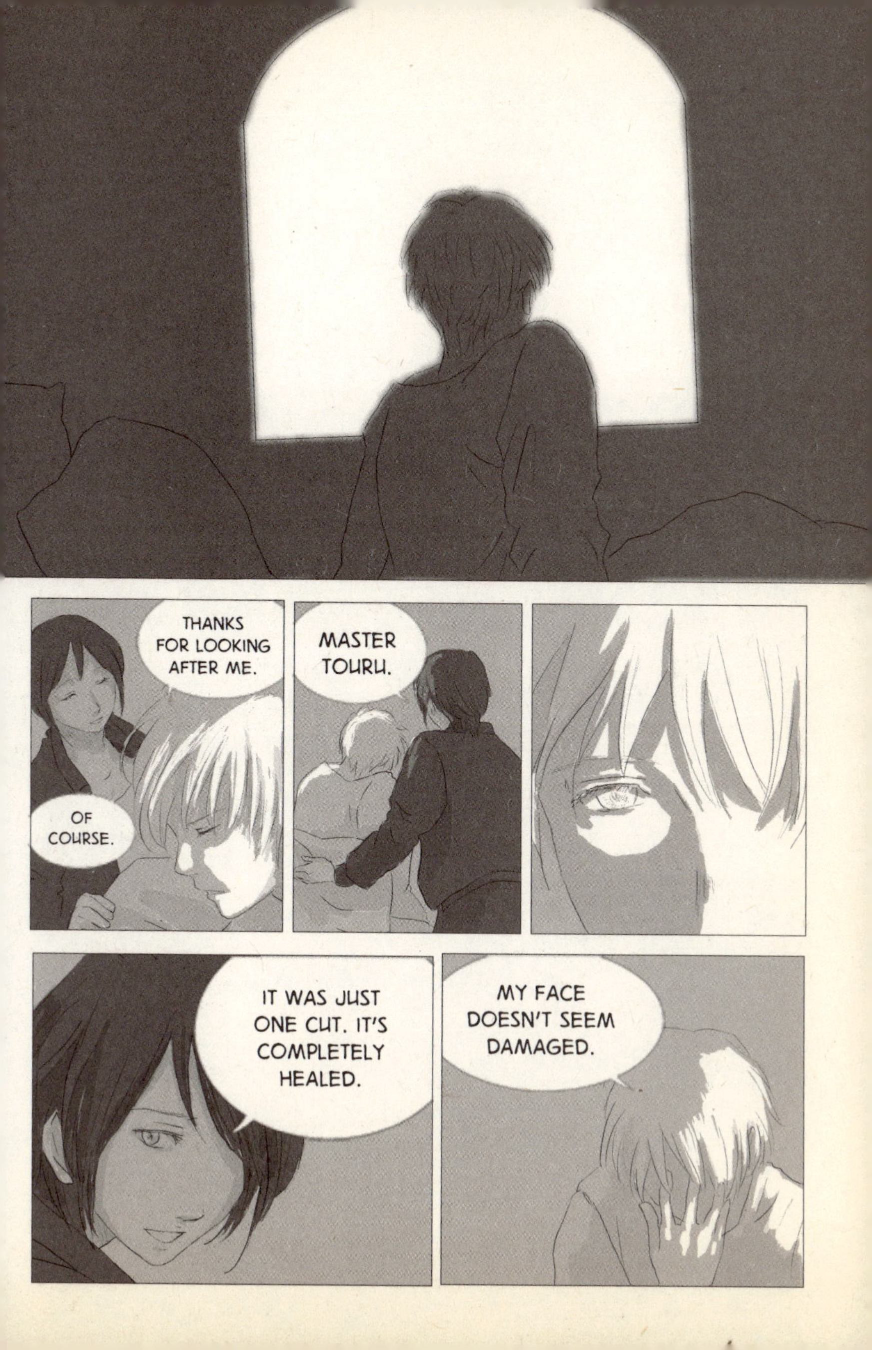
MASTER TOURU.
THANKS FOR LOOKING AFTER ME.
OF COURSE.
MY FACE DOESN'T SEEM DAMAGED.
IT WAS JUST ONE CUT. IT'S COMPLETELY HEALED.

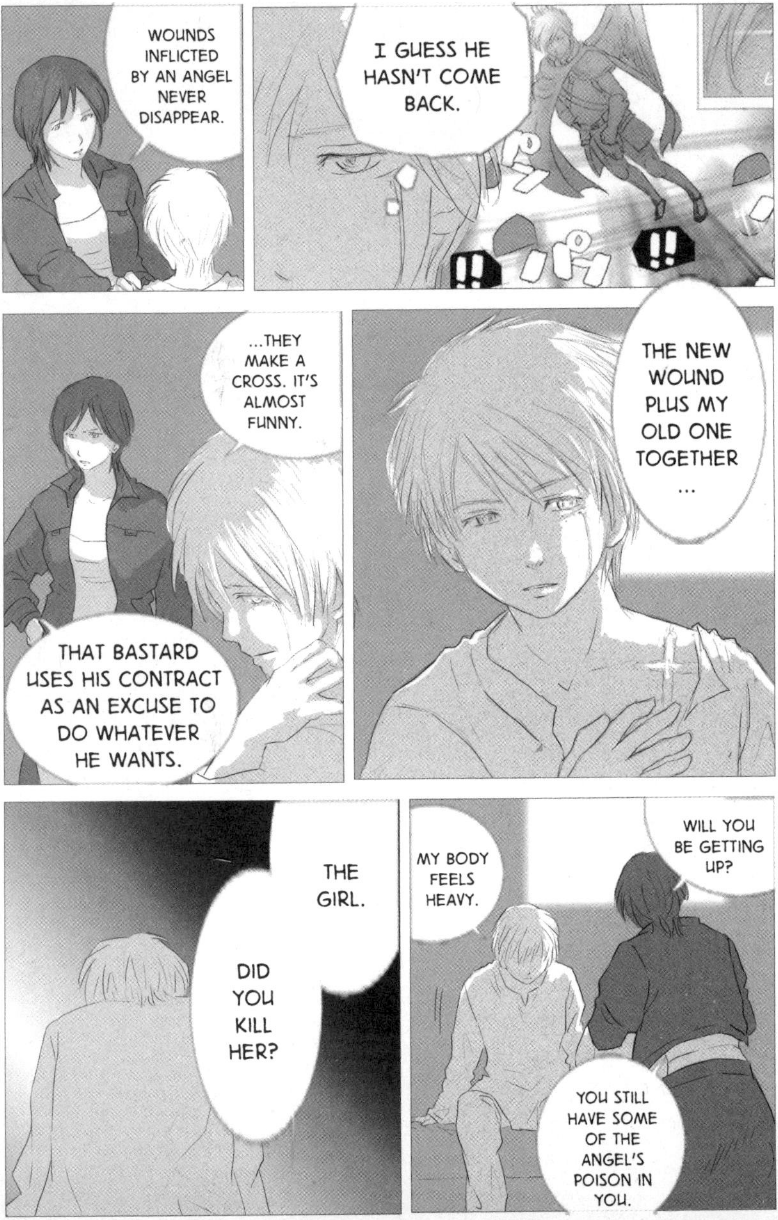
I GUESS HE HASN'T COME BACK.
WOUNDS INFLICTED BY AN ANGEL NEVER DISAPPEAR.
THE NEW WOUND PLUS MY OLD ONE TOGETHER ...
...THEY MAKE A CROSS. IT'S ALMOST FUNNY.
THAT BASTARD USES HIS CONTRACT AS AN EXCUSE TO DO WHATEVER HE WANTS.
WILL YOU BE GETTING UP?
MY BODY FEELS HEAVY.
YOU STILL HAVE SOME OF THE ANGEL'S POISON IN YOU.
THE GIRL.
DID YOU KILL HER?

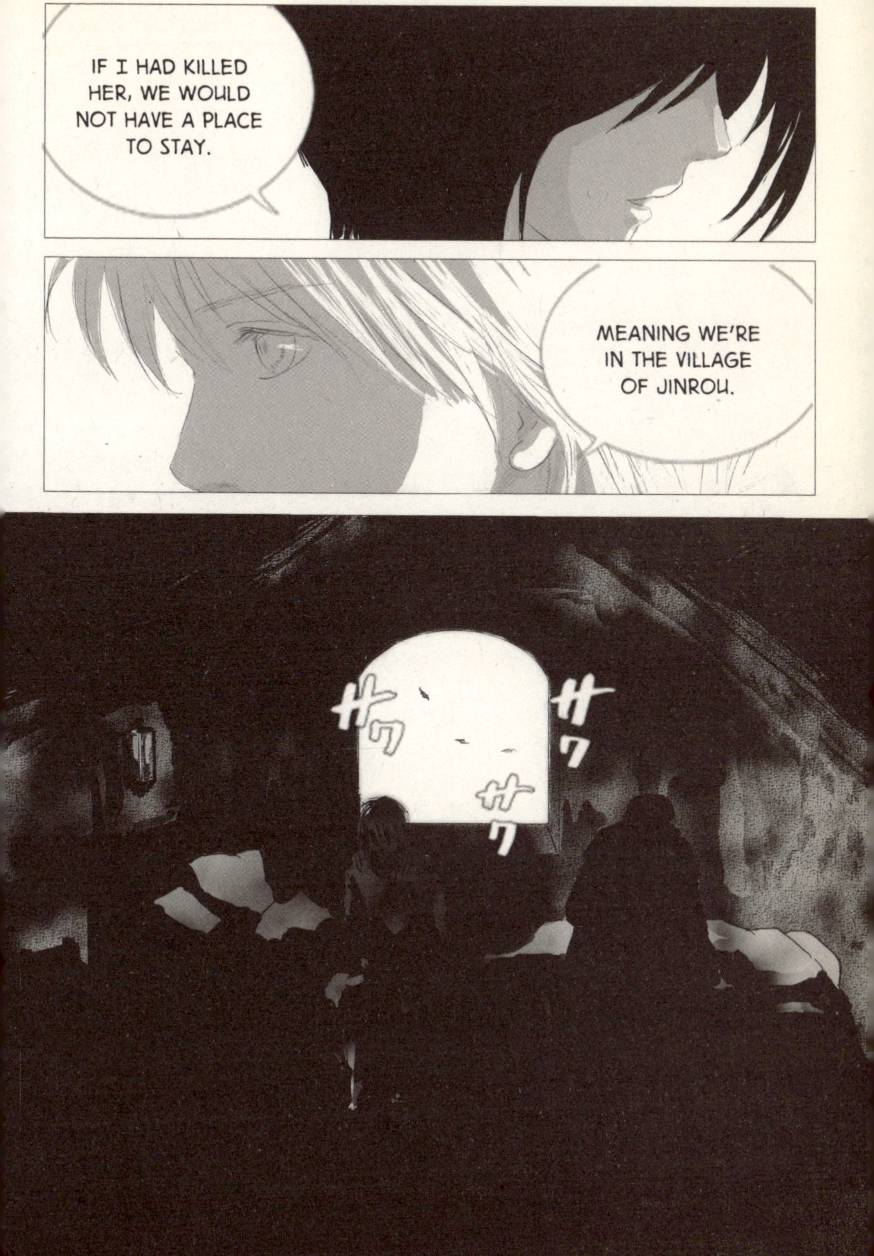
IF I HAD KILLED HER, WE WOULD NOT HAVE A PLACE TO STAY.
MEANING WE'RE IN THE VILLAGE OF JINROU.
サワ
サワ
サワ

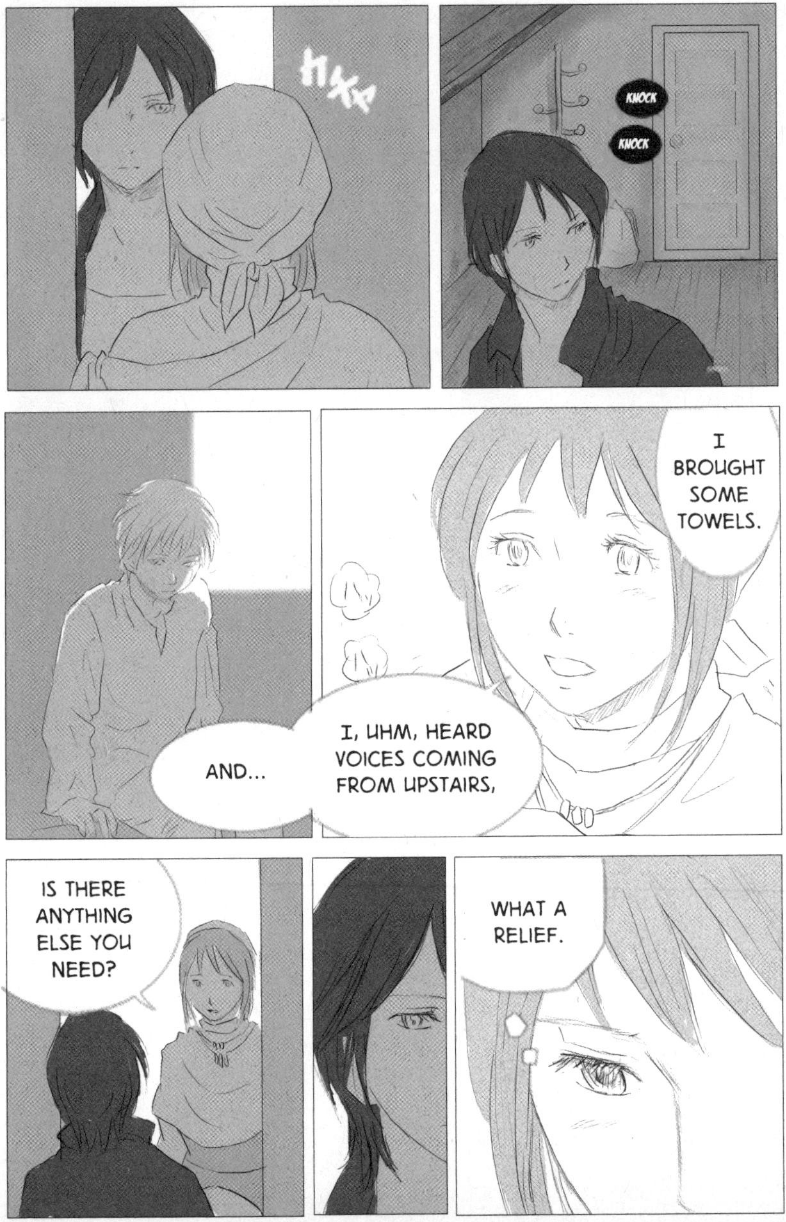
KNOCK
KNOCK
I BROUGHT SOME TOWELS.
I, UHM, HEARD VOICES COMING FROM UPSTAIRS,
AND...
IS THERE ANYTHING ELSE YOU NEED?
WHAT A RELIEF.

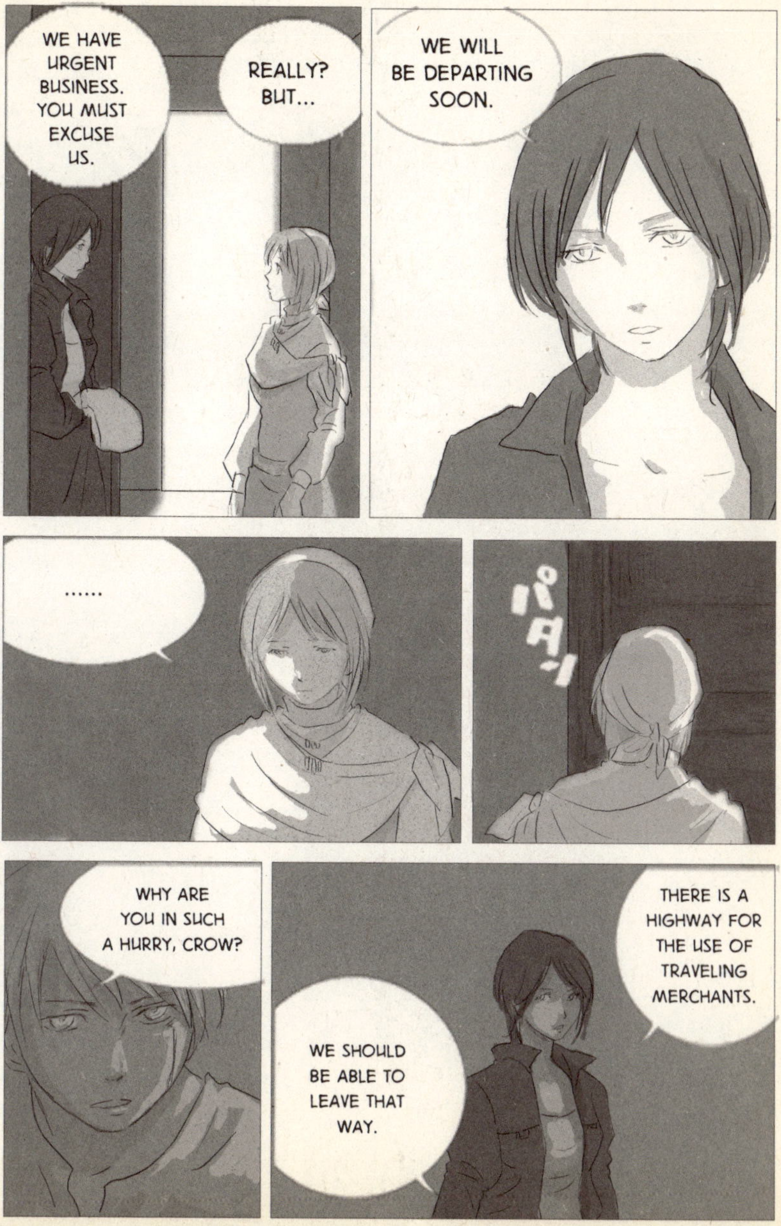
WE HAVE URGENT BUSINESS. YOU MUST EXCUSE US.
REALLY? BUT...
WE WILL BE DEPARTING SOON.
......
パタッ
WHY ARE YOU IN SUCH A HURRY, CROW?
THERE IS A HIGHWAY FOR THE USE OF TRAVELING MERCHANTS.
WE SHOULD BE ABLE TO LEAVE THAT WAY.

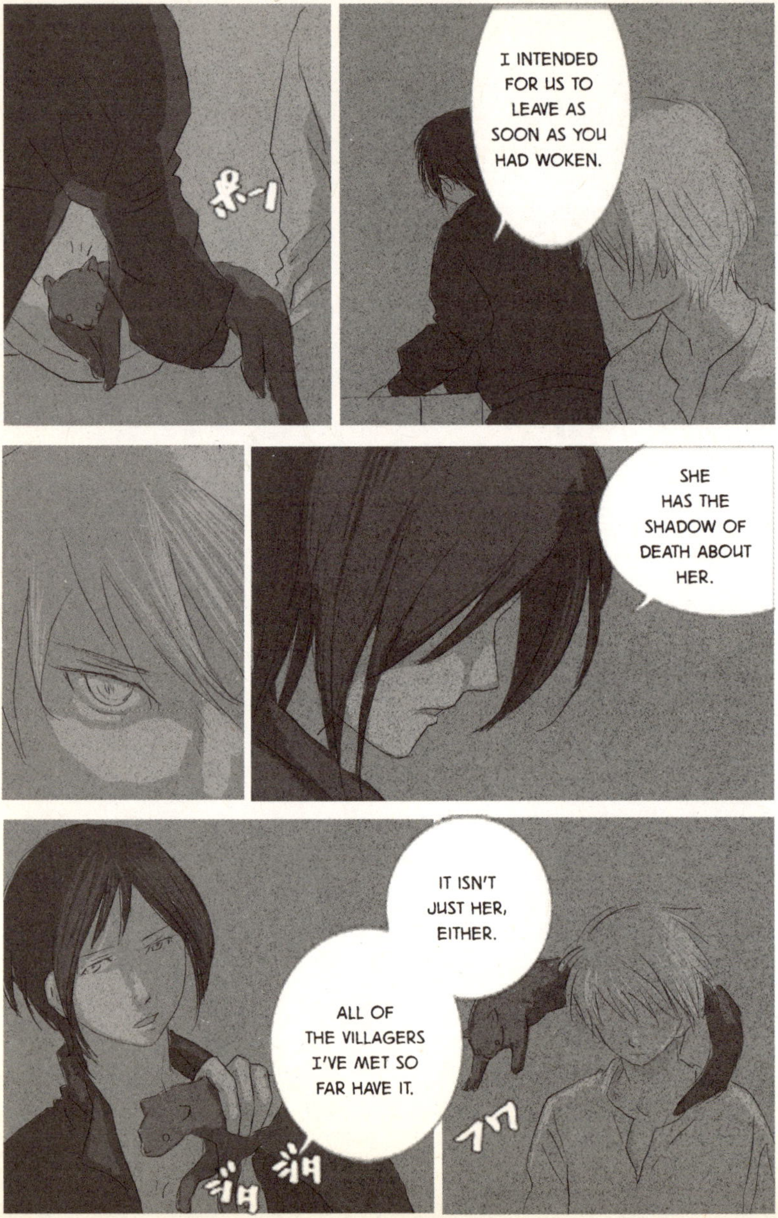

I INTENDED FOR US TO LEAVE AS SOON AS YOU HAD WOKEN.
SHE HAS THE SHADOW OF DEATH ABOUT HER.
IT ISN'T JUST HER, EITHER.
ALL OF THE VILLAGERS I'VE MET SO FAR HAVE IT.

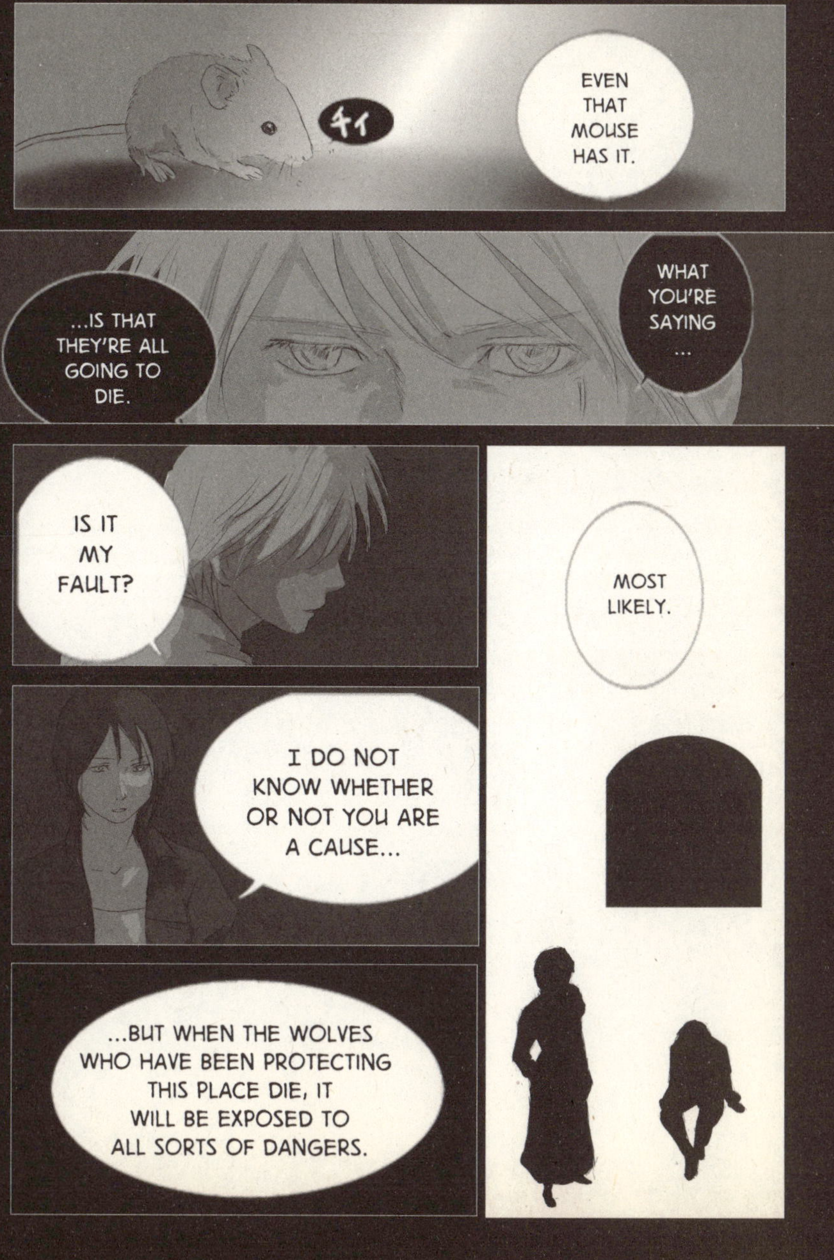
EVEN THAT MOUSE HAS IT.
チィ
WHAT YOU'RE SAYING ...
...IS THAT THEY'RE ALL GOING TO DIE.
MOST LIKELY.
IS IT MY FAULT?
I DO NOT KNOW WHETHER OR NOT YOU ARE A CAUSE...
...BUT WHEN THE WOLVES WHO HAVE BEEN PROTECTING THIS PLACE DIE, IT WILL BE EXPOSED TO ALL SORTS OF DANGERS.

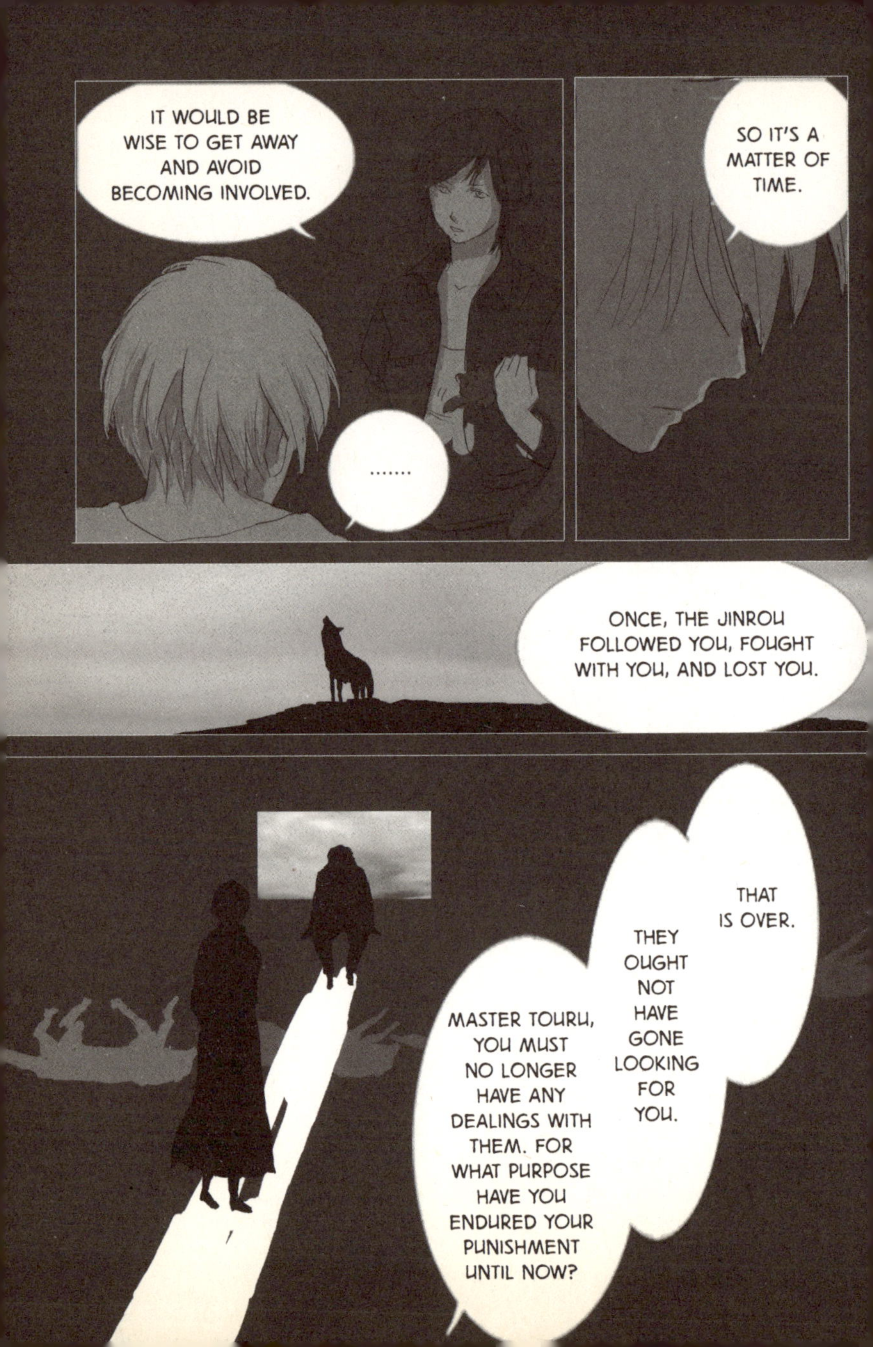
SO IT'S A MATTER OF TIME.
IT WOULD BE WISE TO GET AWAY AND AVOID BECOMING INVOLVED.
....
ONCE, THE JINROU FOLLOWED YOU, FOUGHT WITH YOU, AND LOST YOU.
THAT IS OVER.
THEY OUGHT NOT HAVE GONE LOOKING FOR YOU.
MASTER TOURU, YOU MUST NO LONGER HAVE ANY DEALINGS WITH THEM. FOR WHAT PURPOSE HAVE YOU ENDURED YOUR PUNISHMENT UNTIL NOW?

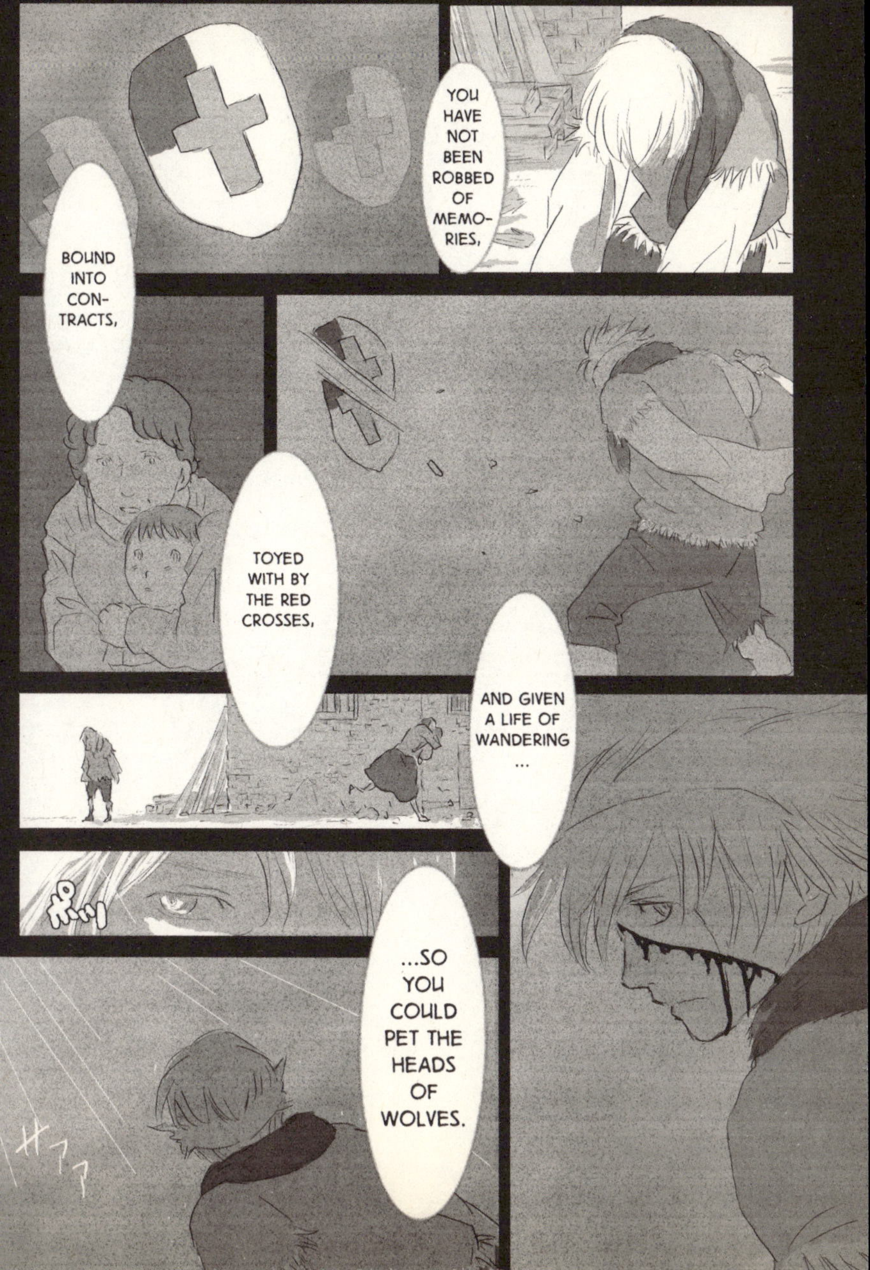
YOU HAVE NOT BEEN ROBBED OF MEMO-RIES,
BOUND INTO CON-TRACTS,
TOYED WITH BY THE RED CROSSES,
AND GIVEN A LIFE OF WANDERING ...
ポッ
...SO YOU COULD PET THE HEADS OF WOLVES.
サァァ

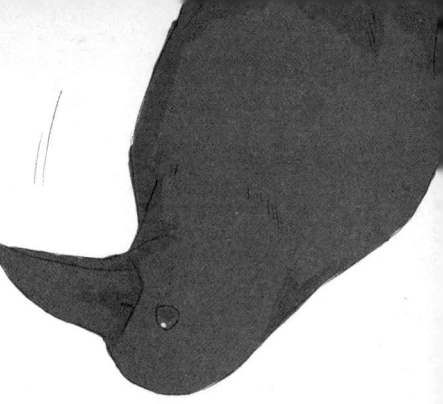

I'M SORRY, CROW.

IT DOES NOT SEEM WE CAN USE OUR CURRENCY HERE. I AM GOING TO FIND A MONEYLENDER.

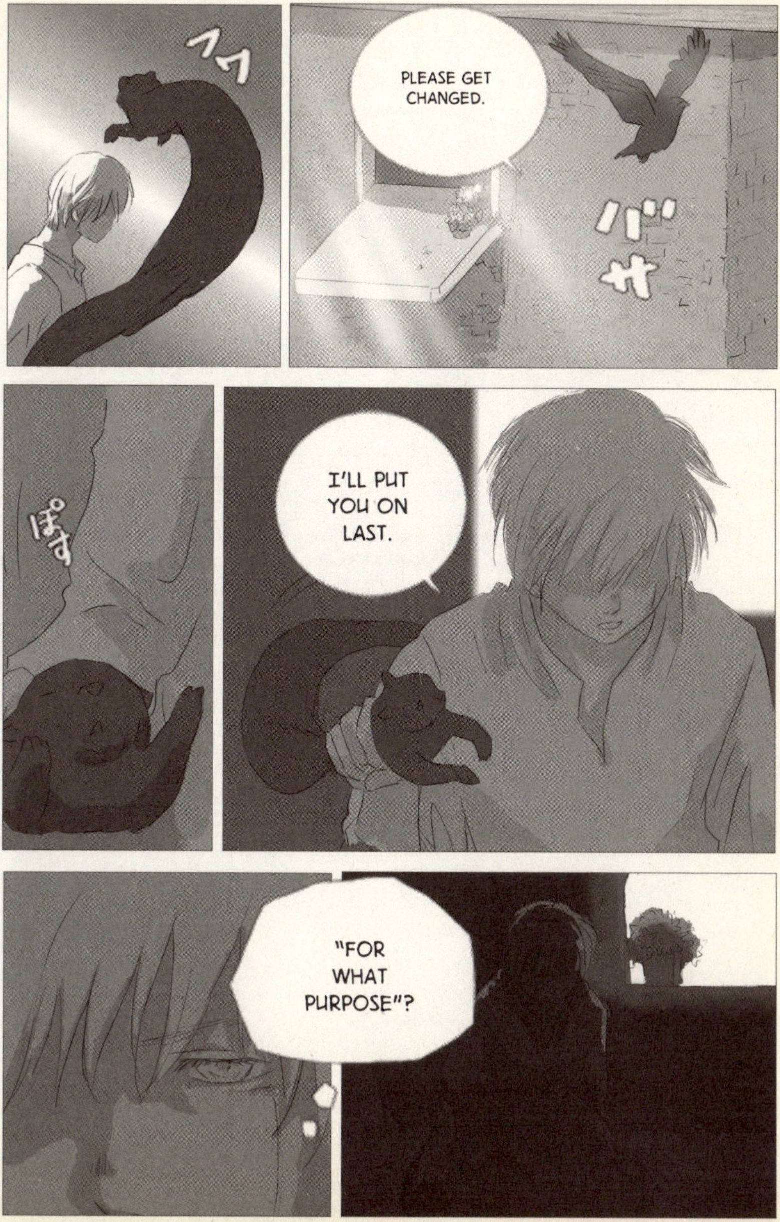
バサ
PLEASE GET CHANGED.
ぽす
I'LL PUT YOU ON LAST.
"FOR WHAT PURPOSE"?

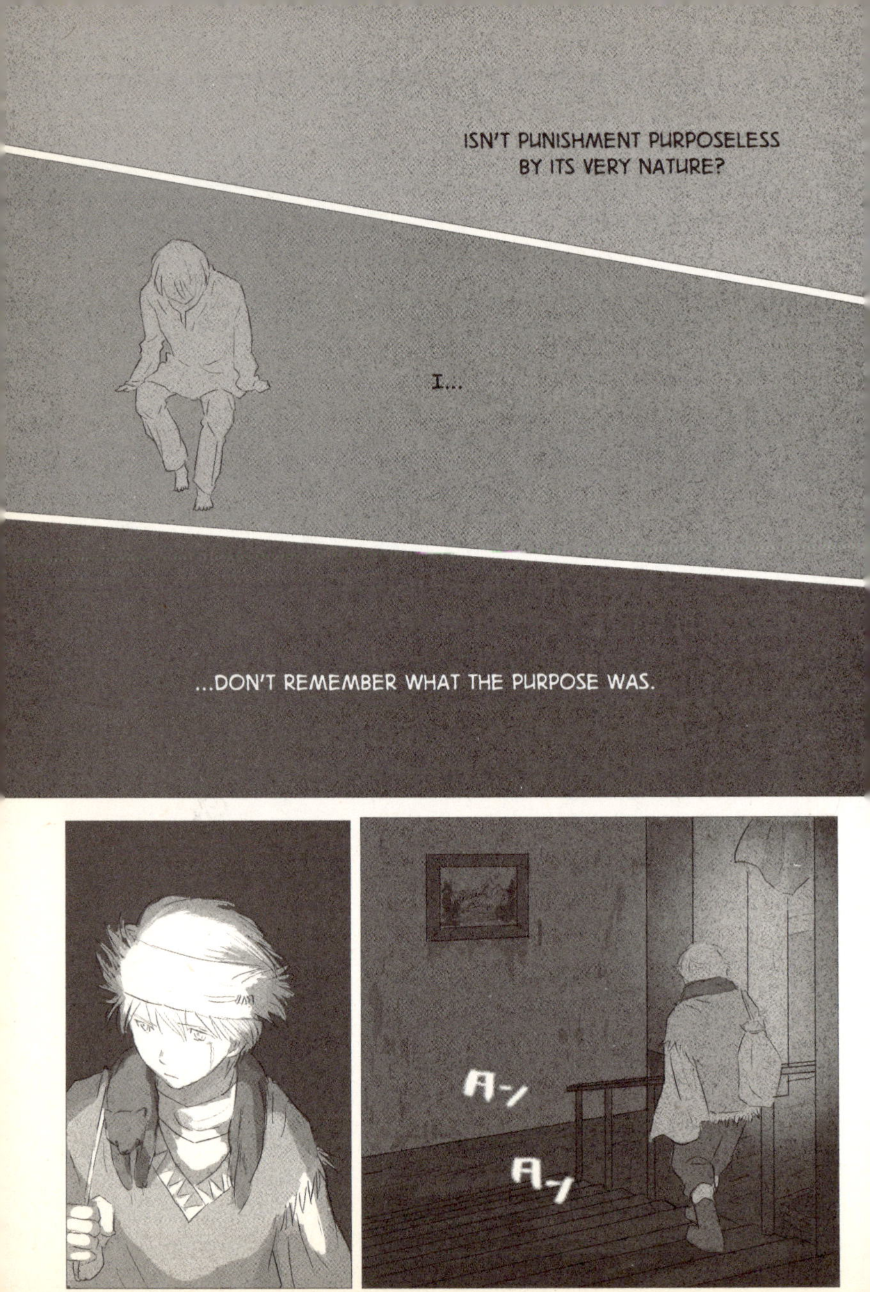
ISN'T PUNISHMENT PURPOSELESS BY ITS VERY NATURE?
I...
...DON'T REMEMBER WHAT THE PURPOSE WAS.

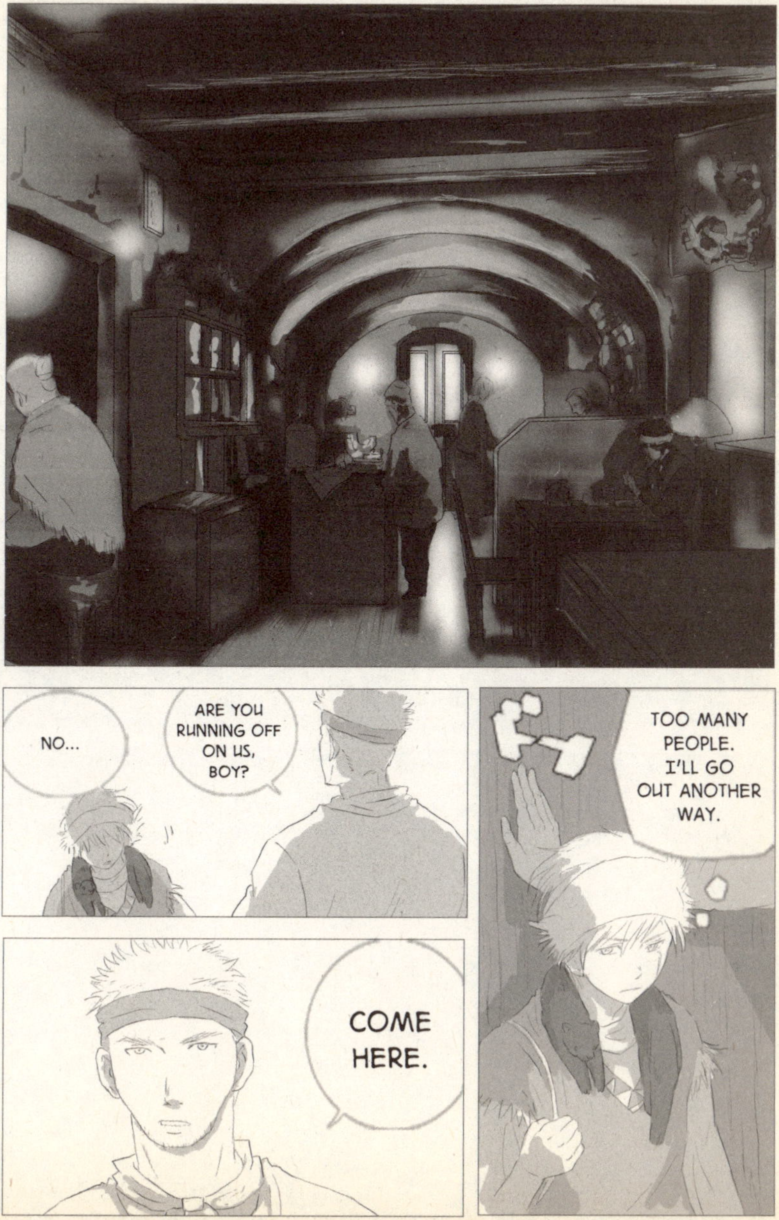
TOO MANY PEOPLE. I'LL GO OUT ANOTHER WAY.
ARE YOU RUNNING OFF ON US, BOY?
NO...
COME HERE.

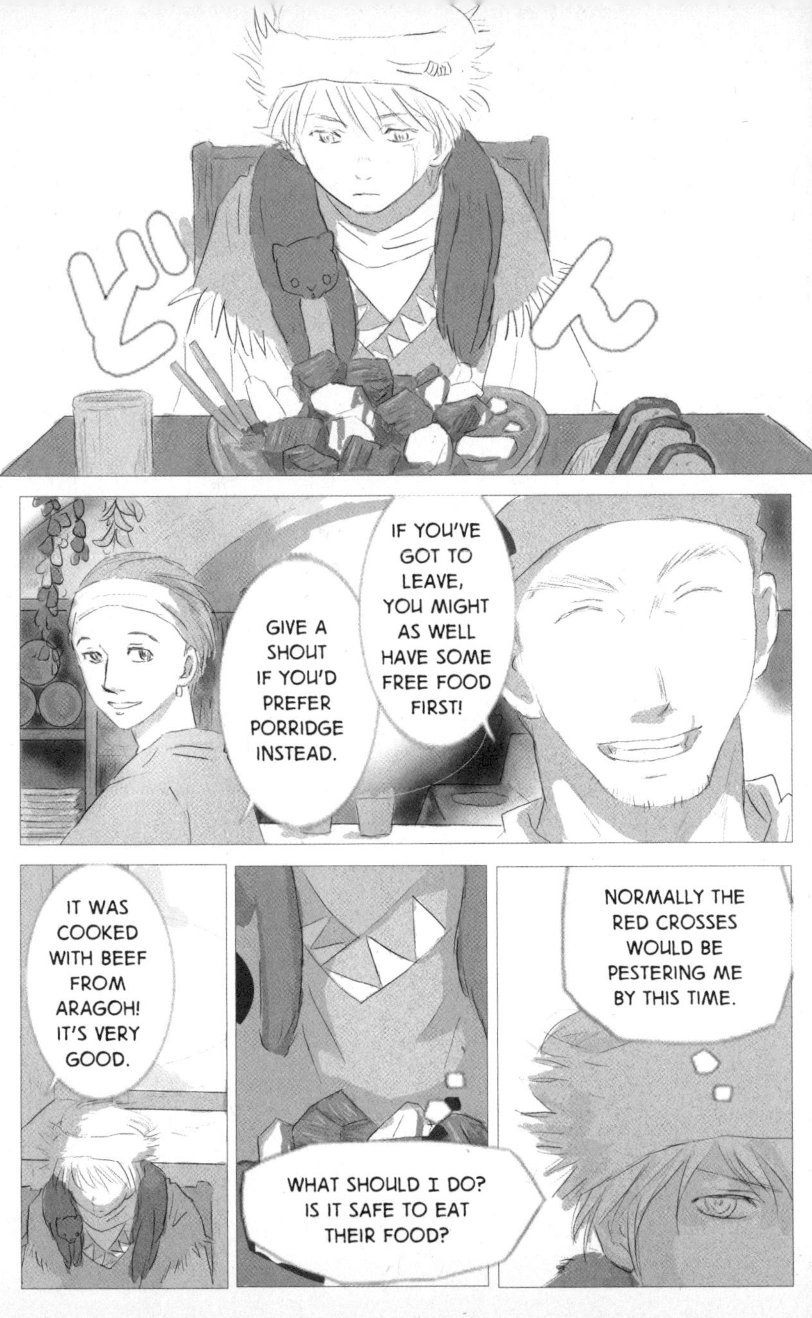
どん
IF YOU'VE GOT TO LEAVE, YOU MIGHT AS WELL HAVE SOME FREE FOOD FIRST!
GIVE A SHOUT IF YOU'D PREFER PORRIDGE INSTEAD.
NORMALLY THE RED CROSSES WOULD BE PESTERING ME BY THIS TIME.
WHAT SHOULD I DO? IS IT SAFE TO EAT THEIR FOOD?
IT WAS COOKED WITH BEEF FROM ARAGOH! IT'S VERY GOOD.

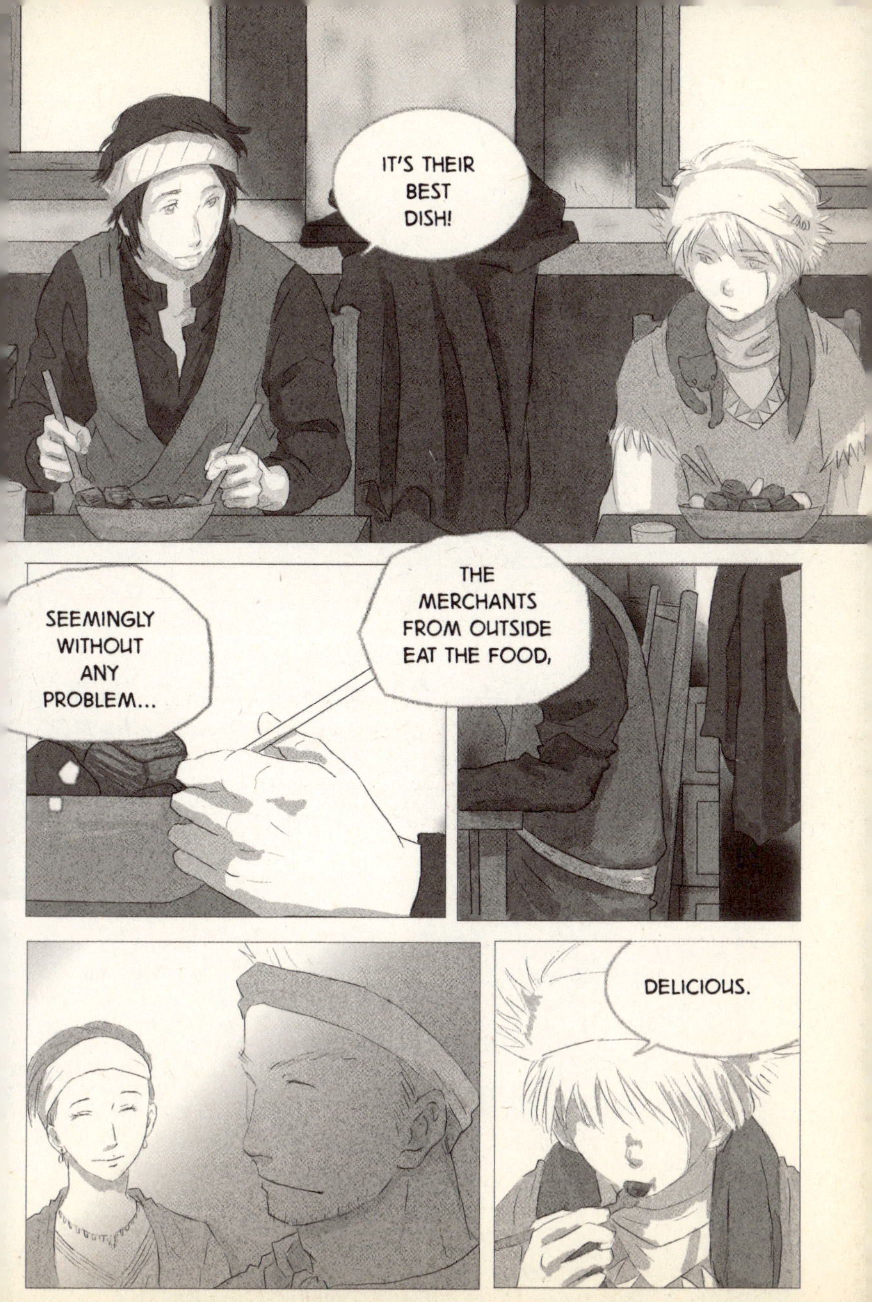
IT'S THEIR BEST DISH!
THE MERCHANTS FROM OUTSIDE EAT THE FOOD,
SEEMINGLY WITHOUT ANY PROBLEM...
DELICIOUS.

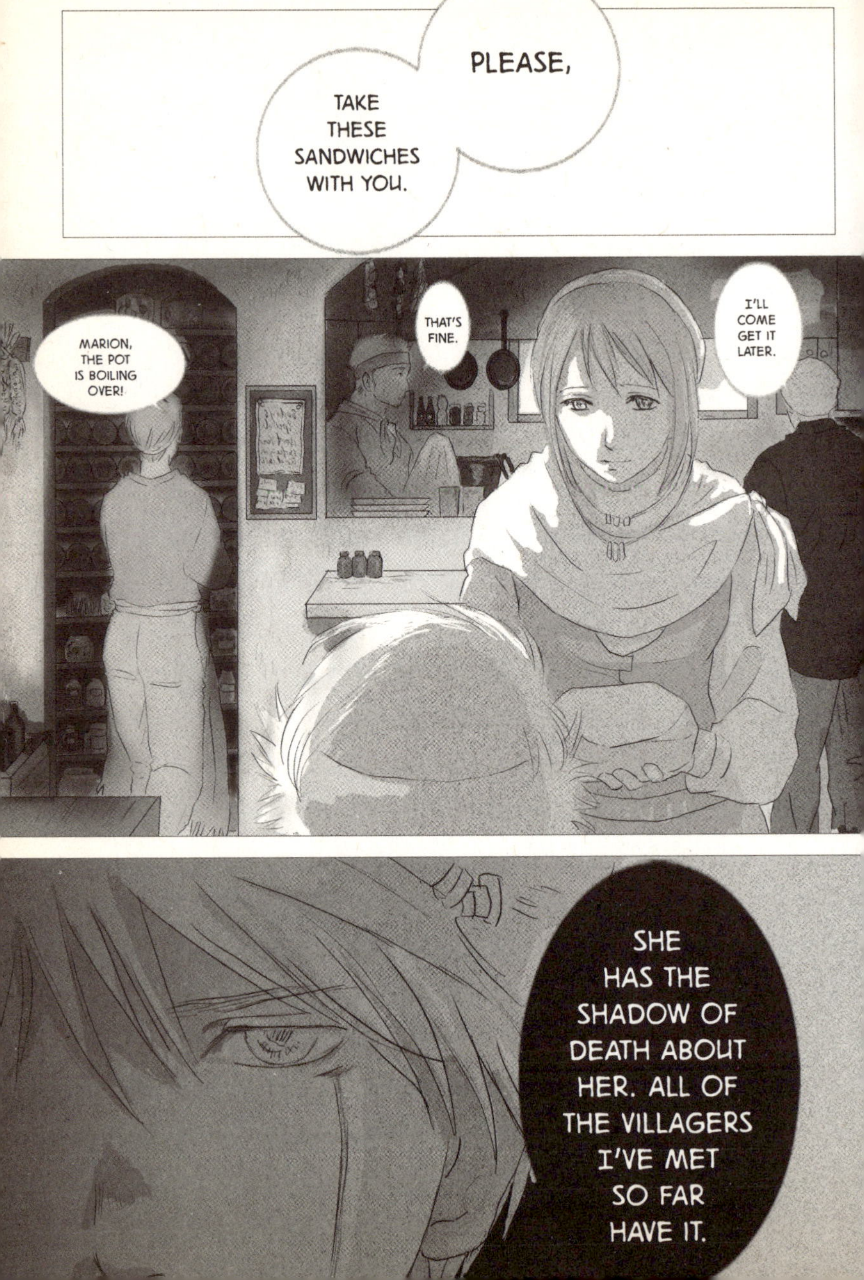
PLEASE,
TAKE THESE SANDWICHES WITH YOU.
I'LL COME GET IT LATER.
THAT'S FINE.
MARION, THE POT IS BOILING OVER!
SHE HAS THE SHADOW OF DEATH ABOUT HER. ALL OF THE VILLAGERS I'VE MET SO FAR HAVE IT.

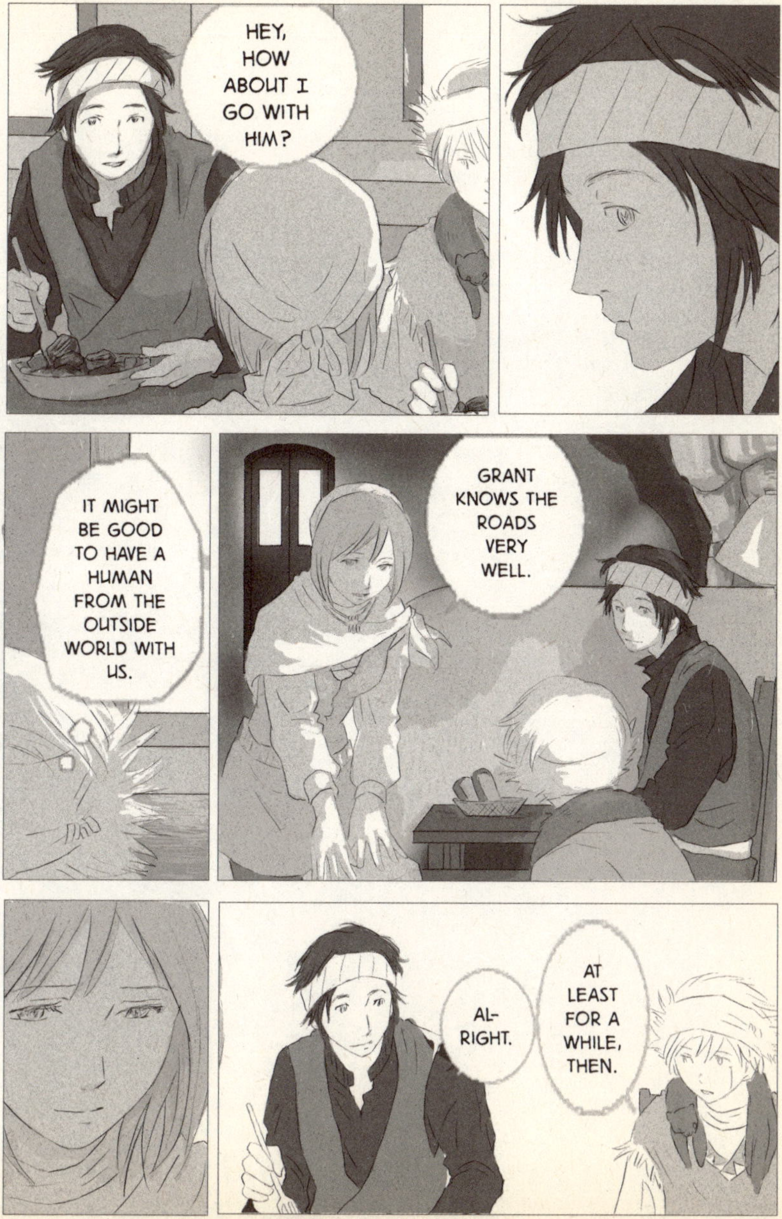
HEY, HOW ABOUT I GO WITH HIM?
GRANT KNOWS THE ROADS VERY WELL.
IT MIGHT BE GOOD TO HAVE A HUMAN FROM THE OUTSIDE WORLD WITH US.
AT LEAST FOR A WHILE, THEN.
AL-RIGHT.

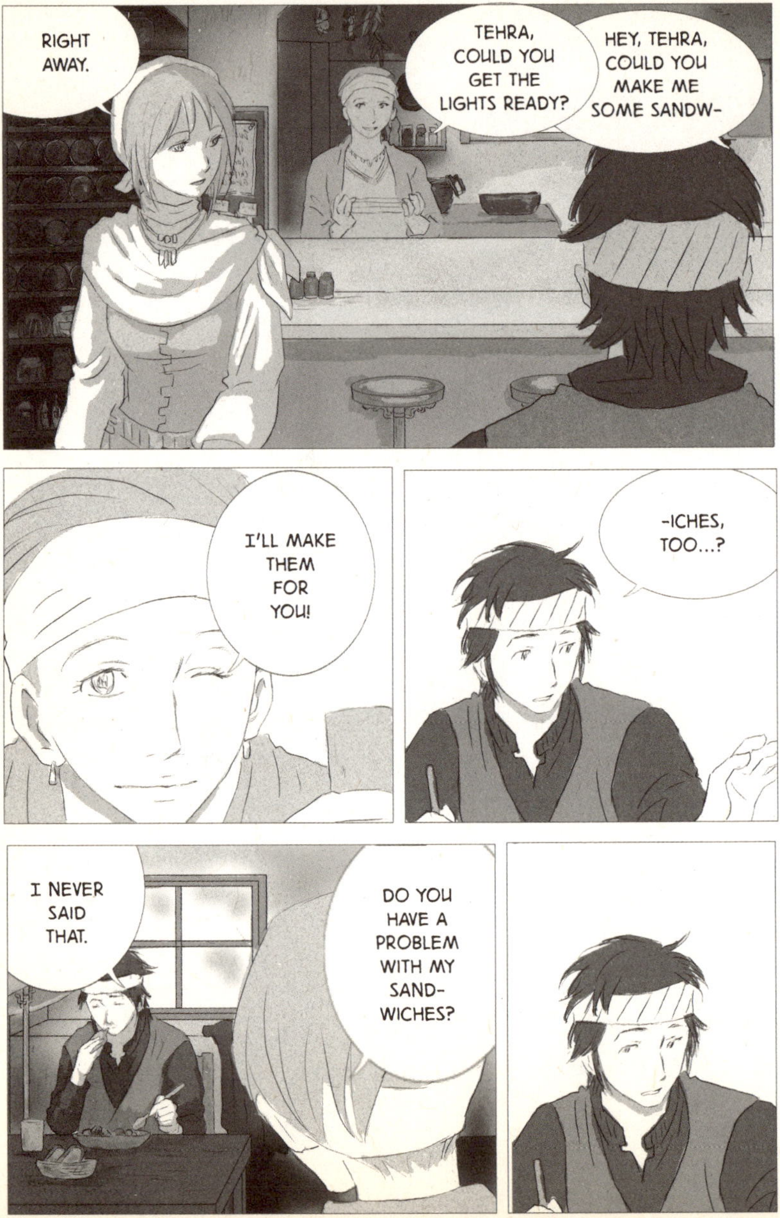
HEY, TEHRA, COULD YOU MAKE ME SOME SANDW-
TEHRA, COULD YOU GET THE LIGHTS READY?
RIGHT AWAY.
-ICHES, TOO...?
I'LL MAKE THEM FOR YOU!
DO YOU HAVE A PROBLEM WITH MY SAND-WICHES?
I NEVER SAID THAT.

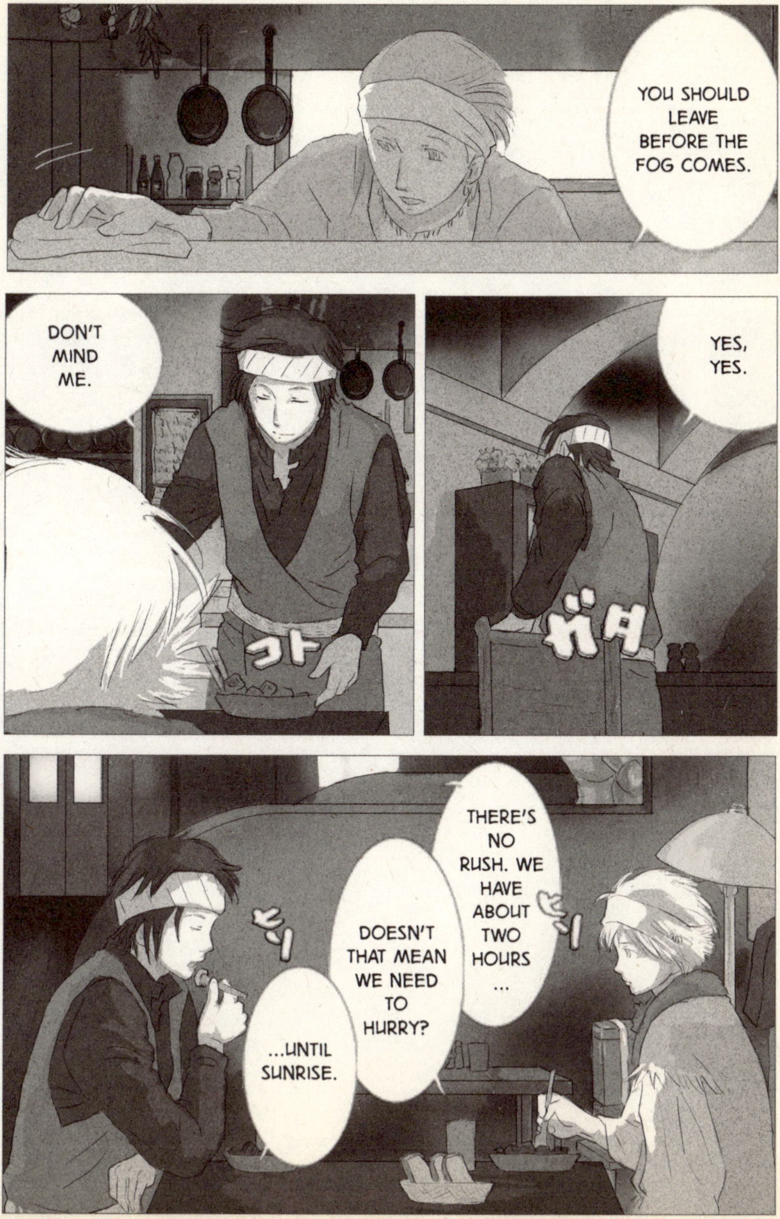
YOU SHOULD LEAVE BEFORE THE FOG COMES.
YES, YES.
DON'T MIND ME.
THERE'S NO RUSH. WE HAVE ABOUT TWO HOURS ...
DOESN'T THAT MEAN WE NEED TO HURRY?
...UNTIL SUNRISE.

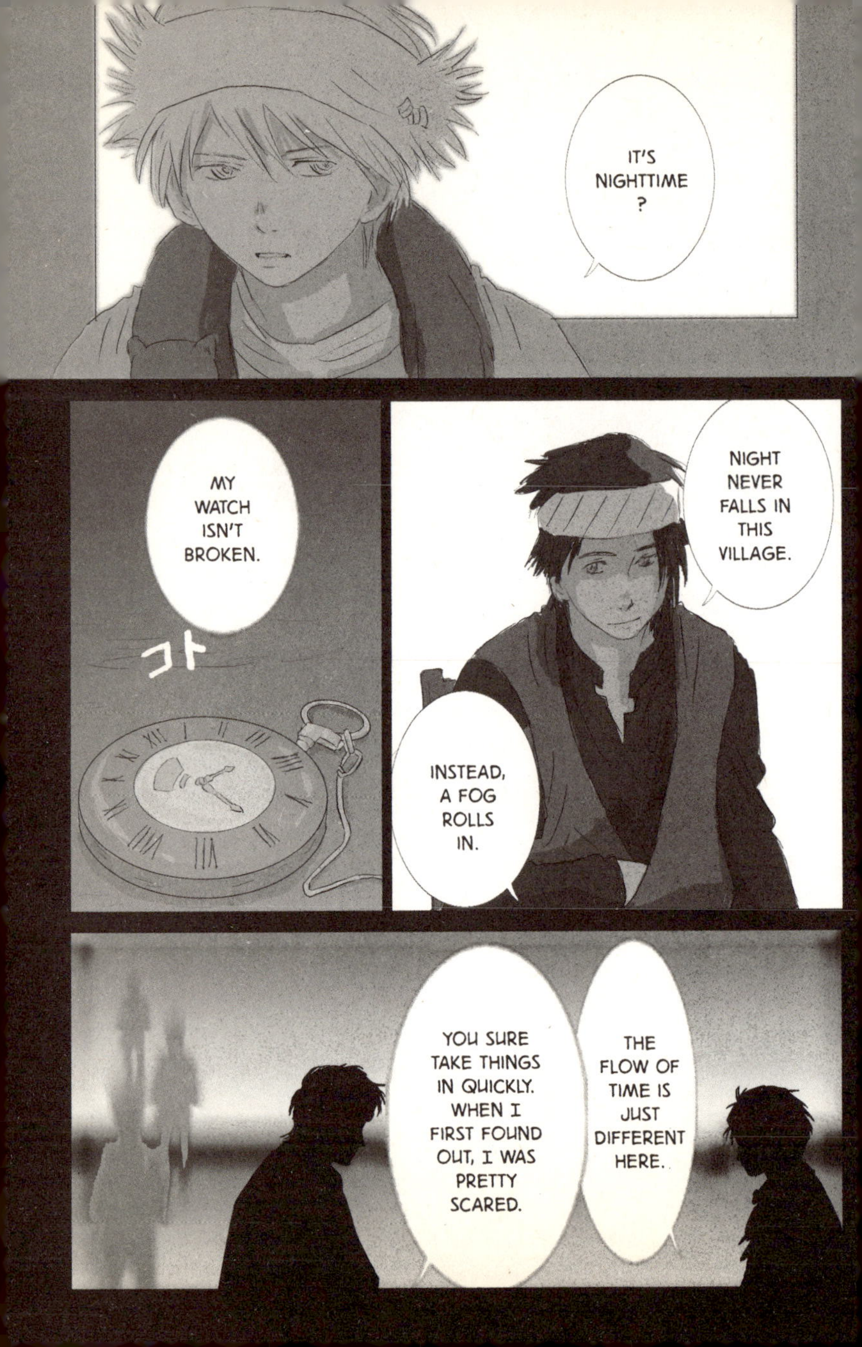
IT'S NIGHTTIME ?
NIGHT NEVER FALLS IN THIS VILLAGE.
INSTEAD, A FOG ROLLS IN.
MY WATCH ISN'T BROKEN.
コト
THE FLOW OF TIME IS JUST DIFFERENT HERE.
YOU SURE TAKE THINGS IN QUICKLY. WHEN I FIRST FOUND OUT, I WAS PRETTY SCARED.

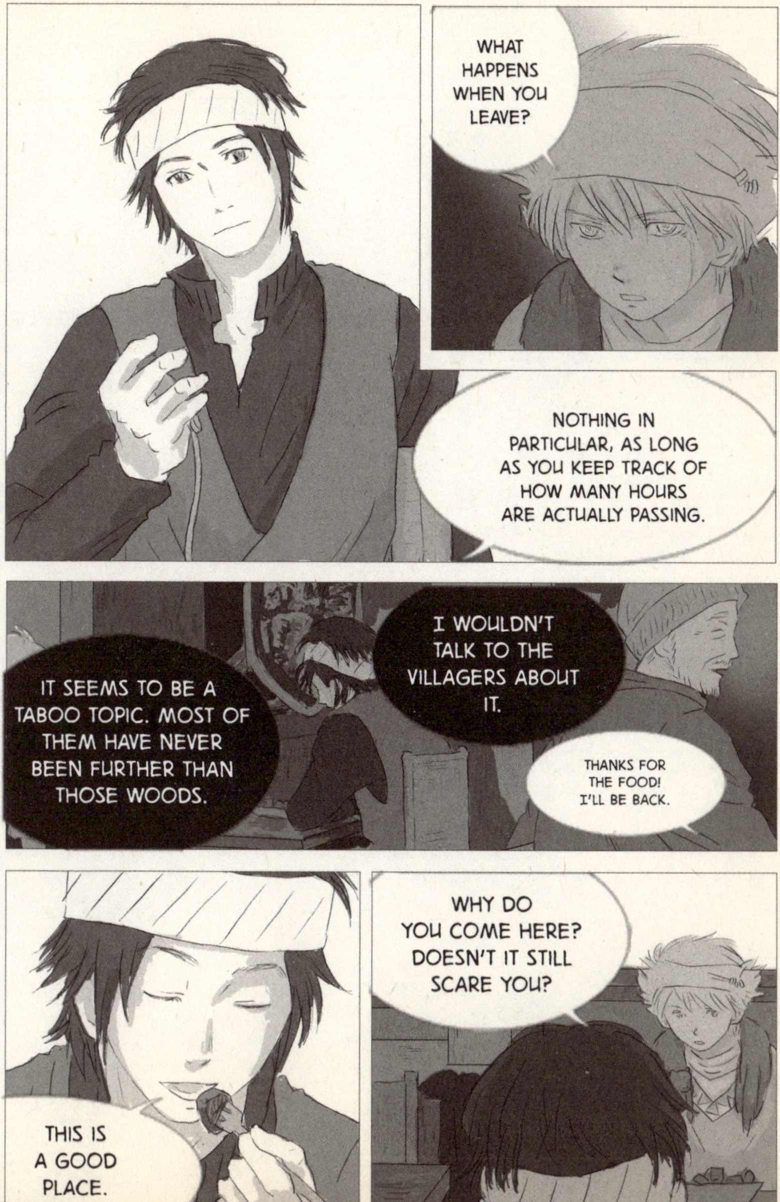
WHAT HAPPENS WHEN YOU LEAVE?
NOTHING IN PARTICULAR, AS LONG AS YOU KEEP TRACK OF HOW MANY HOURS ARE ACTUALLY PASSING.
I WOULDN'T TALK TO THE VILLAGERS ABOUT IT.
IT SEEMS TO BE A TABOO TOPIC. MOST OF THEM HAVE NEVER BEEN FURTHER THAN THOSE WOODS.
THANKS FOR THE FOOD! I'LL BE BACK.
WHY DO YOU COME HERE? DOESN'T IT STILL SCARE YOU?
THIS IS A GOOD PLACE.

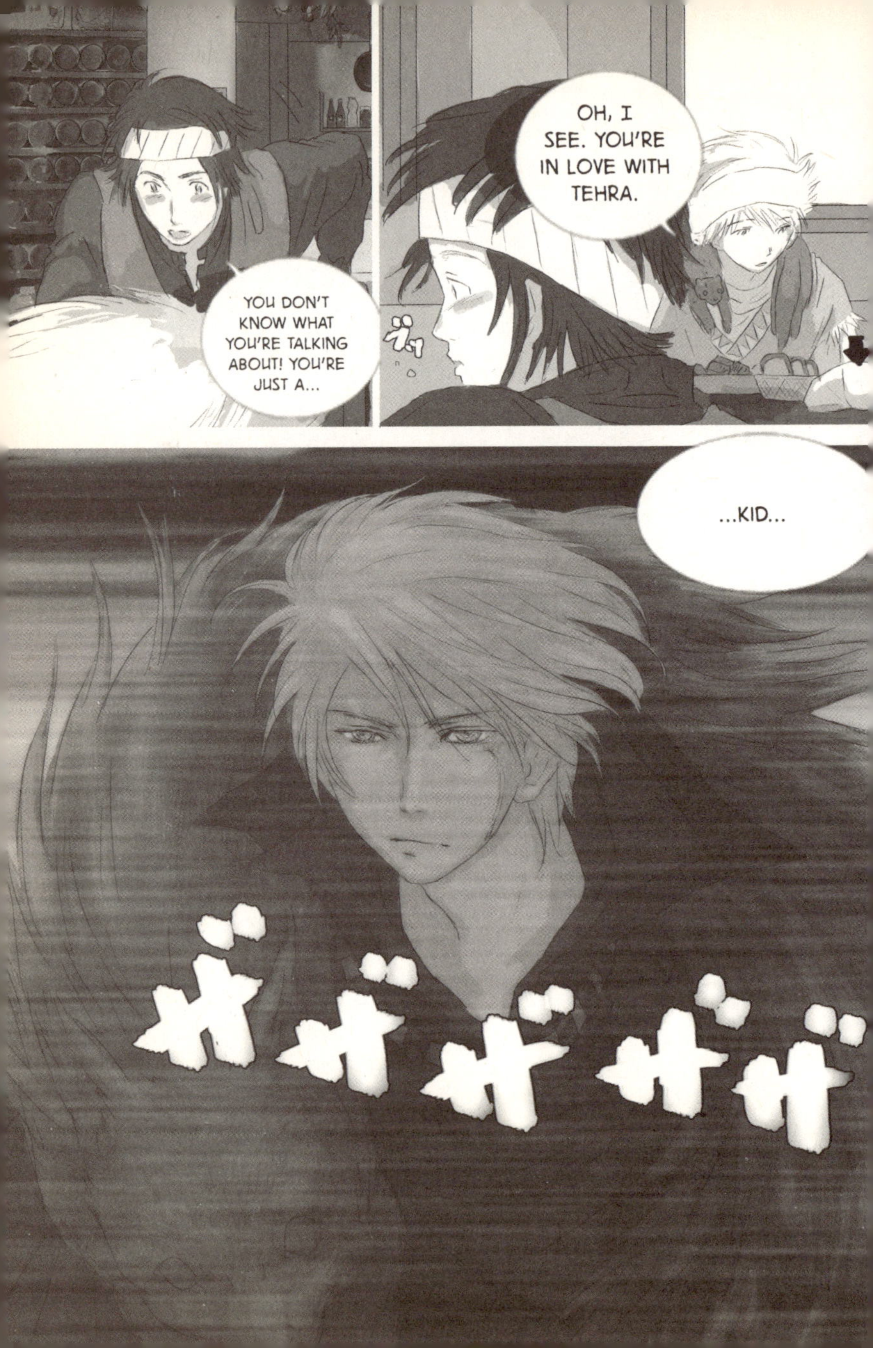
OH, I SEE. YOU'RE IN LOVE WITH TEHRA.
YOU DON'T KNOW WHAT YOU'RE TALKING ABOUT! YOU'RE JUST A...
...KID...
ザザザザ

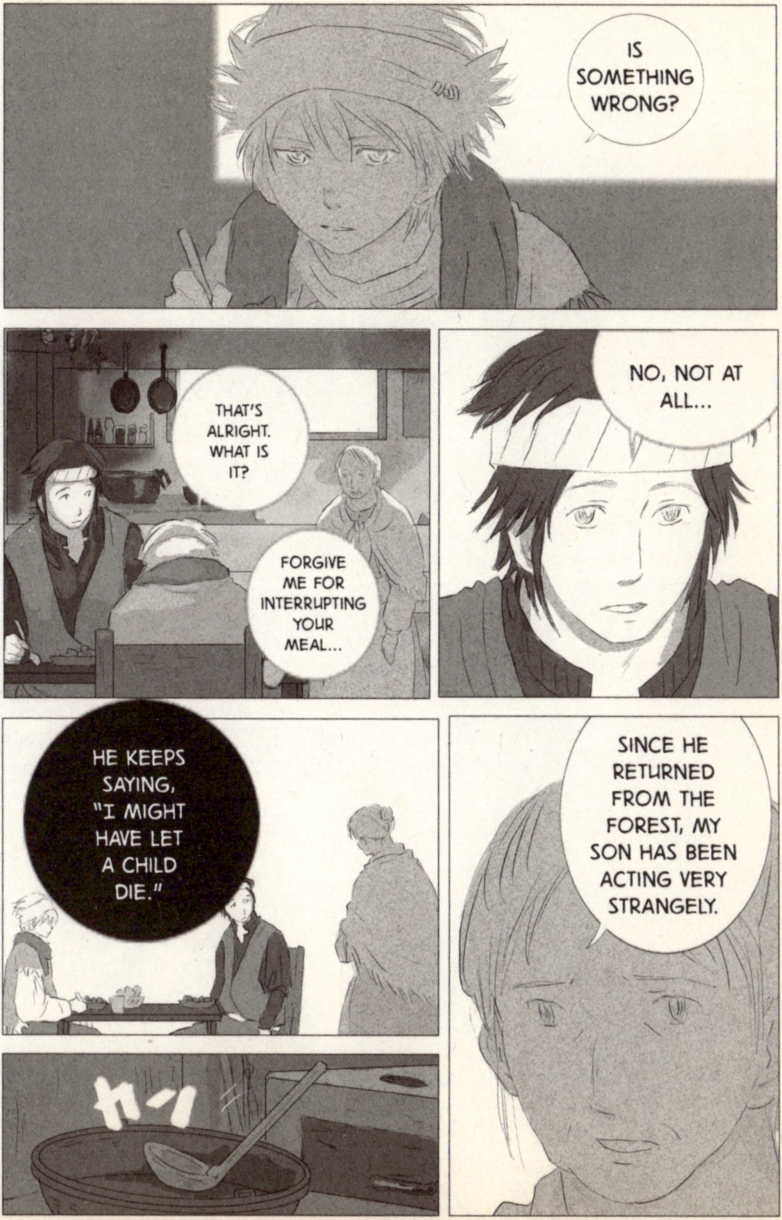
IS SOMETHING WRONG?
NO, NOT AT ALL...
THAT'S ALRIGHT. WHAT IS IT?
FORGIVE ME FOR INTERRUPTING YOUR MEAL...
SINCE HE RETURNED FROM THE FOREST, MY SON HAS BEEN ACTING VERY STRANGELY.
HE KEEPS SAYING, "I MIGHT HAVE LET A CHILD DIE."

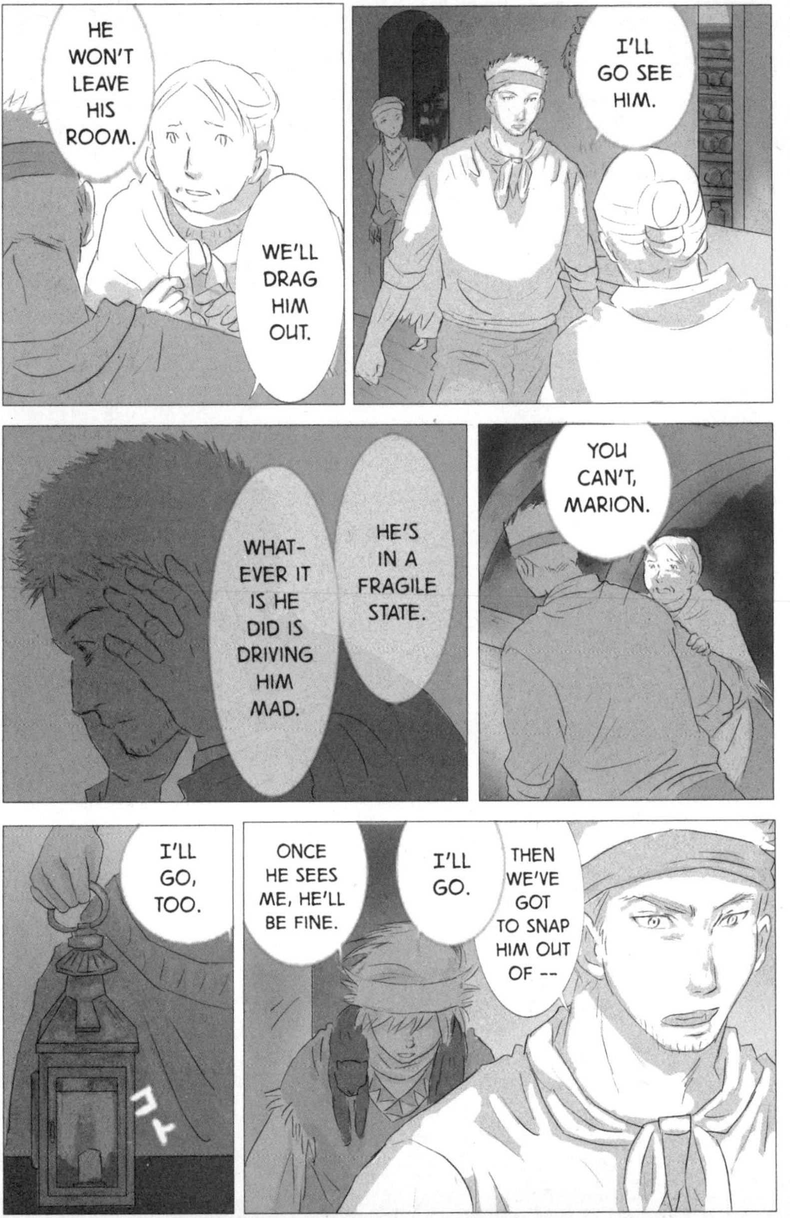
I'LL GO SEE HIM.
HE WON'T LEAVE HIS ROOM.
WE'LL DRAG HIM OUT.
YOU CAN'T, MARION.
HE'S IN A FRAGILE STATE.
WHAT-EVER IT IS HE DID IS DRIVING HIM MAD.
THEN WE'VE GOT TO SNAP HIM OUT OF --
I'LL GO.
ONCE HE SEES ME, HE'LL BE FINE.
I'LL GO, TOO.

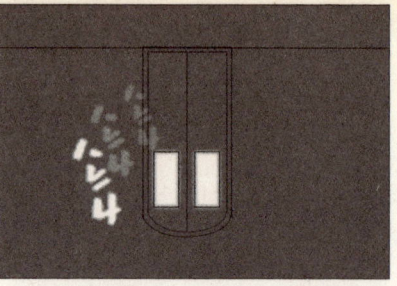

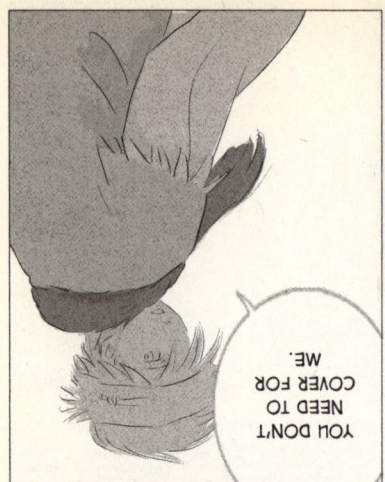

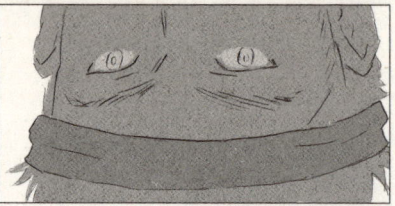

DON'T WORRY, MARION.
BYE FOR NOW.
I'M SORRY FOR THE BOTHER.
WE DON'T MIND.
YOU DON'T NEED TO COVER FOR ME.

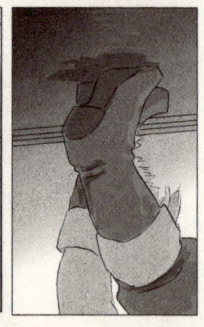

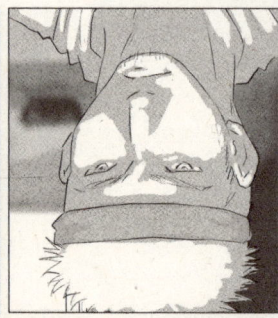

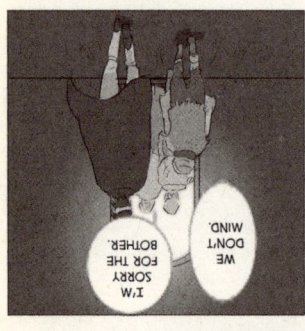

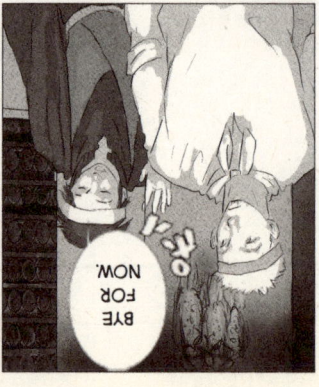

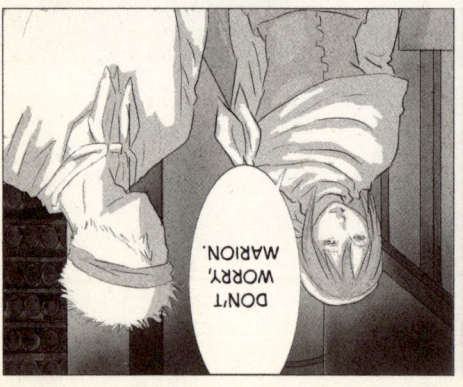

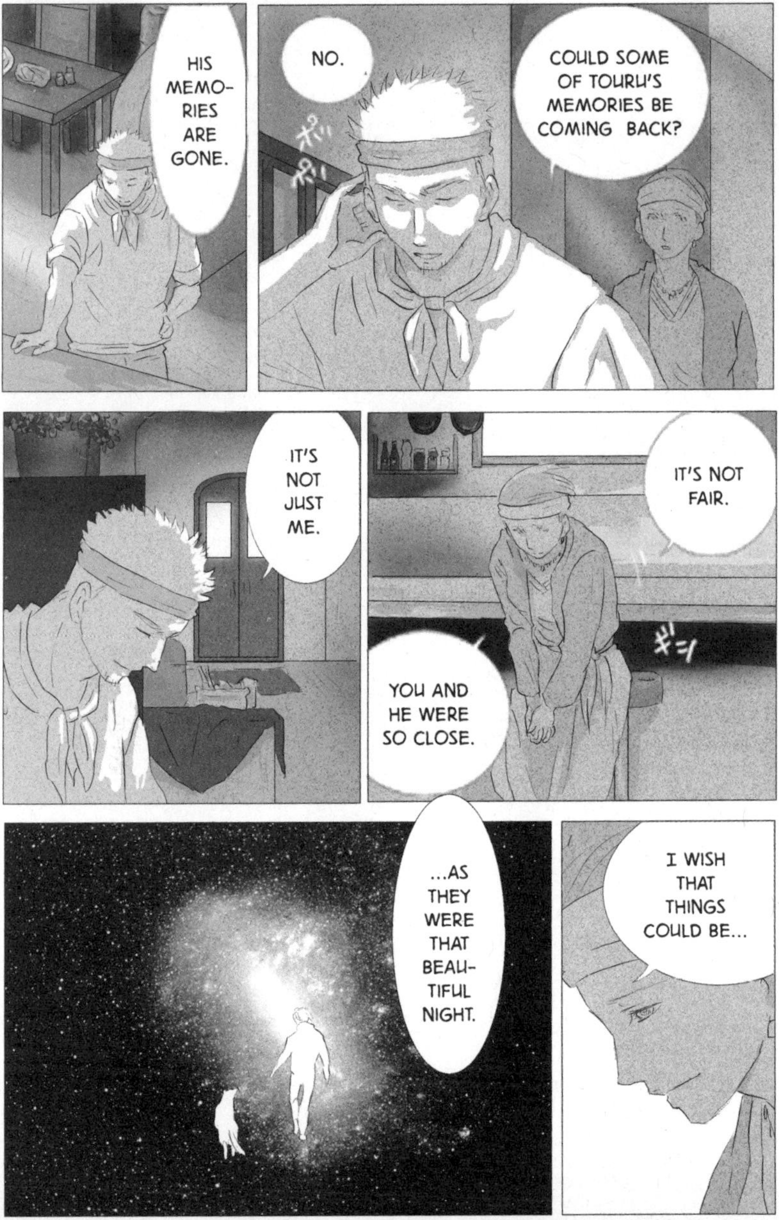
COULD SOME OF TOURU'S MEMORIES BE COMING BACK?
NO.
HIS MEMORIES ARE GONE.
IT'S NOT FAIR.
YOU AND HE WERE SO CLOSE.
IT'S NOT JUST ME.
I WISH THAT THINGS COULD BE...
...AS THEY WERE THAT BEAUTIFUL NIGHT.

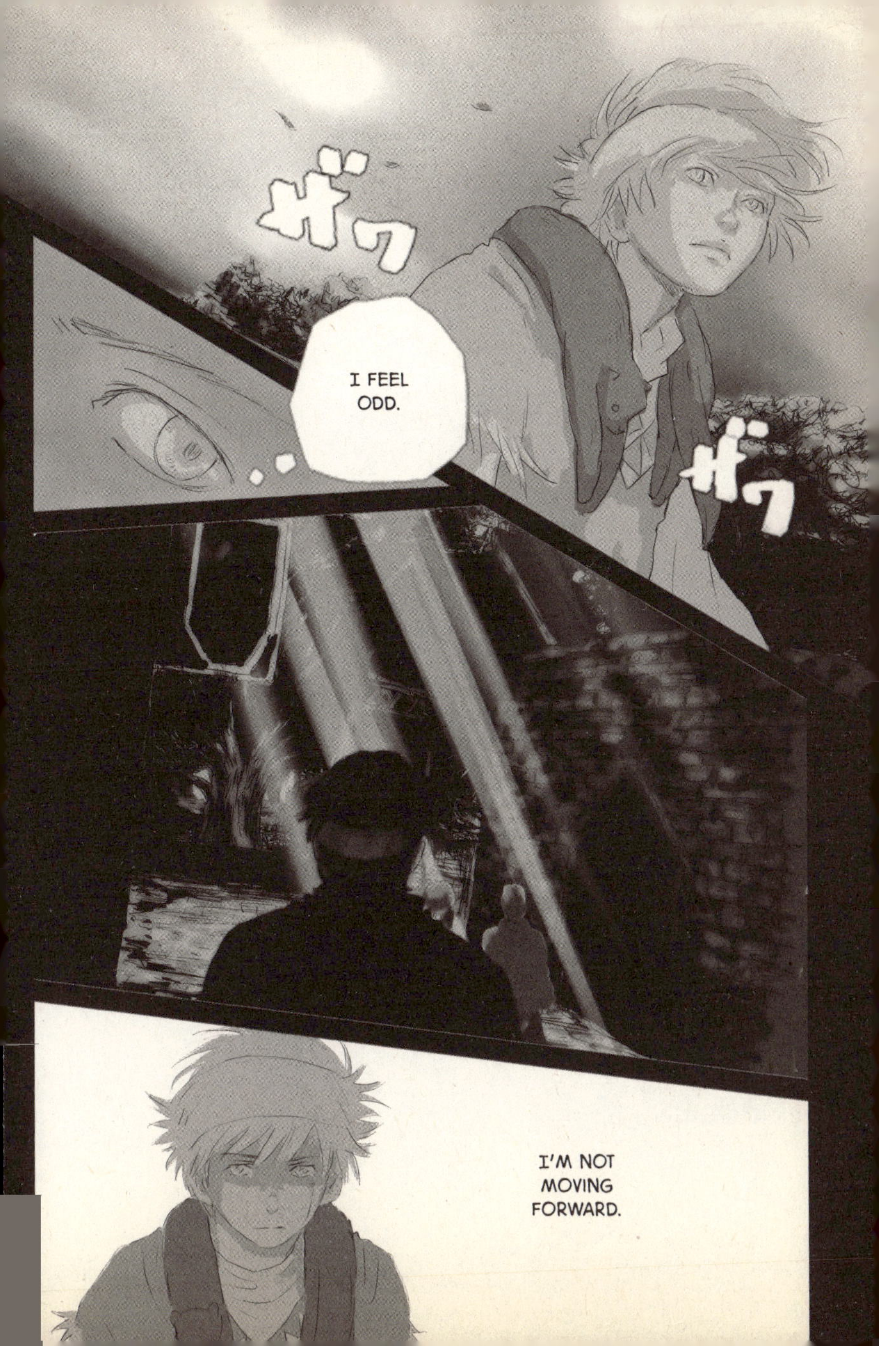
ザワ
ザワ
I FEEL ODD.
I'M NOT MOVING FORWARD.

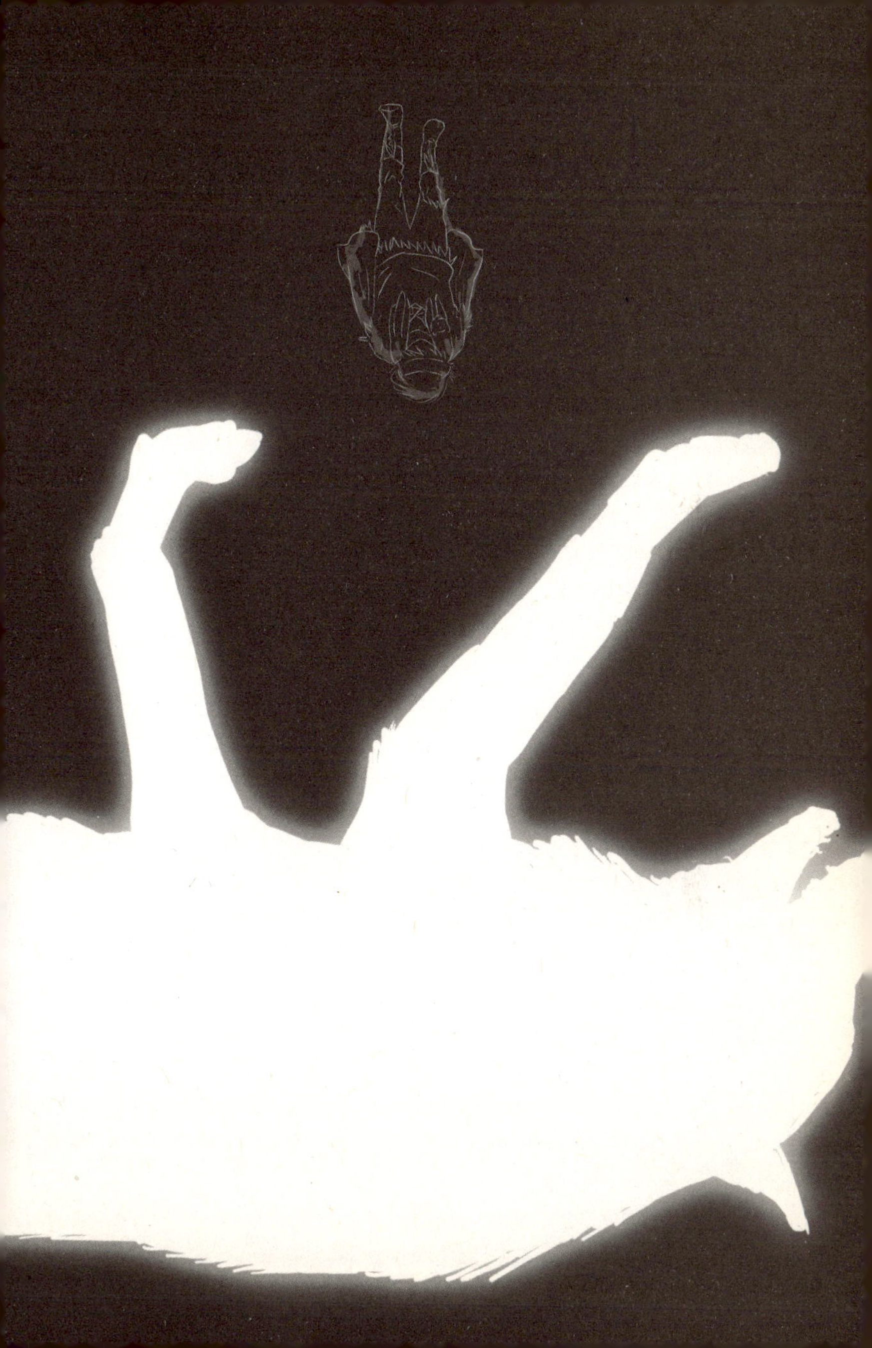

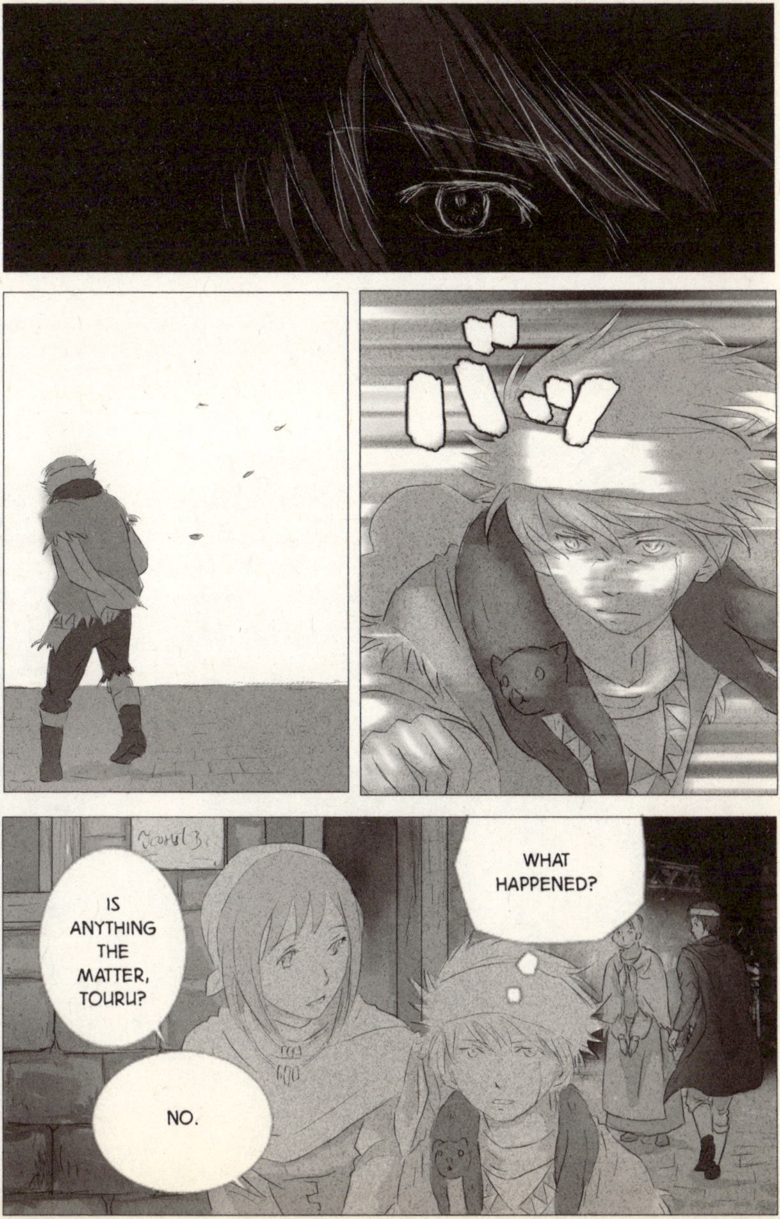
WHAT HAPPENED?
IS ANYTHING THE MATTER, TOURU?
NO.

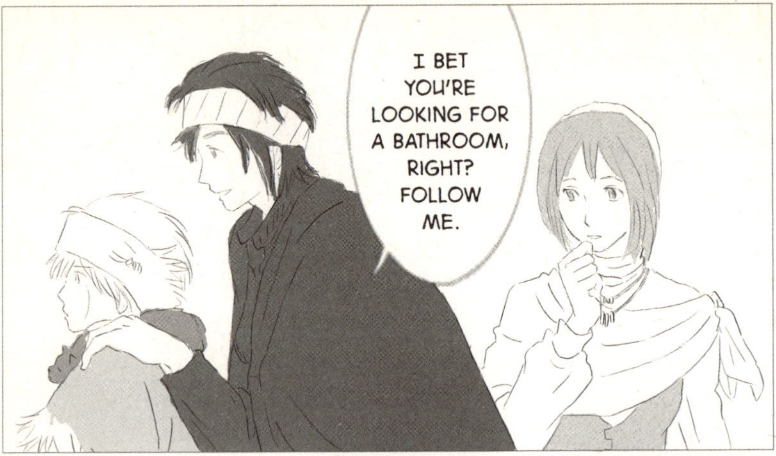
I BET YOU'RE LOOKING FOR A BATHROOM, RIGHT? FOLLOW ME.

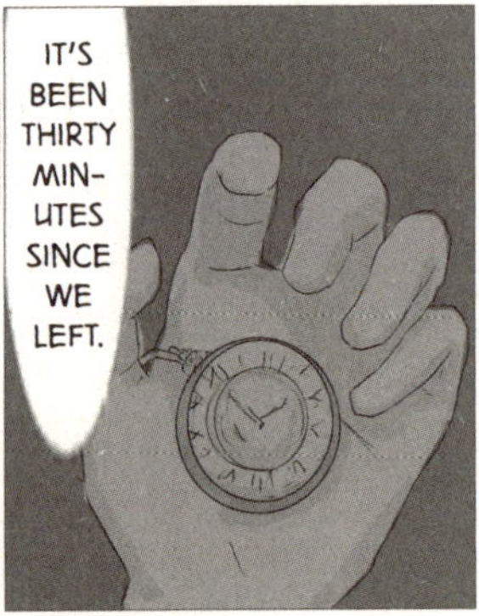
IT'S BEEN THIRTY MIN-UTES SINCE WE LEFT.

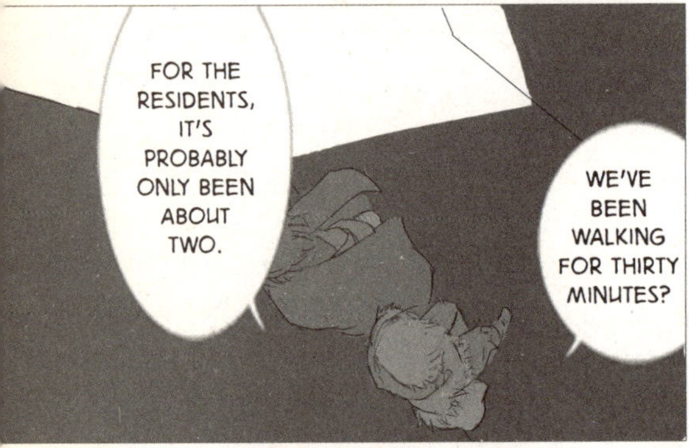
WE'VE BEEN WALKING FOR THIRTY MINUTES?
FOR THE RESIDENTS, IT'S PROBABLY ONLY BEEN ABOUT TWO.

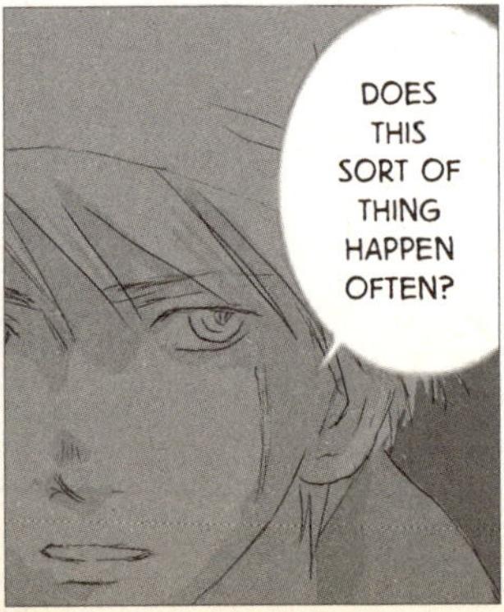
DOES THIS SORT OF THING HAPPEN OFTEN?

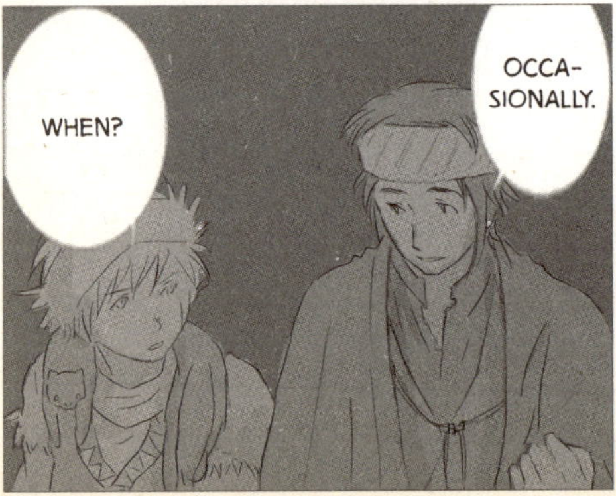
OCCA-SIONALLY.
WHEN?

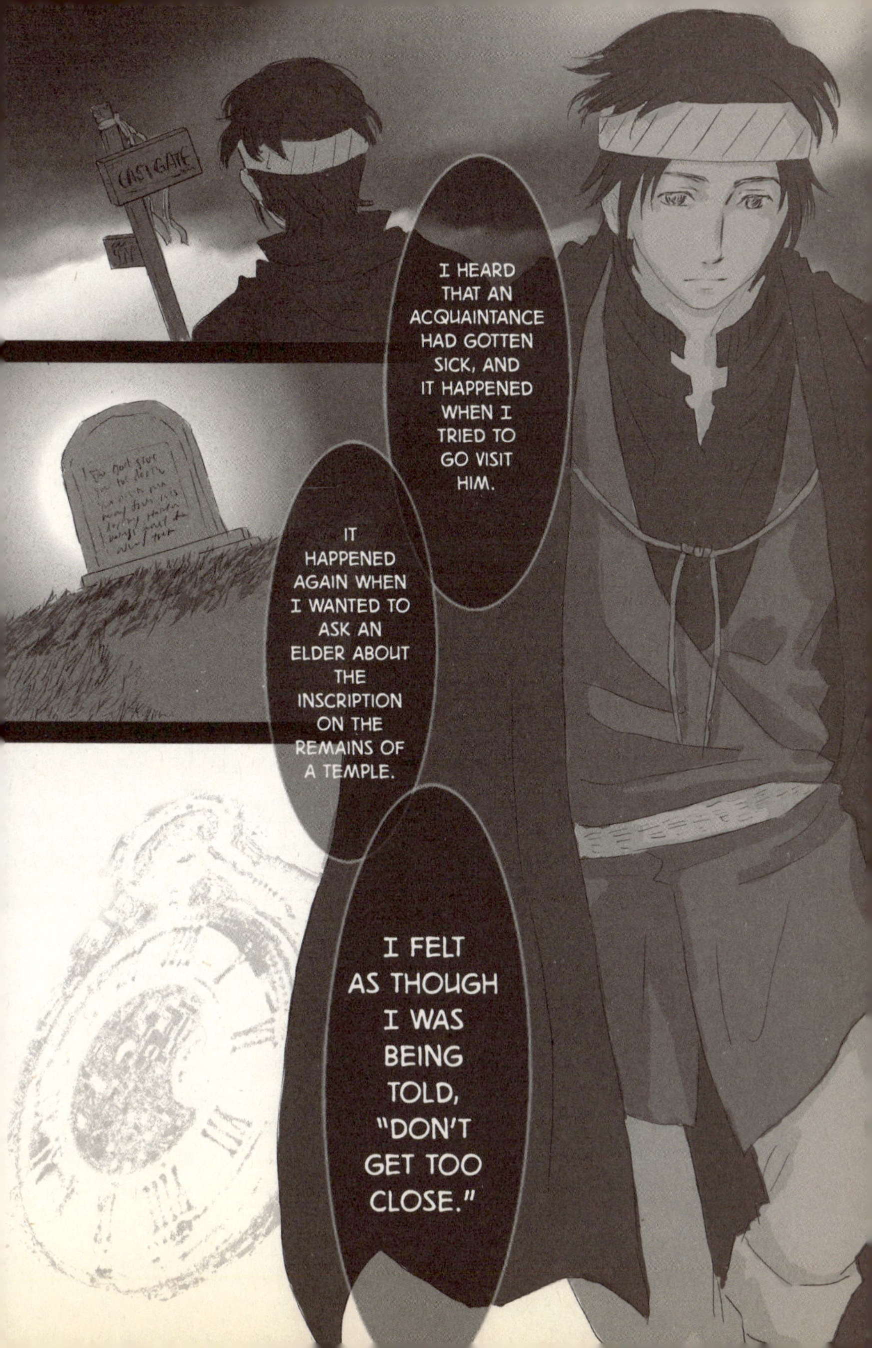
I HEARD THAT AN ACQUAINTANCE HAD GOTTEN SICK, AND IT HAPPENED WHEN I TRIED TO GO VISIT HIM.
IT HAPPENED AGAIN WHEN I WANTED TO ASK AN ELDER ABOUT THE INSCRIPTION ON THE REMAINS OF A TEMPLE.
I FELT AS THOUGH I WAS BEING TOLD, "DON'T GET TOO CLOSE."

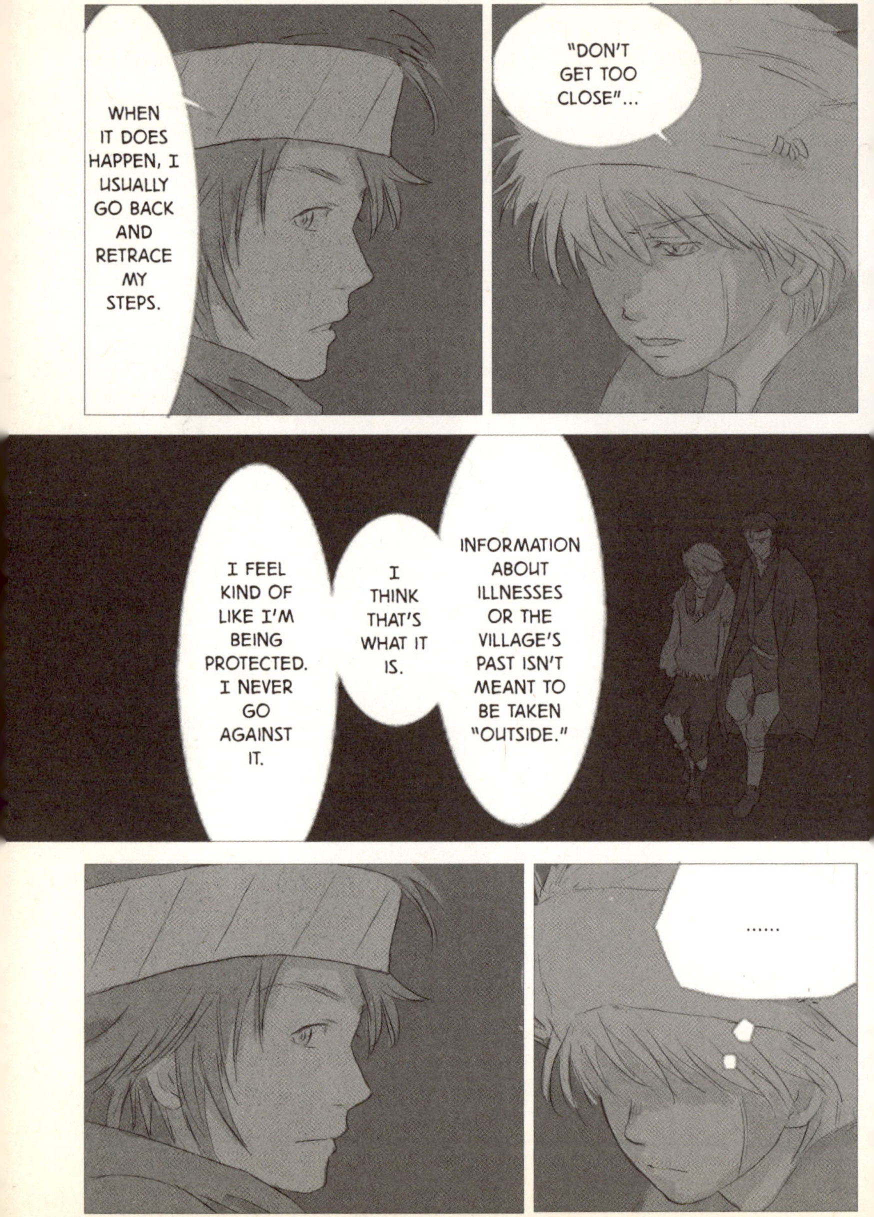
"DON'T GET TOO CLOSE"...
WHEN IT DOES HAPPEN, I USUALLY GO BACK AND RETRACE MY STEPS.
INFORMATION ABOUT ILLNESSES OR THE VILLAGE'S PAST ISN'T MEANT TO BE TAKEN "OUTSIDE."
I THINK THAT'S WHAT IT IS.
I FEEL KIND OF LIKE I'M BEING PROTECTED. I NEVER GO AGAINST IT.
......

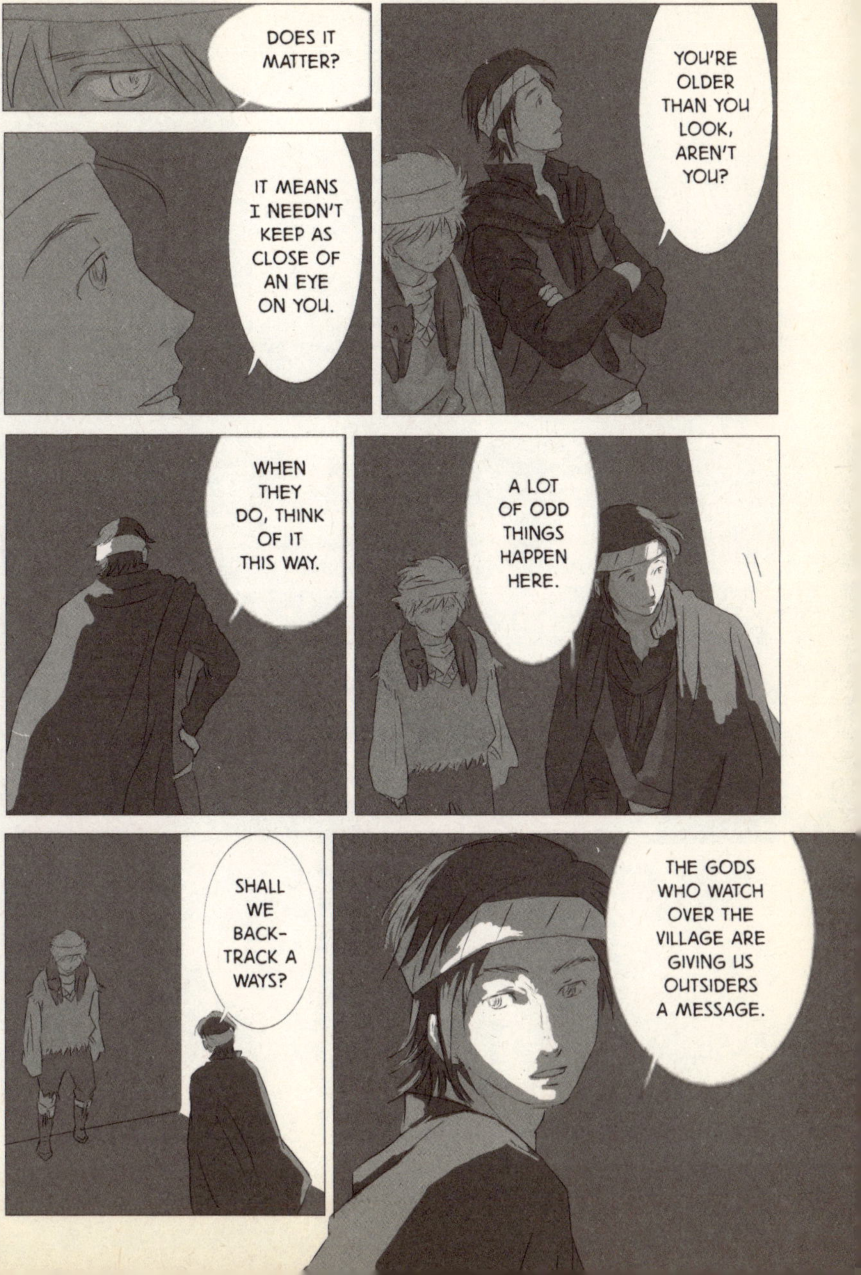
YOU'RE OLDER THAN YOU LOOK, AREN'T YOU?
DOES IT MATTER?
IT MEANS I NEEDN'T KEEP AS CLOSE OF AN EYE ON YOU.
A LOT OF ODD THINGS HAPPEN HERE.
WHEN THEY DO, THINK OF IT THIS WAY.
THE GODS WHO WATCH OVER THE VILLAGE ARE GIVING US OUTSIDERS A MESSAGE.
SHALL WE BACK-TRACK A WAYS?

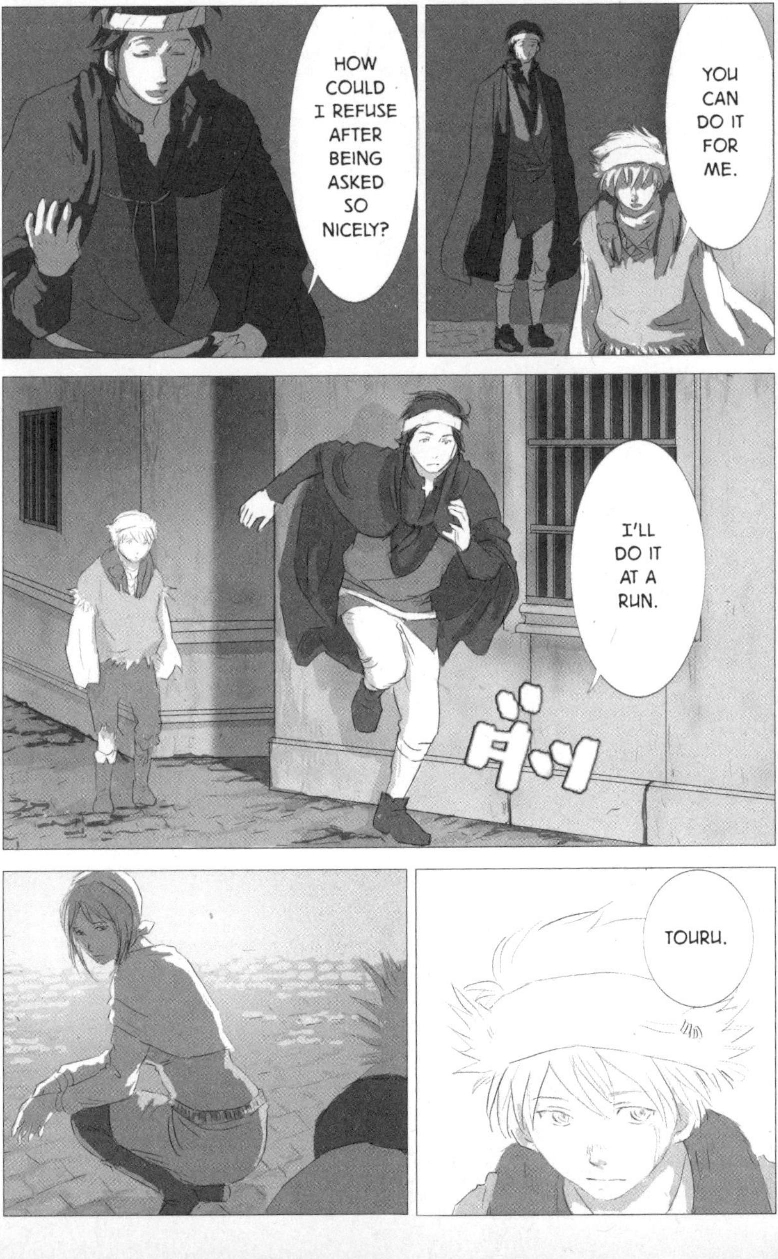
YOU CAN DO IT FOR ME.
HOW COULD I REFUSE AFTER BEING ASKED SO NICELY?
I'LL DO IT AT A RUN.
ダッ
TOURU.

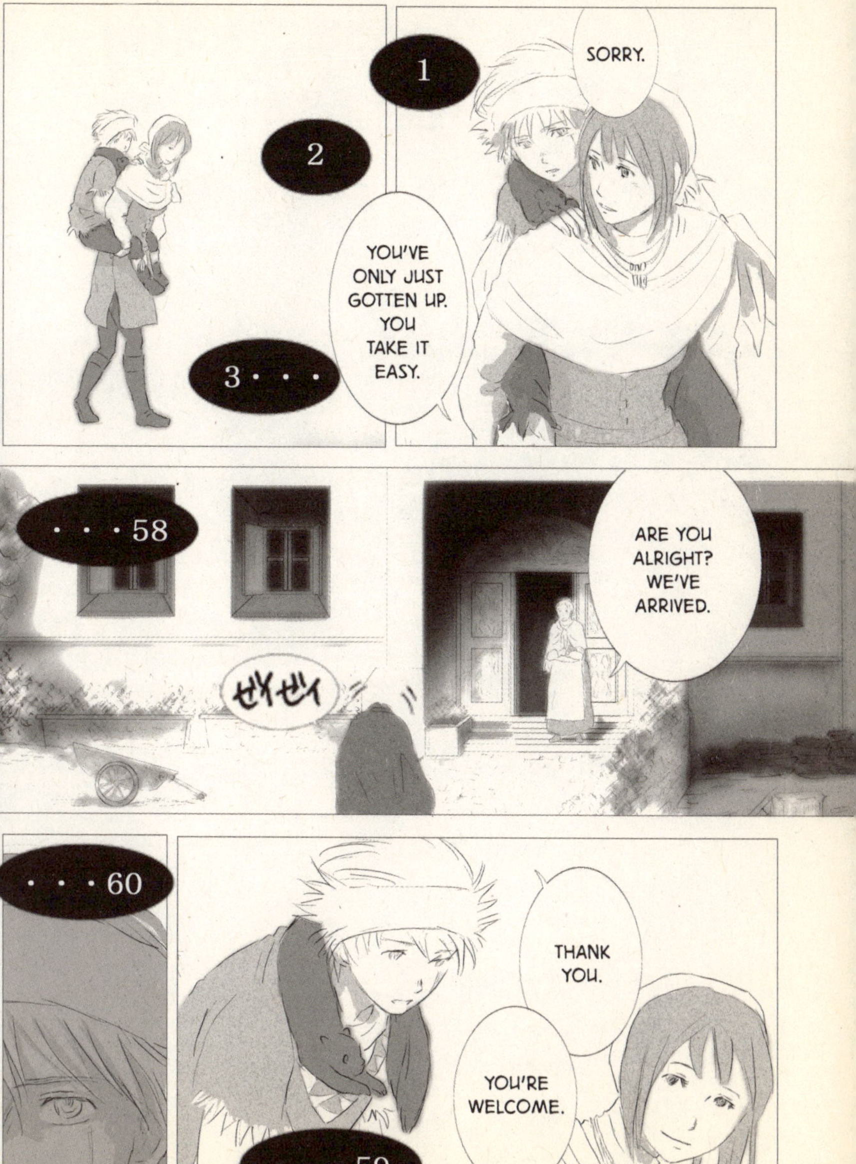
SORRY.
1
YOU'VE ONLY JUST GOTTEN UP. YOU TAKE IT EASY.
2
3 · · ·
ARE YOU ALRIGHT? WE'VE ARRIVED.
ゼイゼイ
· · · 58
THANK YOU.
YOU'RE WELCOME.
· · · 59
· · · 60

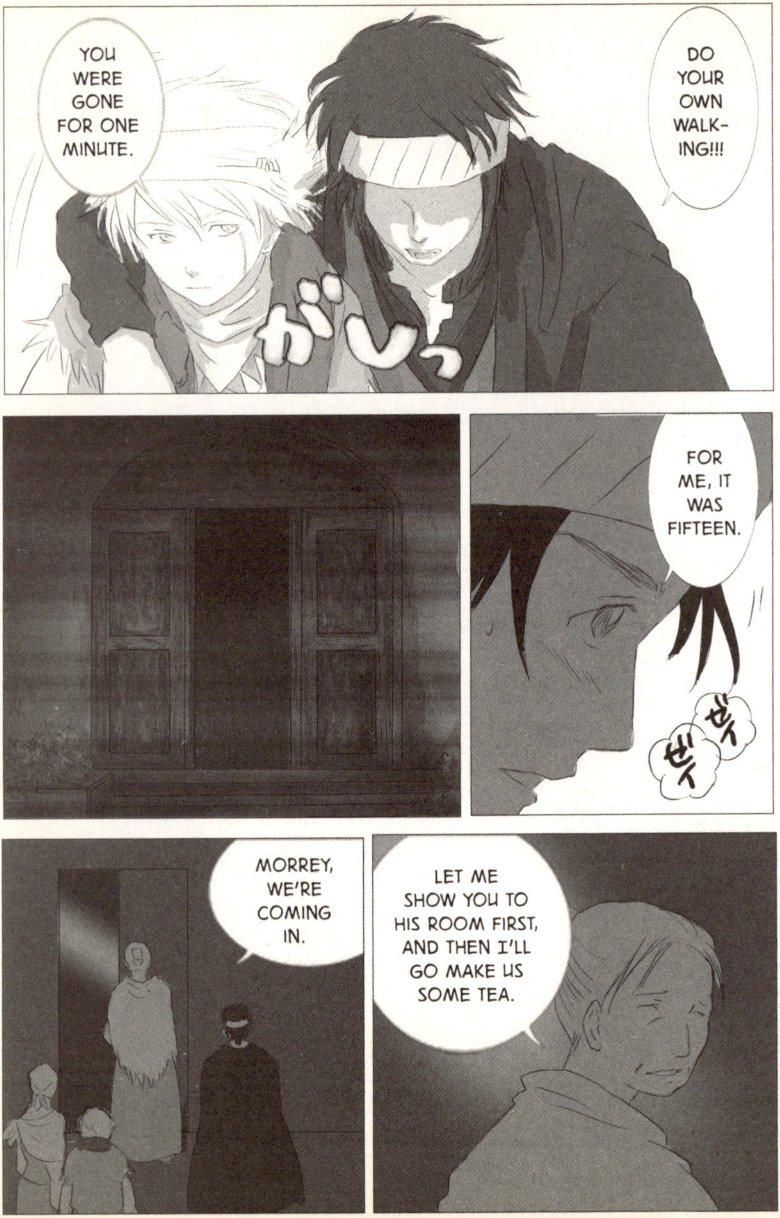
DO YOUR OWN WALK-ING!!!
YOU WERE GONE FOR ONE MINUTE.
がしっ
FOR ME, IT WAS FIFTEEN.
ゼイ ゼイ
LET ME SHOW YOU TO HIS ROOM FIRST, AND THEN I'LL GO MAKE US SOME TEA.
MORREY, WE'RE COMING IN.

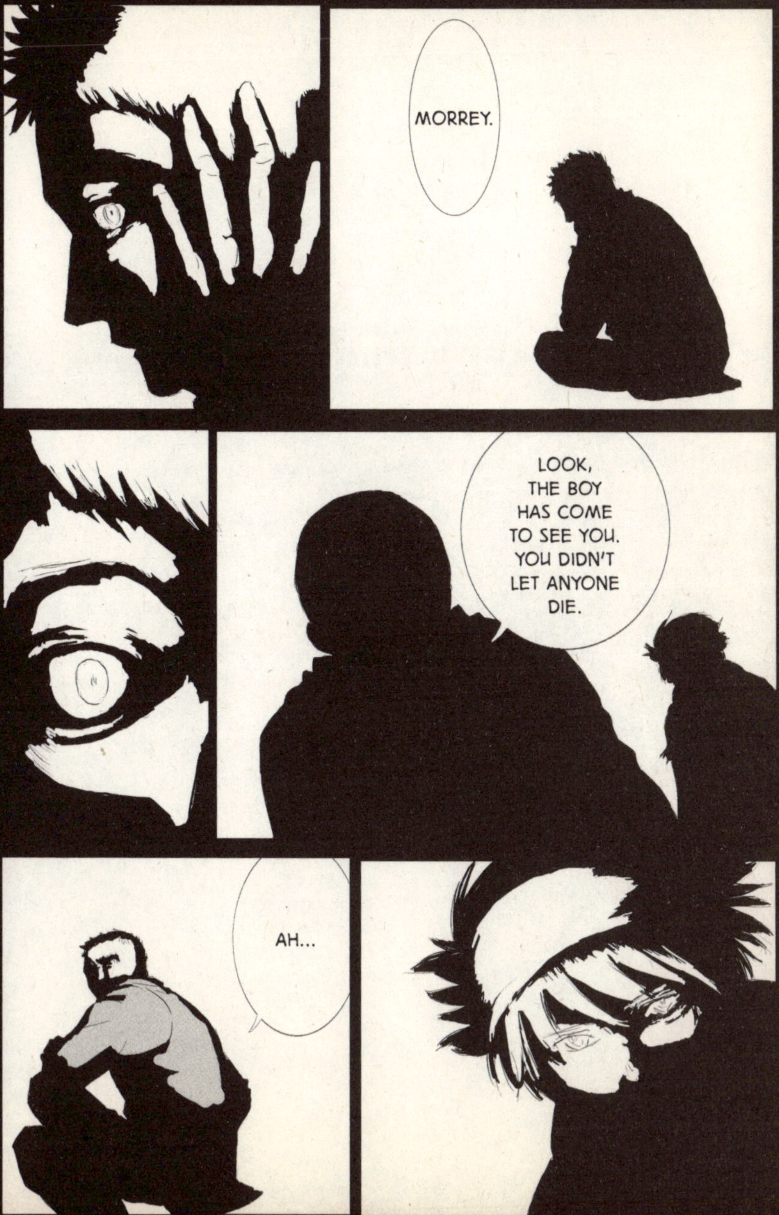
MORREY.
LOOK, THE BOY HAS COME TO SEE YOU. YOU DIDN'T LET ANYONE DIE.
AH...

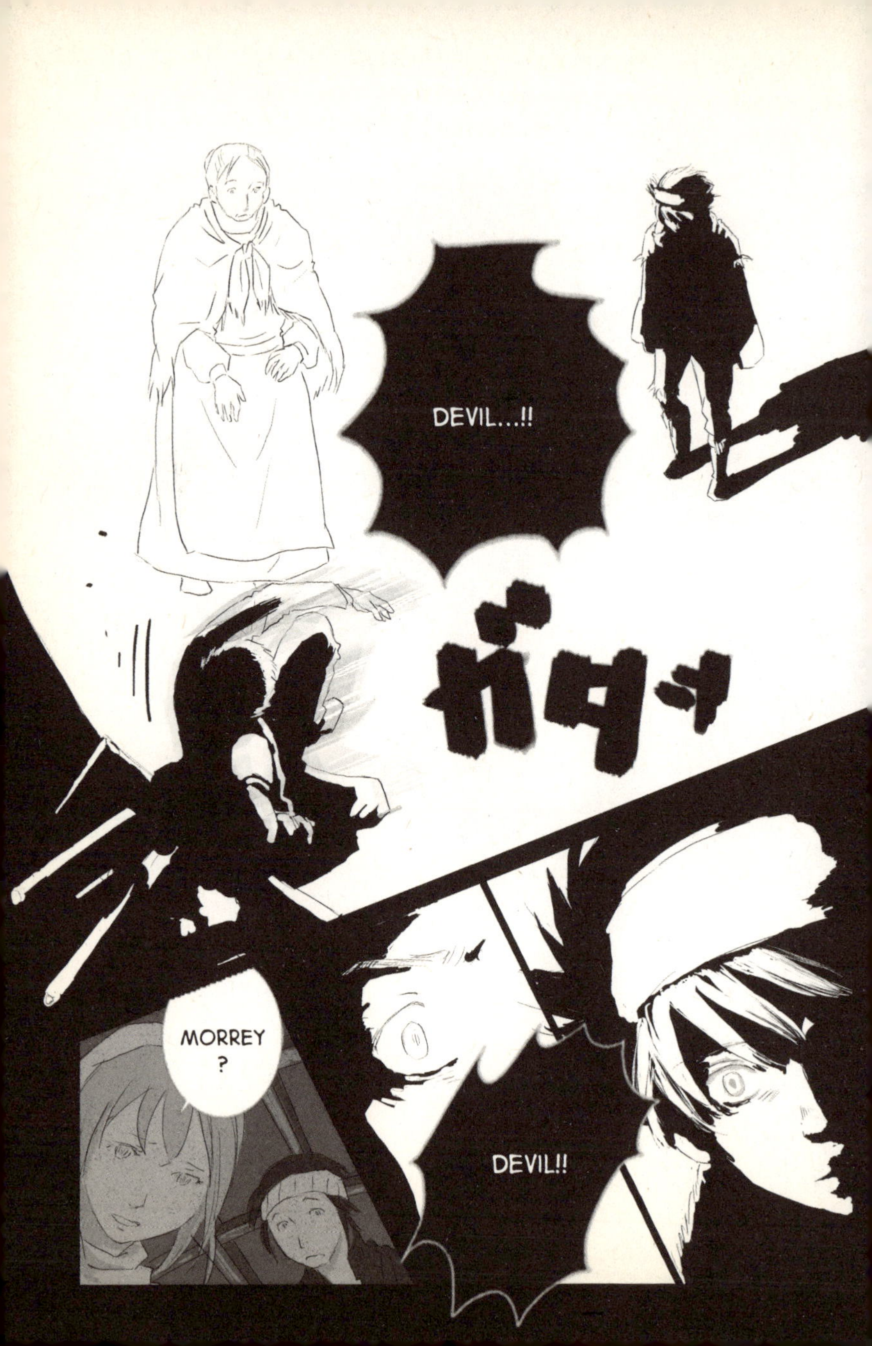
DEVIL...!!
ガタッ
DEVIL!!
MORREY ?

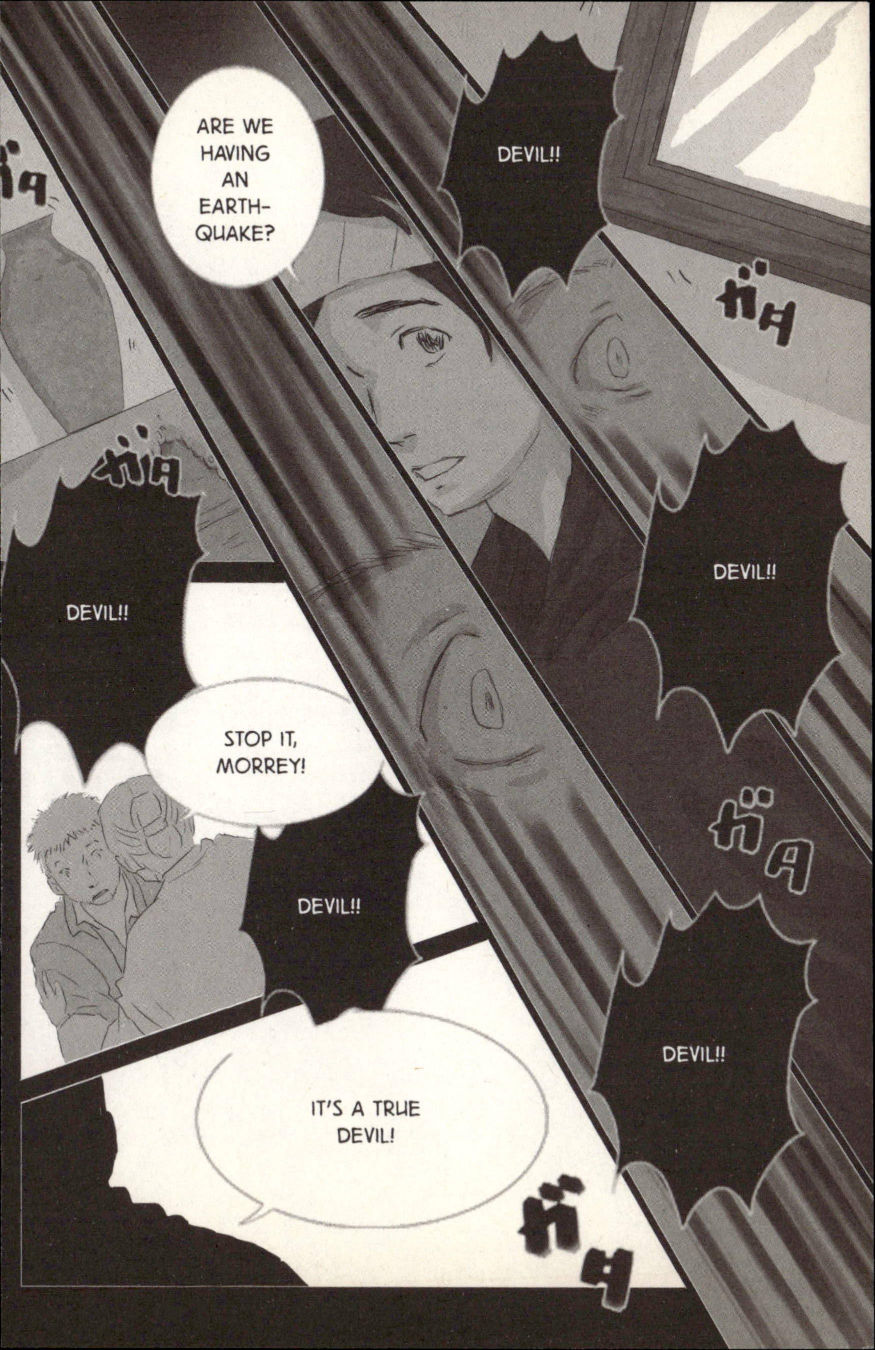
DEVIL!!
ガタ
ARE WE HAVING AN EARTH-QUAKE?
ガタ
DEVIL!!
ガタ
DEVIL!!
STOP IT, MORREY!
DEVIL!!
DEVIL!!
ガタ
IT'S A TRUE DEVIL!

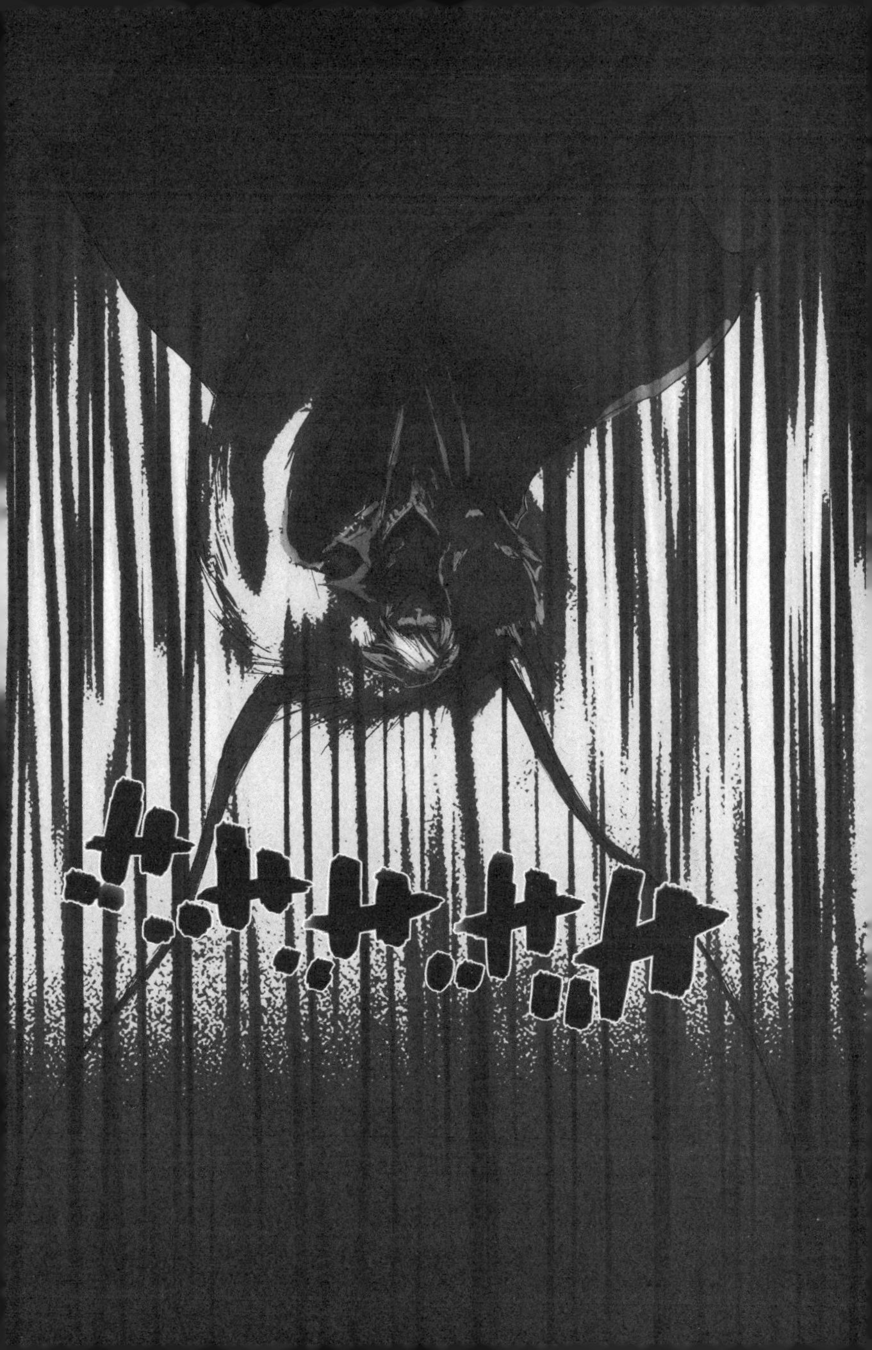
H..H..H..H..H

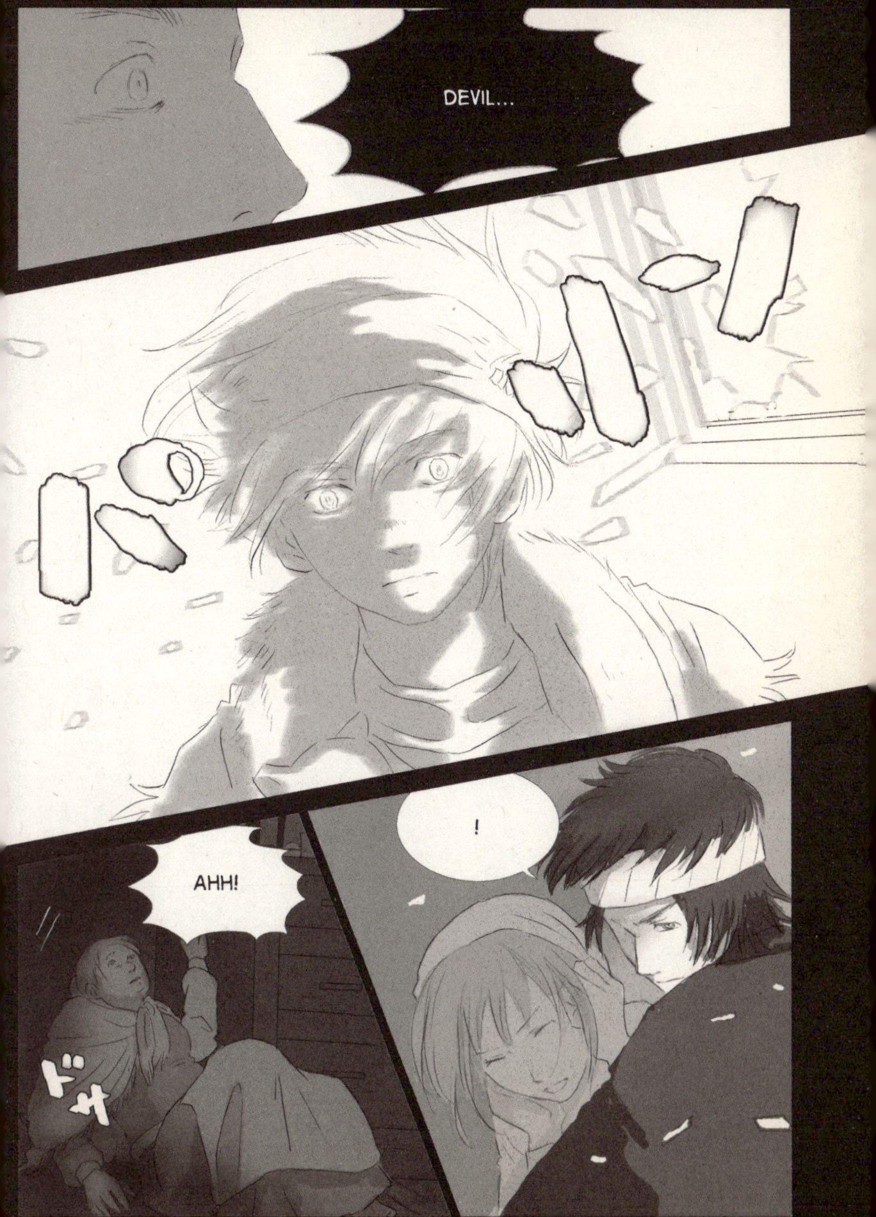
DEVIL...
!
AHH!
ドサ

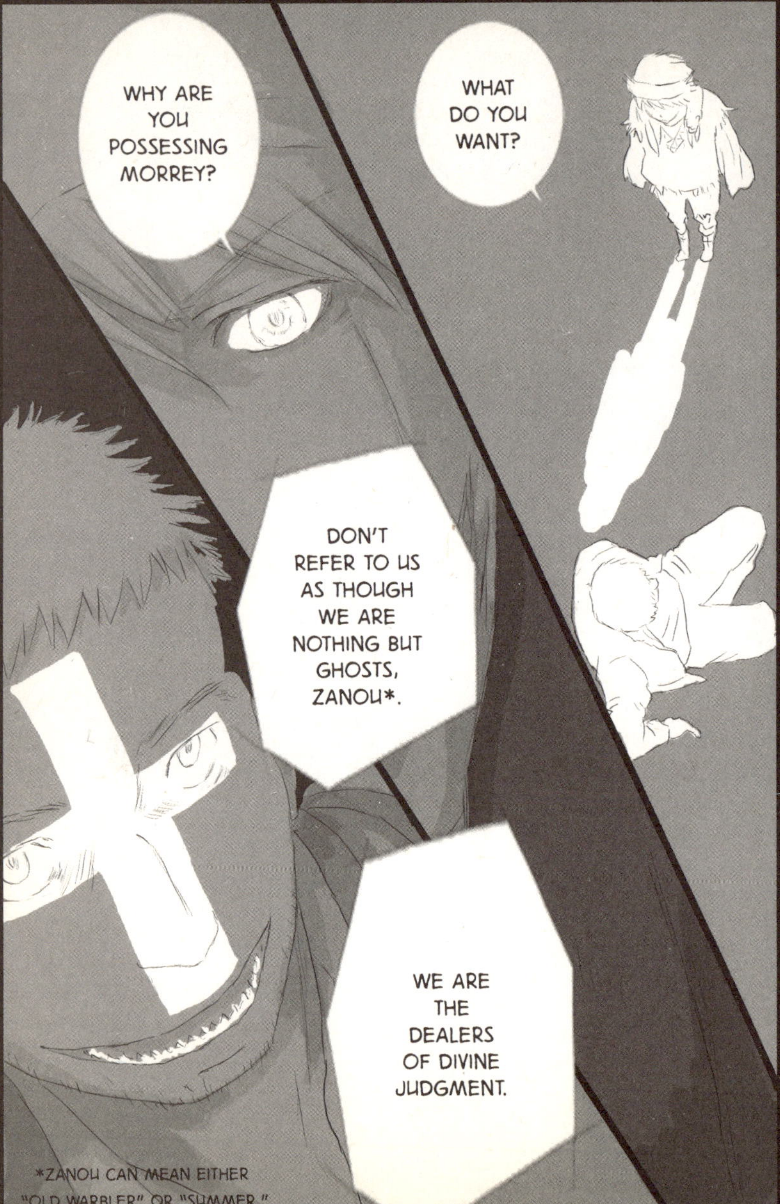
WHAT DO YOU WANT?
WHY ARE YOU POSSESSING MORREY?
DON'T REFER TO US AS THOUGH WE ARE NOTHING BUT GHOSTS, ZANOU*.
WE ARE THE DEALERS OF DIVINE JUDGMENT.

*ZANOU CAN MEAN EITHER "OLD WARBLER" OR "SUMMER."

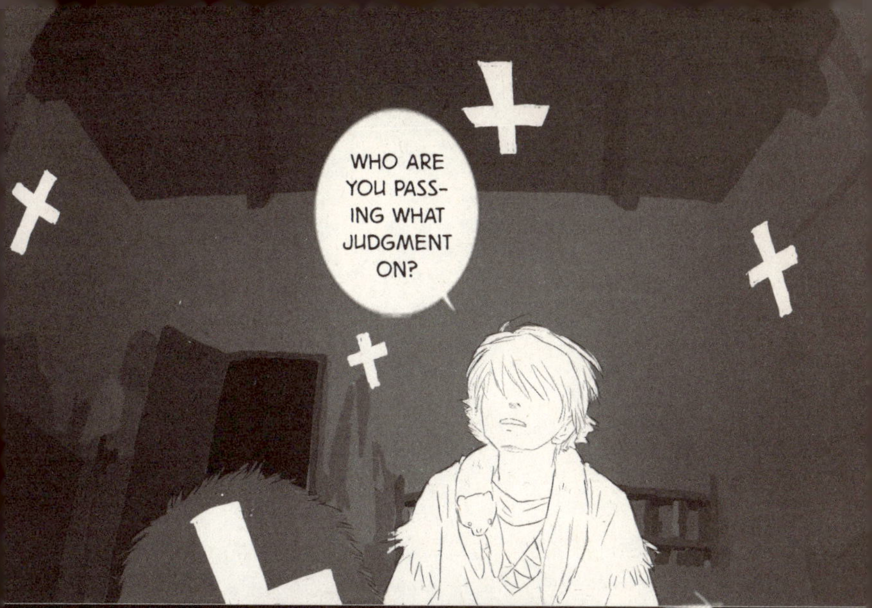
WHO ARE YOU PASSING WHAT JUDGMENT ON?
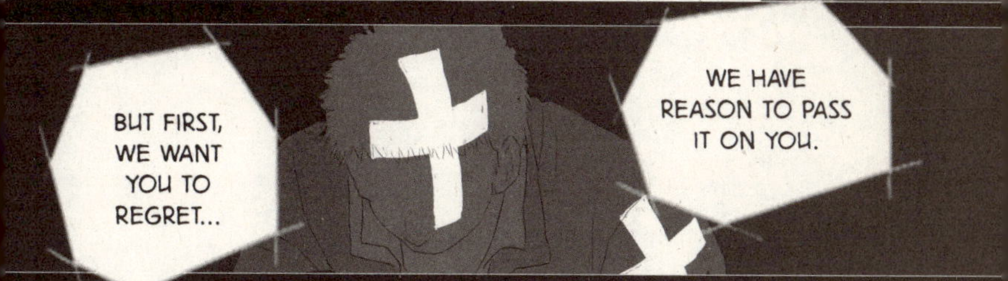
WE HAVE REASON TO PASS IT ON YOU.
BUT FIRST, WE WANT YOU TO REGRET...
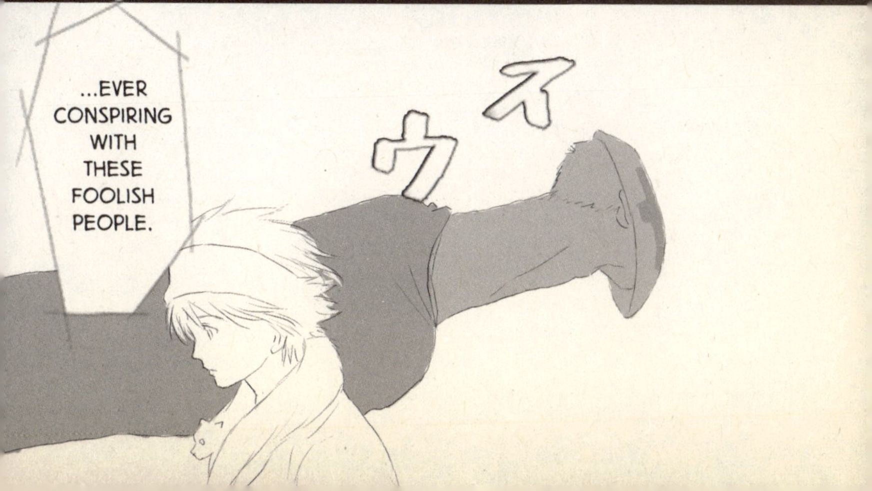
スウ
...EVER CONSPIRING WITH THESE FOOLISH PEOPLE.

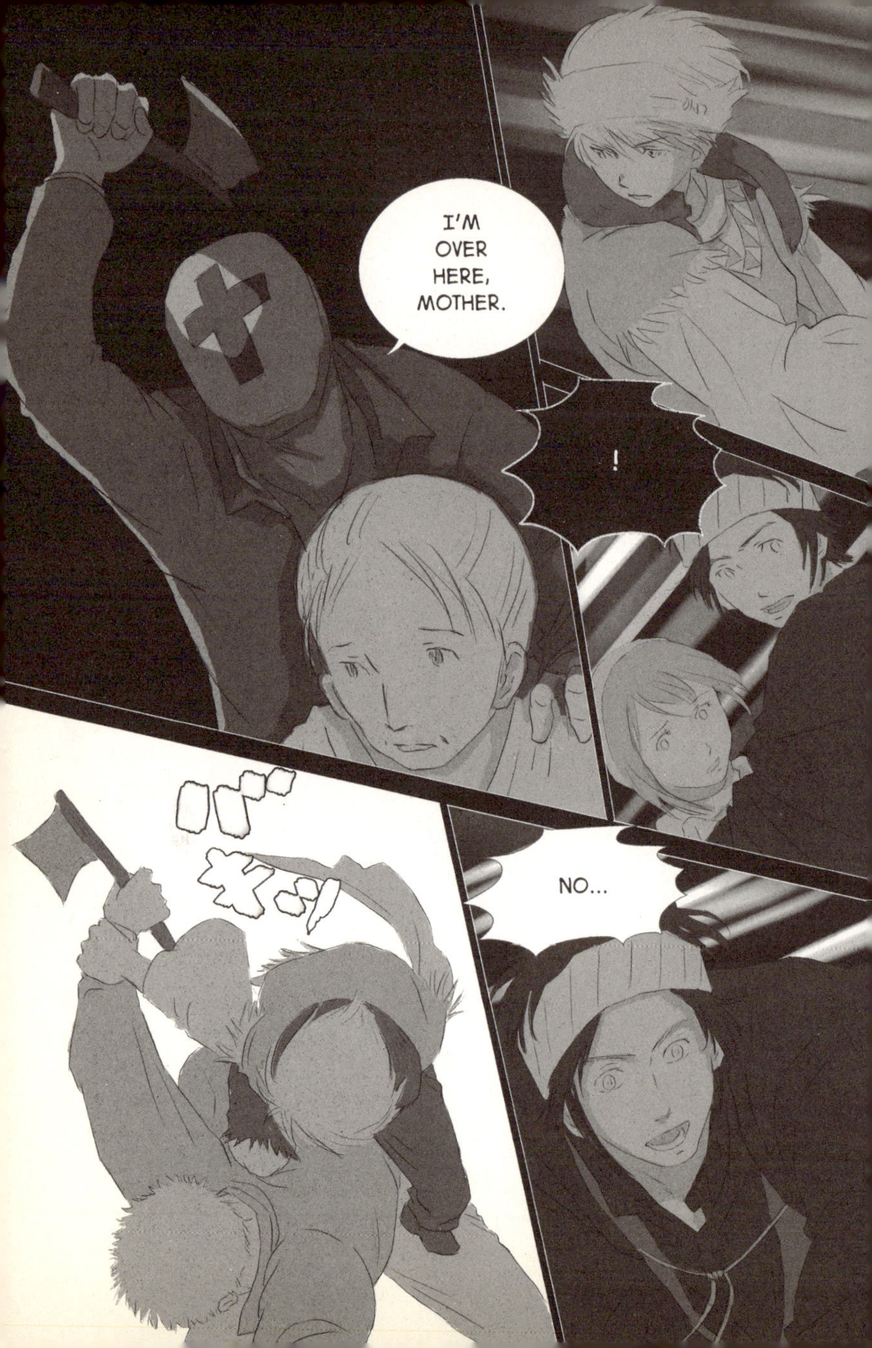
I'M OVER HERE, MOTHER.
!
NO...

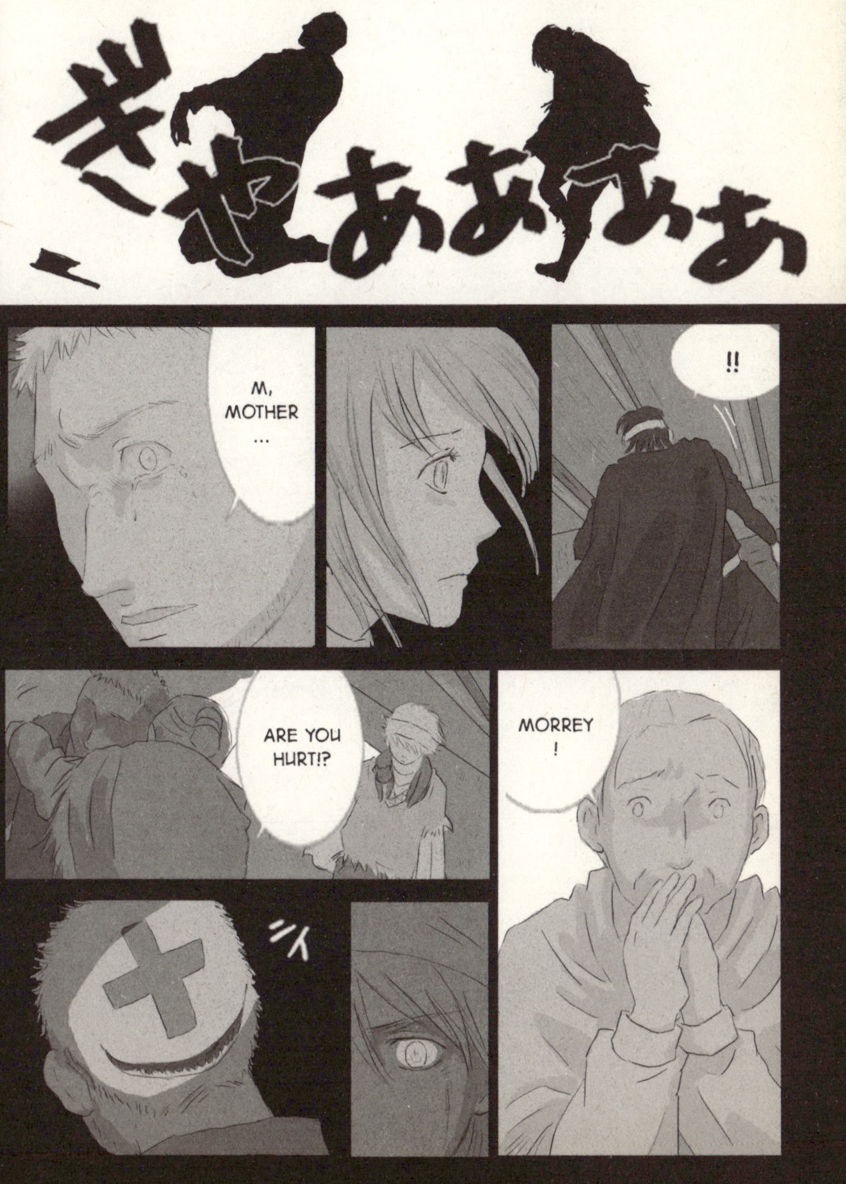
ぎゃああああ
!!
M, MOTHER ...
MORREY !
ARE YOU HURT!?

YOU ARE NO LONGER USEFUL.
BE JUDGED BY THE PEOPLE, AND GO TO YOUR MISERABLE LITTLE DIRT GRAVE.
YOU MURDERER !!
CALM DOWN, EMMET!

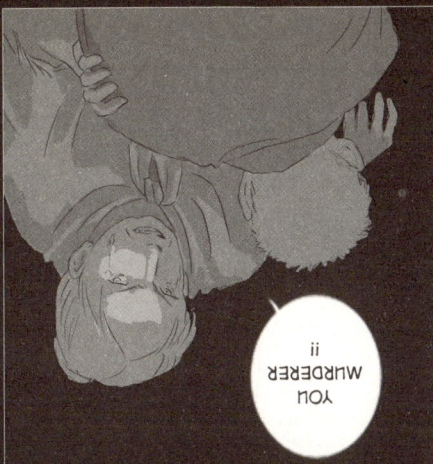

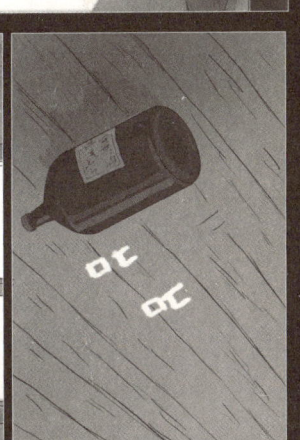

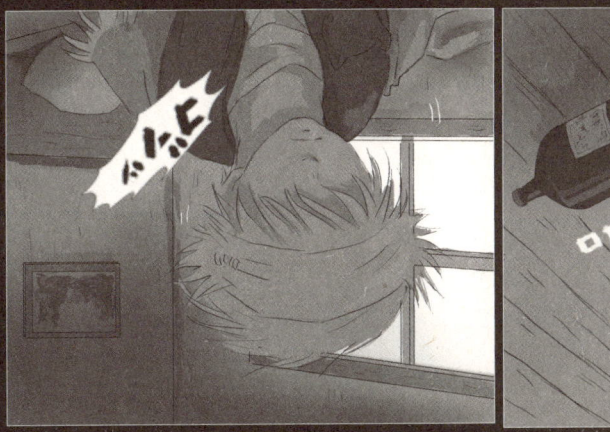

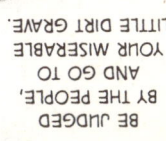

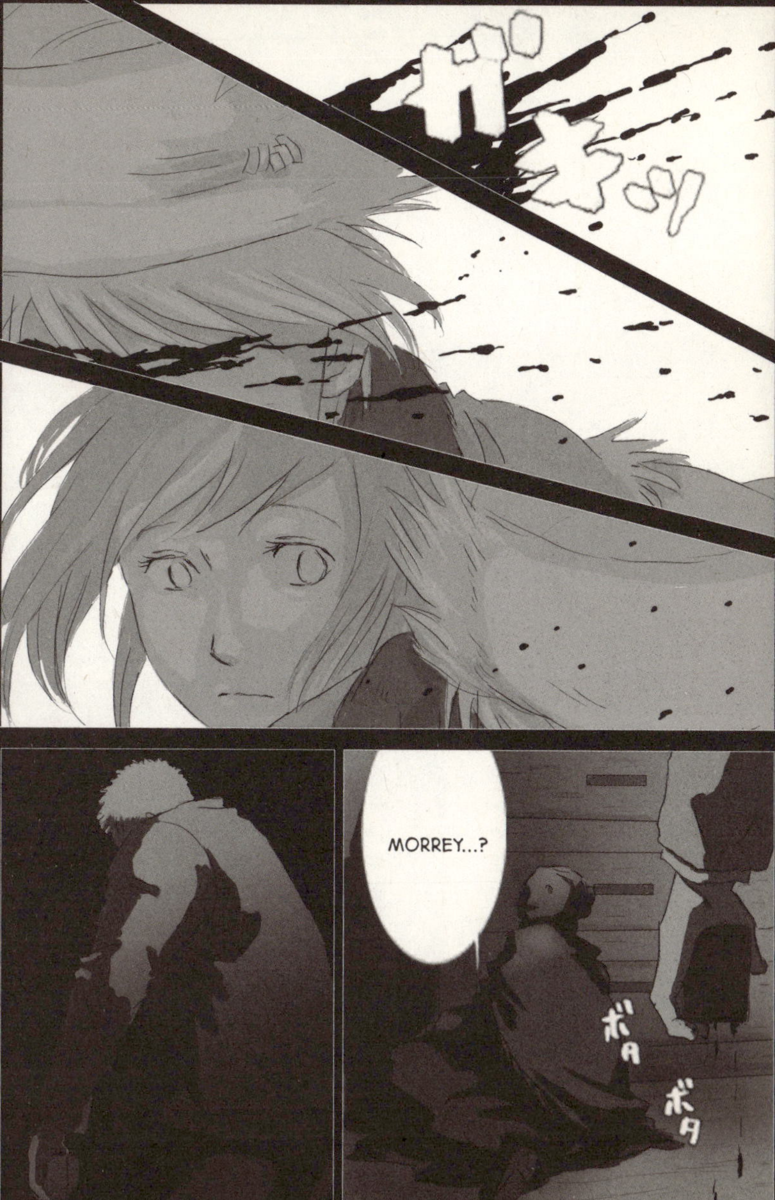
ガキッ
MORREY...?
ボタ
ボタ

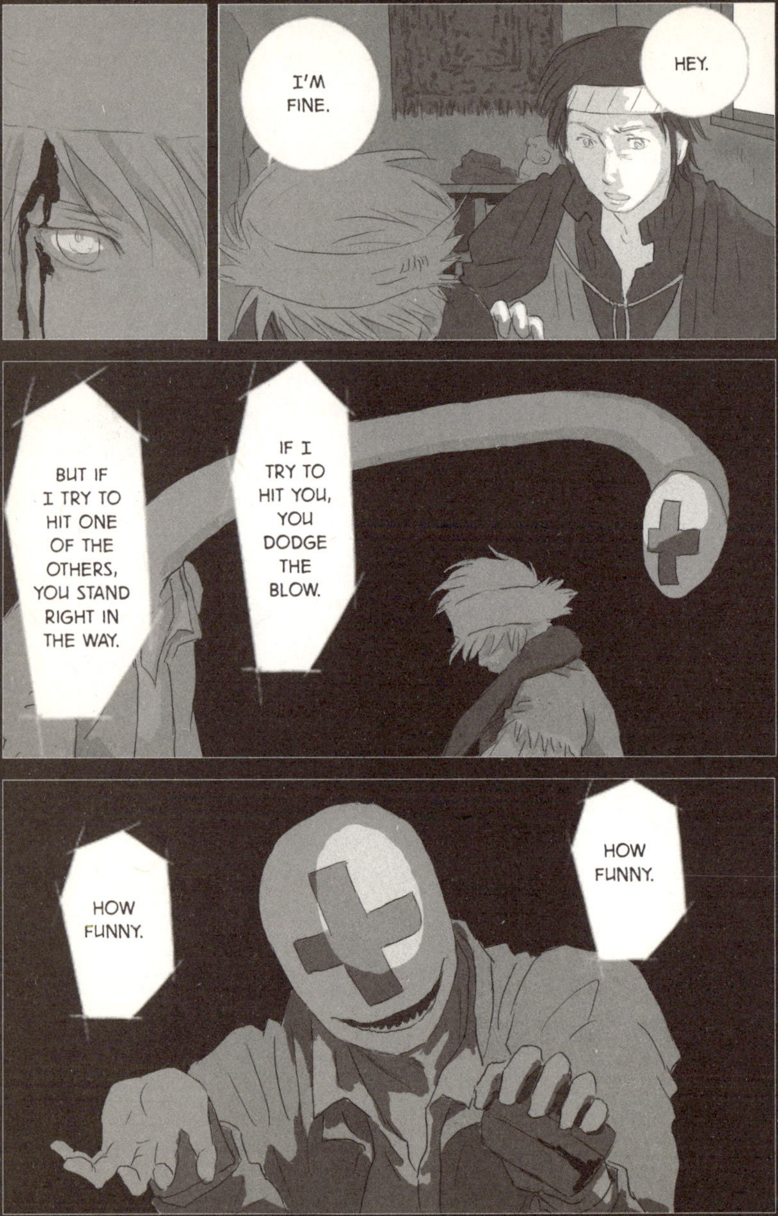
HEY.
I'M FINE.
IF I TRY TO HIT YOU, YOU DODGE THE BLOW.
BUT IF I TRY TO HIT ONE OF THE OTHERS, YOU STAND RIGHT IN THE WAY.
HOW FUNNY.
HOW FUNNY.

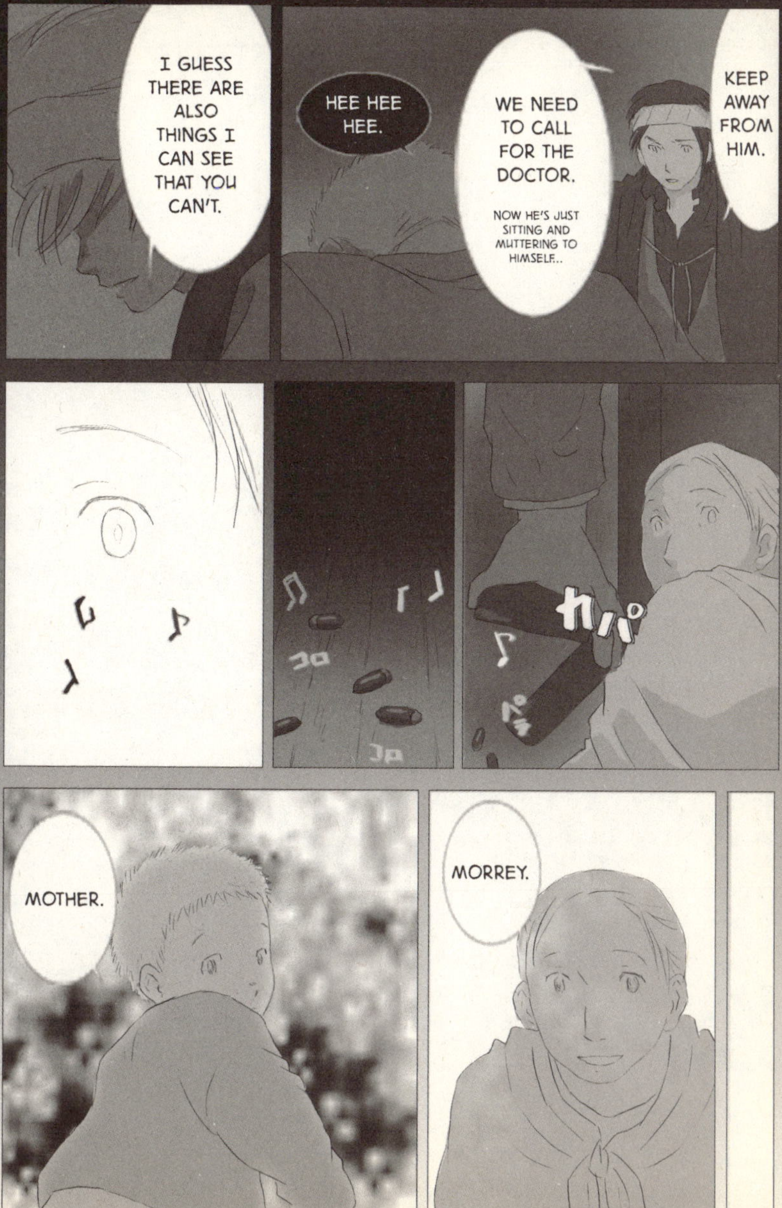
KEEP AWAY FROM HIM.
WE NEED TO CALL FOR THE DOCTOR.
NOW HE'S JUST SITTING AND MUTTERING TO HIMSELF...
HEE HEE HEE.
I GUESS THERE ARE ALSO THINGS I CAN SEE THAT YOU CAN'T.
カパ
コロ
コロ
MORREY.
MOTHER.

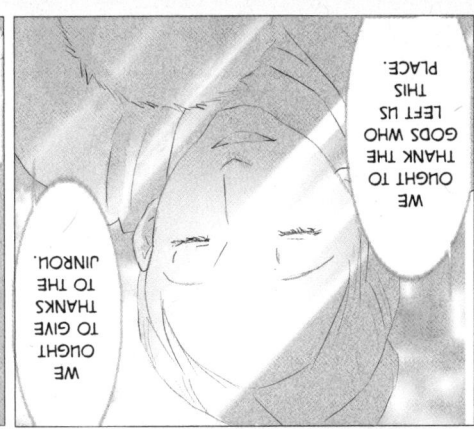

I GATHERED UP A BUNCH OF ACORNS!
ACORNS?
I'M GIVING THEM TO SQUIRR-ELS.
IS THAT SO?
THEY WON'T BE ABLE TO LEAVE THE VILLAGE IF YOU DO.
THEY WON'T MIND. I LOVE IT HERE.
IT'S SO EASY TO MAKE FRIENDS.
WE OUGHT TO GIVE THANKS TO THE JINROU.
WE OUGHT TO THANK THE GODS WHO LEFT US THIS PLACE.

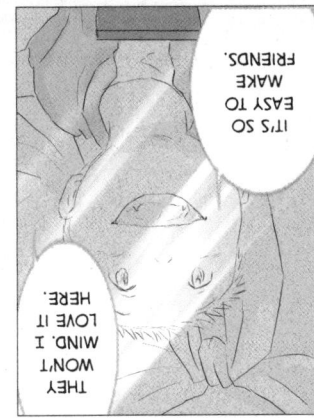

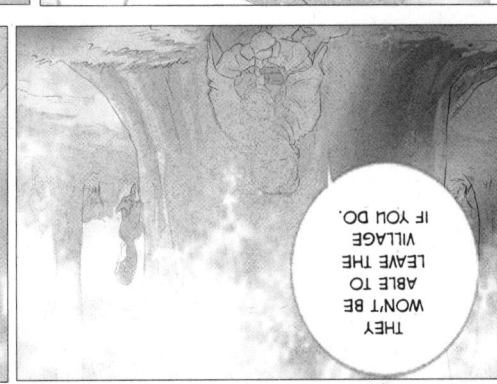

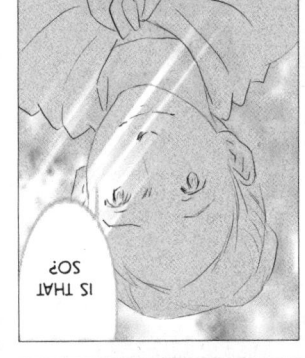

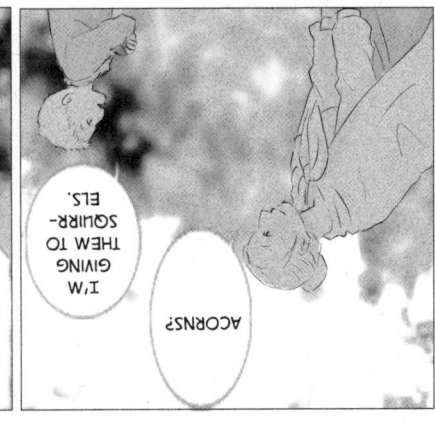

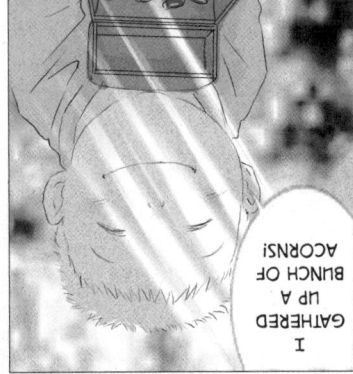

GO!
QUICKLY!
I...
...WILL DEAL WITH MY CHILD!
FORGIVE ME...
ポタ
メキ
...FOR HAVING TROUBLED YOU WITH THIS.
EMMET!
DON'T...

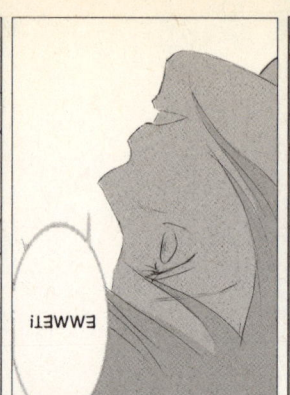

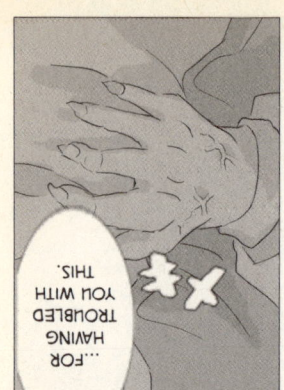

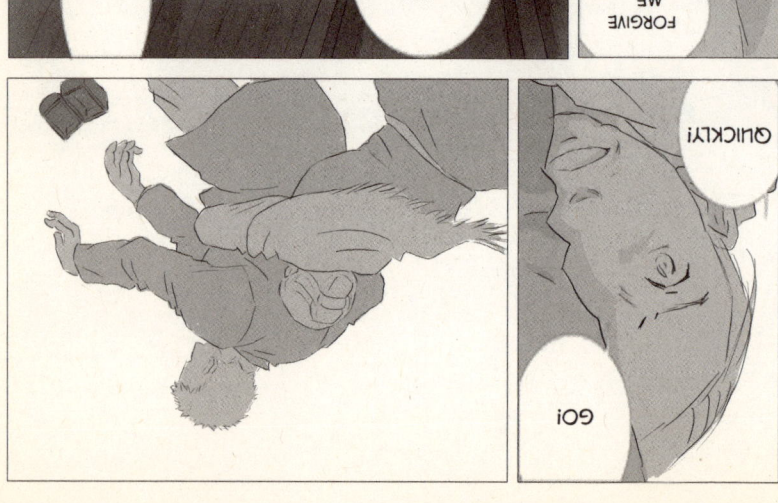

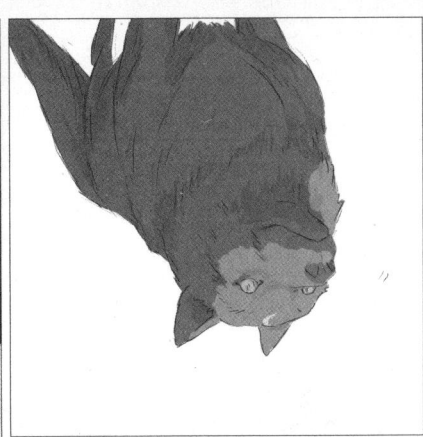

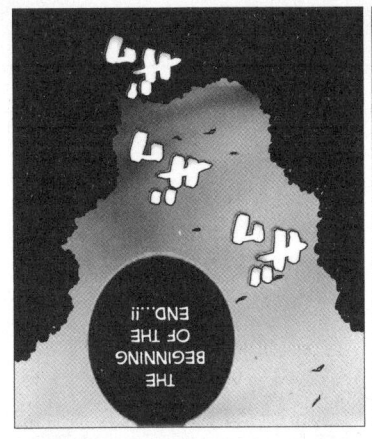

THE BEGINNING OF THE END...!!

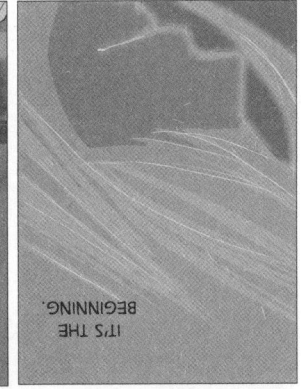

IT'S THE BEGINNING.

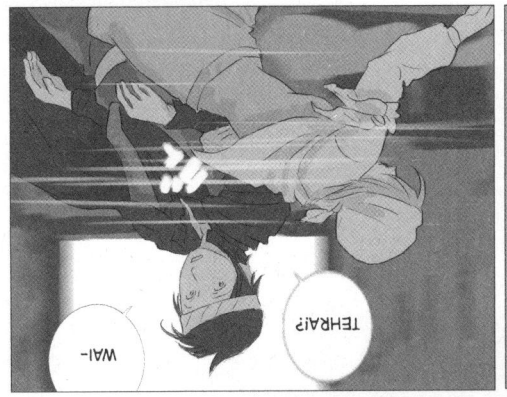

TEHRA?!

WAI–

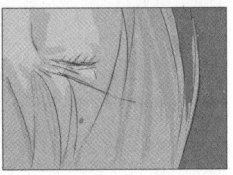

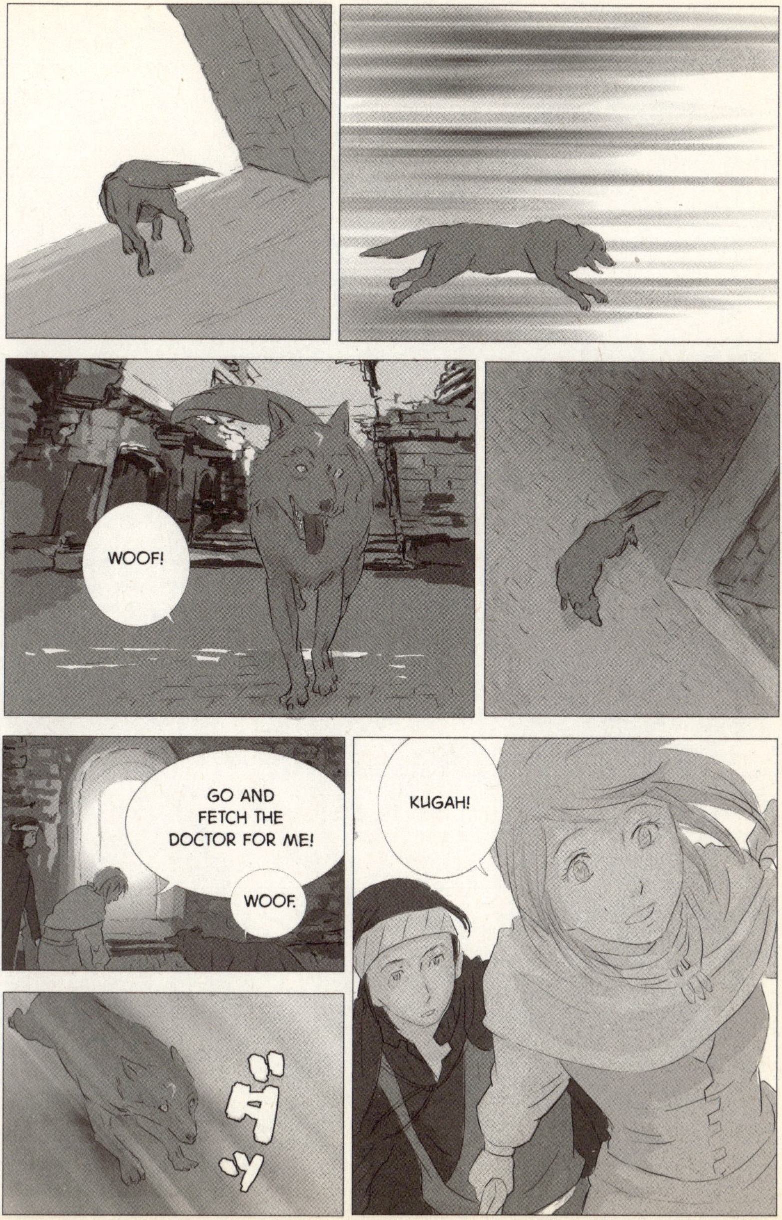
WOOF!
KUGAH!
GO AND FETCH THE DOCTOR FOR ME!
WOOF.
ダッ

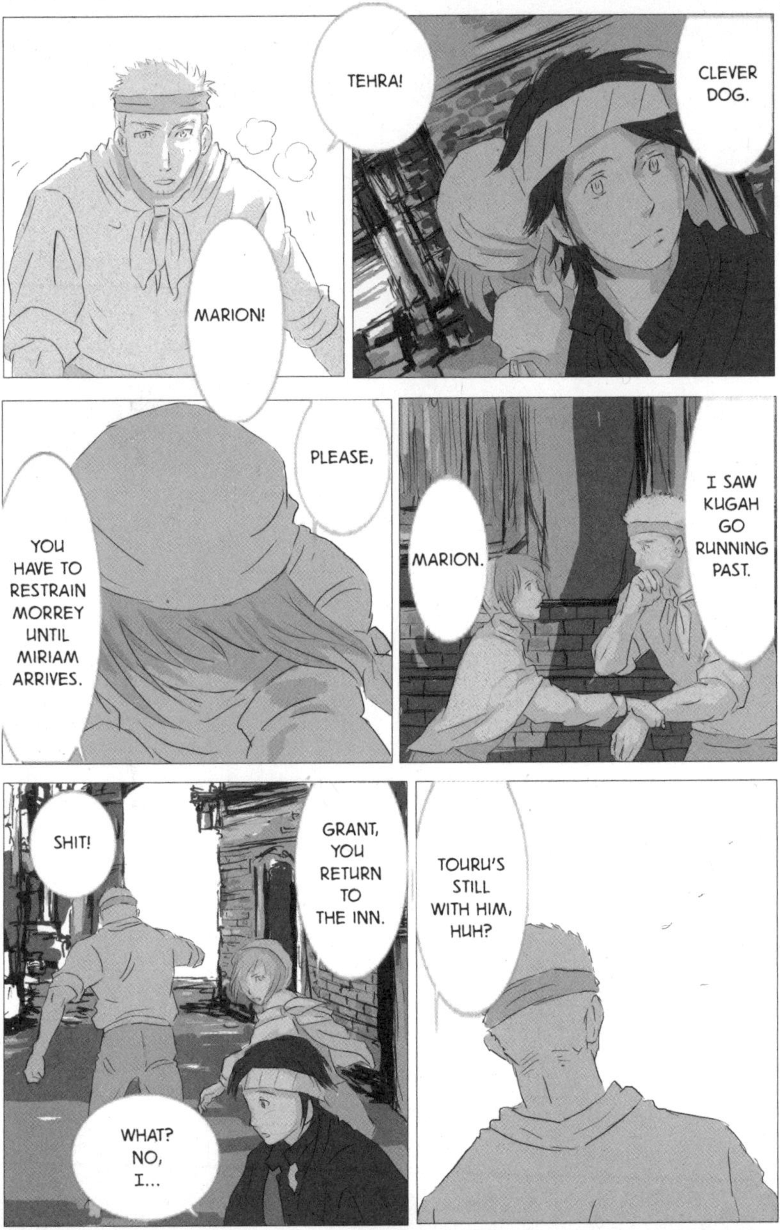
CLEVER DOG.
TEHRA!
MARION!
I SAW KUGAH GO RUNNING PAST.
MARION.
PLEASE,
YOU HAVE TO RESTRAIN MORREY UNTIL MIRIAM ARRIVES.
TOURU'S STILL WITH HIM, HUH?
GRANT, YOU RETURN TO THE INN.
SHIT!
WHAT? NO, I...

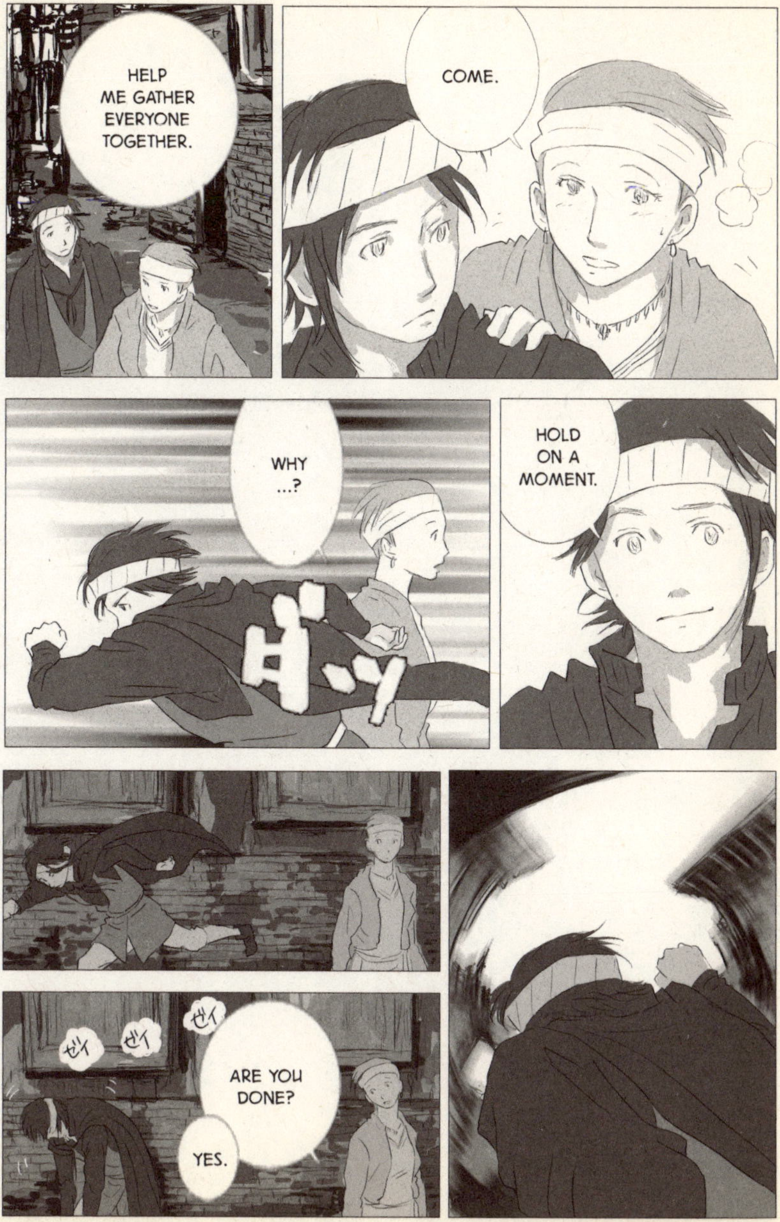
COME.
HELP ME GATHER EVERYONE TOGETHER.
HOLD ON A MOMENT.
WHY ...?
ダッ
ゼイ
ゼイ
ゼイ
ARE YOU DONE?
YES.

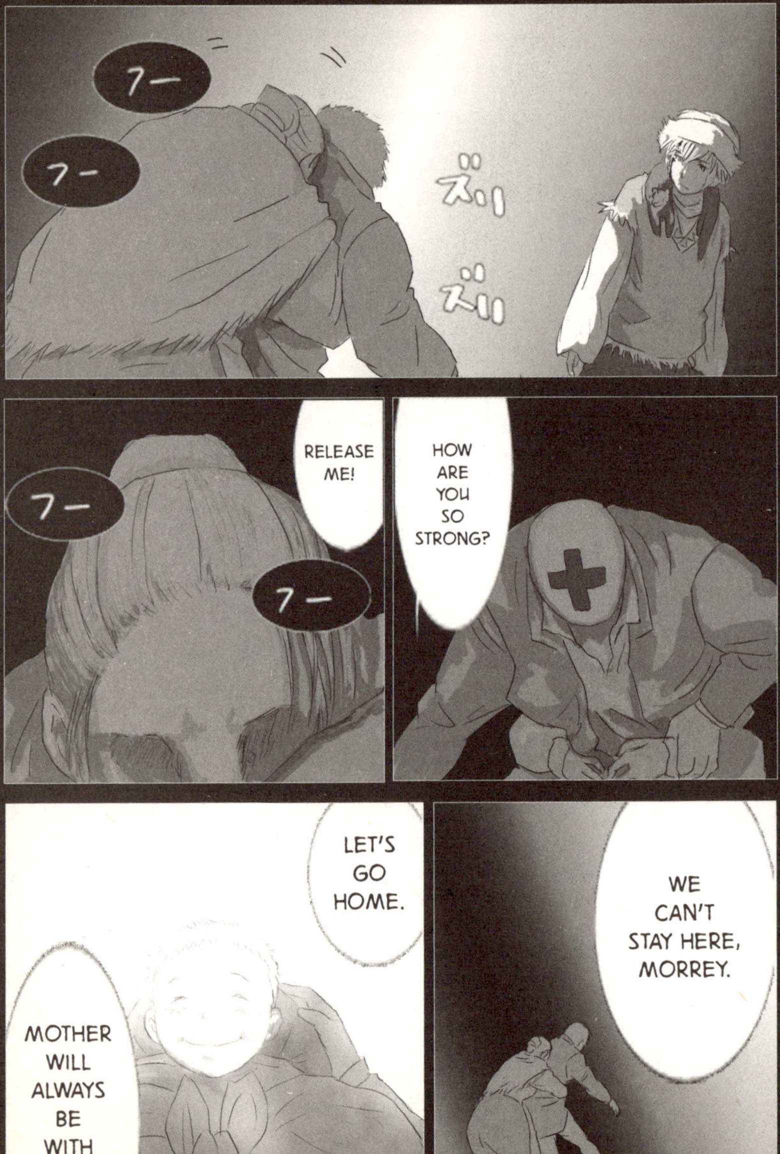
フー
フー
HOW ARE YOU SO STRONG?
RELEASE ME!
フー
フー
WE CAN'T STAY HERE, MORREY.
LET'S GO HOME.
MOTHER WILL ALWAYS BE WITH YOU.

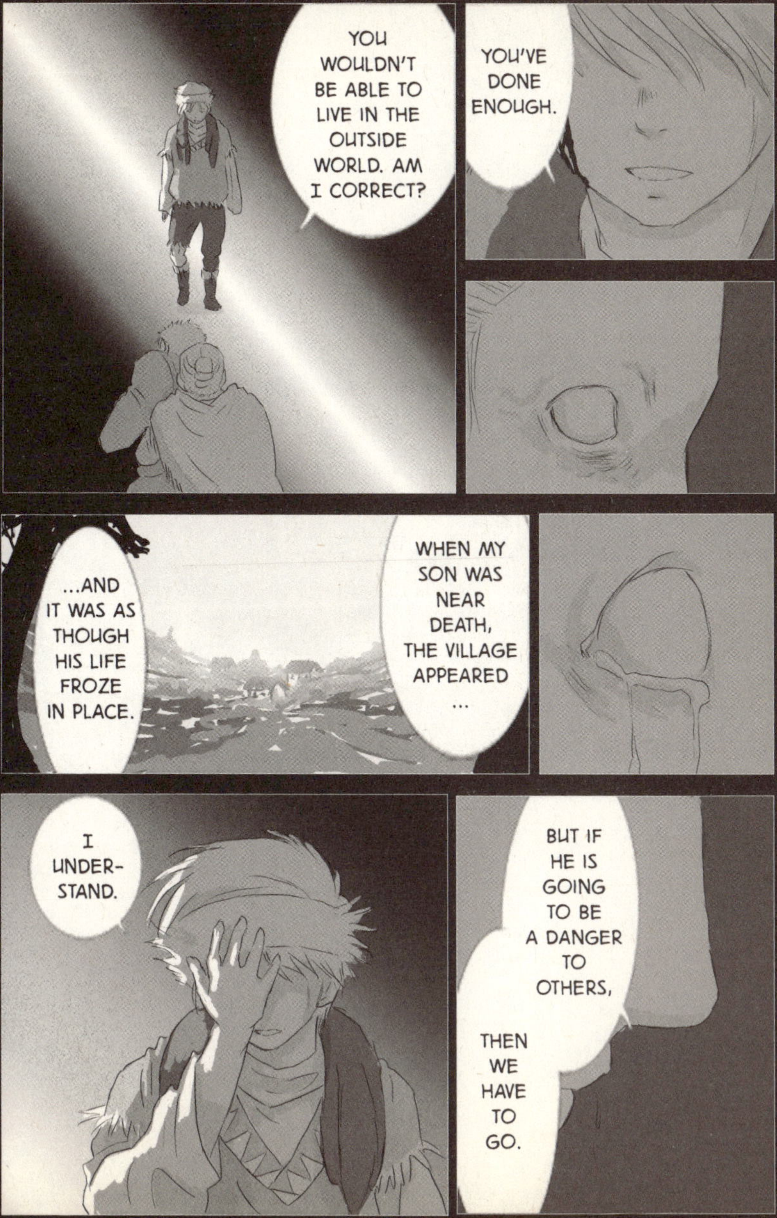
YOU'VE DONE ENOUGH.
YOU WOULDN'T BE ABLE TO LIVE IN THE OUTSIDE WORLD. AM I CORRECT?
WHEN MY SON WAS NEAR DEATH, THE VILLAGE APPEARED ...
...AND IT WAS AS THOUGH HIS LIFE FROZE IN PLACE.
BUT IF HE IS GOING TO BE A DANGER TO OTHERS,
THEN WE HAVE TO GO.
I UNDER-STAND.

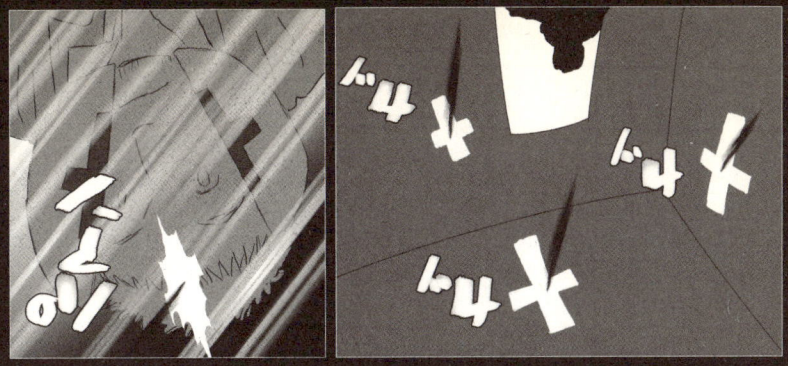
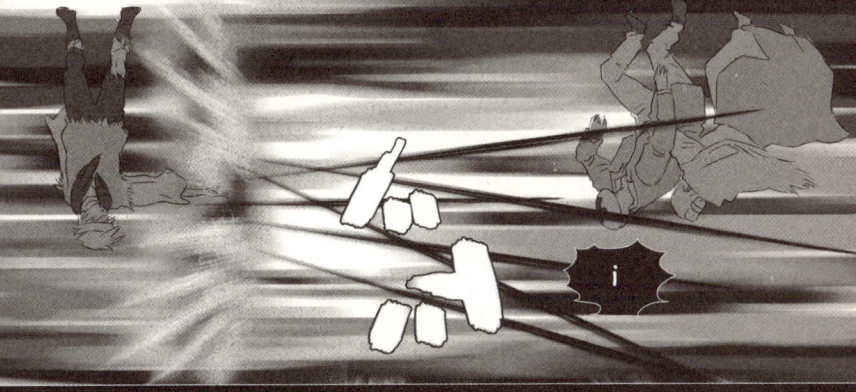

HOWEVER, YOU TWO WILL NOT BE THE ONES LEAVING.

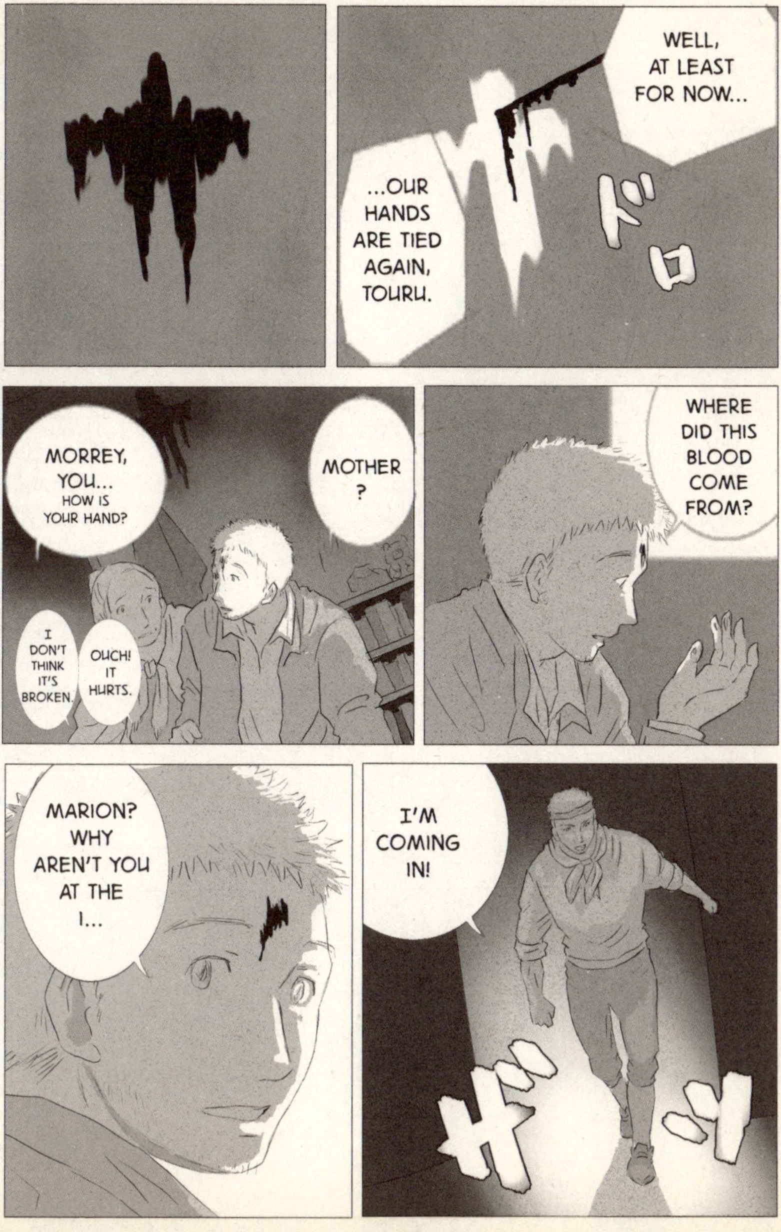
WELL, AT LEAST FOR NOW...
...OUR HANDS ARE TIED AGAIN, TOURU.
ドロ
WHERE DID THIS BLOOD COME FROM?
MOTHER ?
MORREY, YOU... HOW IS YOUR HAND?
OUCH! IT HURTS.
I DON'T THINK IT'S BROKEN.
I'M COMING IN!
ザッ
MARION? WHY AREN'T YOU AT THE I...

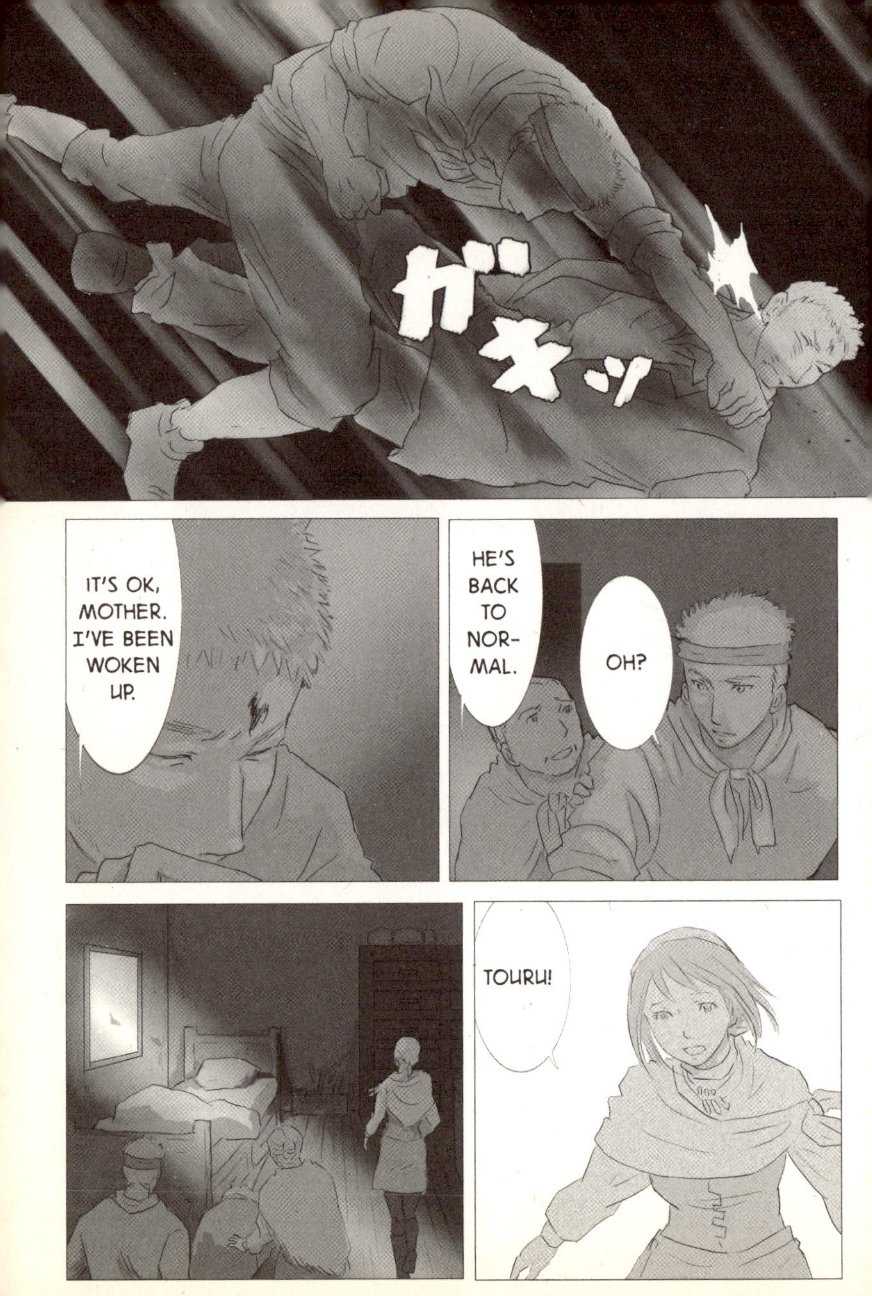
ガスッ
HE'S BACK TO NOR-MAL.
OH?
IT'S OK, MOTHER. I'VE BEEN WOKEN UP.
TOURU!

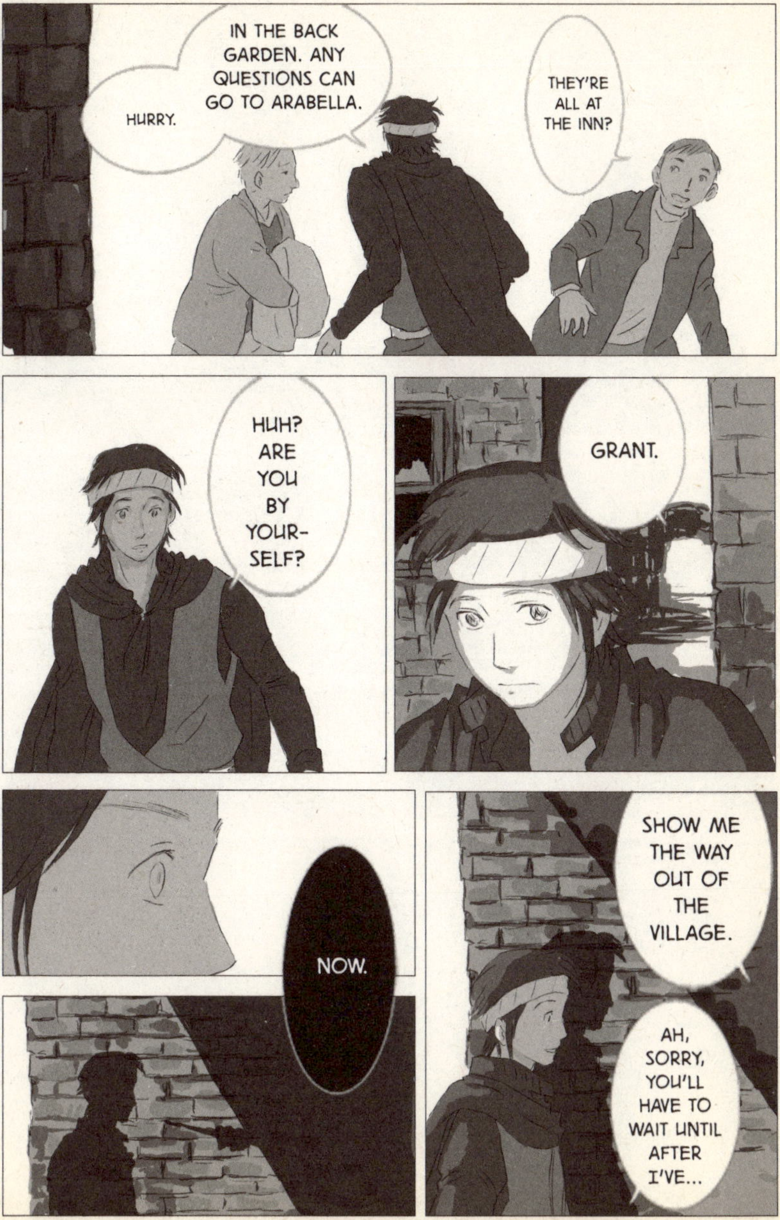
THEY'RE ALL AT THE INN?
IN THE BACK GARDEN. ANY QUESTIONS CAN GO TO ARABELLA.
HURRY.
GRANT.
HUH? ARE YOU BY YOUR-SELF?
SHOW ME THE WAY OUT OF THE VILLAGE.
AH, SORRY, YOU'LL HAVE TO WAIT UNTIL AFTER I'VE...
NOW.

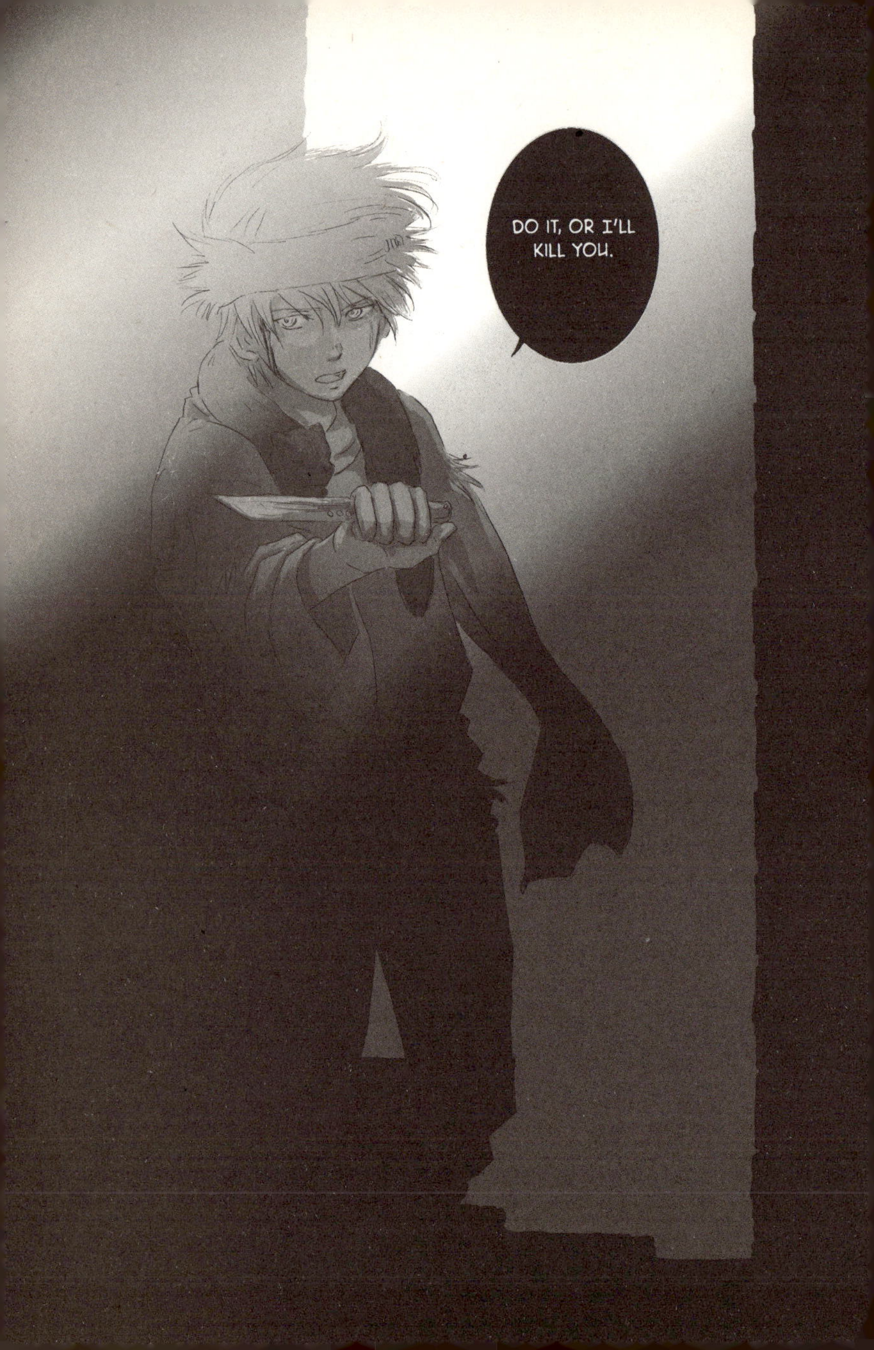
DO IT, OR I'LL KILL YOU.

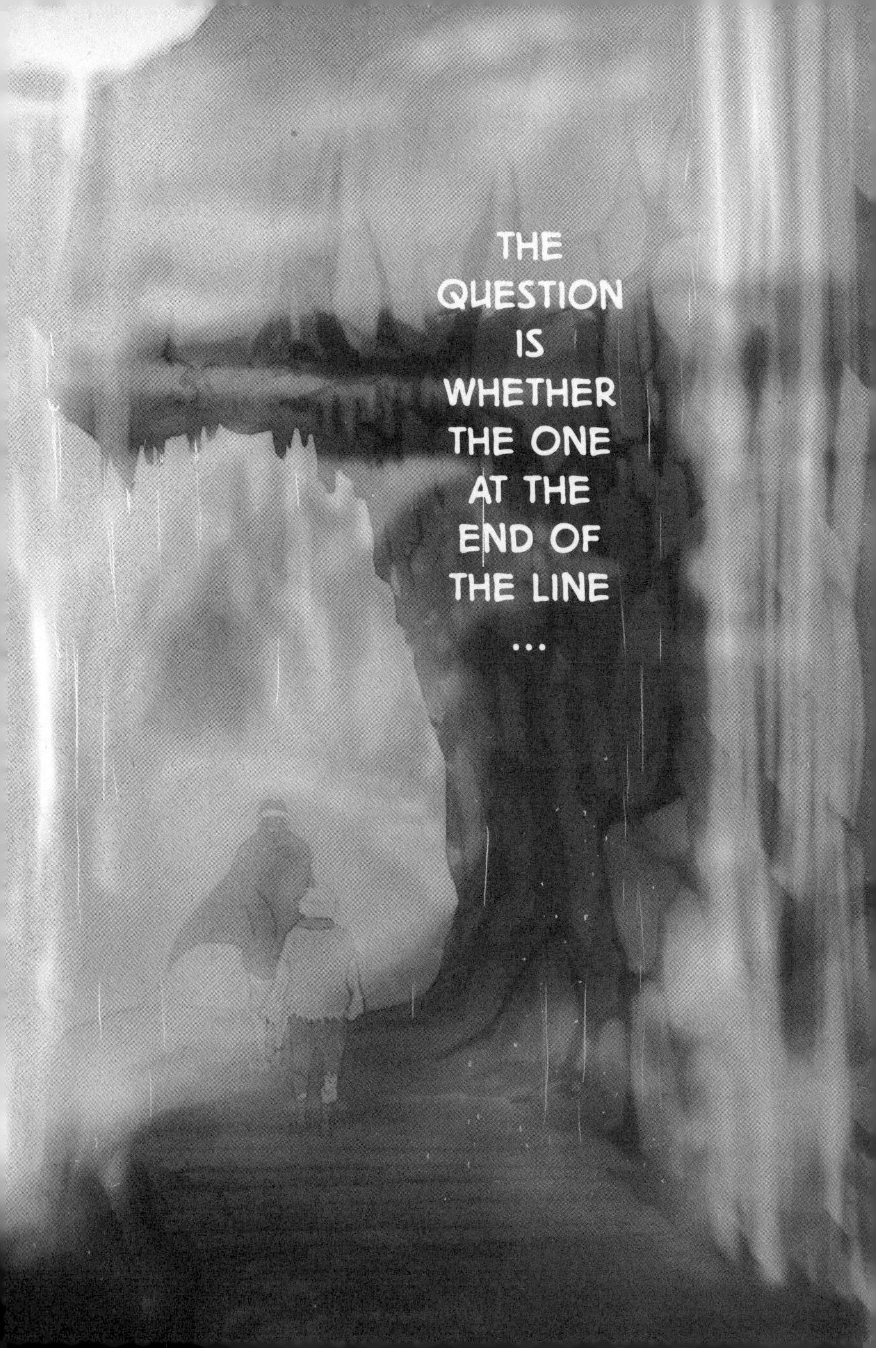
THE QUESTION IS WHETHER THE ONE AT THE END OF THE LINE ...

STAGE 3
PARADE OF THE GODS OF DEATH

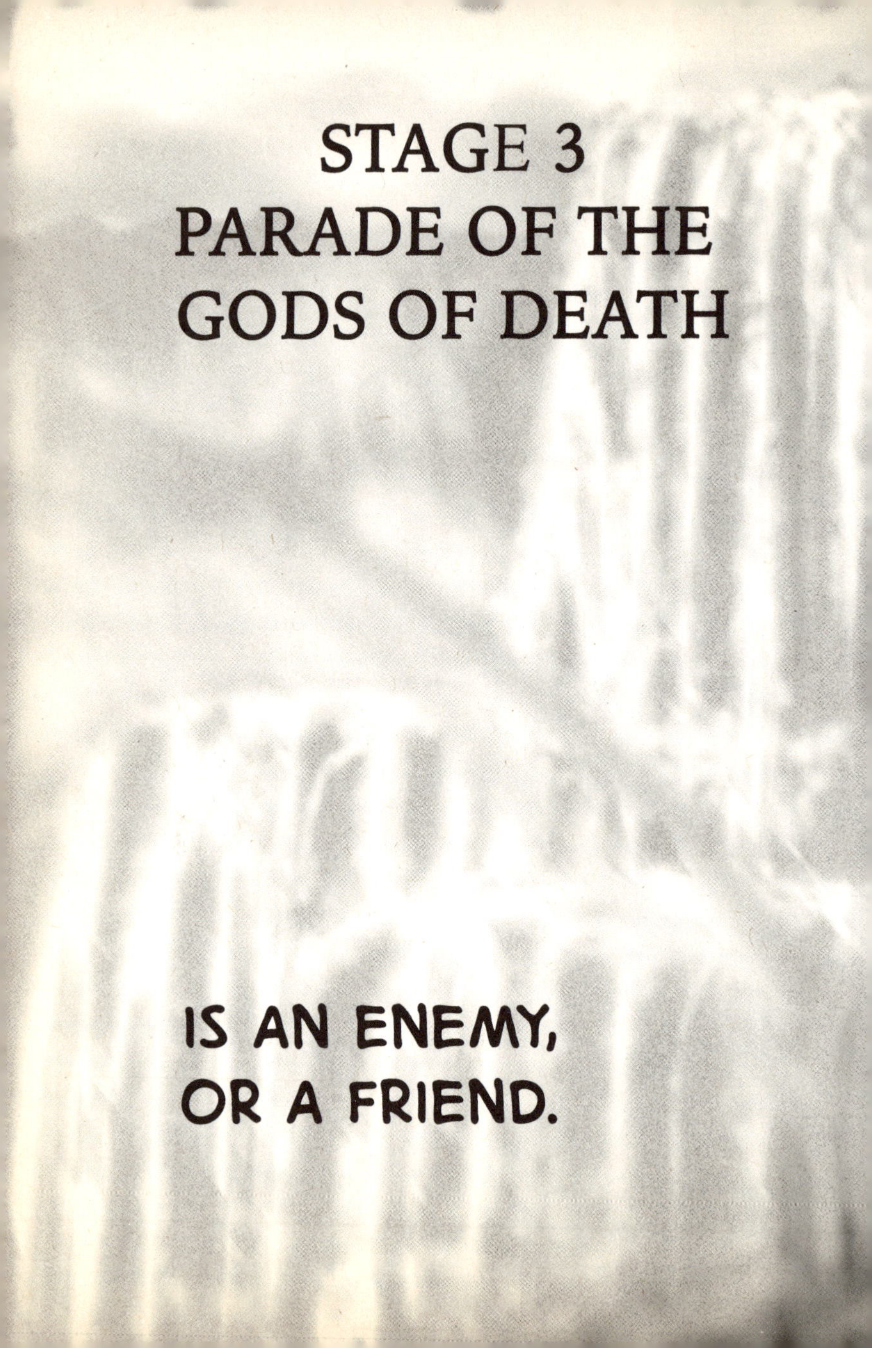

IS AN ENEMY,
OR A FRIEND.

ザザザザ
ピチャ
ドドドド
ARE YOU SURE WE'RE GOING IN THE RIGHT DIRECTION?

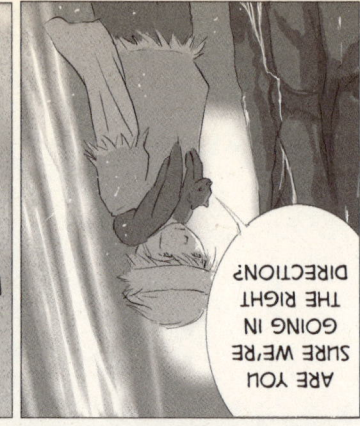

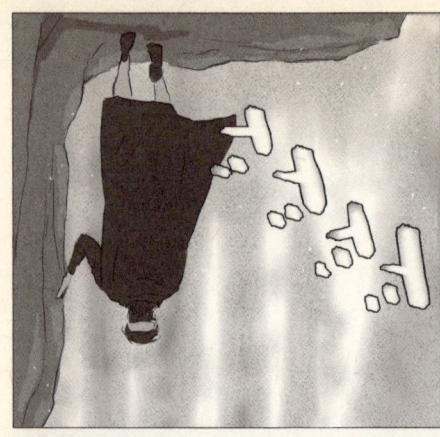

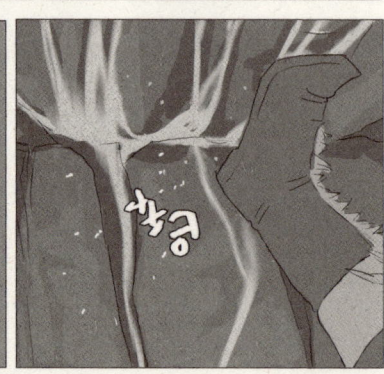

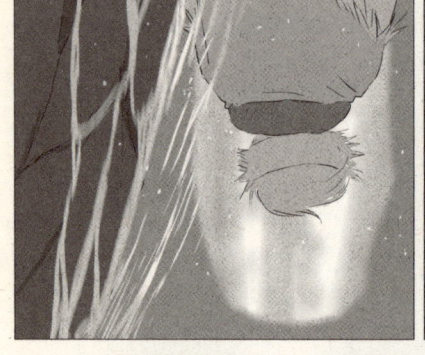

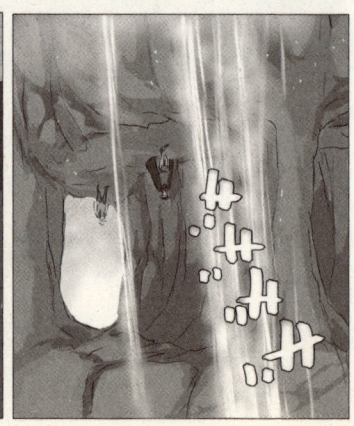

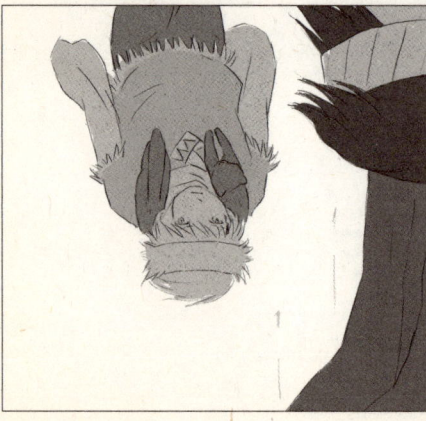

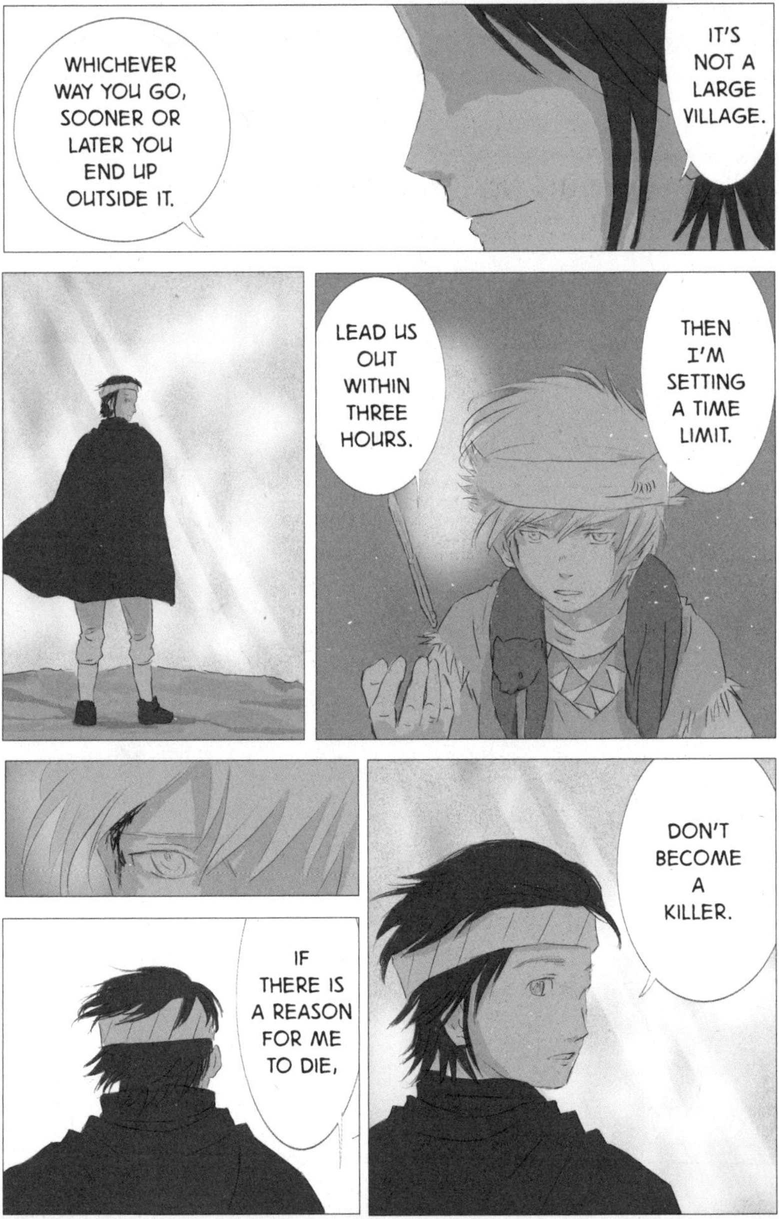
IT'S NOT A LARGE VILLAGE.
WHICHEVER WAY YOU GO, SOONER OR LATER YOU END UP OUTSIDE IT.
THEN I'M SETTING A TIME LIMIT.
LEAD US OUT WITHIN THREE HOURS.
DON'T BECOME A KILLER.
IF THERE IS A REASON FOR ME TO DIE,

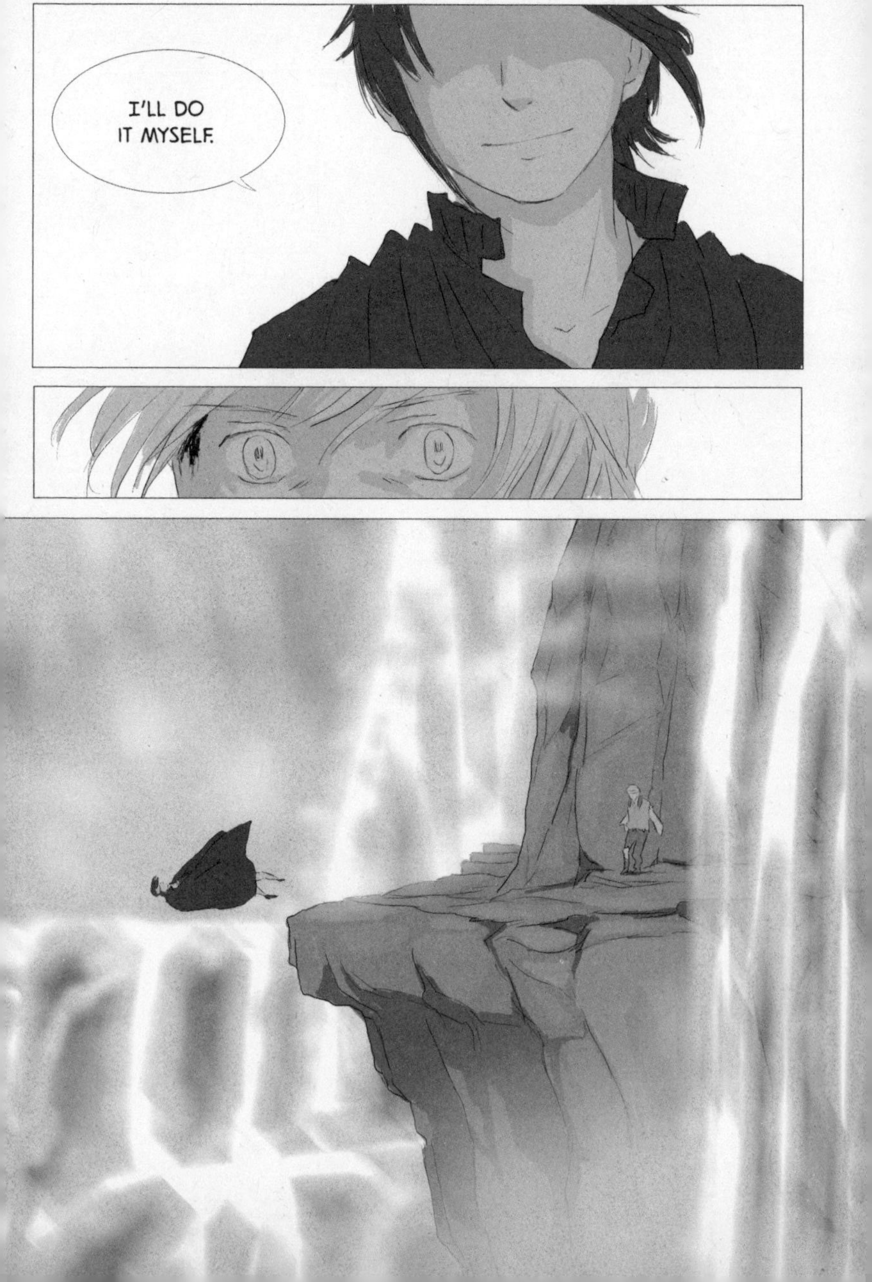
I'LL DO IT MYSELF.

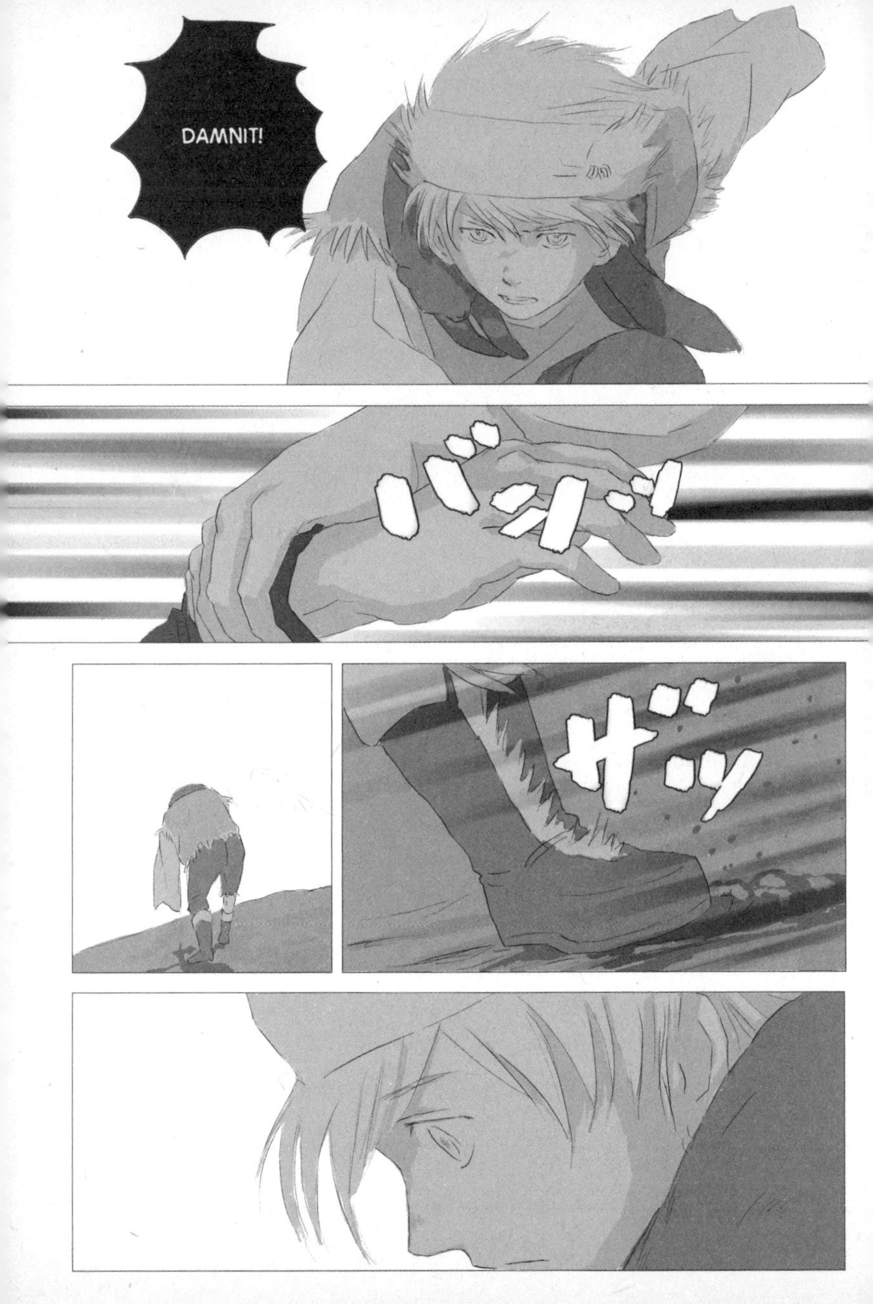
DAMNIT!
バッ
ザッ

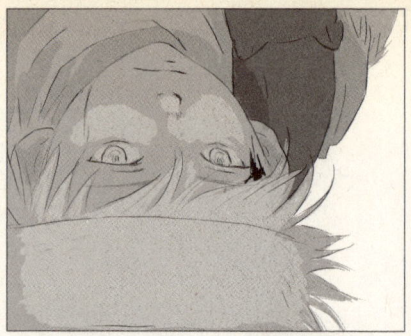

YOU DON'T REALLY INTEND TO KILL ME, DO YOU.

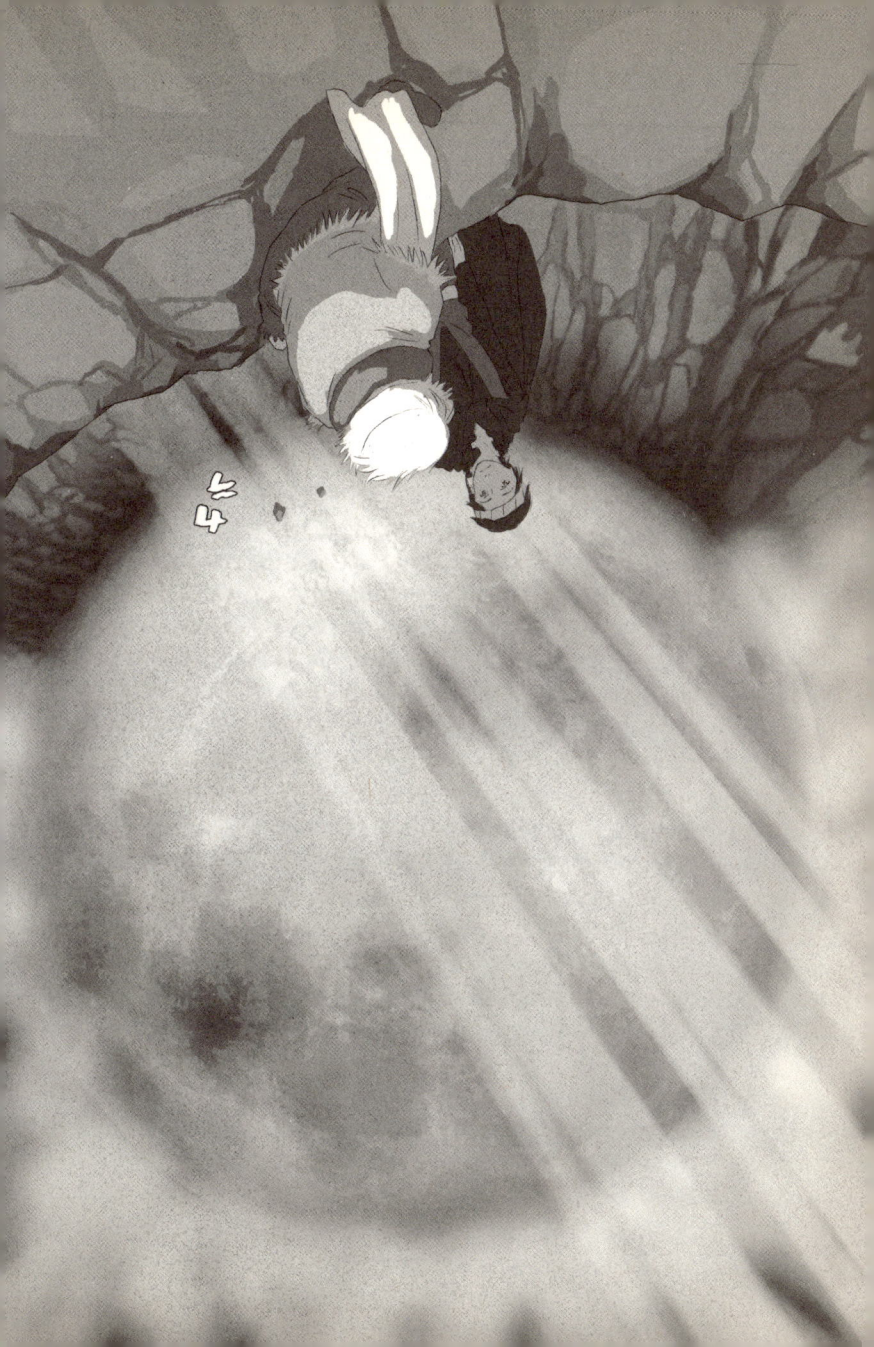

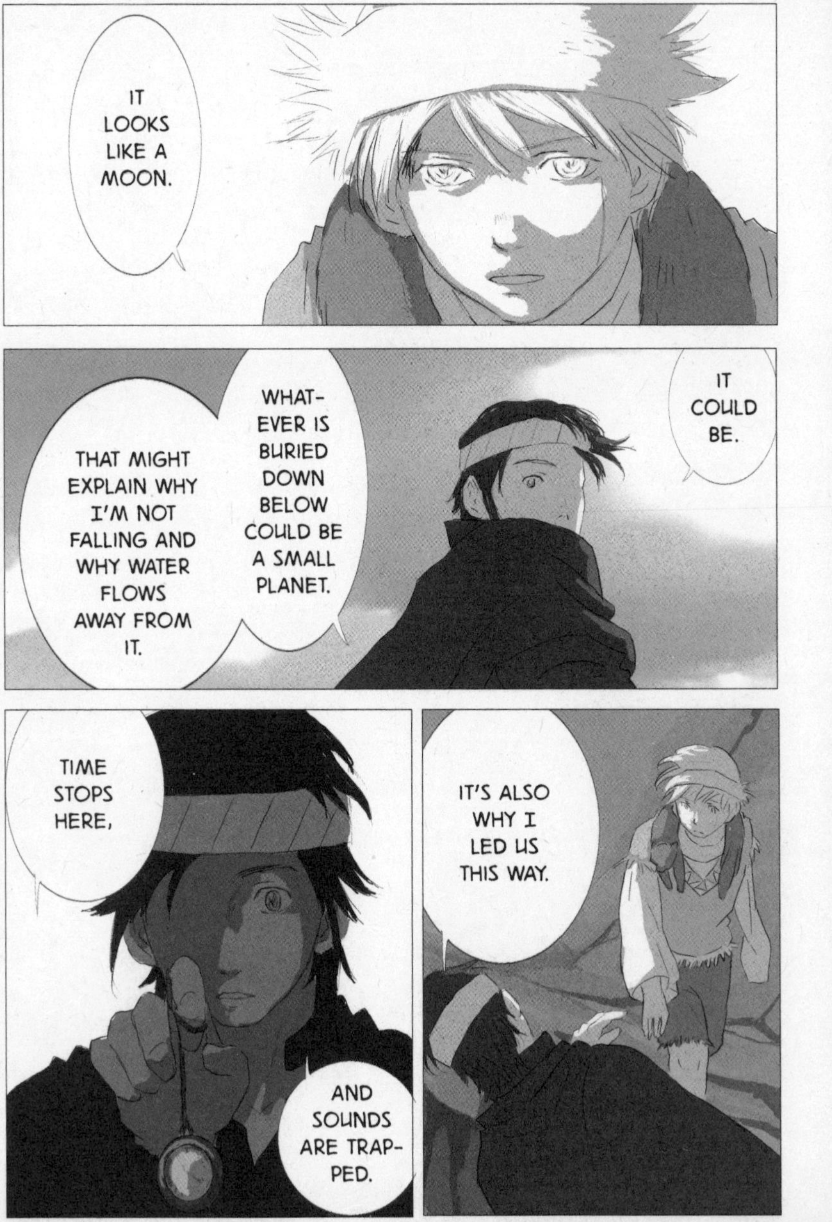
IT LOOKS LIKE A MOON.
IT COULD BE.
WHATEVER IS BURIED DOWN BELOW COULD BE A SMALL PLANET.
THAT MIGHT EXPLAIN WHY I'M NOT FALLING AND WHY WATER FLOWS AWAY FROM IT.
IT'S ALSO WHY I LED US THIS WAY.
TIME STOPS HERE,
AND SOUNDS ARE TRAP-PED.

THROW.
IF YOU WEREN'T HOLDING MY HAND, YOU PROBABLY WOULDN'T BE ABLE TO HEAR ME EITHER.
I HEARD A "CLUNK" WHEN IT HIT THE ROCK WALL. DID YOU?
NO.
WE'RE IN THE PERFECT PLACE TO SPEAK PRIVATE-LY.
EXA-CTLY.

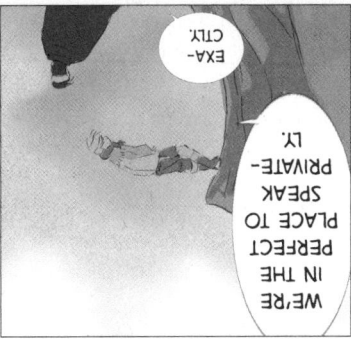

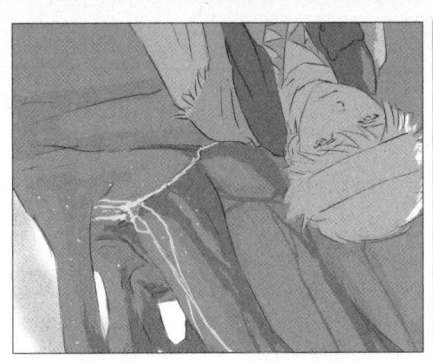

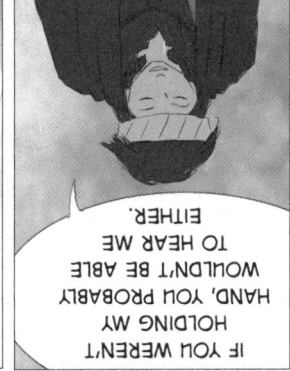

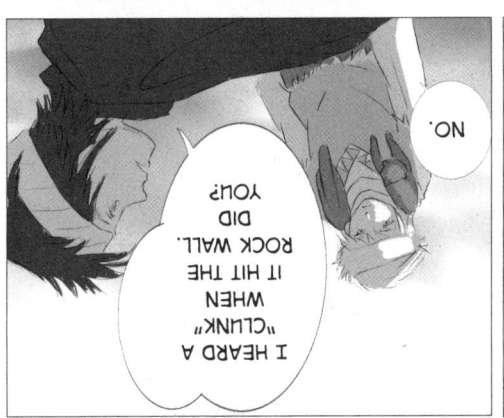

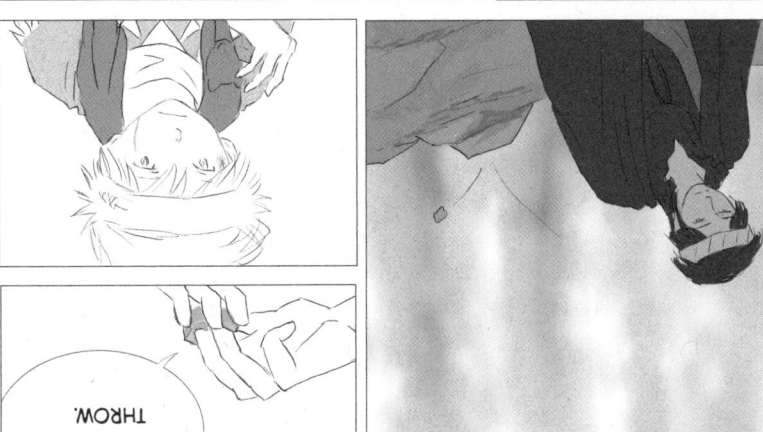

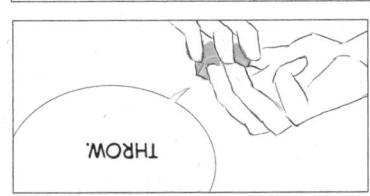

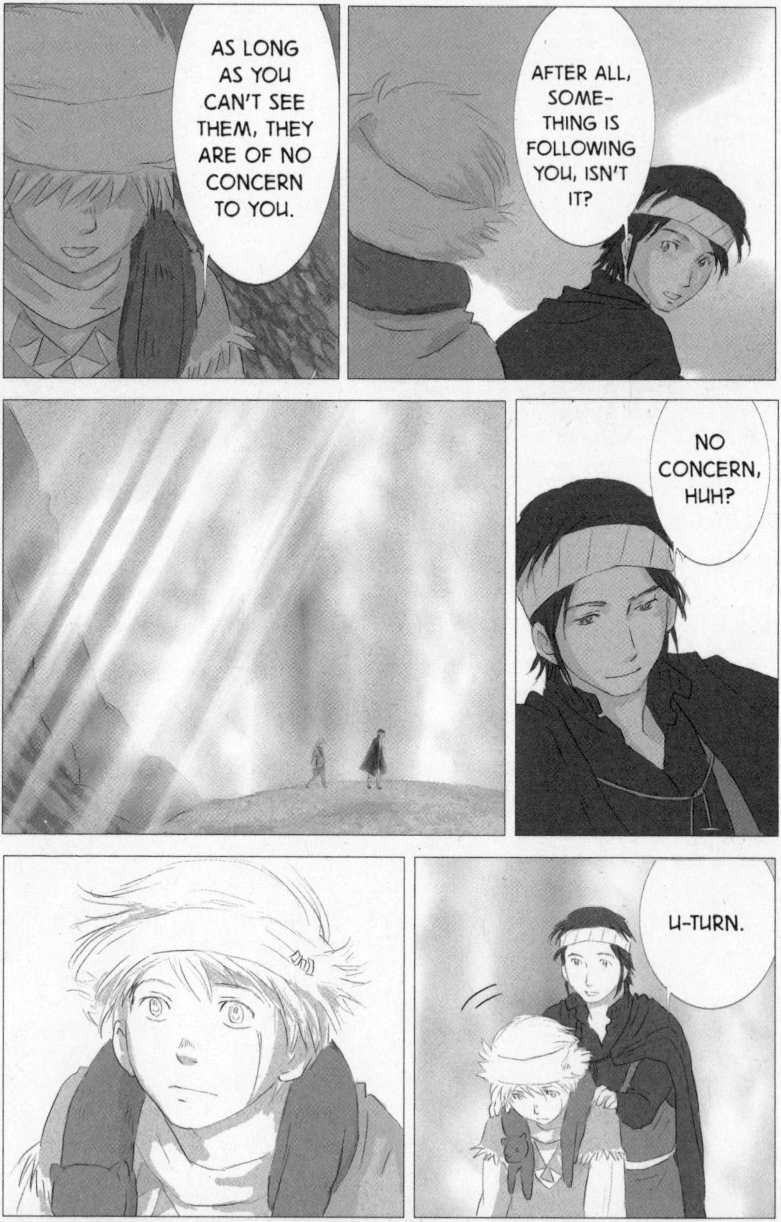
AFTER ALL, SOME-THING IS FOLLOWING YOU, ISN'T IT?
AS LONG AS YOU CAN'T SEE THEM, THEY ARE OF NO CONCERN TO YOU.
NO CONCERN, HUH?
U-TURN.

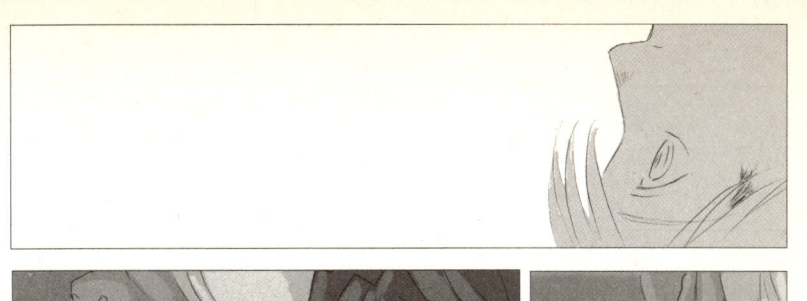

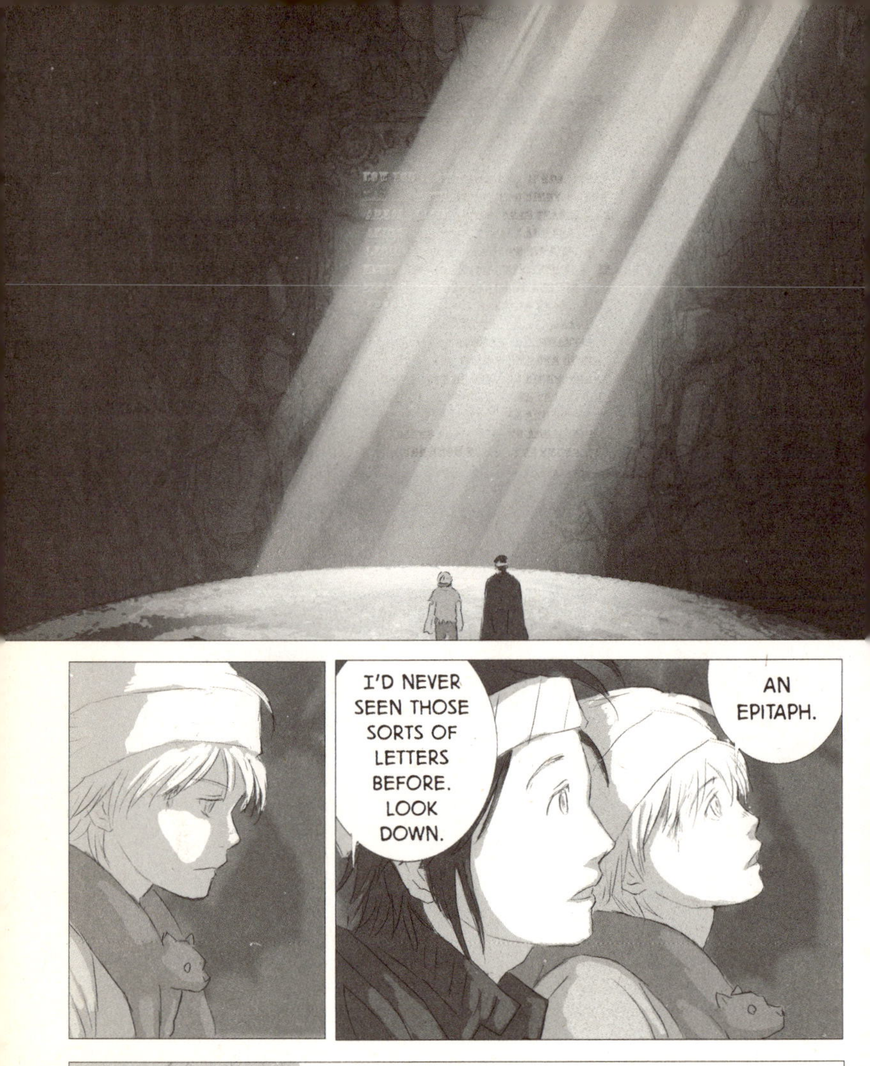
AN EPITAPH.
I'D NEVER SEEN THOSE SORTS OF LETTERS BEFORE. LOOK DOWN.

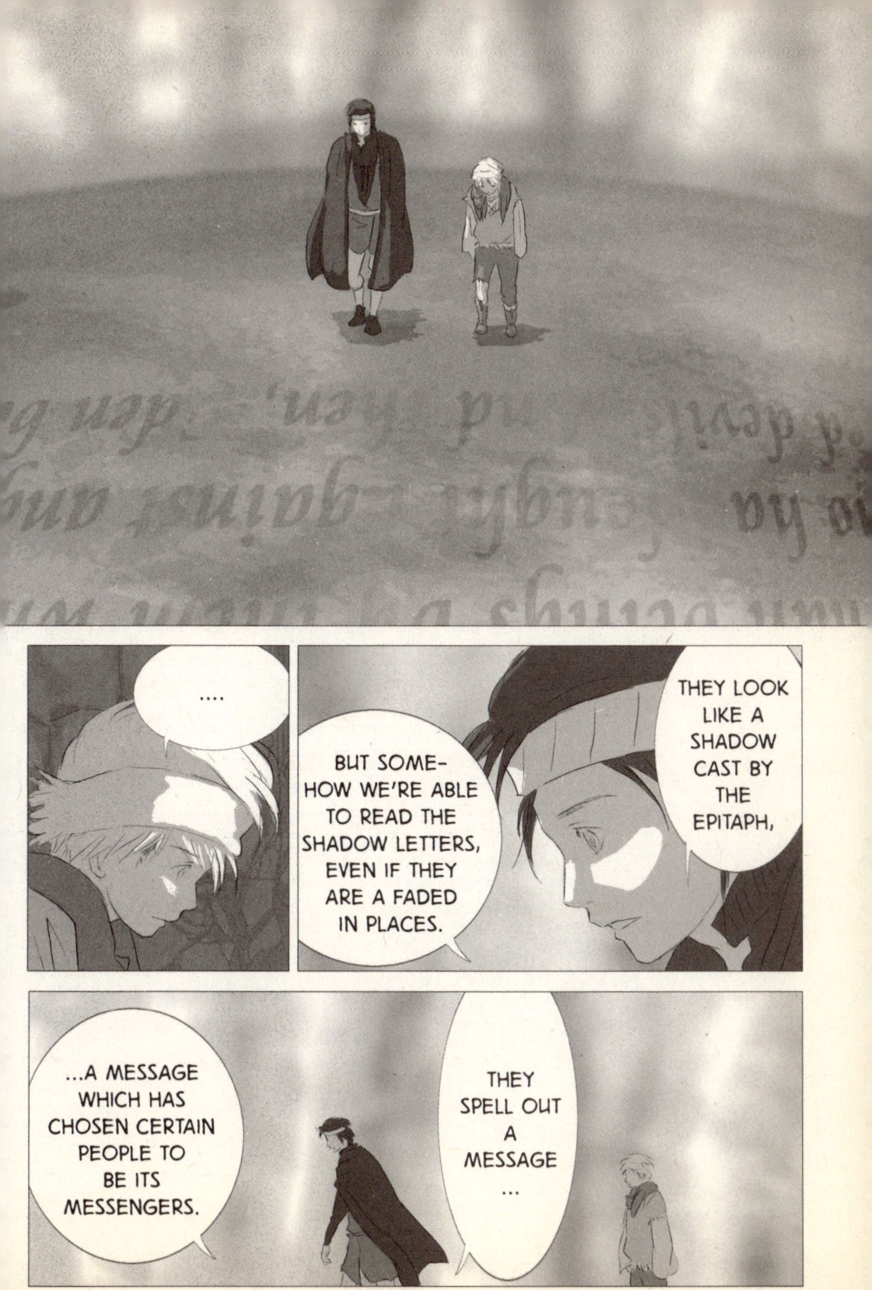
THEY LOOK LIKE A SHADOW CAST BY THE EPITAPH,
BUT SOME-HOW WE'RE ABLE TO READ THE SHADOW LETTERS, EVEN IF THEY ARE A FADED IN PLACES.
....
THEY SPELL OUT A MESSAGE ...
...A MESSAGE WHICH HAS CHOSEN CERTAIN PEOPLE TO BE ITS MESSENGERS.

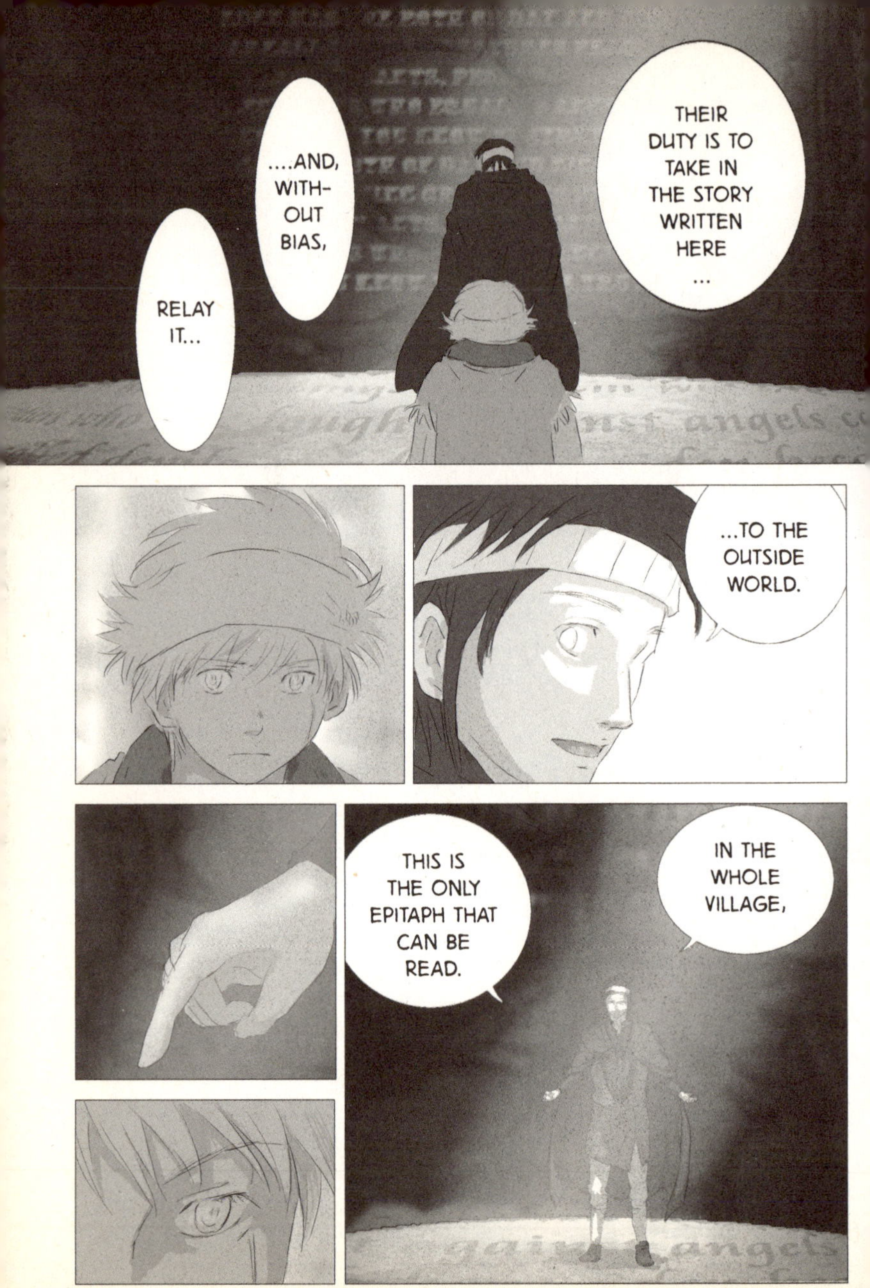
THEIR DUTY IS TO TAKE IN THE STORY WRITTEN HERE ...
....AND, WITH-OUT BIAS,
RELAY IT...
...TO THE OUTSIDE WORLD.
IN THE WHOLE VILLAGE,
THIS IS THE ONLY EPITAPH THAT CAN BE READ.

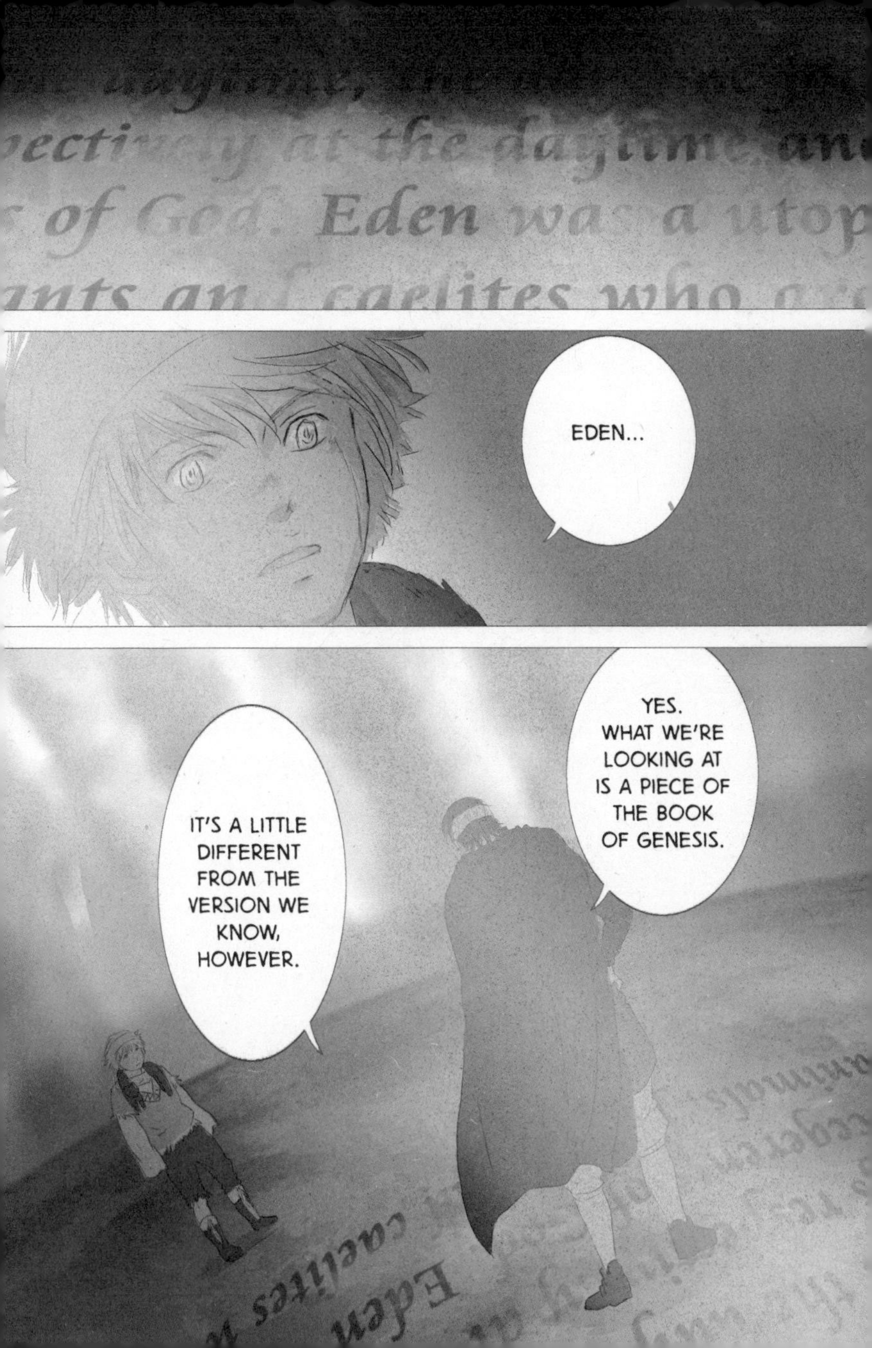
EDEN...
YES. WHAT WE'RE LOOKING AT IS A PIECE OF THE BOOK OF GENESIS.
IT'S A LITTLE DIFFERENT FROM THE VERSION WE KNOW, HOWEVER.

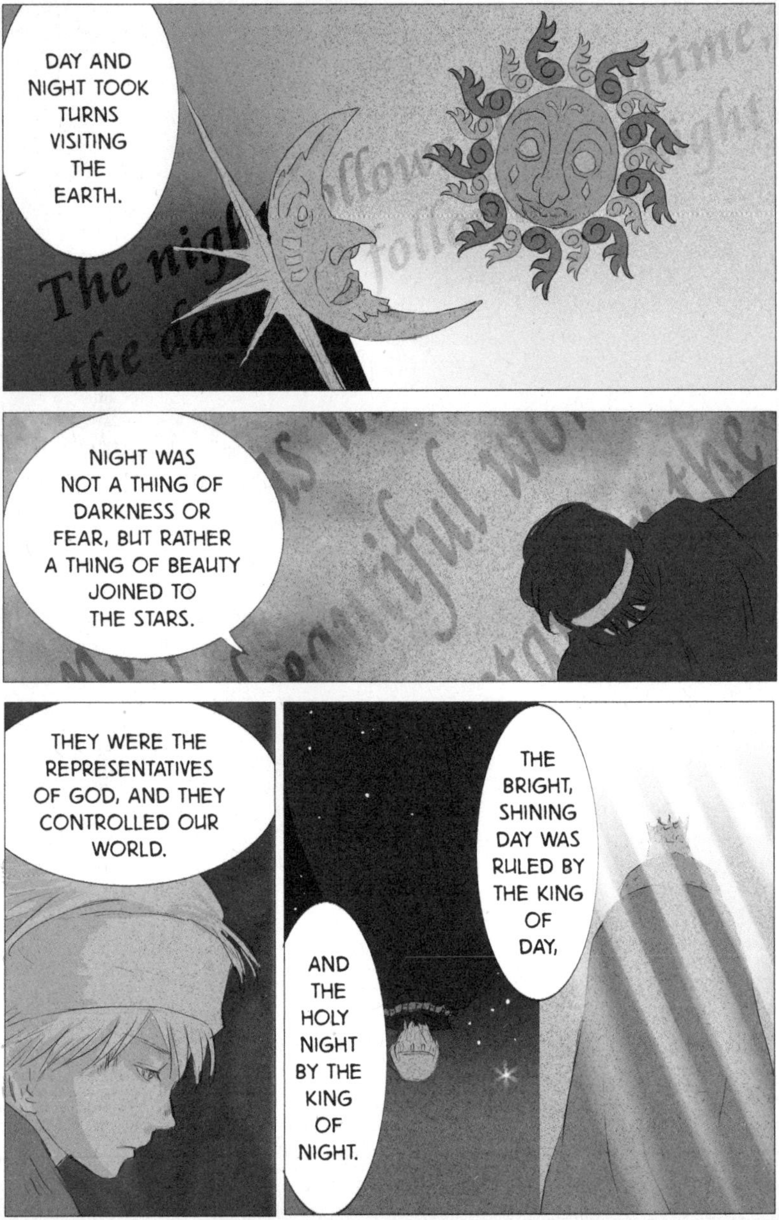
DAY AND NIGHT TOOK TURNS VISITING THE EARTH.
NIGHT WAS NOT A THING OF DARKNESS OR FEAR, BUT RATHER A THING OF BEAUTY JOINED TO THE STARS.
THE BRIGHT, SHINING DAY WAS RULED BY THE KING OF DAY,
AND THE HOLY NIGHT BY THE KING OF NIGHT.
THEY WERE THE REPRESENTATIVES OF GOD, AND THEY CONTROLLED OUR WORLD.

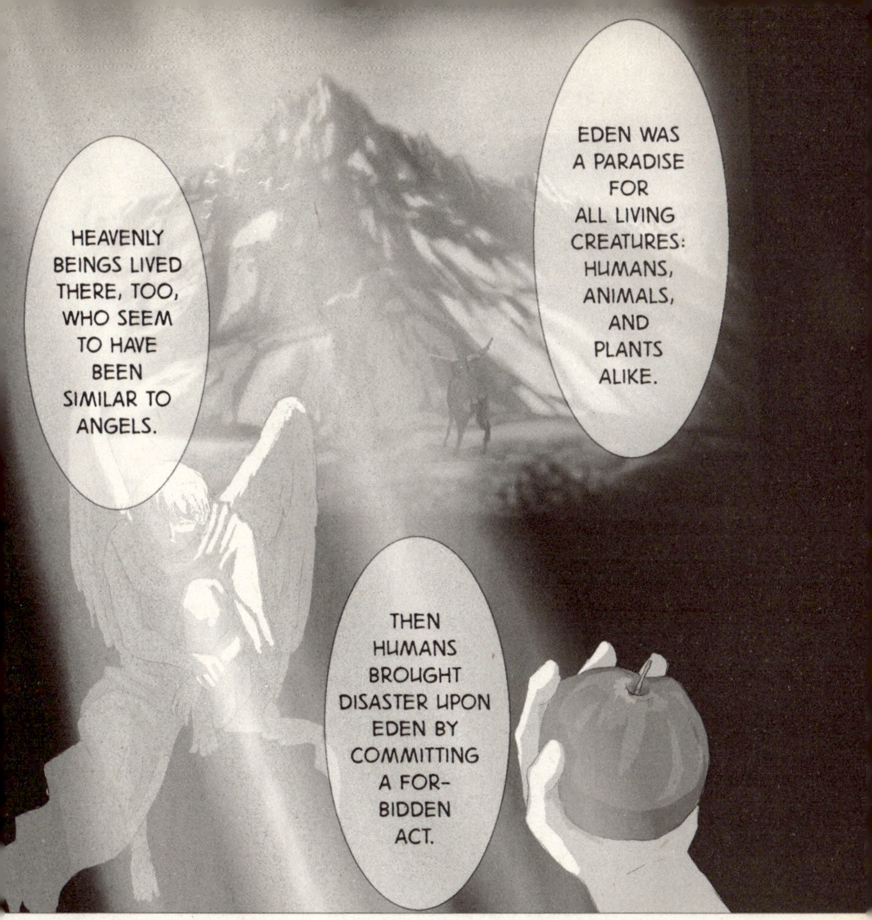
EDEN WAS A PARADISE FOR ALL LIVING CREATURES: HUMANS, ANIMALS, AND PLANTS ALIKE.
HEAVENLY BEINGS LIVED THERE, TOO, WHO SEEM TO HAVE BEEN SIMILAR TO ANGELS.
THEN HUMANS BROUGHT DISASTER UPON EDEN BY COMMITTING A FOR-BIDDEN ACT.
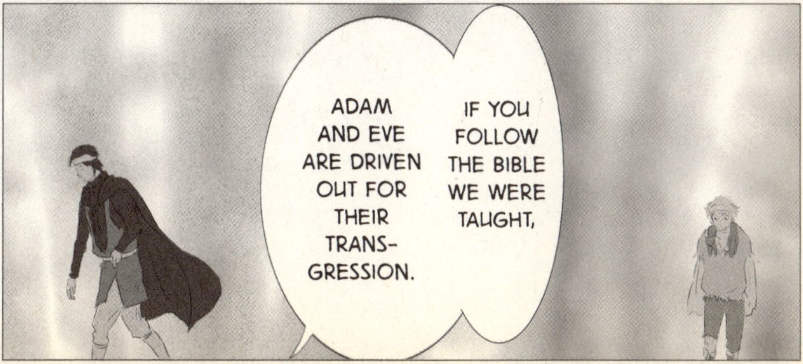
IF YOU FOLLOW THE BIBLE WE WERE TAUGHT,
ADAM AND EVE ARE DRIVEN OUT FOR THEIR TRANS-GRESSION.

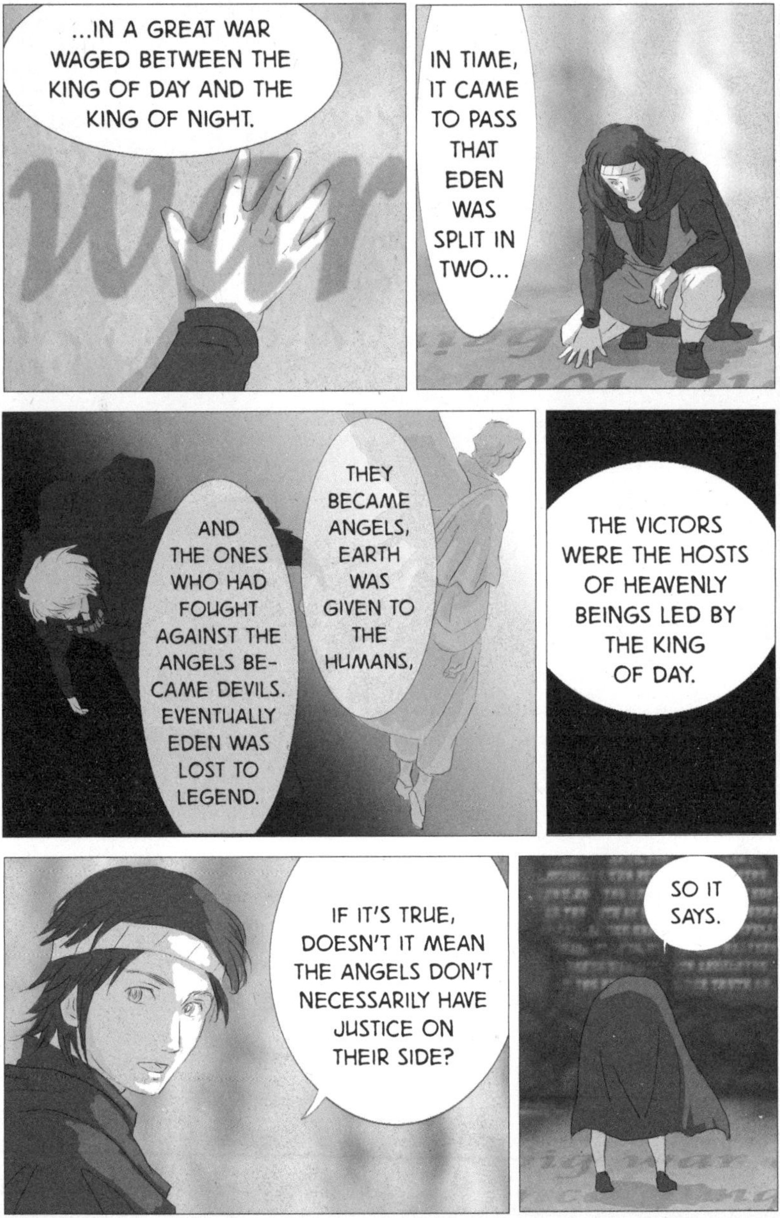
IN TIME, IT CAME TO PASS THAT EDEN WAS SPLIT IN TWO...
...IN A GREAT WAR WAGED BETWEEN THE KING OF DAY AND THE KING OF NIGHT.
war
THE VICTORS WERE THE HOSTS OF HEAVENLY BEINGS LED BY THE KING OF DAY.
THEY BECAME ANGELS, EARTH WAS GIVEN TO THE HUMANS,
AND THE ONES WHO HAD FOUGHT AGAINST THE ANGELS BE-CAME DEVILS. EVENTUALLY EDEN WAS LOST TO LEGEND.
SO IT SAYS.
IF IT'S TRUE, DOESN'T IT MEAN THE ANGELS DON'T NECESSARILY HAVE JUSTICE ON THEIR SIDE?

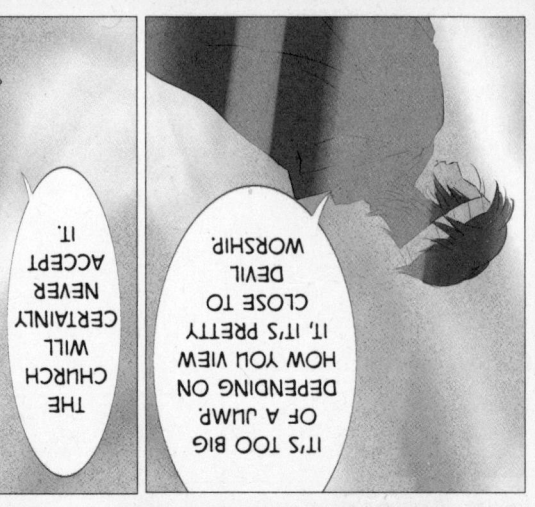

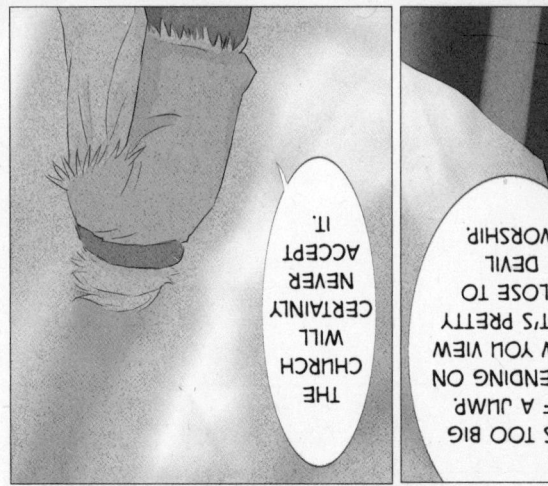

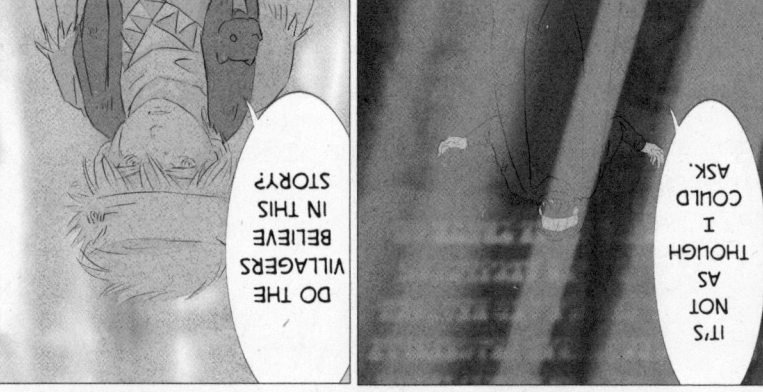

MAYBE THE ONES WHO DESERVE JUDGMENT ARE ANGELS AND HUM-ANS.
ON THE OTHER HAND, AS HUMANS WE ALSO OWE THE ANGELS OUR THANKS.
DO THE VILLAGERS BELIEVE IN THIS STORY?
IT'S NOT AS THOUGH I COULD ASK.
THE CHURCH WILL CERTAINLY NEVER ACCEPT IT.
IT'S TOO BIG OF A JUMP. DEPENDING ON HOW YOU VIEW IT, IT'S PRETTY CLOSE TO DEVIL WORSHIP.

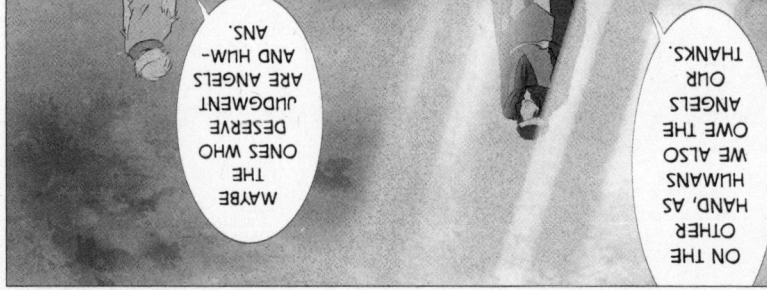

Eden was lost in the legend
WELL, I'VE SHOWN YOU MY CARDS. YOUR TURN.
TELL ME YOUR SECRETS.
WHAT WILL YOU DO ONCE I'VE TOLD YOU?
I'LL DECIDE WHETHER TO GUIDE YOU OUT, OR GUIDE YOU BACK.

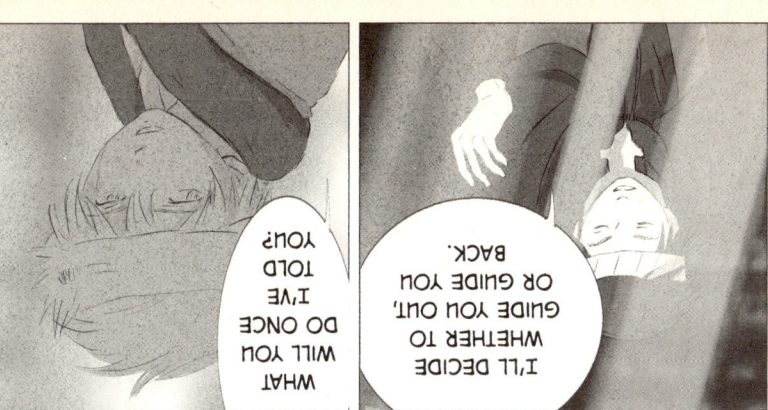

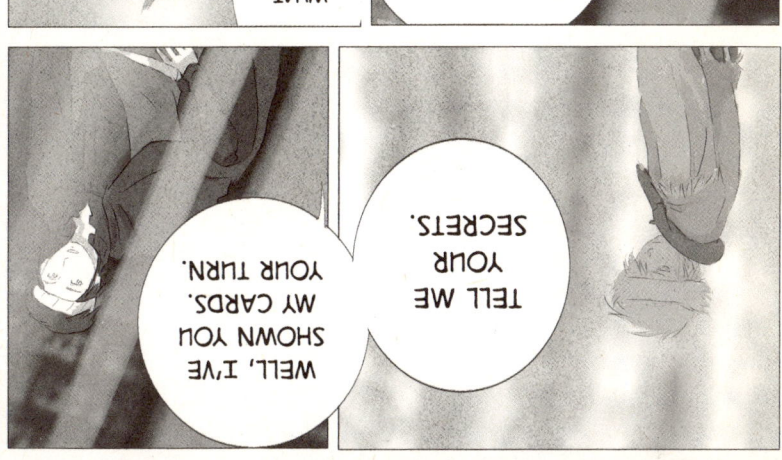

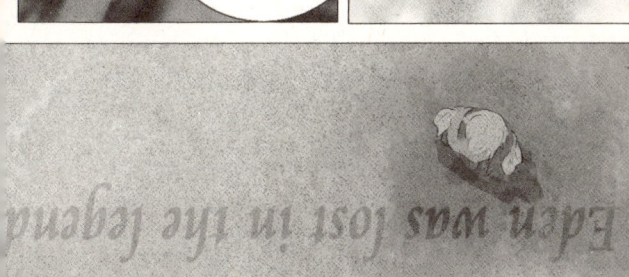

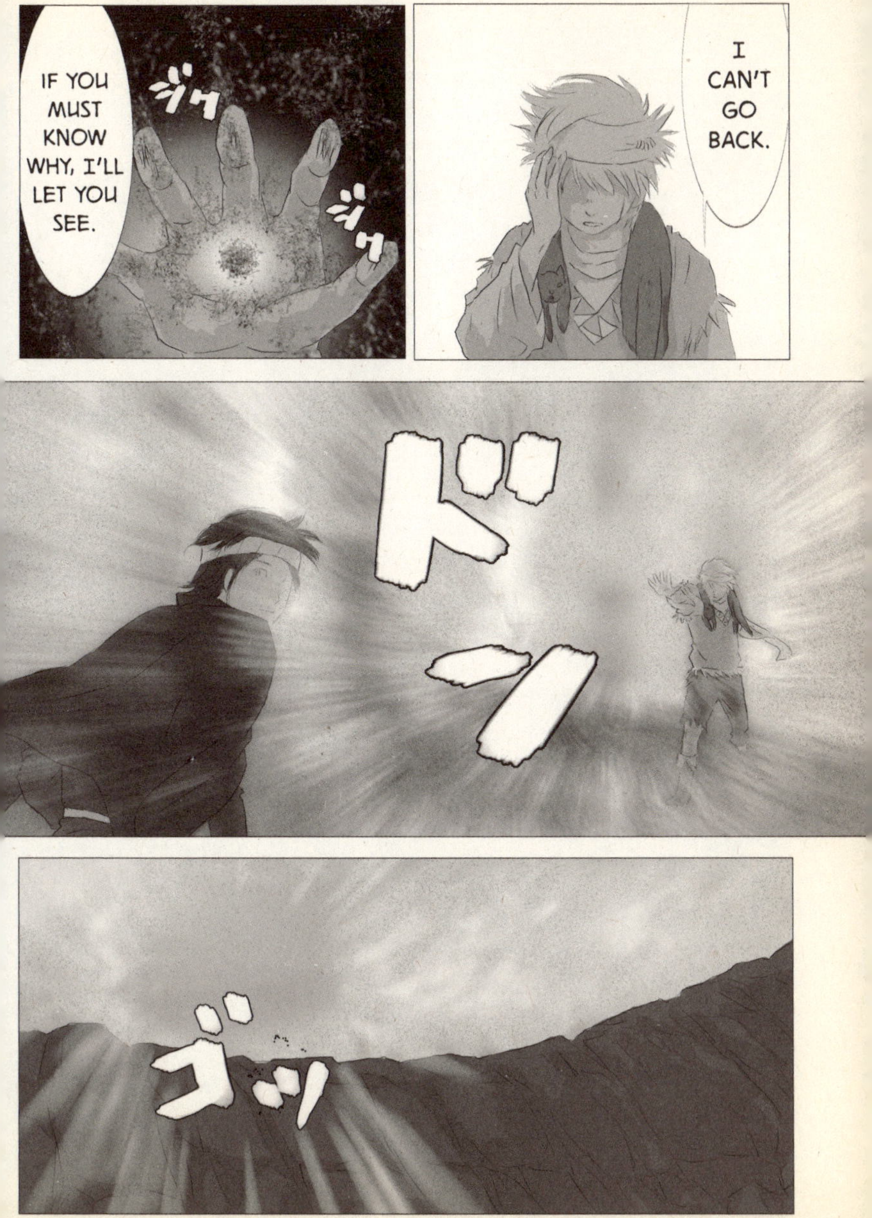
I CAN'T GO BACK.
IF YOU MUST KNOW WHY, I'LL LET YOU SEE.
ドッ
ゴッ

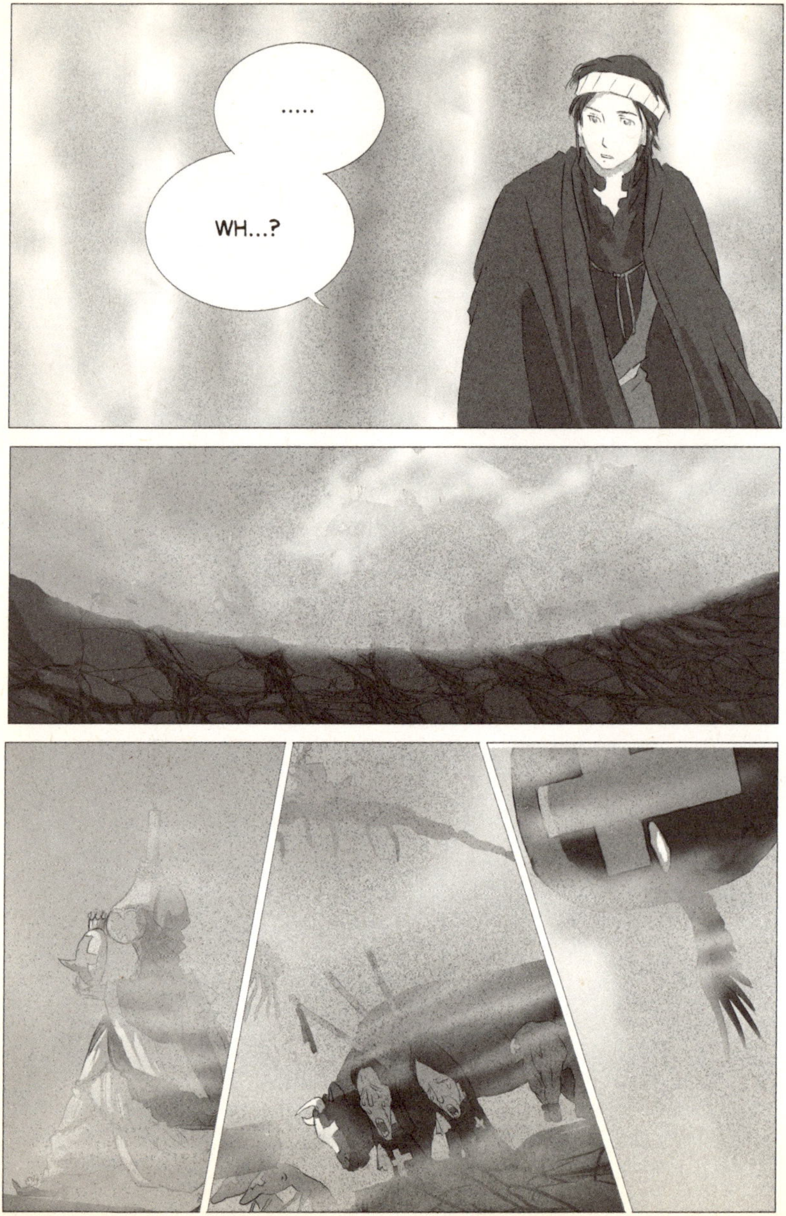
.....
WH...?

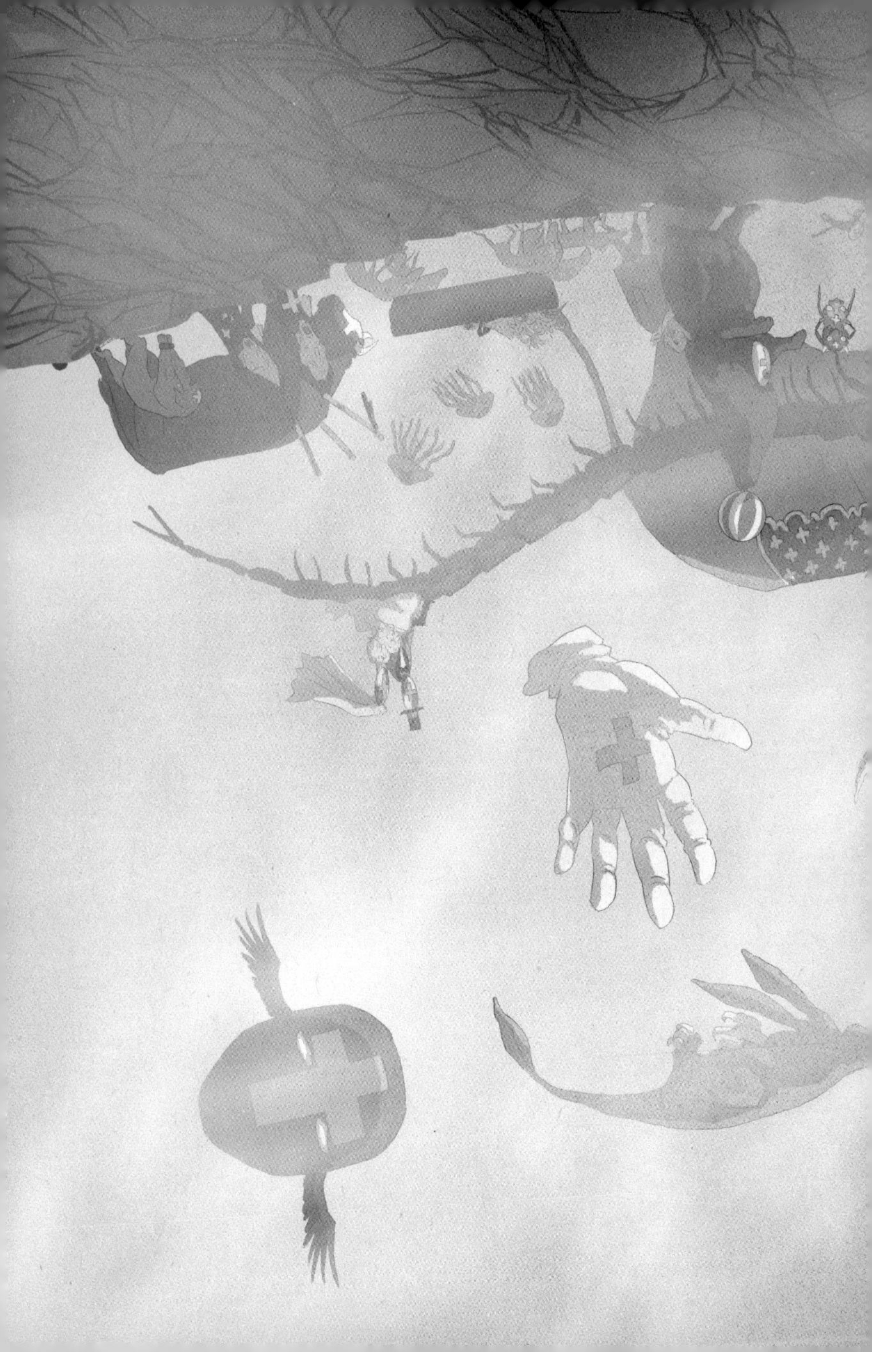

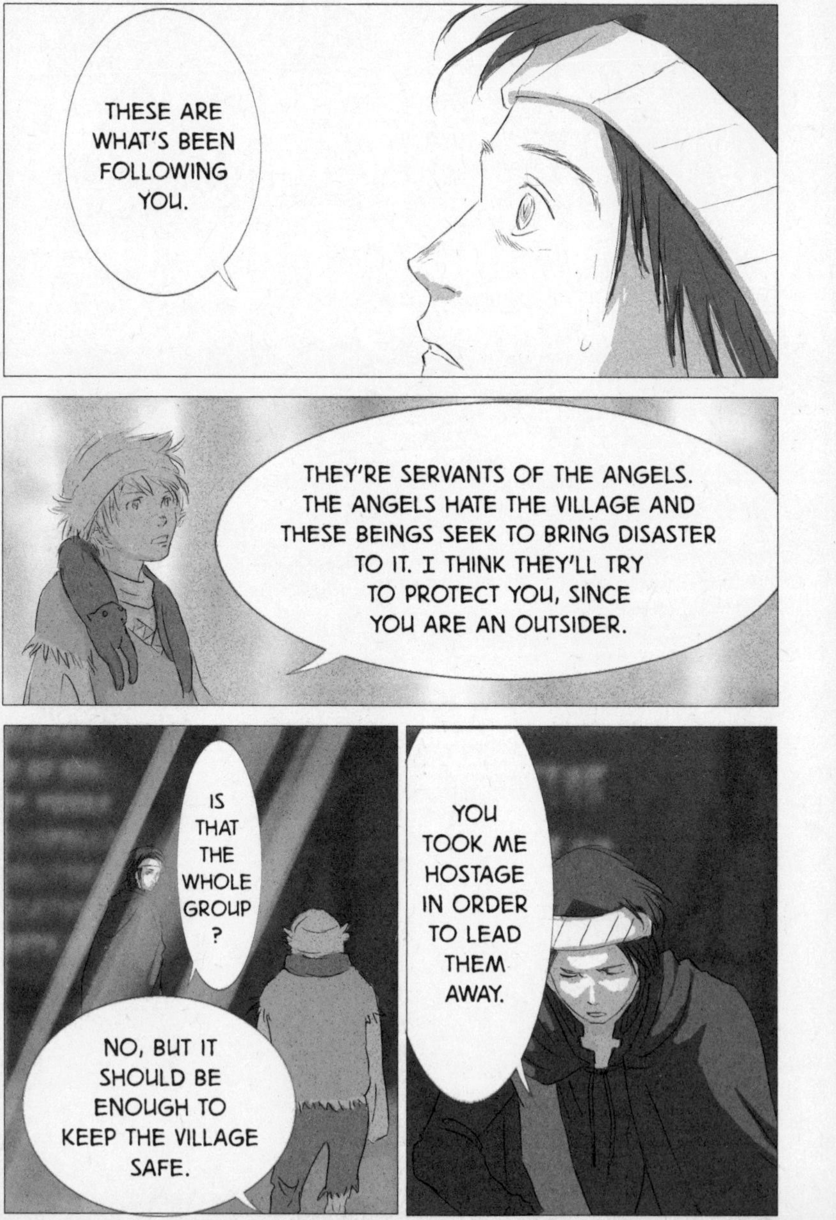
THESE ARE WHAT'S BEEN FOLLOWING YOU.
THEY'RE SERVANTS OF THE ANGELS. THE ANGELS HATE THE VILLAGE AND THESE BEINGS SEEK TO BRING DISASTER TO IT. I THINK THEY'LL TRY TO PROTECT YOU, SINCE YOU ARE AN OUTSIDER.
YOU TOOK ME HOSTAGE IN ORDER TO LEAD THEM AWAY.
IS THAT THE WHOLE GROUP?
NO, BUT IT SHOULD BE ENOUGH TO KEEP THE VILLAGE SAFE.

ALRIGHT, I'VE DECIDED. WE'LL LEAVE.
JUST IGNORE THEM.

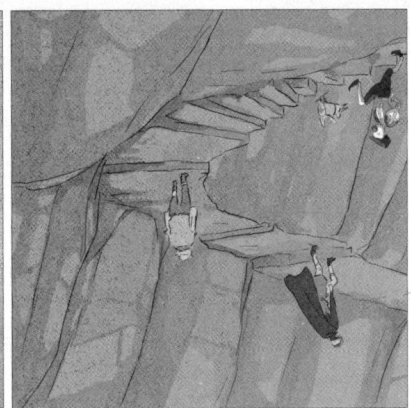

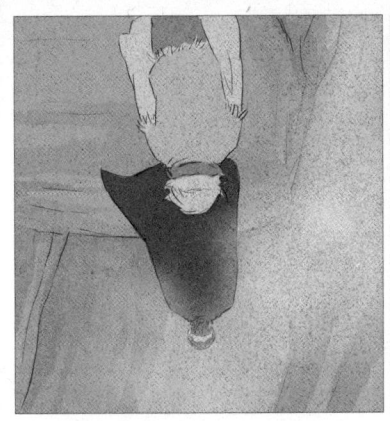

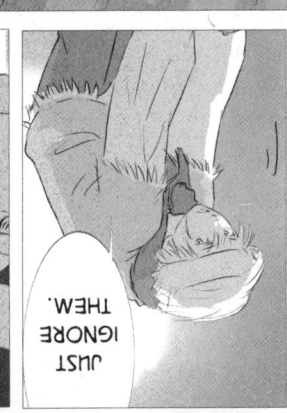

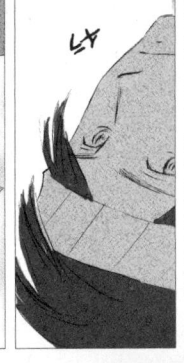

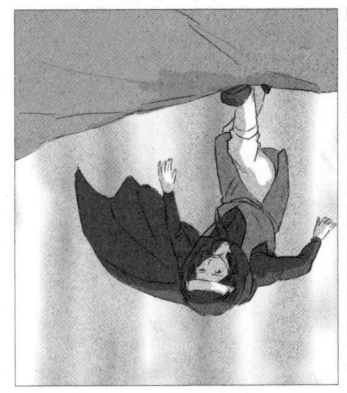

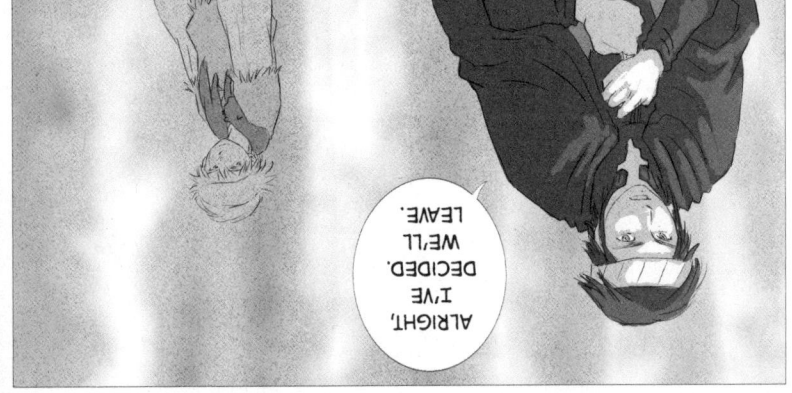

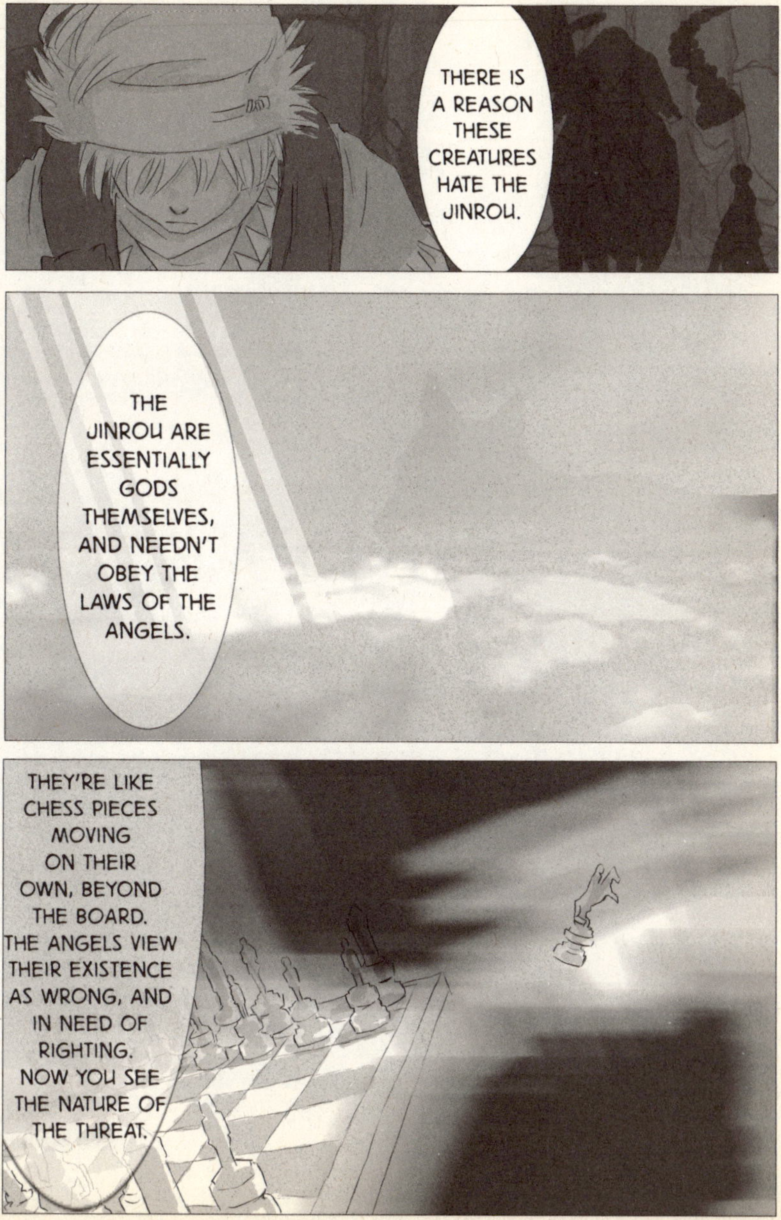
THERE IS A REASON THESE CREATURES HATE THE JINROU.
THE JINROU ARE ESSENTIALLY GODS THEMSELVES, AND NEEDN'T OBEY THE LAWS OF THE ANGELS.
THEY'RE LIKE CHESS PIECES MOVING ON THEIR OWN, BEYOND THE BOARD. THE ANGELS VIEW THEIR EXISTENCE AS WRONG, AND IN NEED OF RIGHTING. NOW YOU SEE THE NATURE OF THE THREAT.

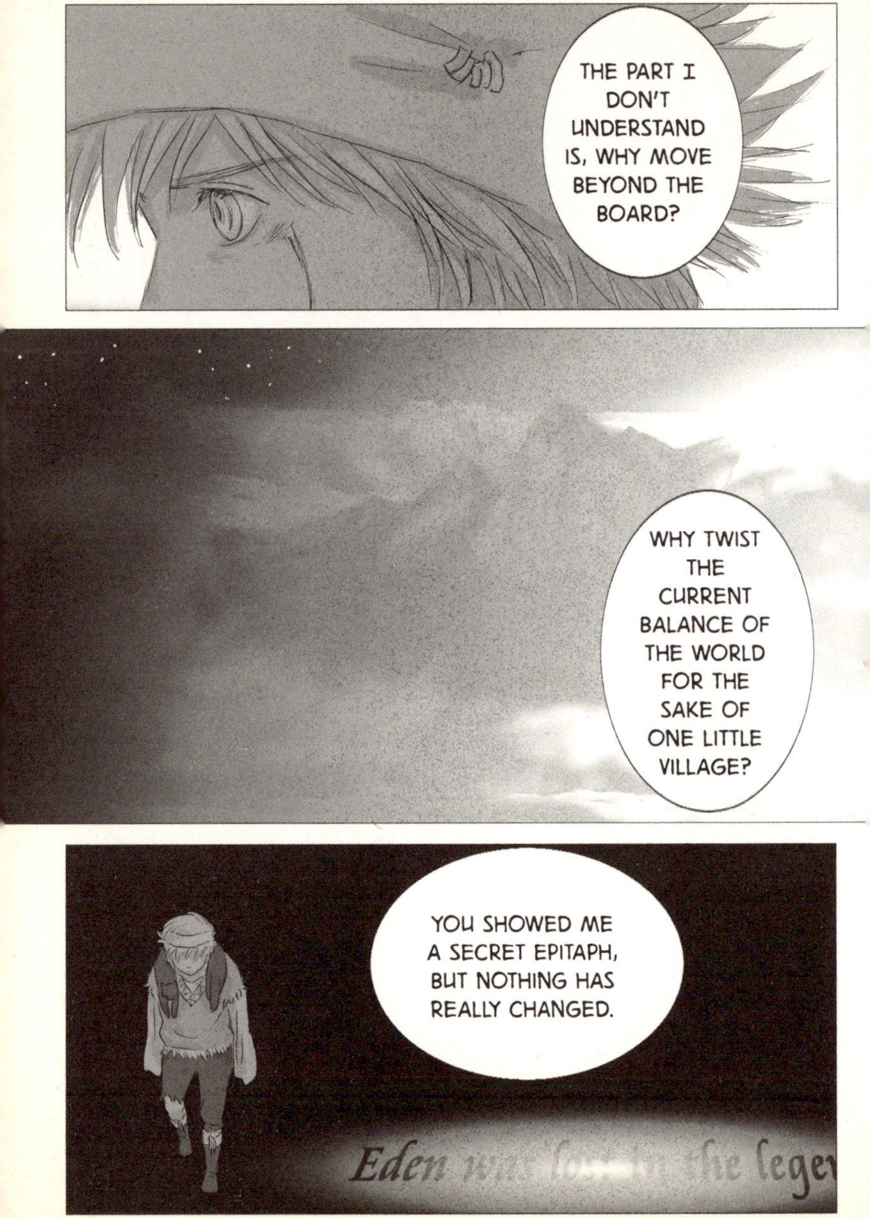
THE PART I DON'T UNDERSTAND IS, WHY MOVE BEYOND THE BOARD?
WHY TWIST THE CURRENT BALANCE OF THE WORLD FOR THE SAKE OF ONE LITTLE VILLAGE?
YOU SHOWED ME A SECRET EPITAPH, BUT NOTHING HAS REALLY CHANGED.

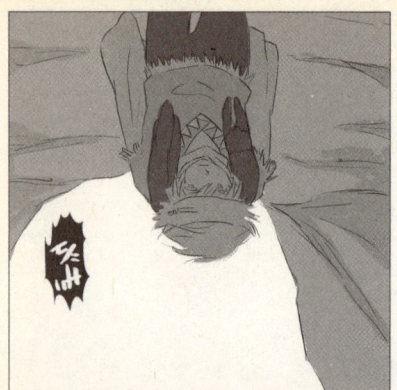

MAYBE THE WAR NEVER TRULY ENDED.

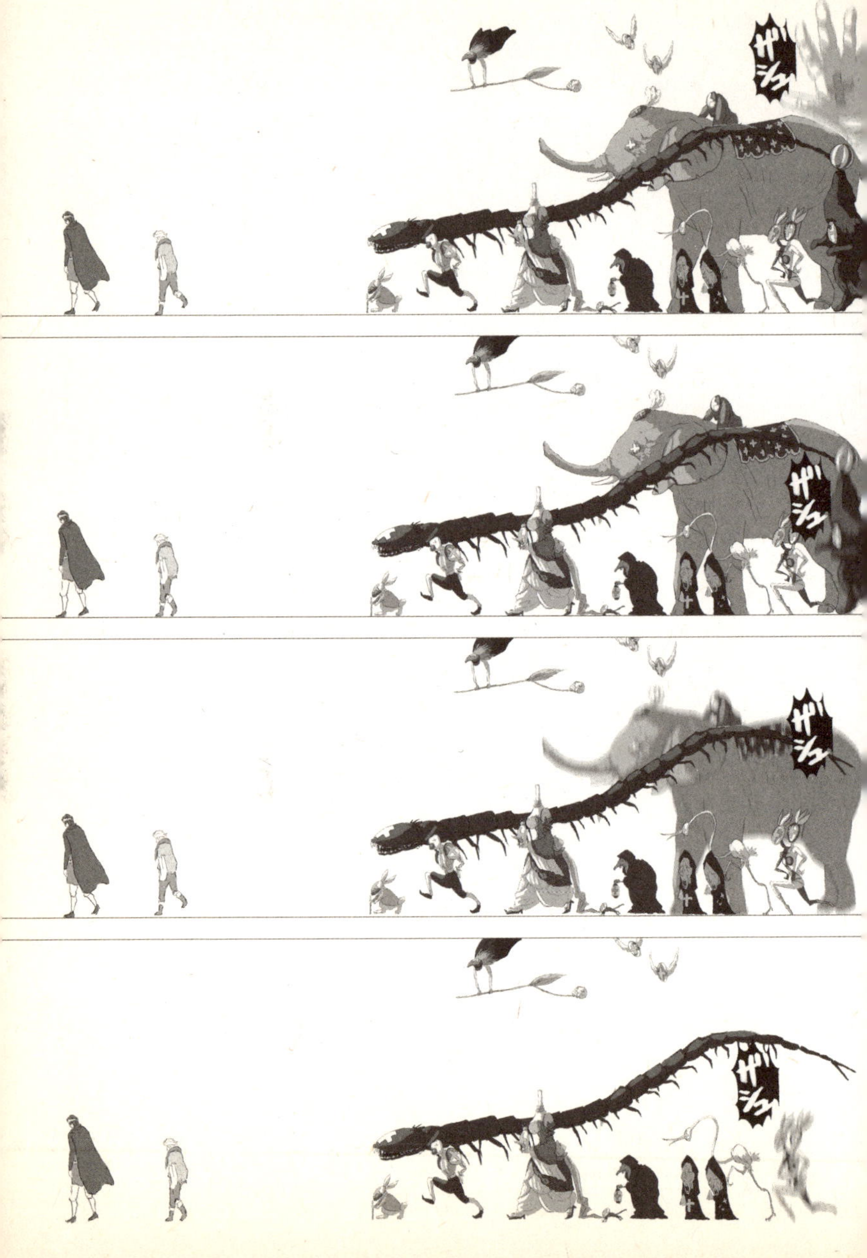
ザシュ
ザシュ
ザシュ
ザシュ

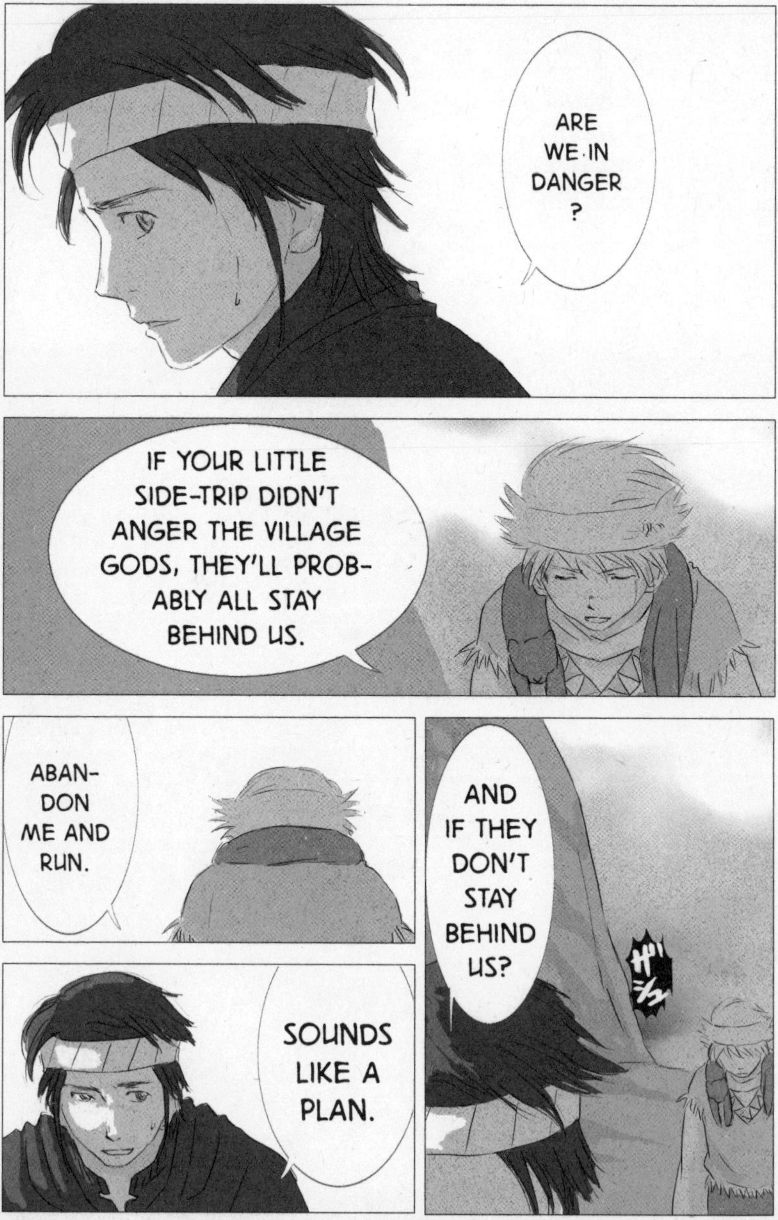
ARE WE IN DANGER ?
IF YOUR LITTLE SIDE-TRIP DIDN'T ANGER THE VILLAGE GODS, THEY'LL PROB- ABLY ALL STAY BEHIND US.
AND IF THEY DON'T STAY BEHIND US?
ABAN- DON ME AND RUN.
SOUNDS LIKE A PLAN.

SOME-
ONE'S
BROKEN
OUT OF
LINE.

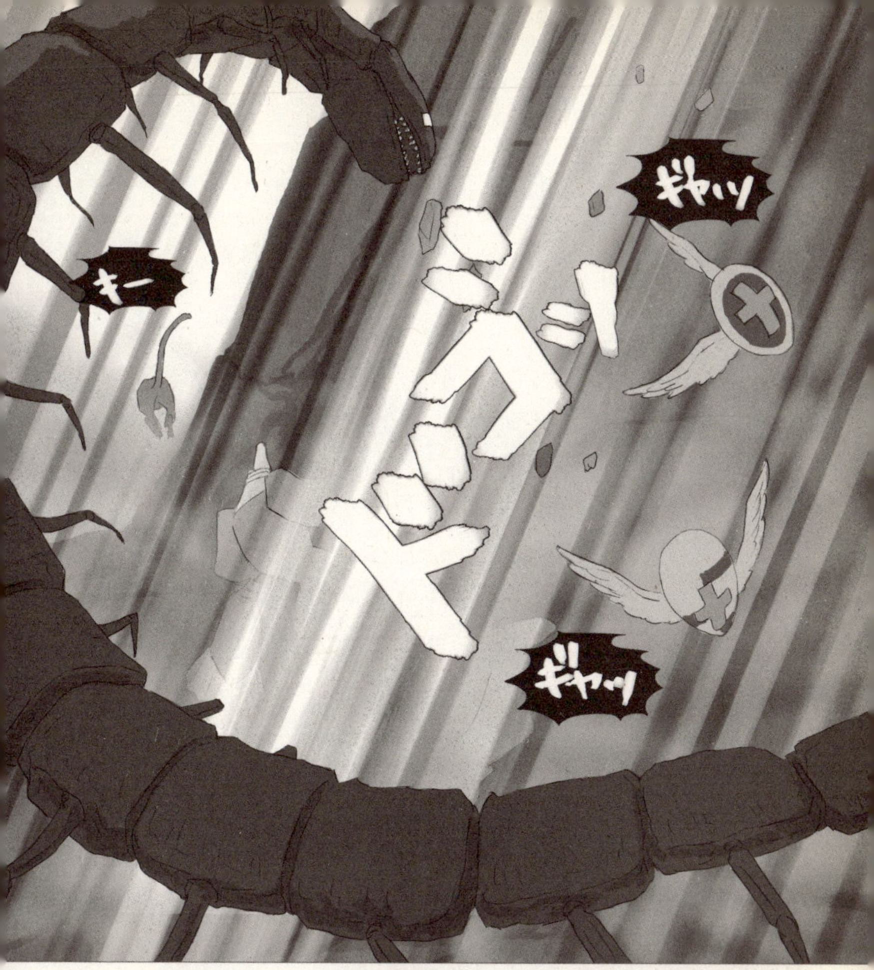
ギャッ
ギャッ
キー
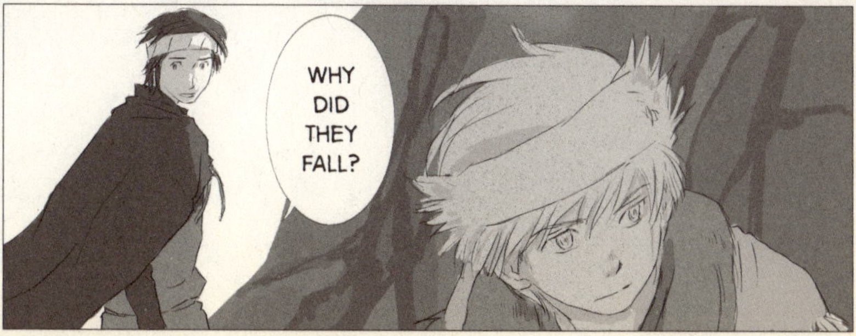
WHY DID THEY FALL?

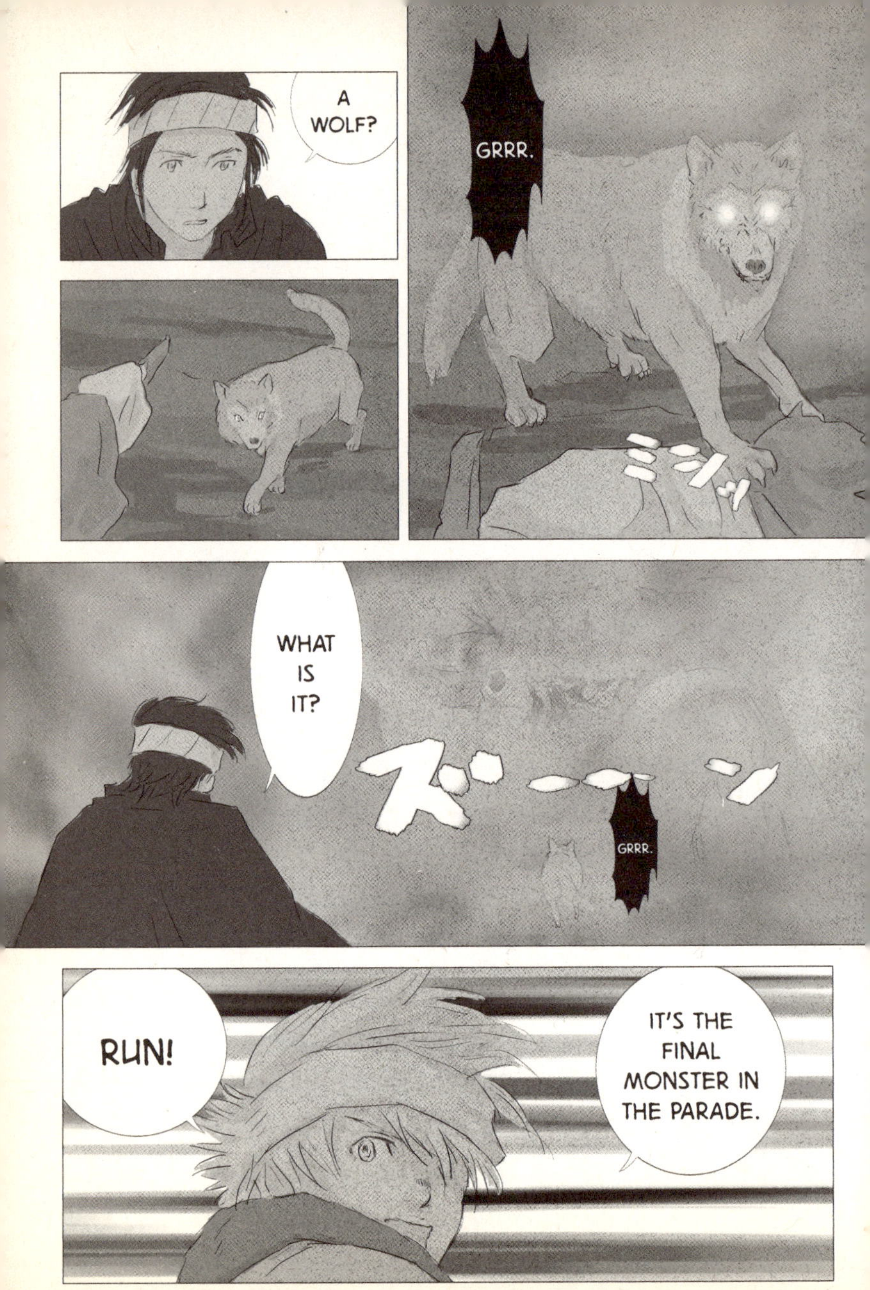
GRRR.
A WOLF?
GRRR.
WHAT IS IT?
IT'S THE FINAL MONSTER IN THE PARADE.
RUN!

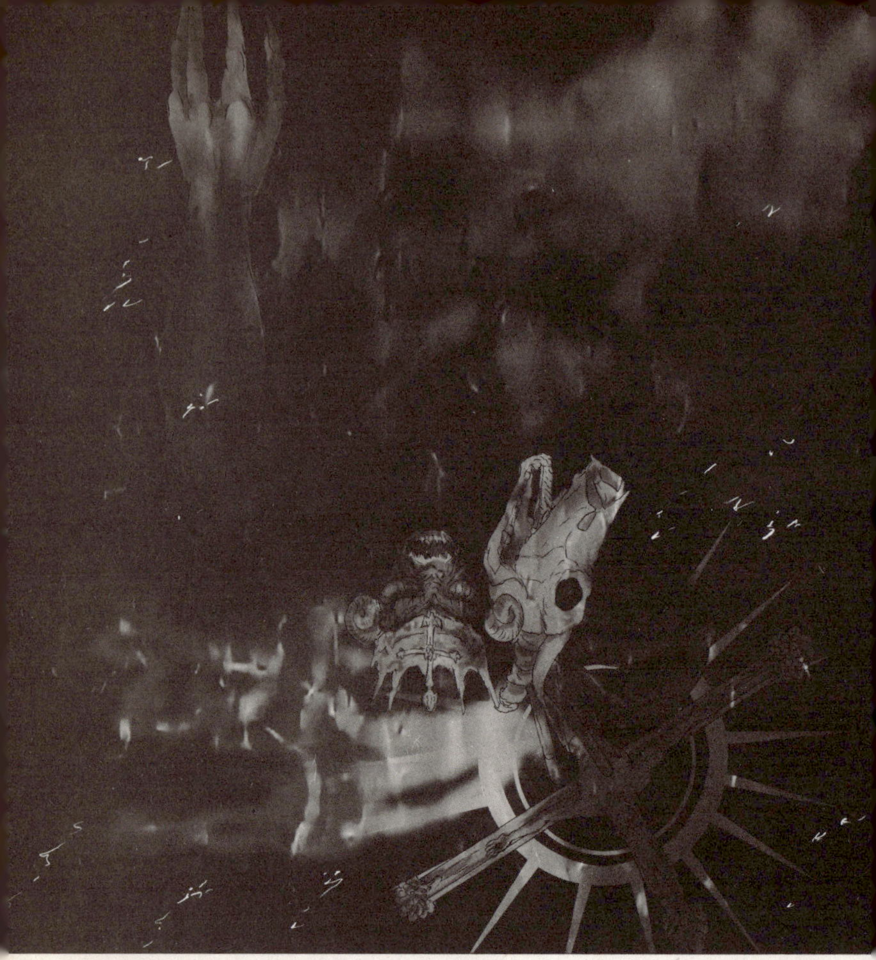

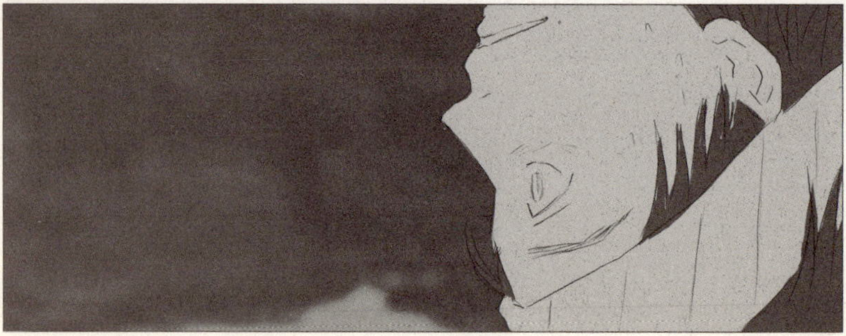

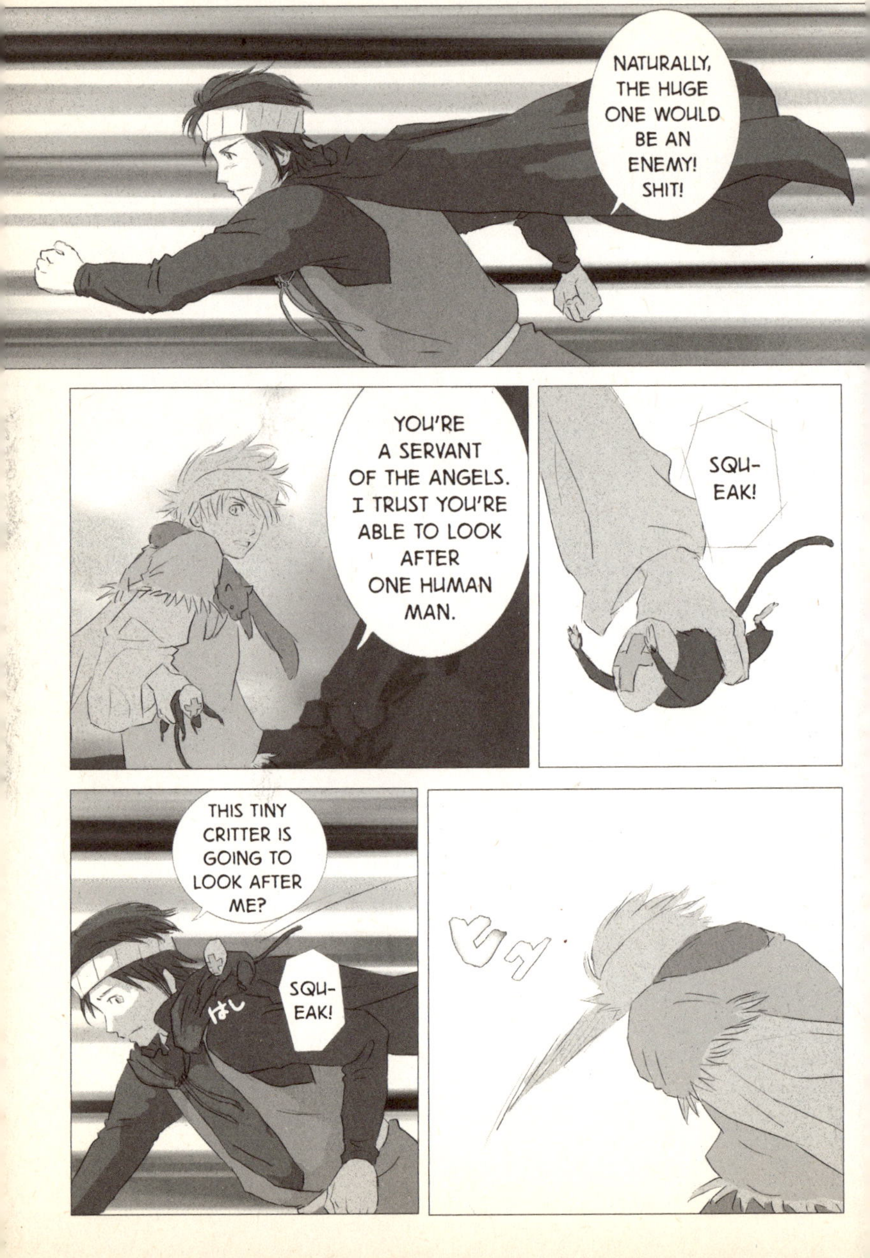
NATURALLY, THE HUGE ONE WOULD BE AN ENEMY! SHIT!
SQU- EAK!
YOU'RE A SERVANT OF THE ANGELS. I TRUST YOU'RE ABLE TO LOOK AFTER ONE HUMAN MAN.
THIS TINY CRITTER IS GOING TO LOOK AFTER ME?
SQU- EAK!

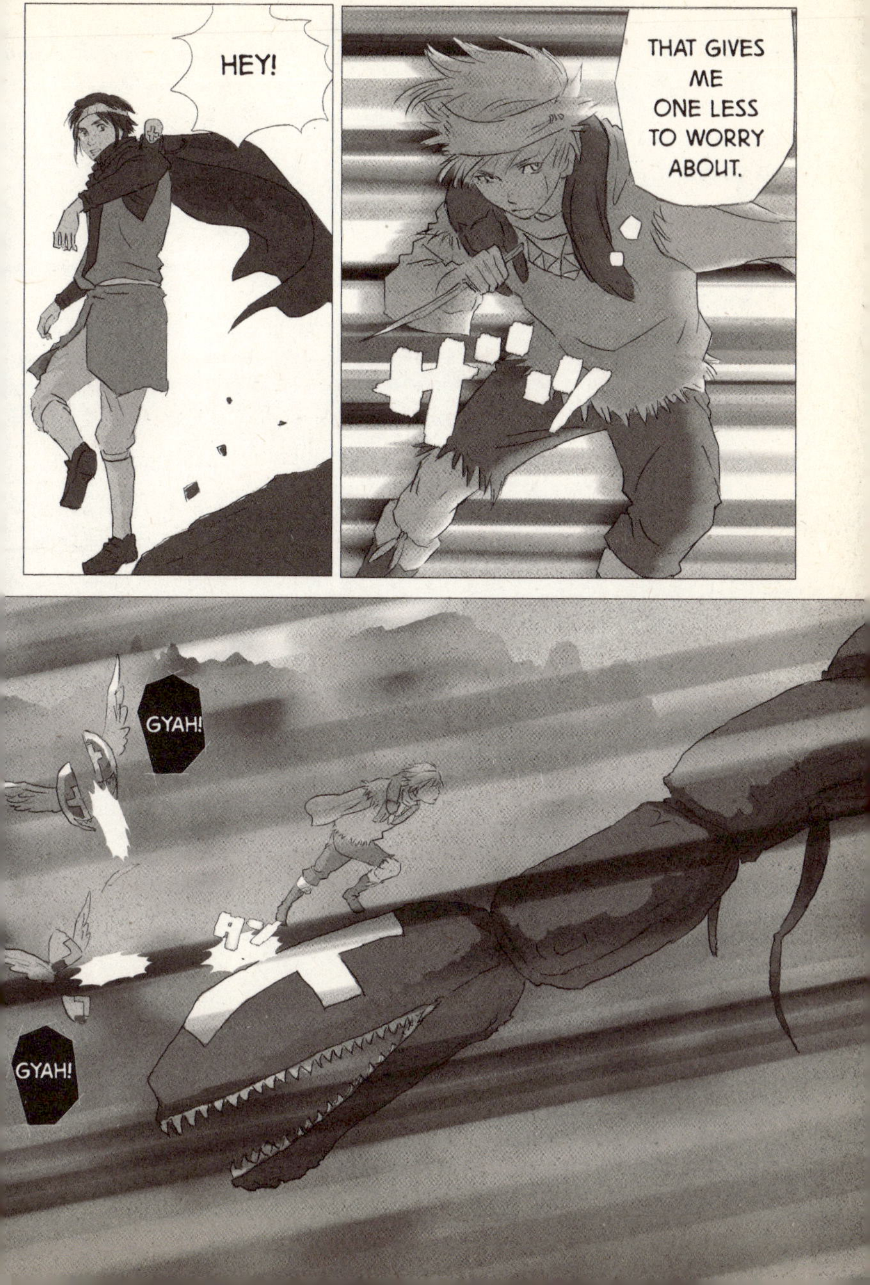
THAT GIVES ME ONE LESS TO WORRY ABOUT.
HEY!
GYAH!
GYAH!

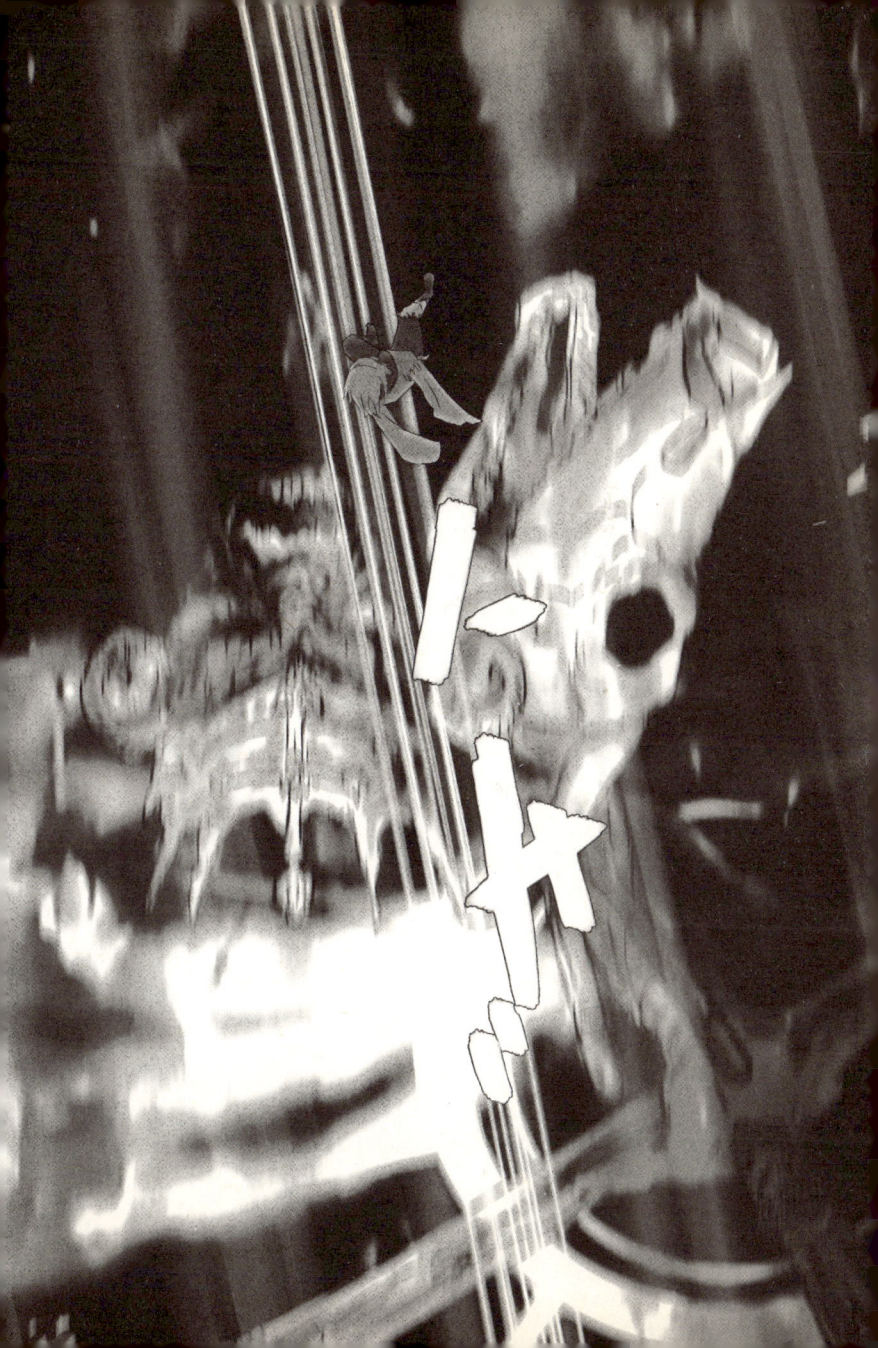

ズザ
パチ
パチ
I
...
...WILL ALWAYS BE.
パチ
パチ
HEE HEE HEE.
KEH KEH KEH.
HEH HEH HEH.

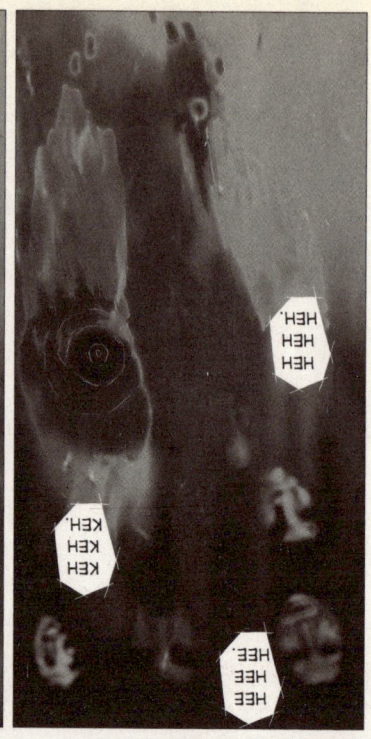

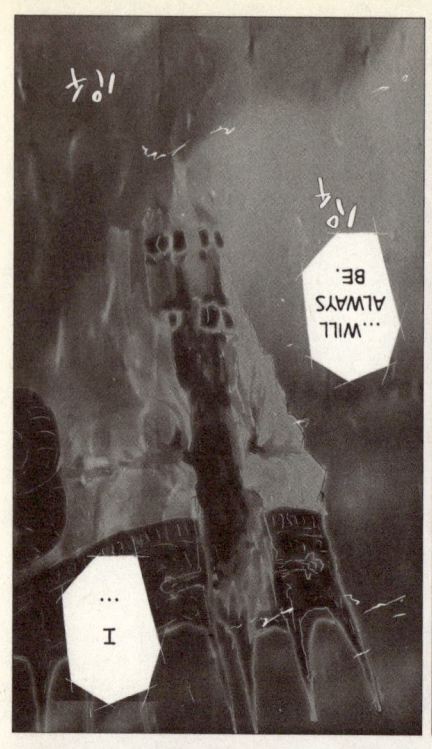

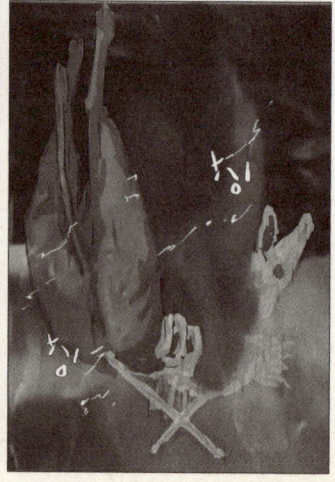

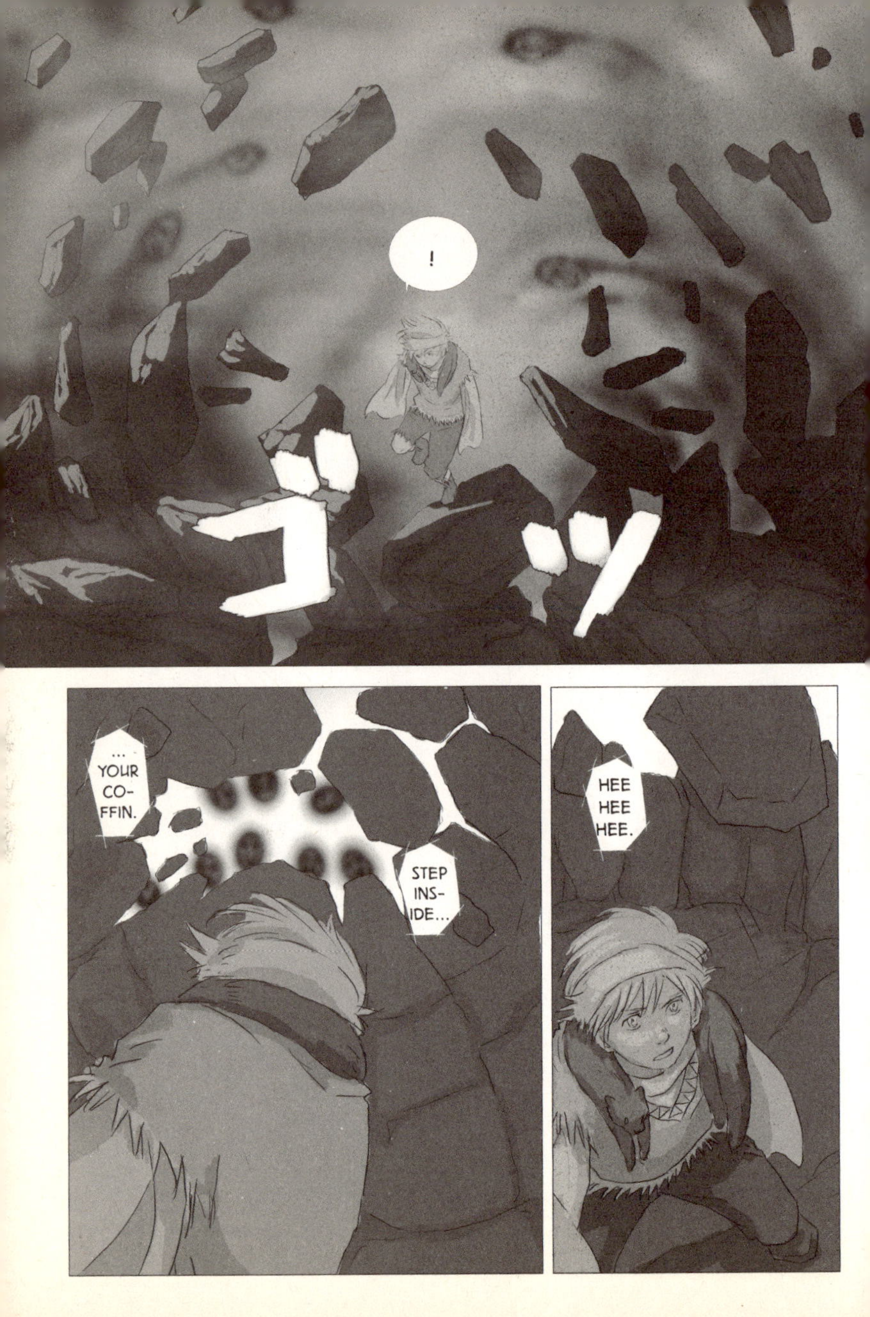
!
ゴッ
HEE HEE HEE.
STEP INS-IDE...
... YOUR CO-FFIN.

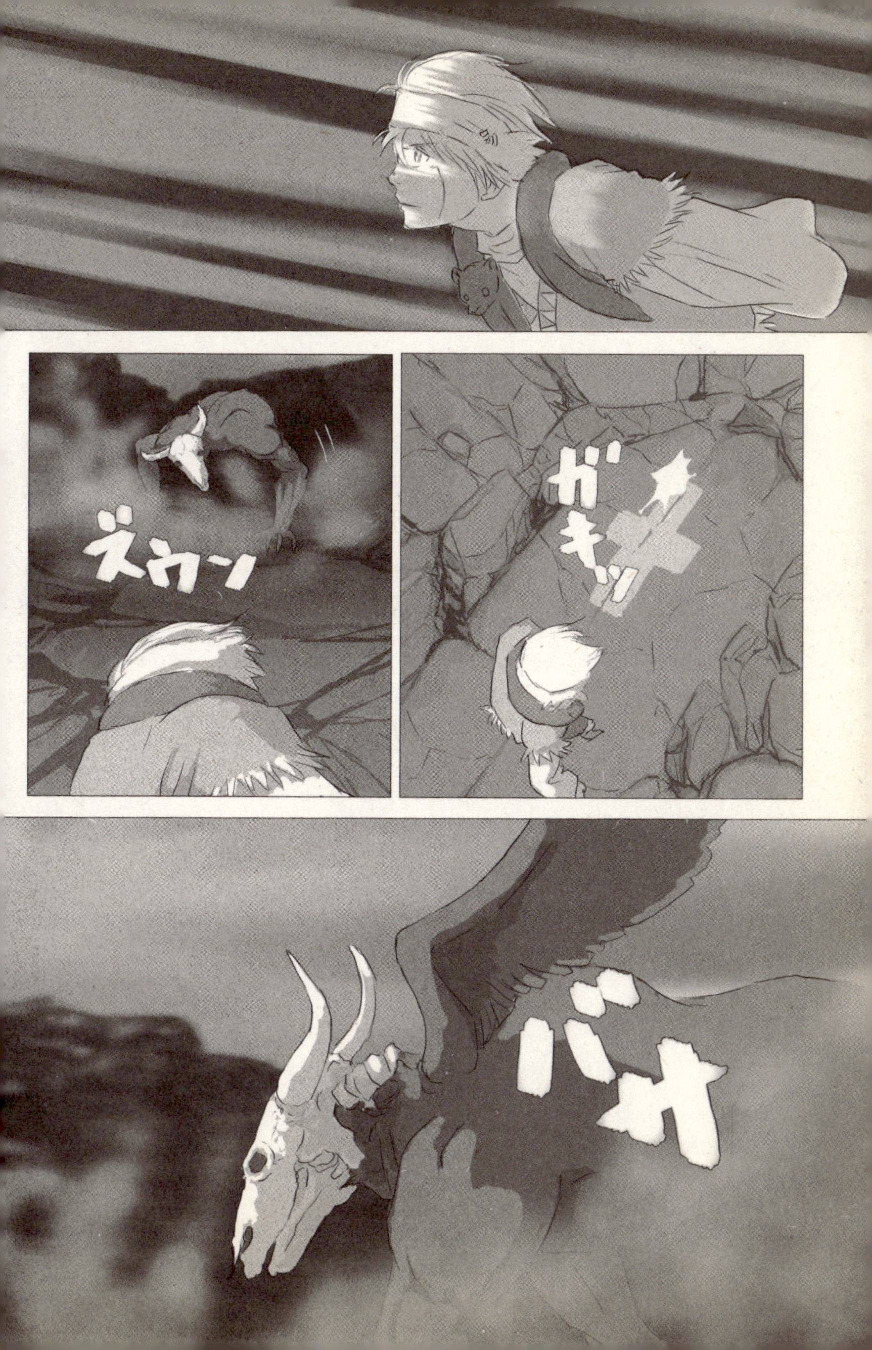
ガキッ
ズウーン
バオ

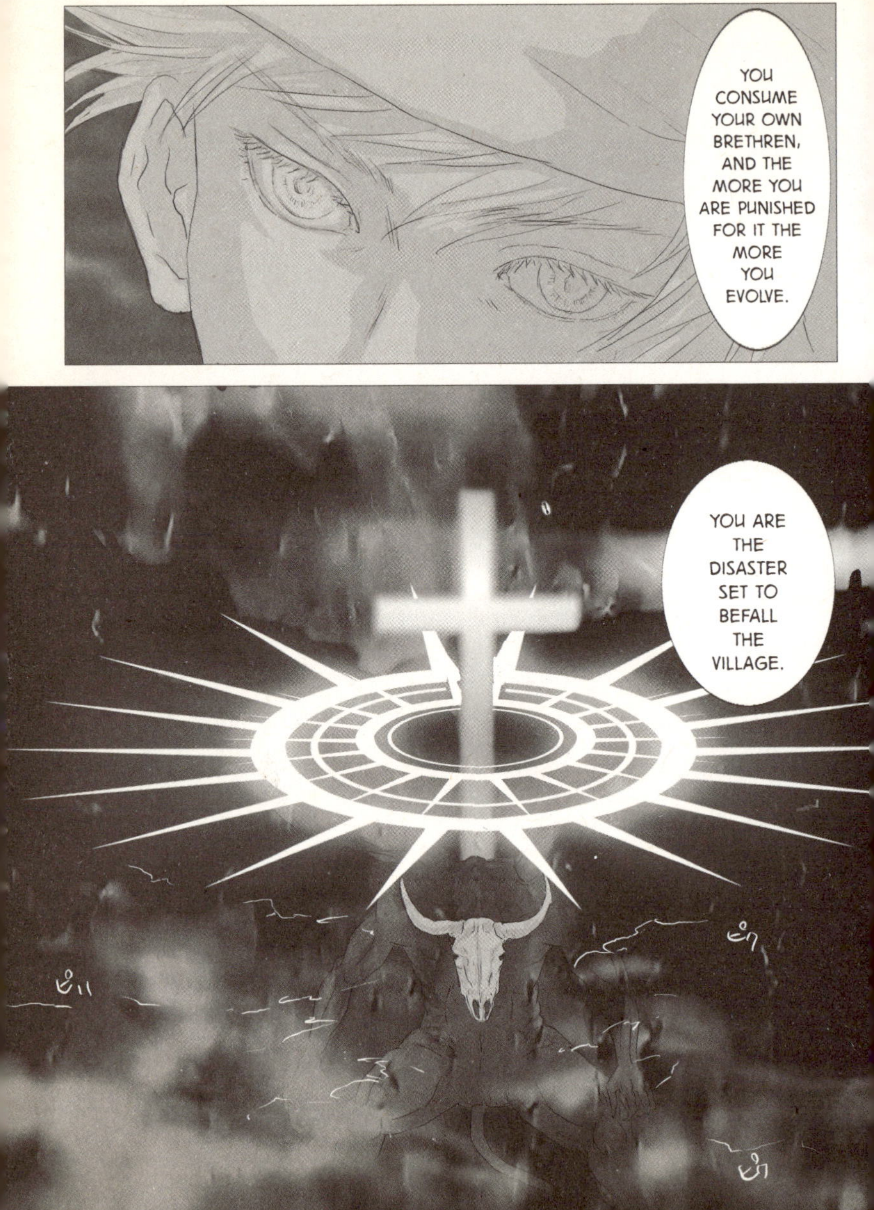
YOU CONSUME YOUR OWN BRETHREN, AND THE MORE YOU ARE PUNISHED FOR IT THE MORE YOU EVOLVE.
YOU ARE THE DISASTER SET TO BEFALL THE VILLAGE.

パアアアアア
HELP MEE ...

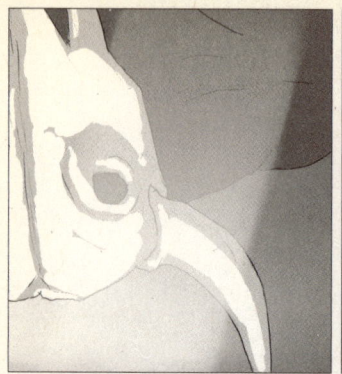

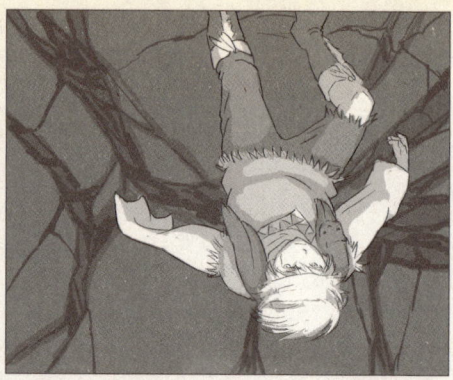

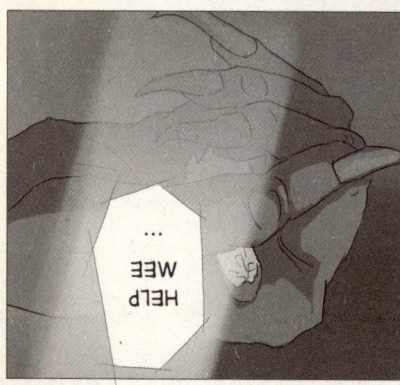

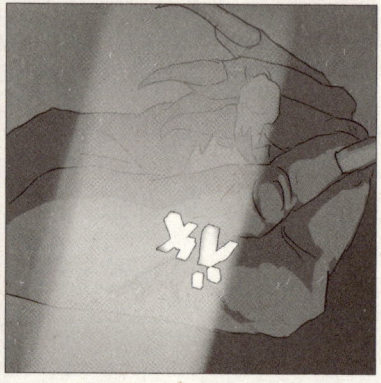

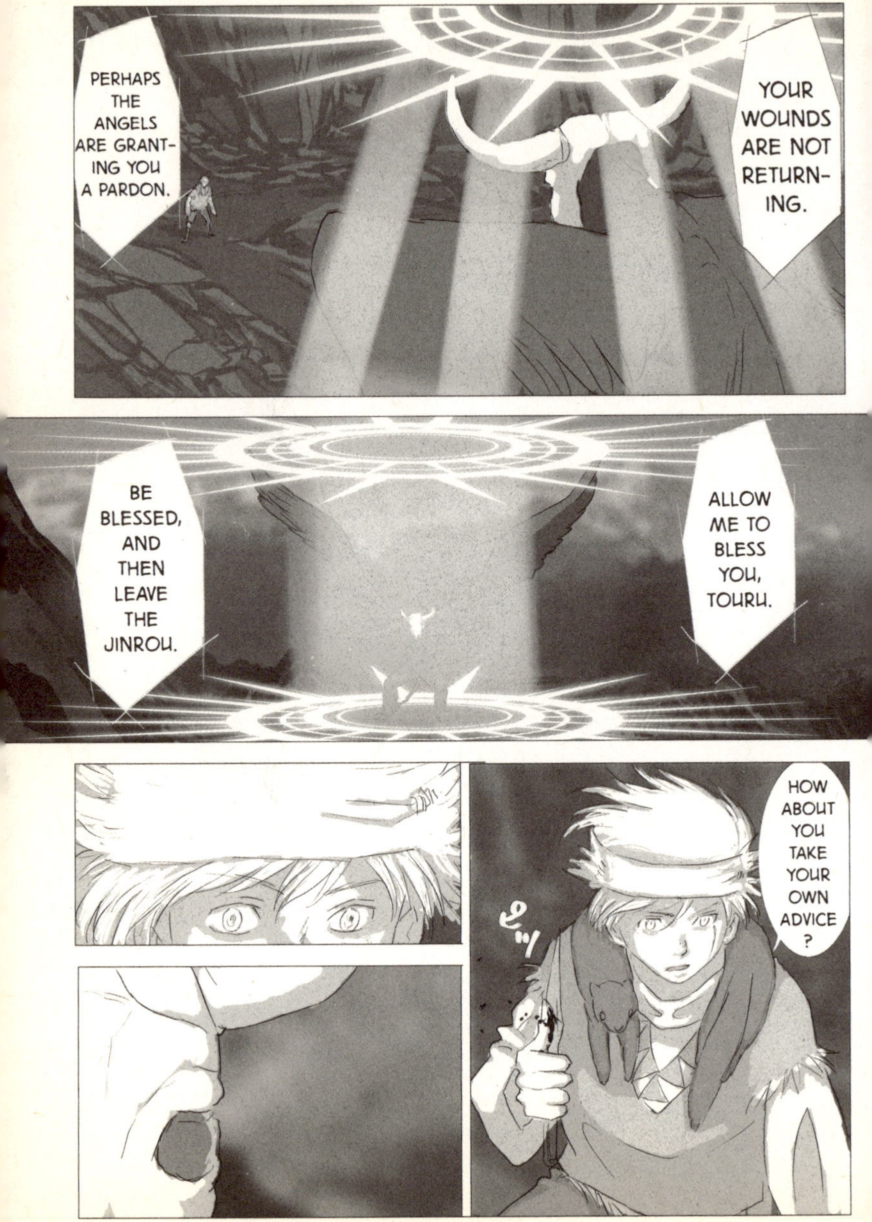
YOUR WOUNDS ARE NOT RETURN-ING.
PERHAPS THE ANGELS ARE GRANT-ING YOU A PARDON.
ALLOW ME TO BLESS YOU, TOURU.
BE BLESSED, AND THEN LEAVE THE JINROU.
HOW ABOUT YOU TAKE YOUR OWN ADVICE?

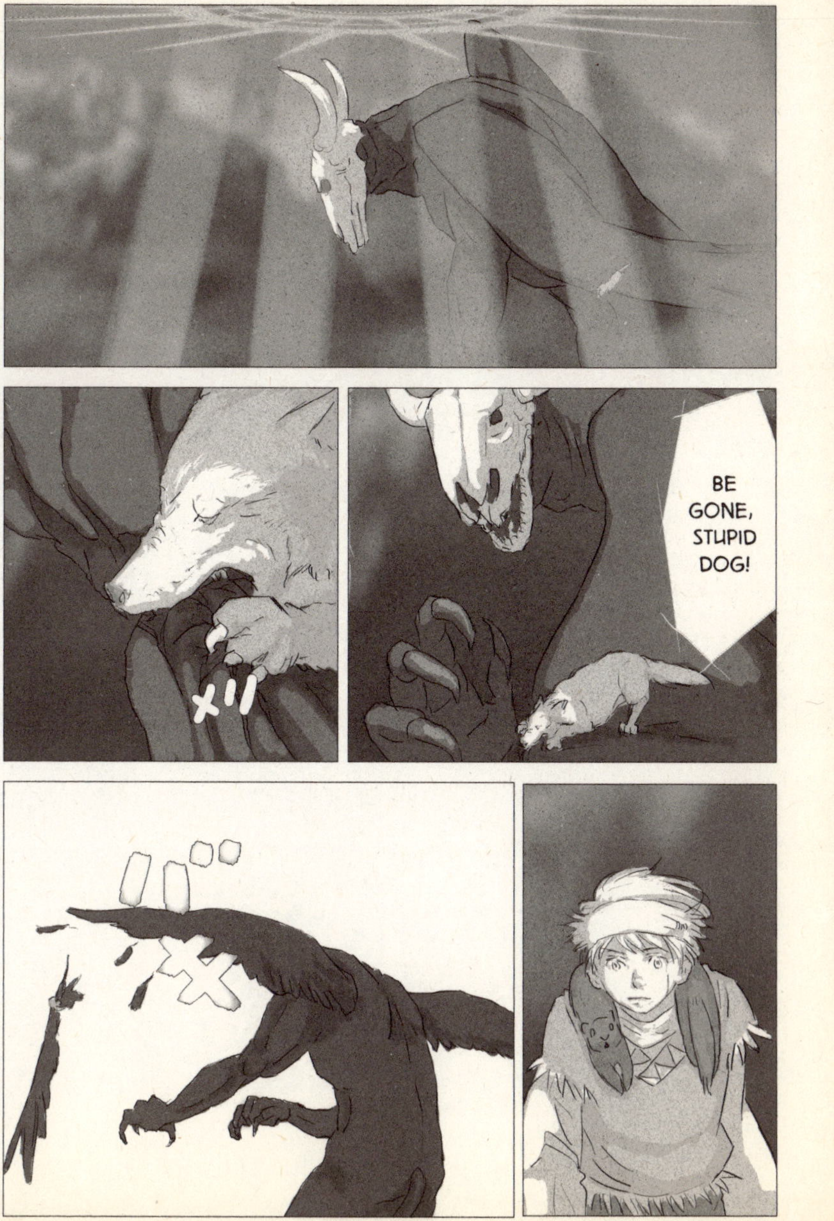
BE GONE, STUPID DOG!
メリ

ズウン
STAY OUT OF THE AFFAIRS OF YOUR BETTERS!
バチ
バチ
GRRR.
GOOD WORK.

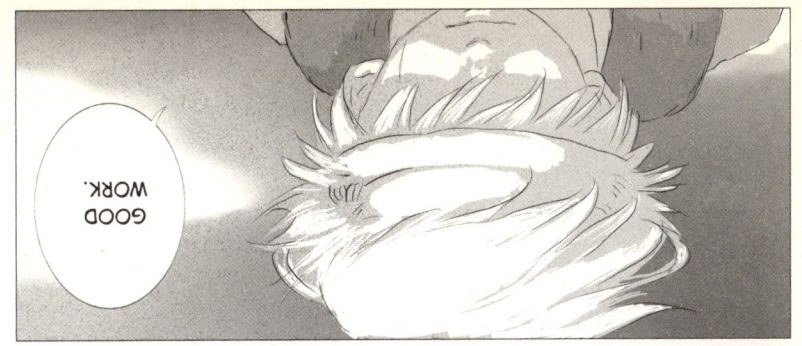

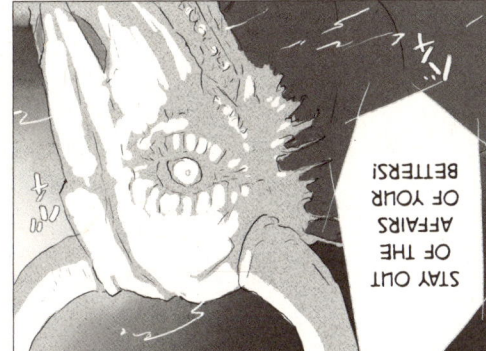

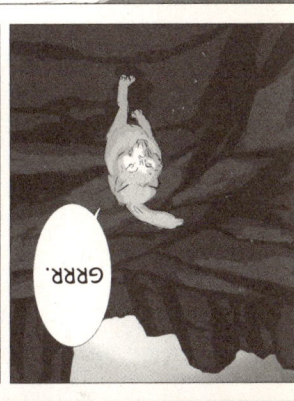

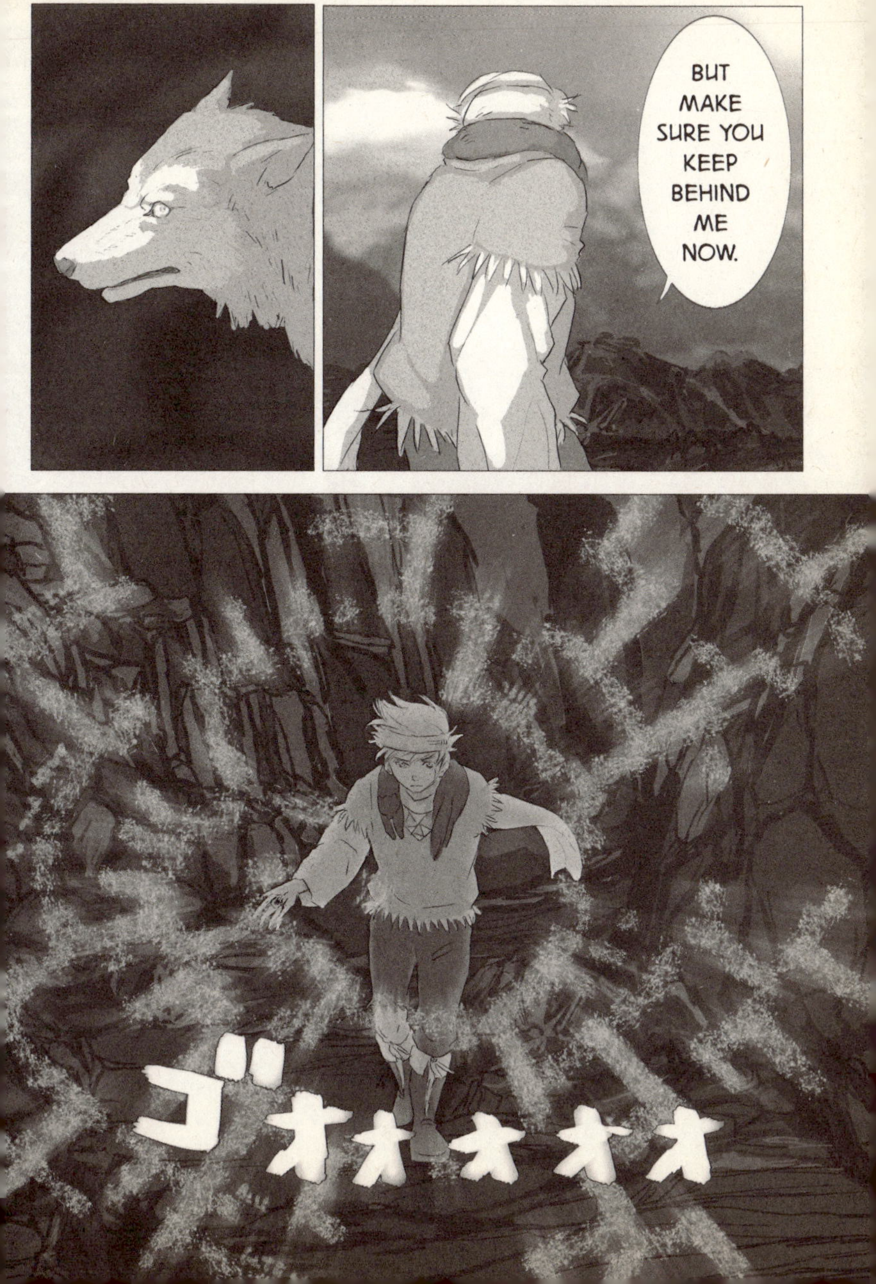
BUT MAKE SURE YOU KEEP BEHIND ME NOW.
ゴオオオオオ

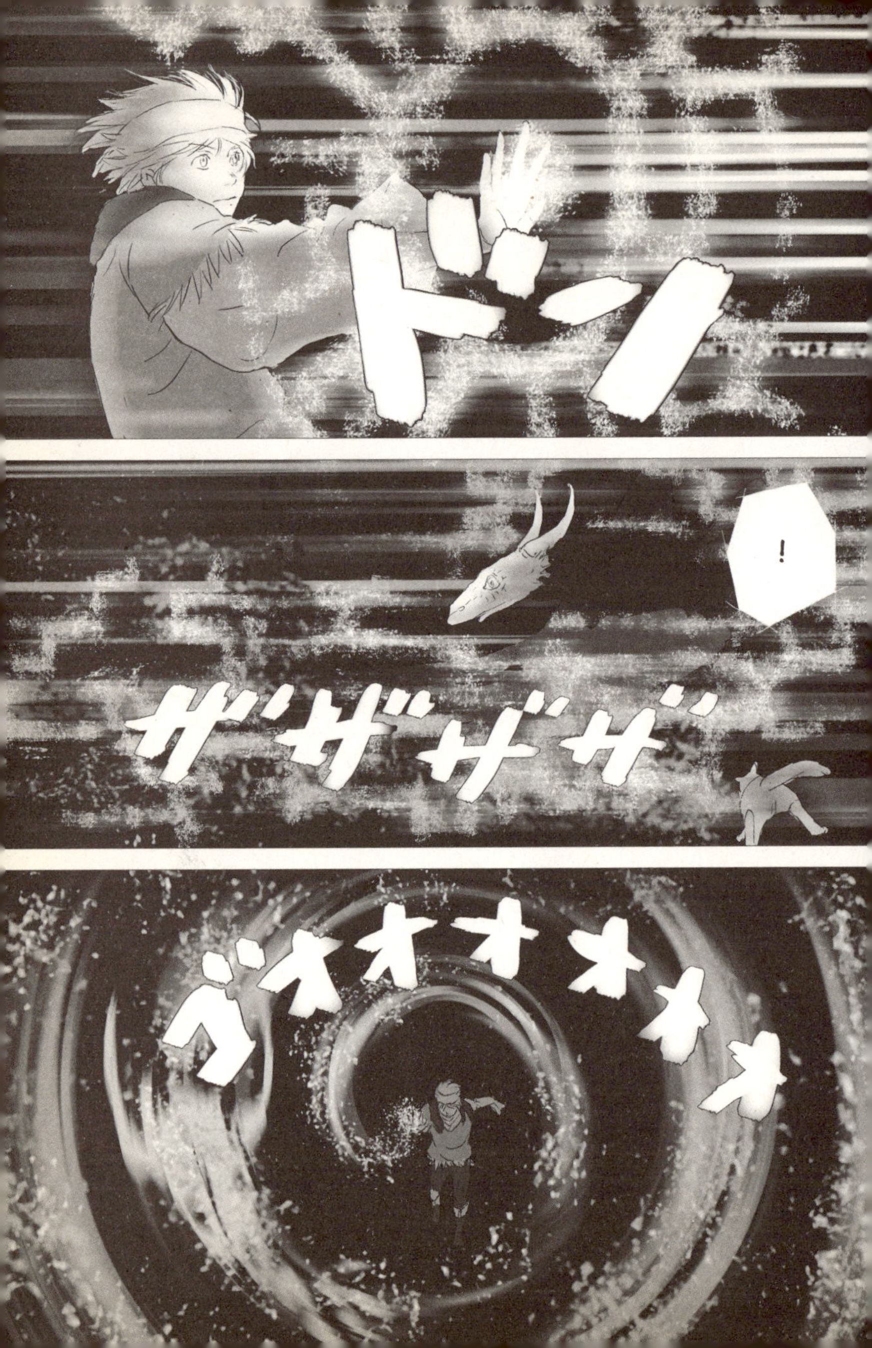
ドン
!
ザザザザ
ヴオオオオオオ

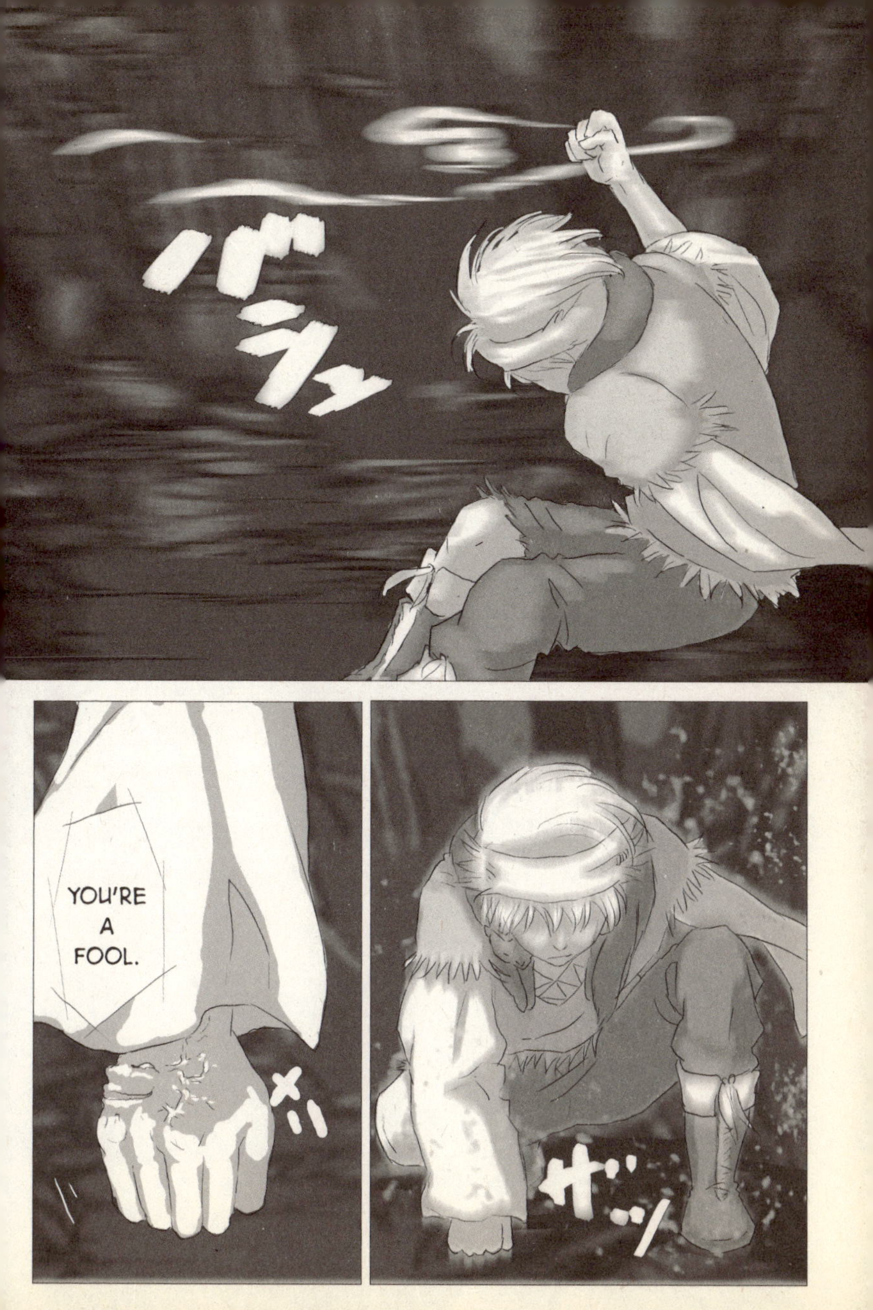
バシュ
ザッ
YOU'RE A FOOL.

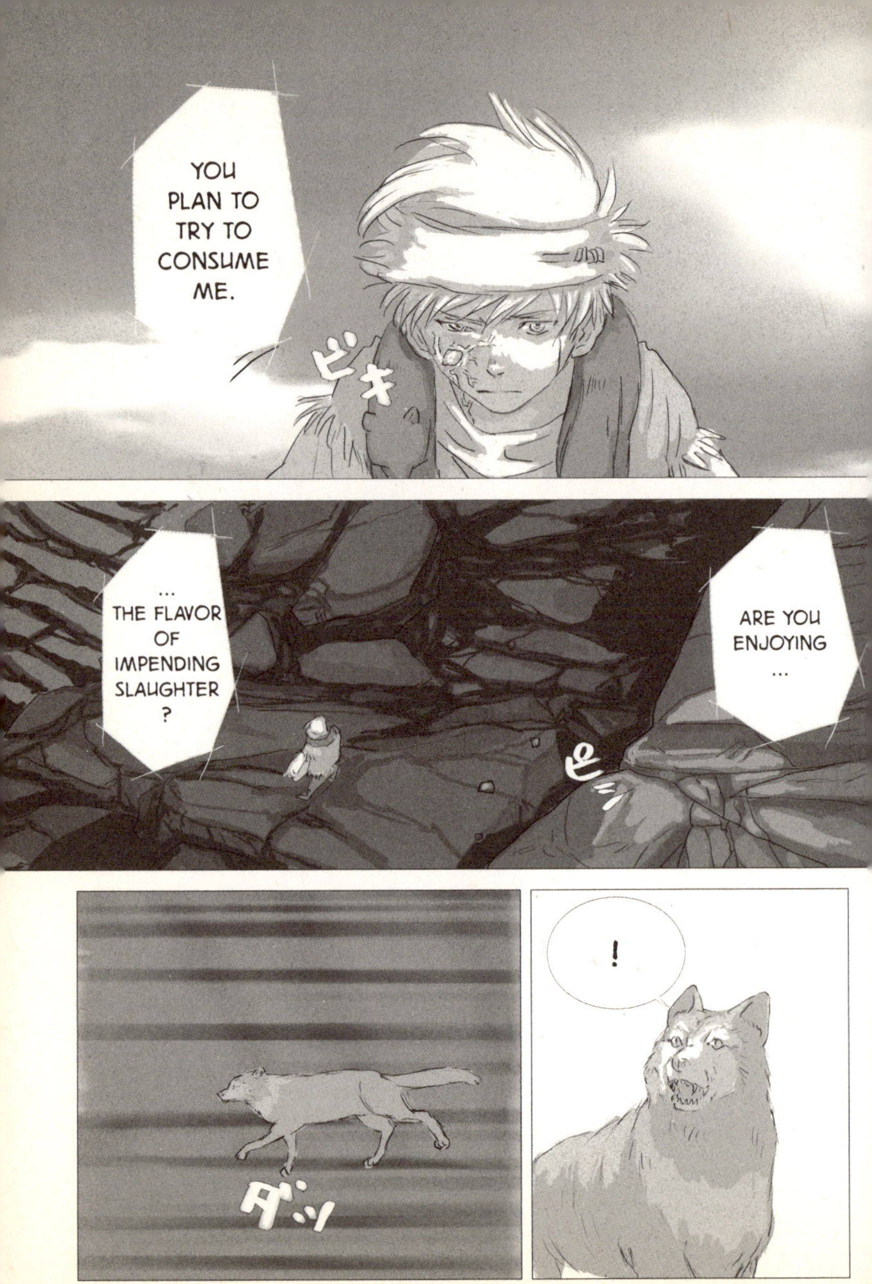
YOU PLAN TO TRY TO CONSUME ME.
ビキ
ARE YOU ENJOYING ...
... THE FLAVOR OF IMPENDING SLAUGHTER ?
ピ
!
ダッ

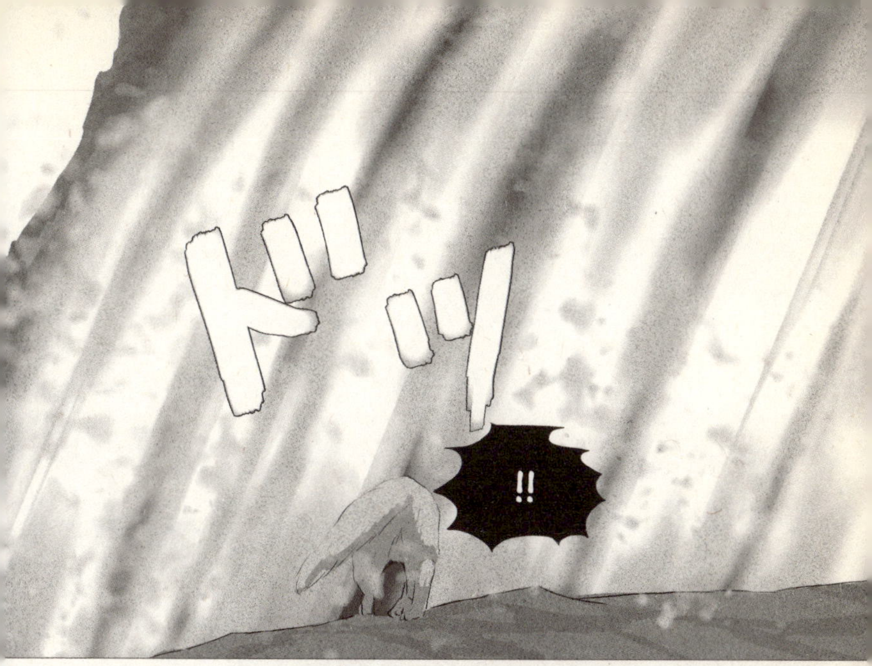
ドッッ
!!
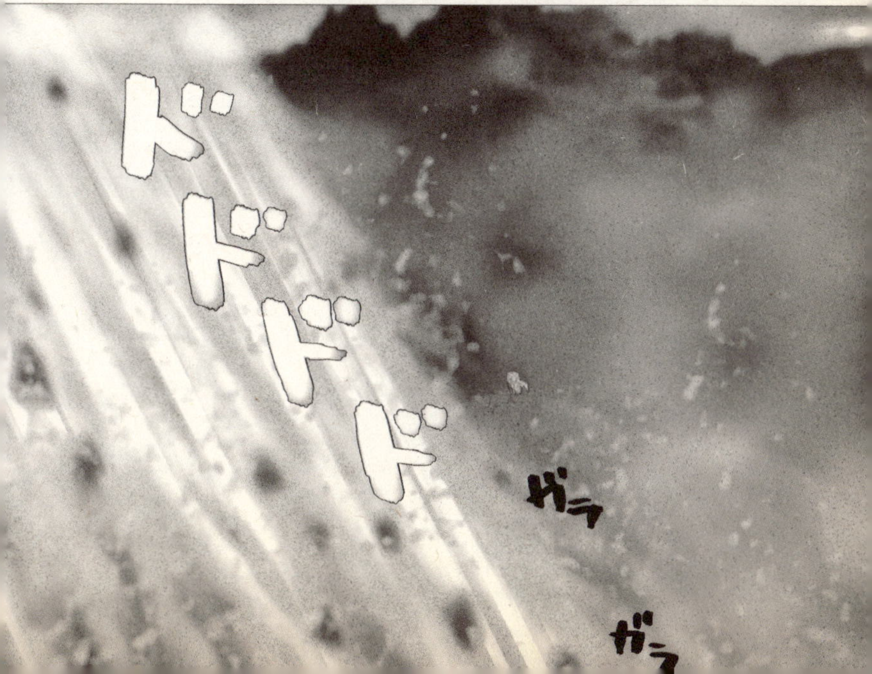
ドドドド
ガラ
ガラ

オオーーン
ドドドドド
ゼイ
ゼイ
ピチャン
ARE YOU OK?
I CAN LOOK AFTER MYSELF, REMEMBER?
!

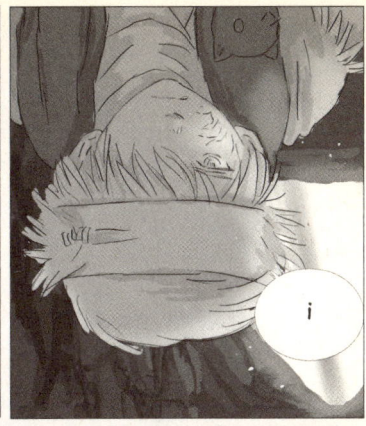

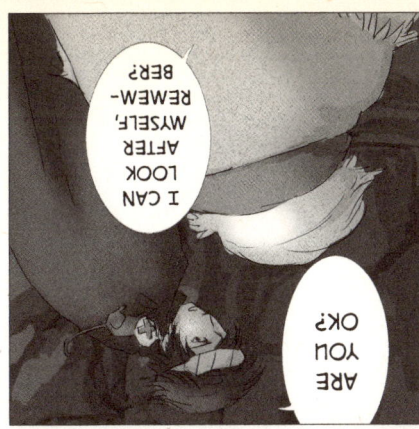

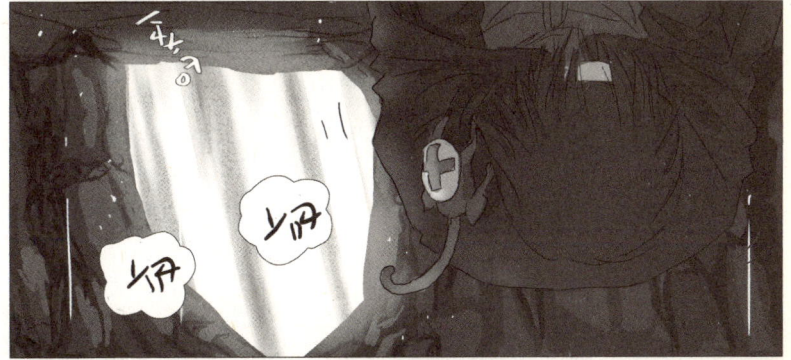

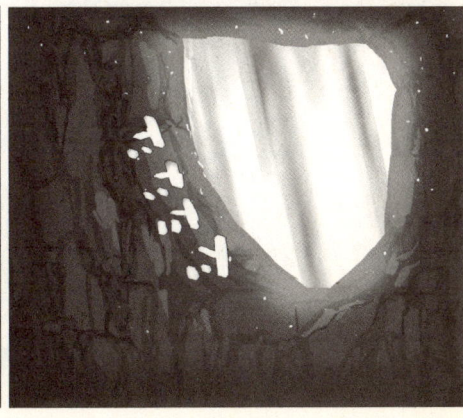

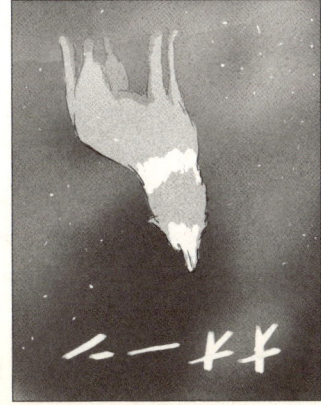

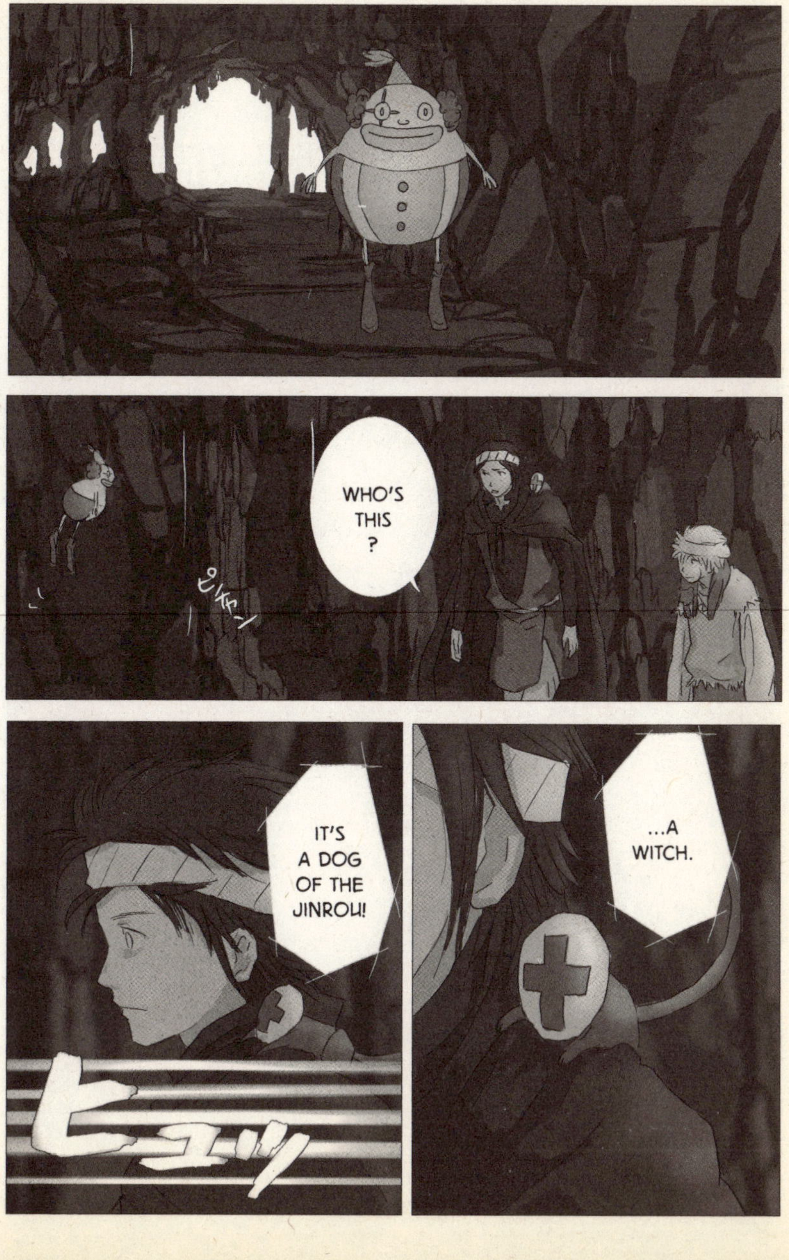
WHO'S THIS ?
...A WITCH.
IT'S A DOG OF THE JINROU!
ヒュッ

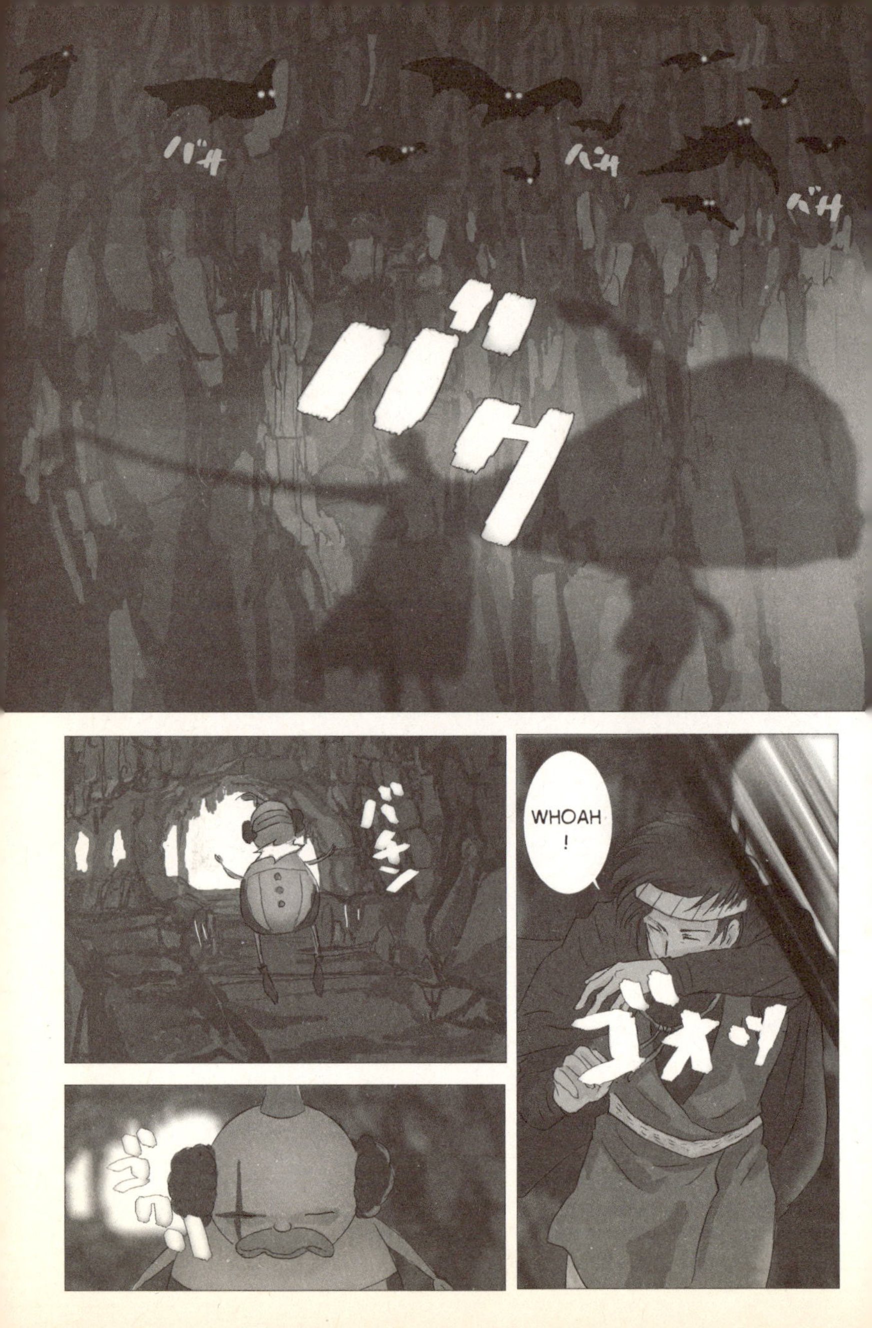
WHOAH !

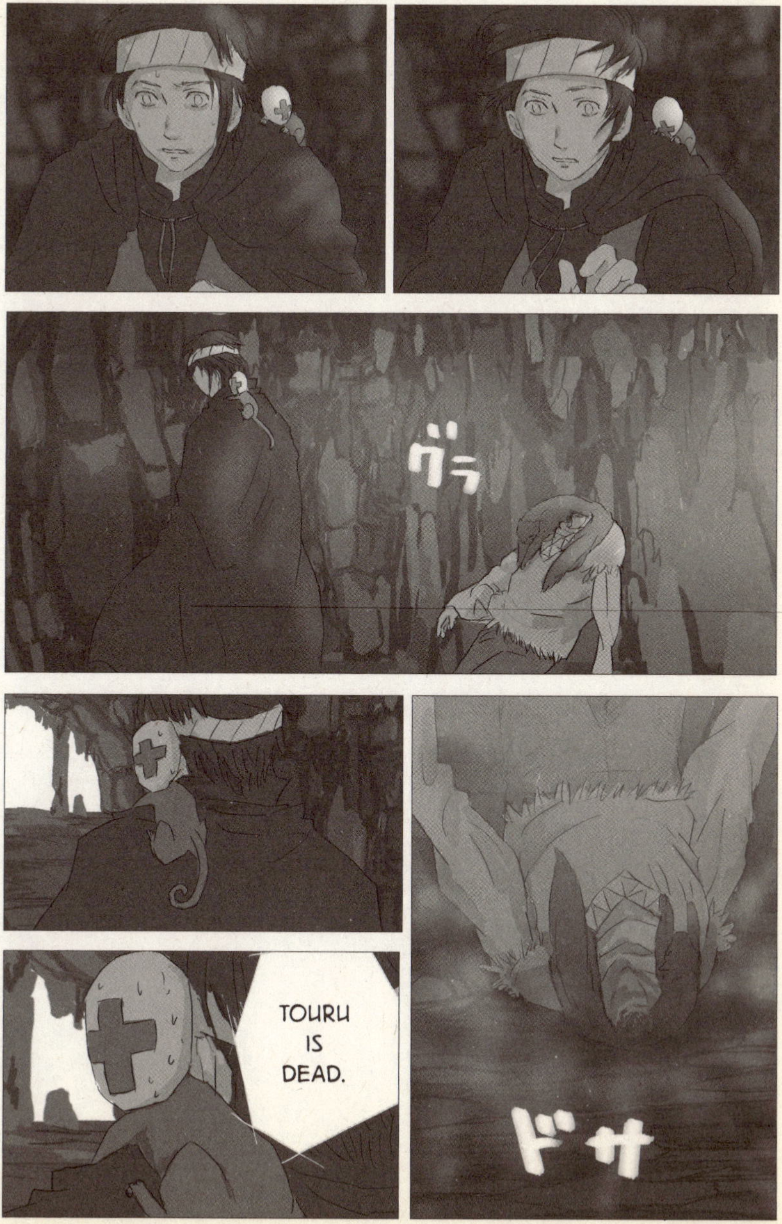
グラ
ドサ
TOURU IS DEAD.

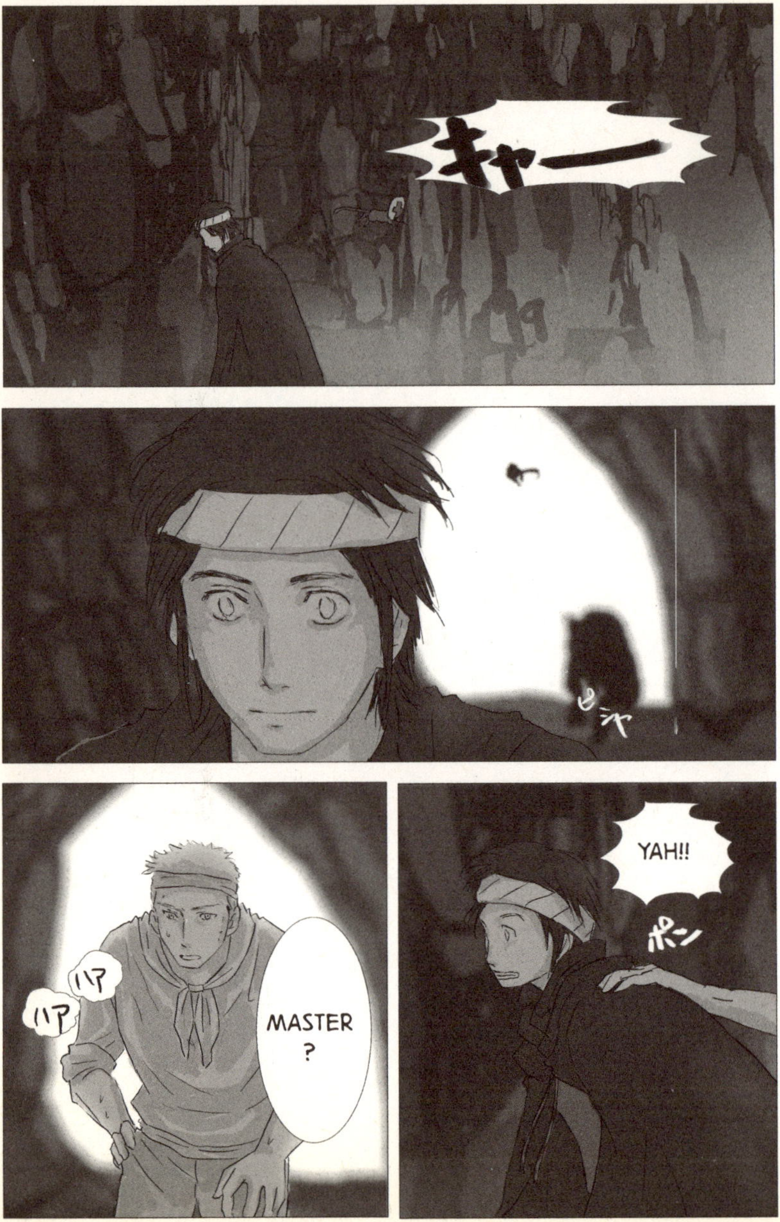
キャー
ピシャ
YAH!!
ポン
MASTER ?
ハア
ハア

HE'S GONE...?

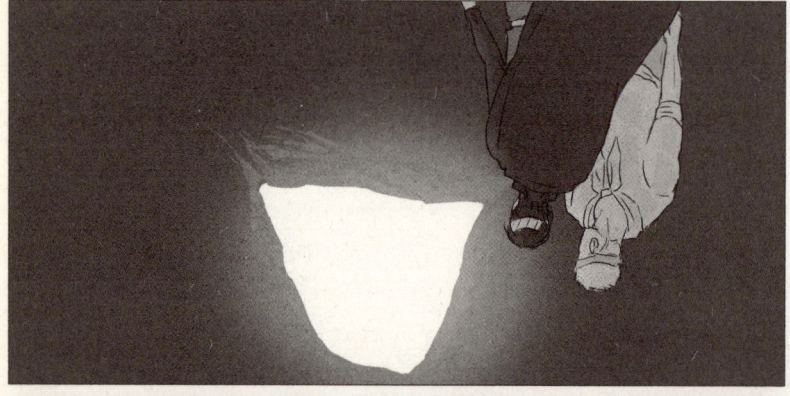

HUH?

WHERE IS TOHRU?

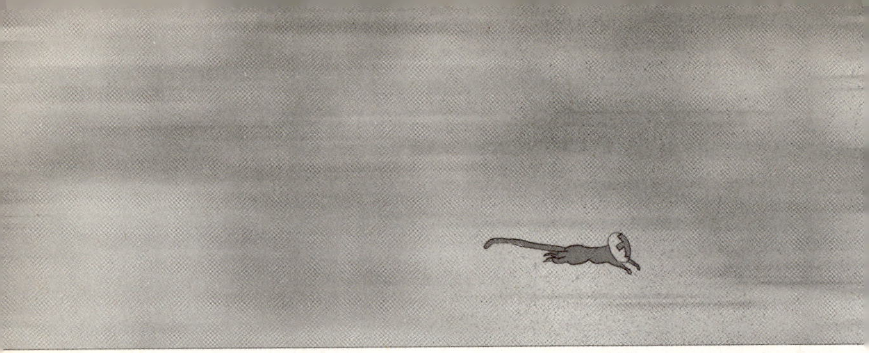
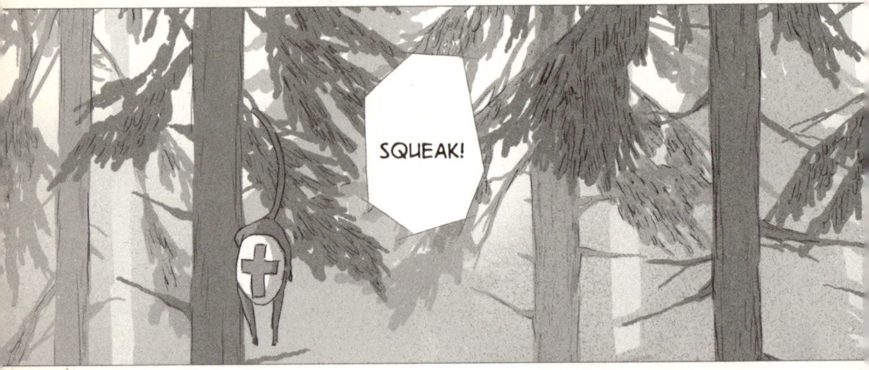
SQUEAK!
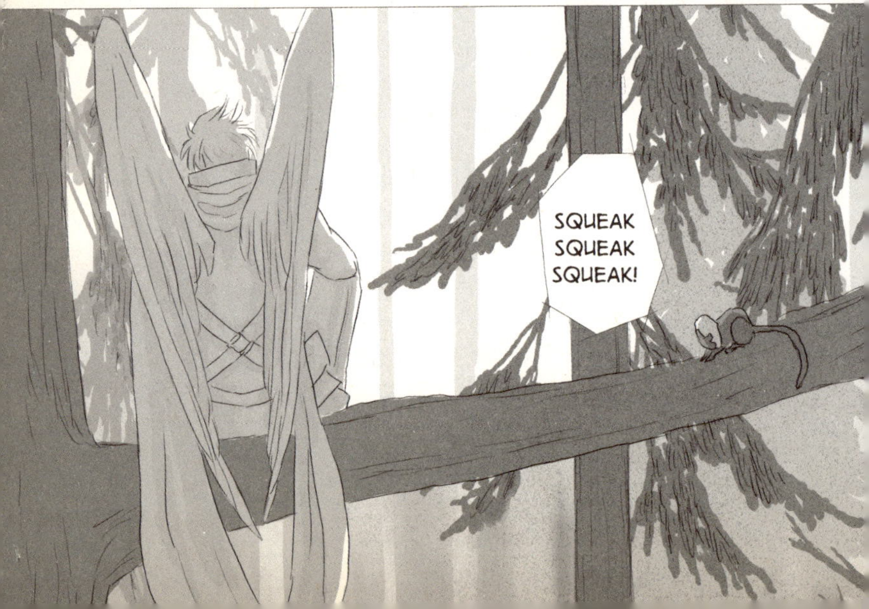
SQUEAK
SQUEAK
SQUEAK!

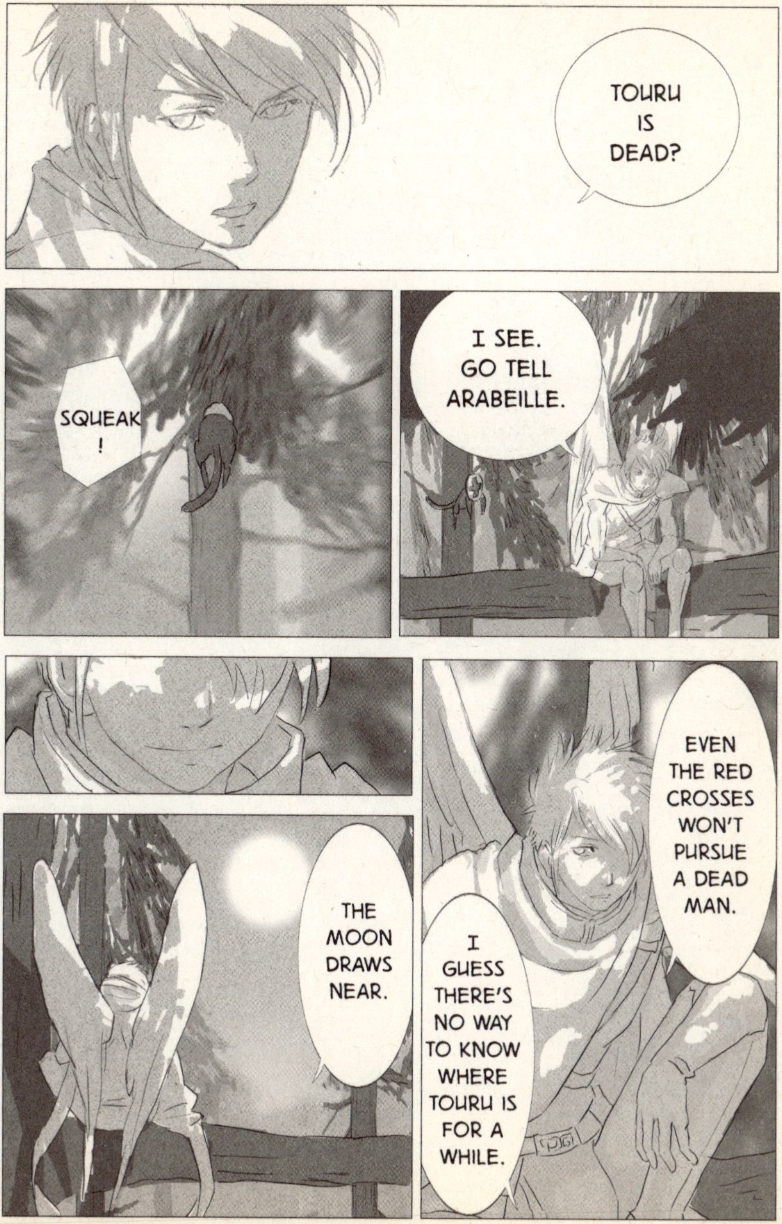
TOURU IS DEAD?
I SEE. GO TELL ARABEILLE.
SQUEAK!
EVEN THE RED CROSSES WON'T PURSUE A DEAD MAN.
I GUESS THERE'S NO WAY TO KNOW WHERE TOURU IS FOR A WHILE.
THE MOON DRAWS NEAR.

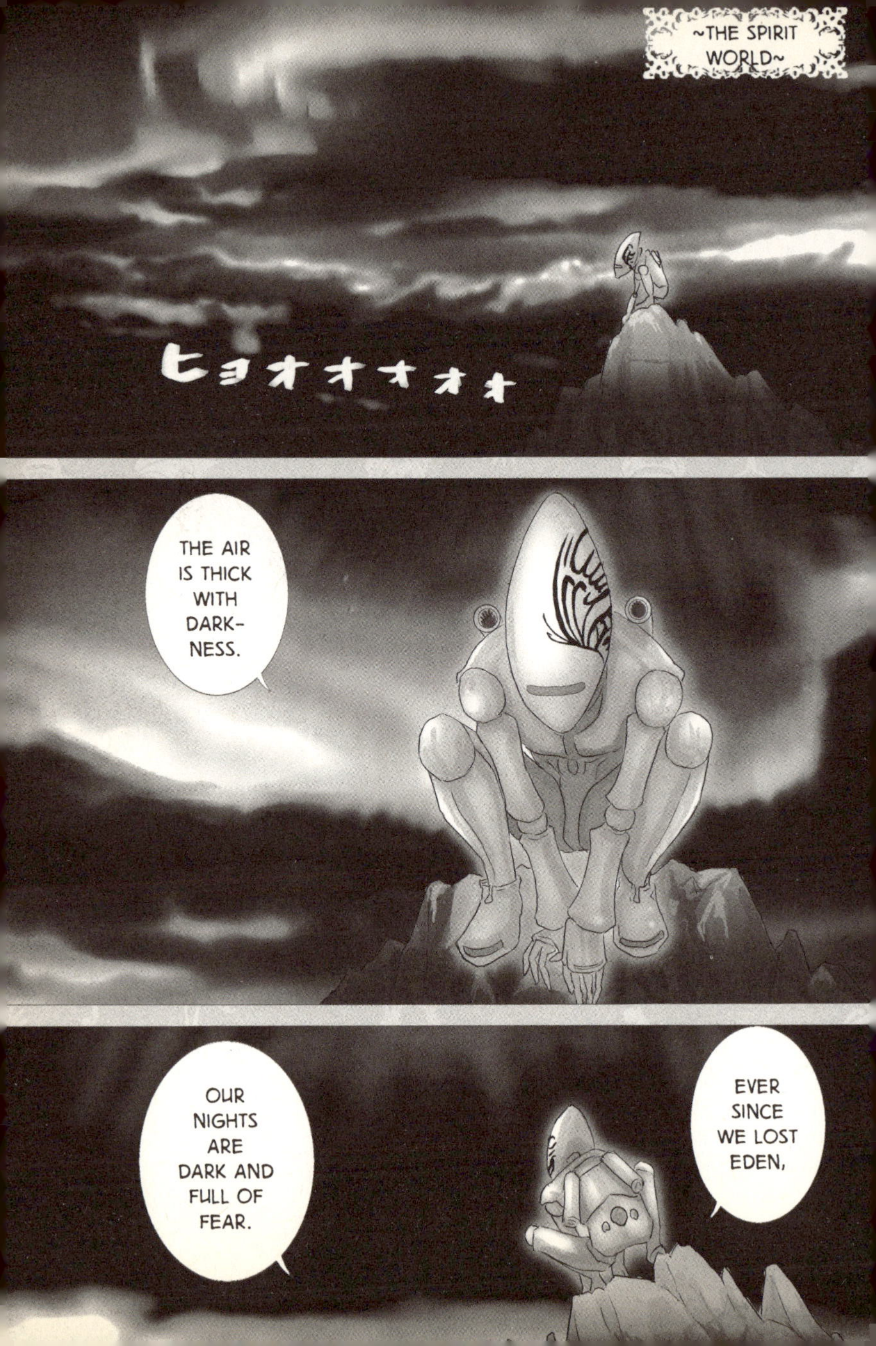
~THE SPIRIT WORLD~
ヒョオオオオオ
THE AIR IS THICK WITH DARK-NESS.
EVER SINCE WE LOST EDEN,
OUR NIGHTS ARE DARK AND FULL OF FEAR.

MY KING, WHY DID YOU LEAVE?
WE ...
...CAN STILL FIGHT.
O3!
WIFFIE IS OUT OF CONTROL!
PLEASE, WE NEED YOUR HELP!

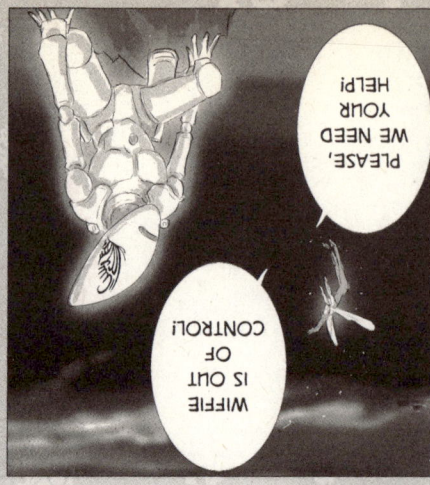

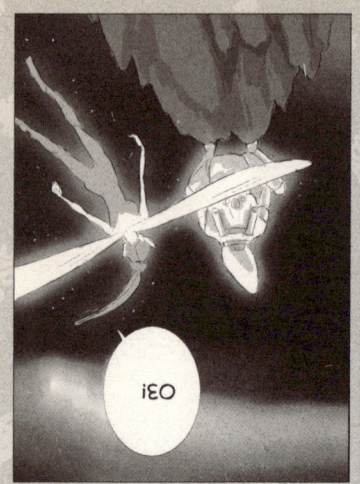

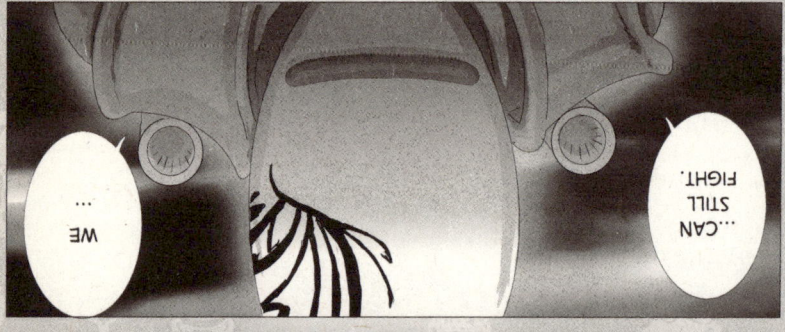

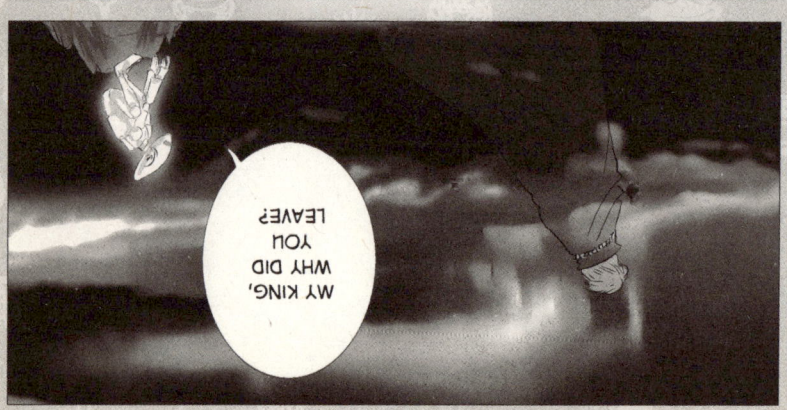

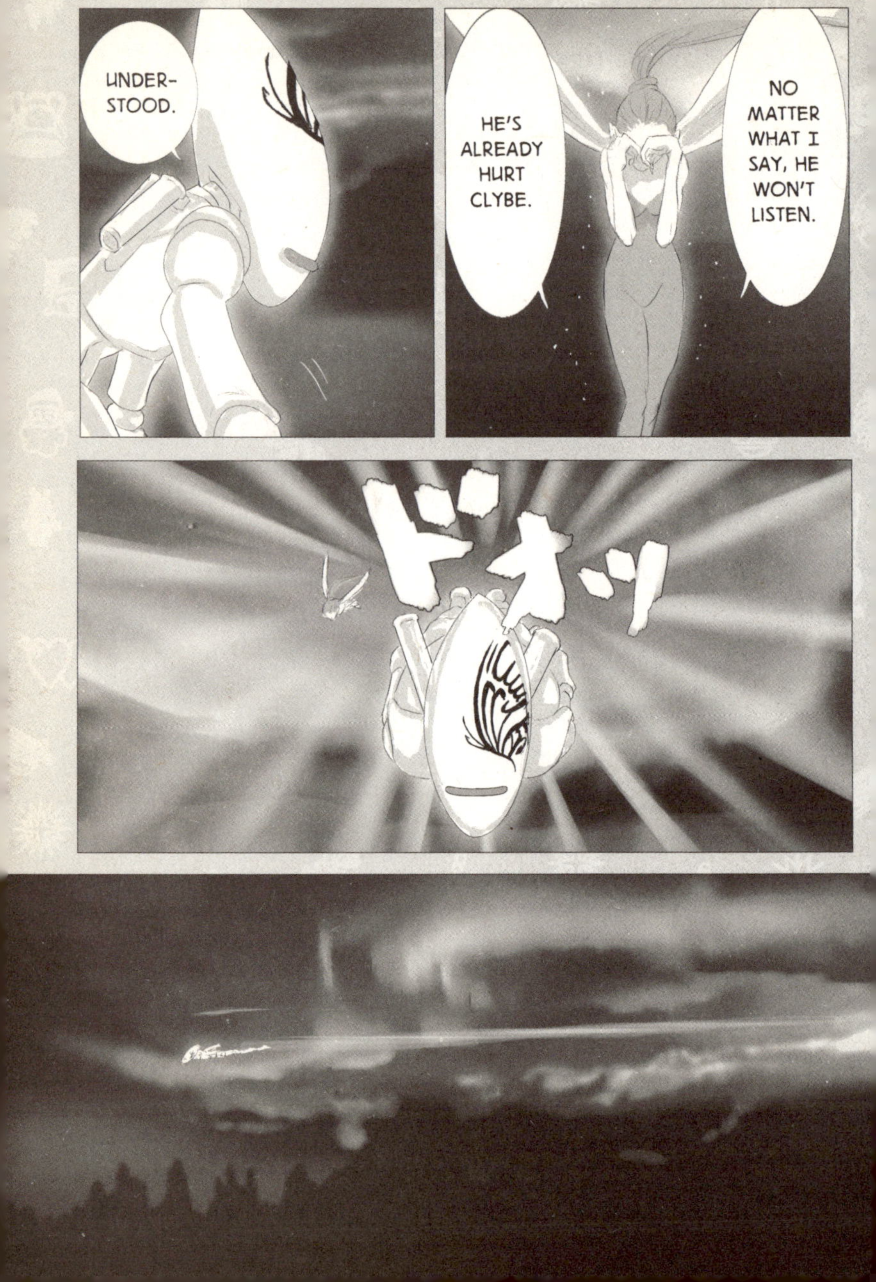
NO MATTER WHAT I SAY, HE WON'T LISTEN.
HE'S ALREADY HURT CLYBE.
UNDER-STOOD.

OVER THERE!
LOOK AT HIS BODY.
HE'S CHANGED INTO A DEMON!

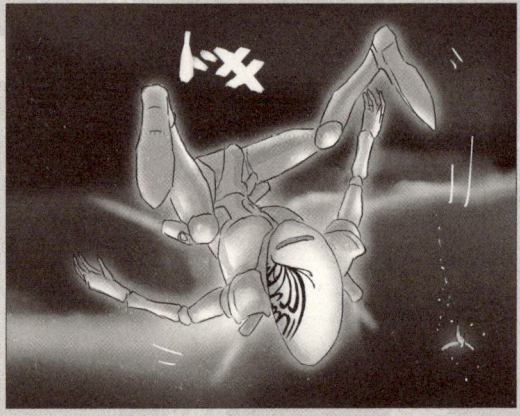

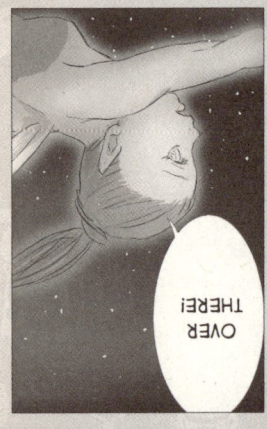

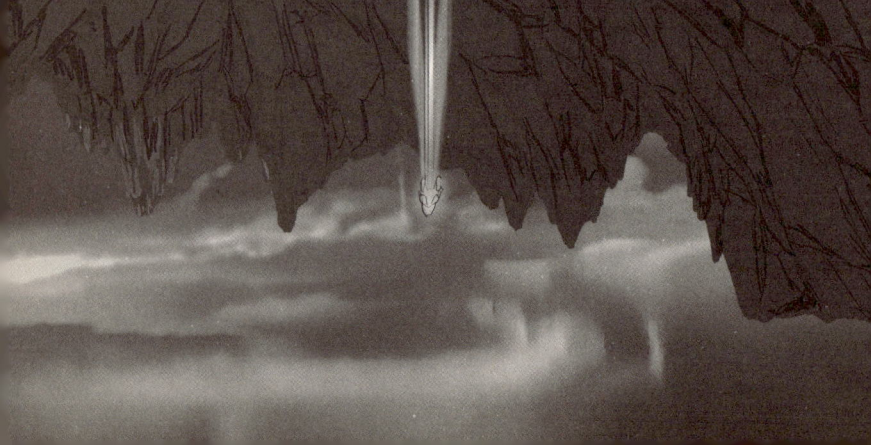

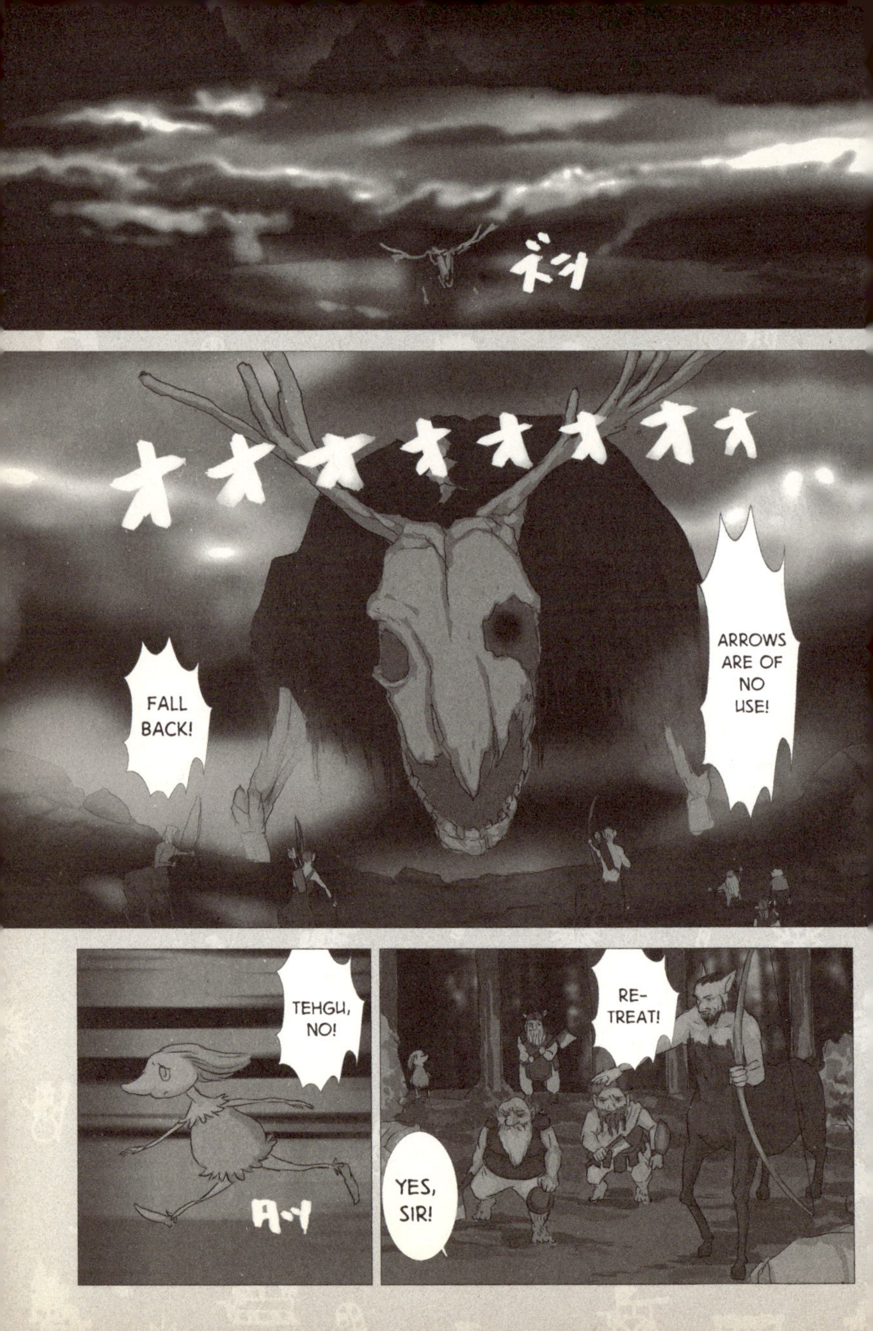
オオオオオオオオ
ARROWS ARE OF NO USE!
FALL BACK!
RE-TREAT!
YES, SIR!
TEHGU, NO!

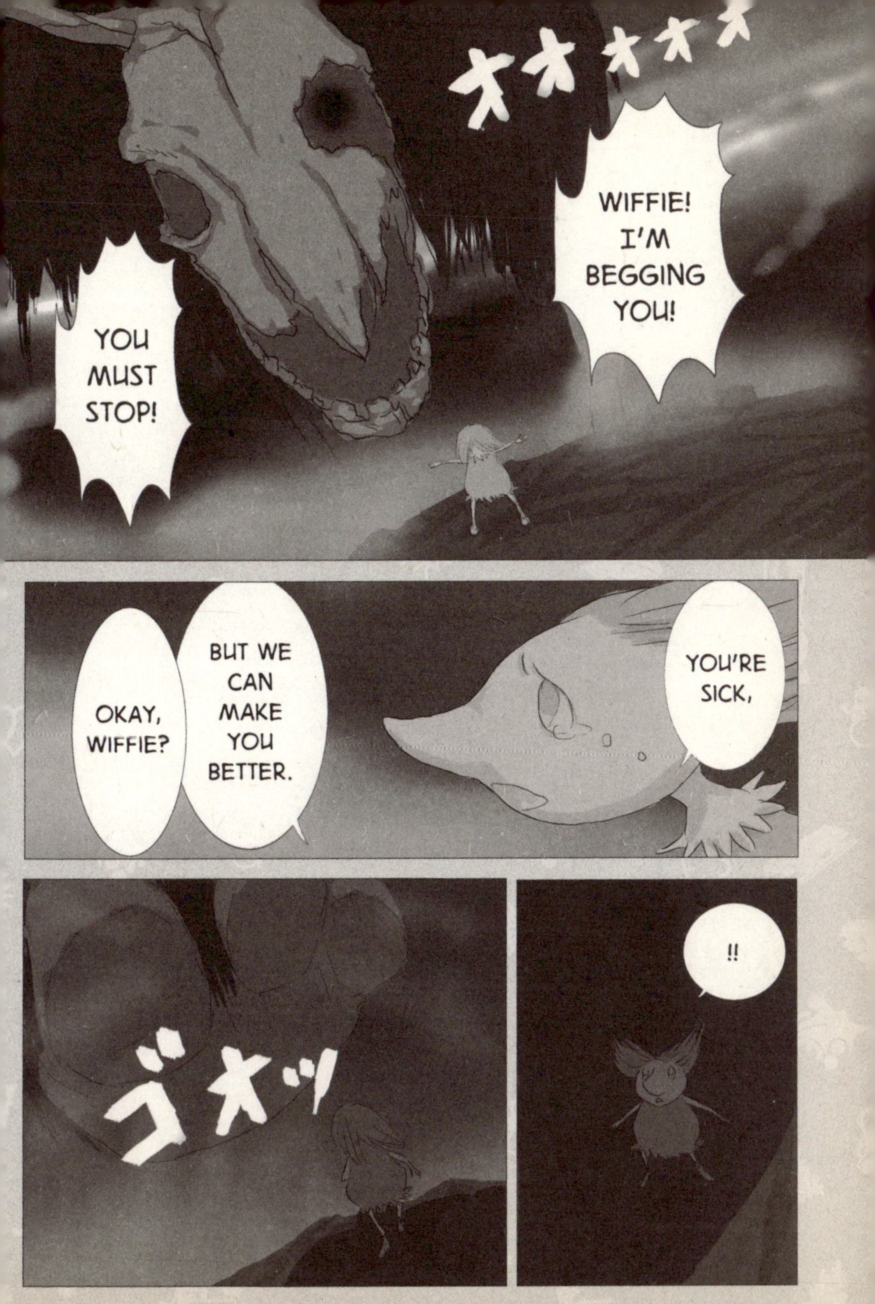
オオオオオ
WIFFIE! I'M BEGGING YOU!
YOU MUST STOP!
YOU'RE SICK,
BUT WE CAN MAKE YOU BETTER.
OKAY, WIFFIE?
!!
ゴオッ

!O3!

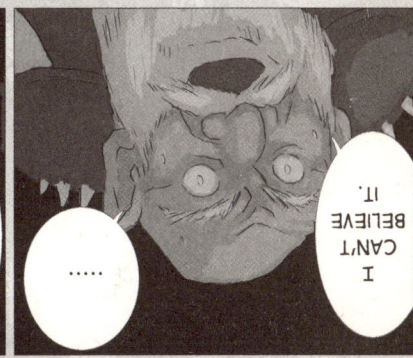

WH...!

HE STEP-PED ON TENGU!

......

I CAN'T BELIEVE IT.

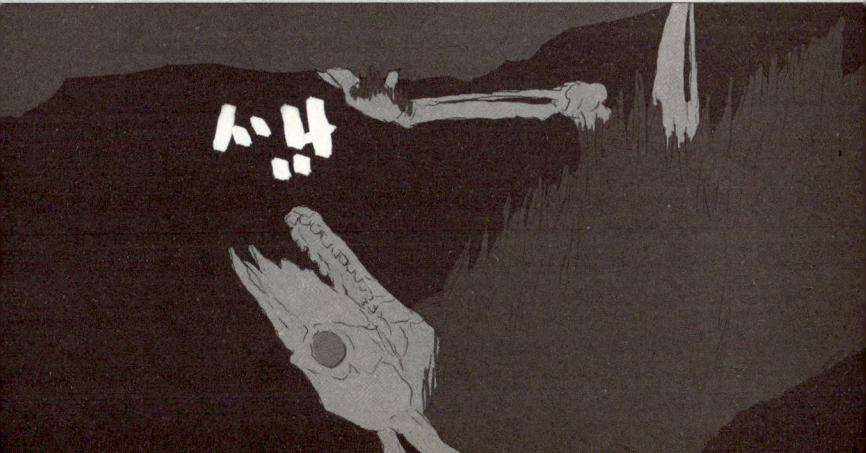

I'M GOING TO RETURN WIFFIE TO THE KING.
IT'S WHAT THE SPIRIT WORLD THINKS IS BEST.
WILL WIFFIE BE NORMAL AFTER-WARDS? WILL HE COME HOME?
I DO NOT KNOW.
BUT ...
I DO KNOW THAT THE KING AIDS US ALWAYS BY TAKING ...
...THE PAIN AND SADNESS OF THIS WORLD UPON HIMSELF.
LET'S BEGIN.

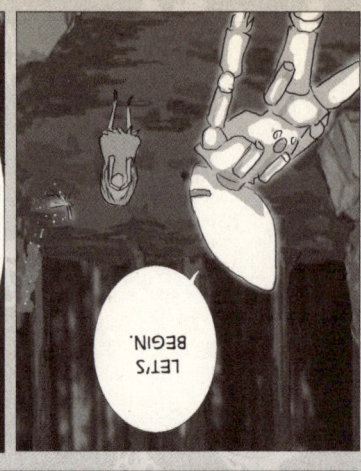

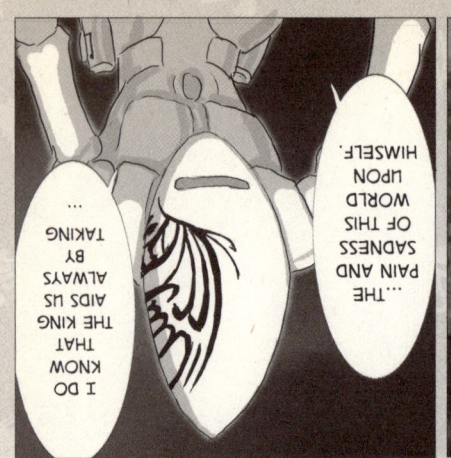

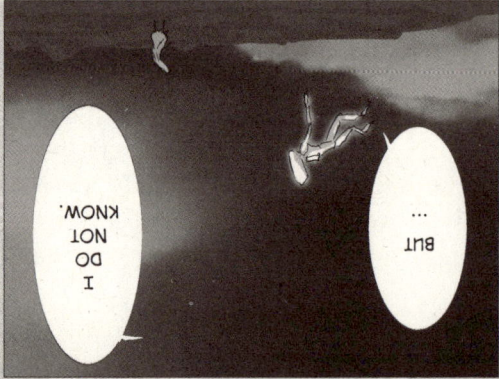

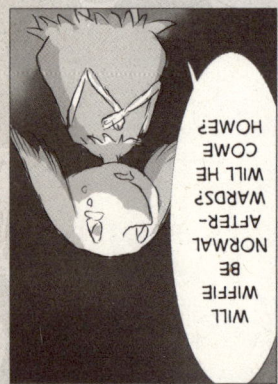

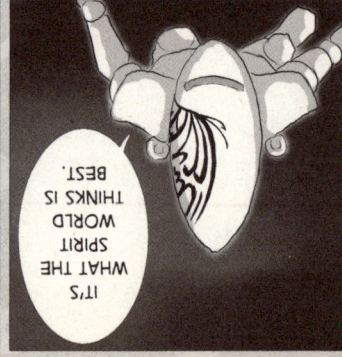

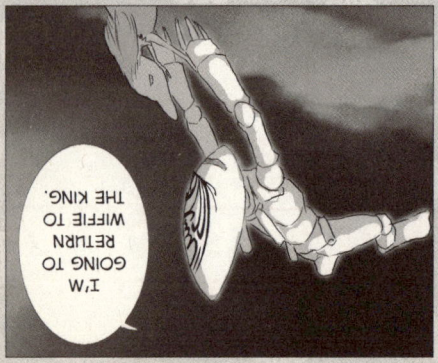

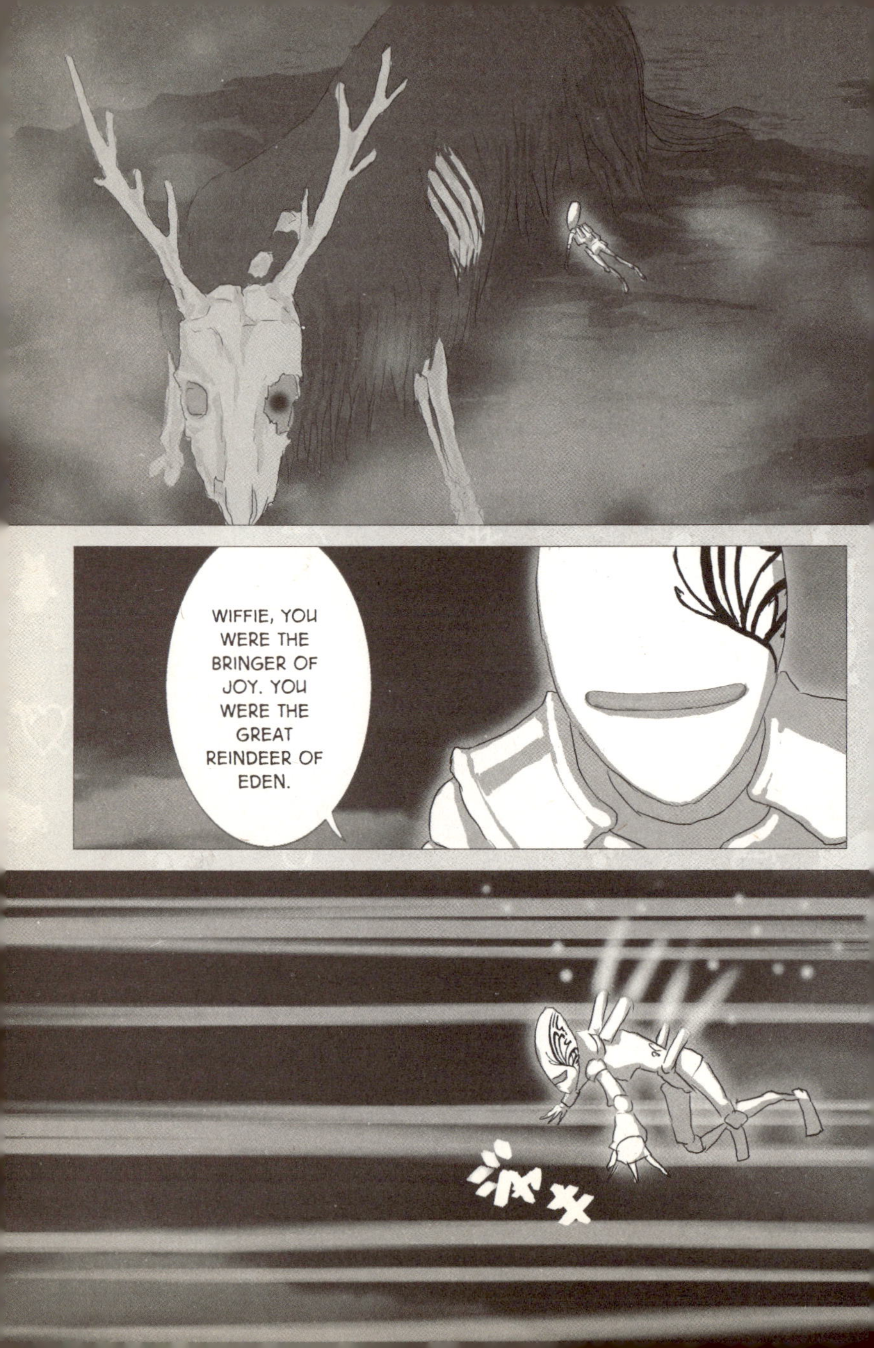
WIFFIE, YOU WERE THE BRINGER OF JOY. YOU WERE THE GREAT REINDEER OF EDEN.

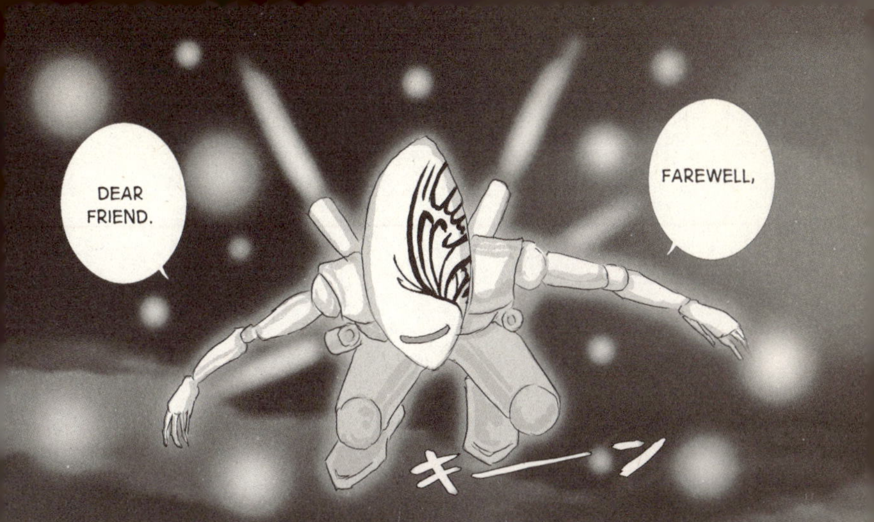
FAREWELL,
DEAR FRIEND.
キーーン

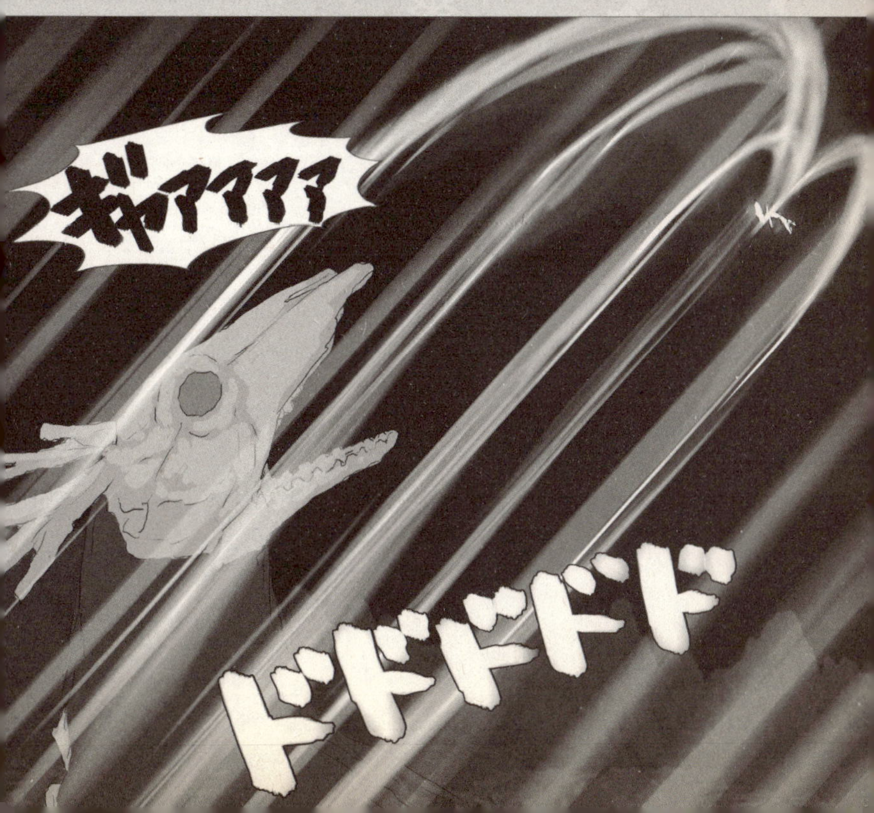
ギャアアアア
ドドドドド

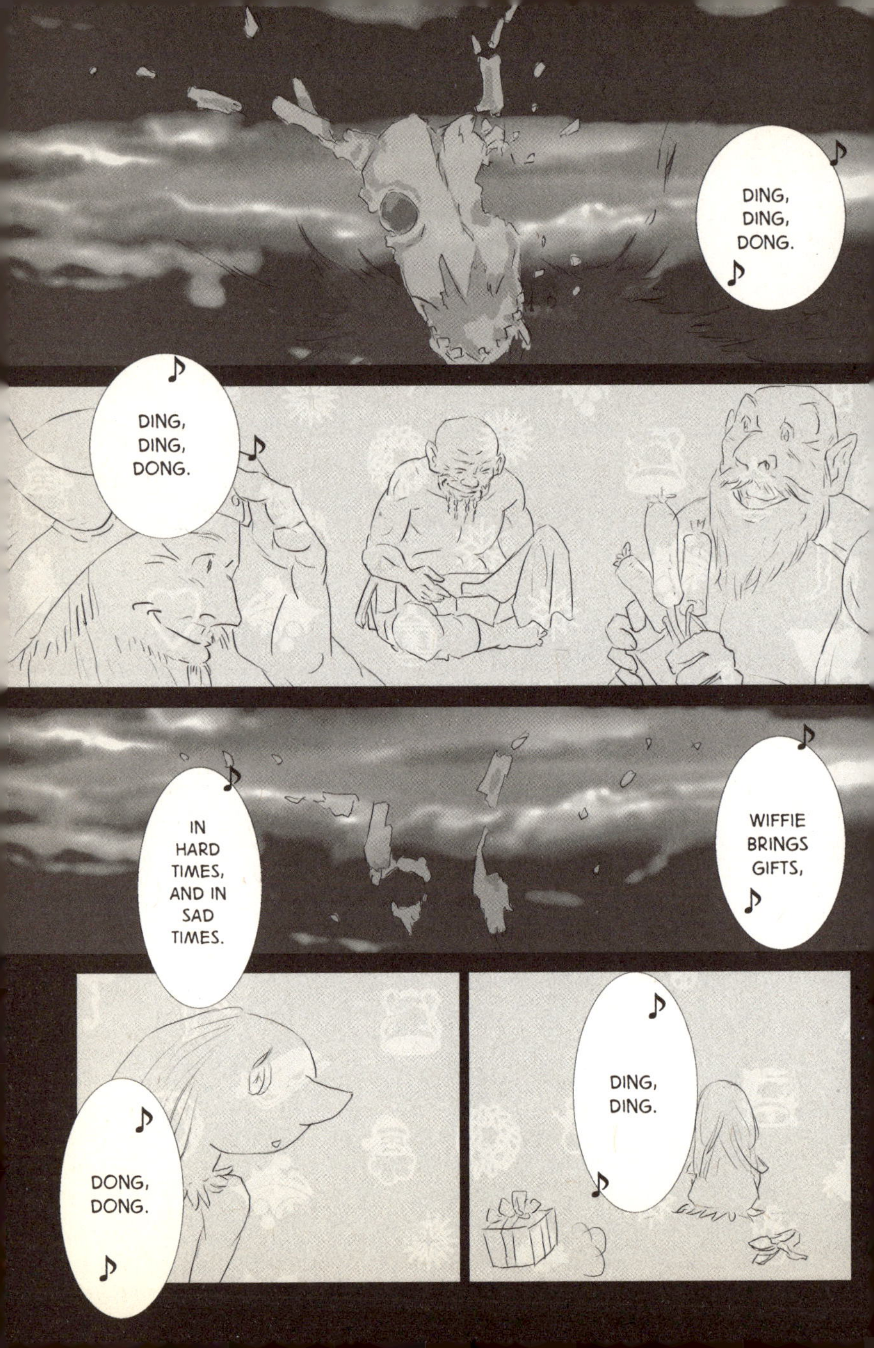
♪ DING, DING, DONG. ♪
♪ DING, DING, DONG. ♪
♪ WIFFIE BRINGS GIFTS, ♪
♪ IN HARD TIMES, AND IN SAD TIMES.
♪ DING, DING. ♪
♪ DONG, DONG. ♪

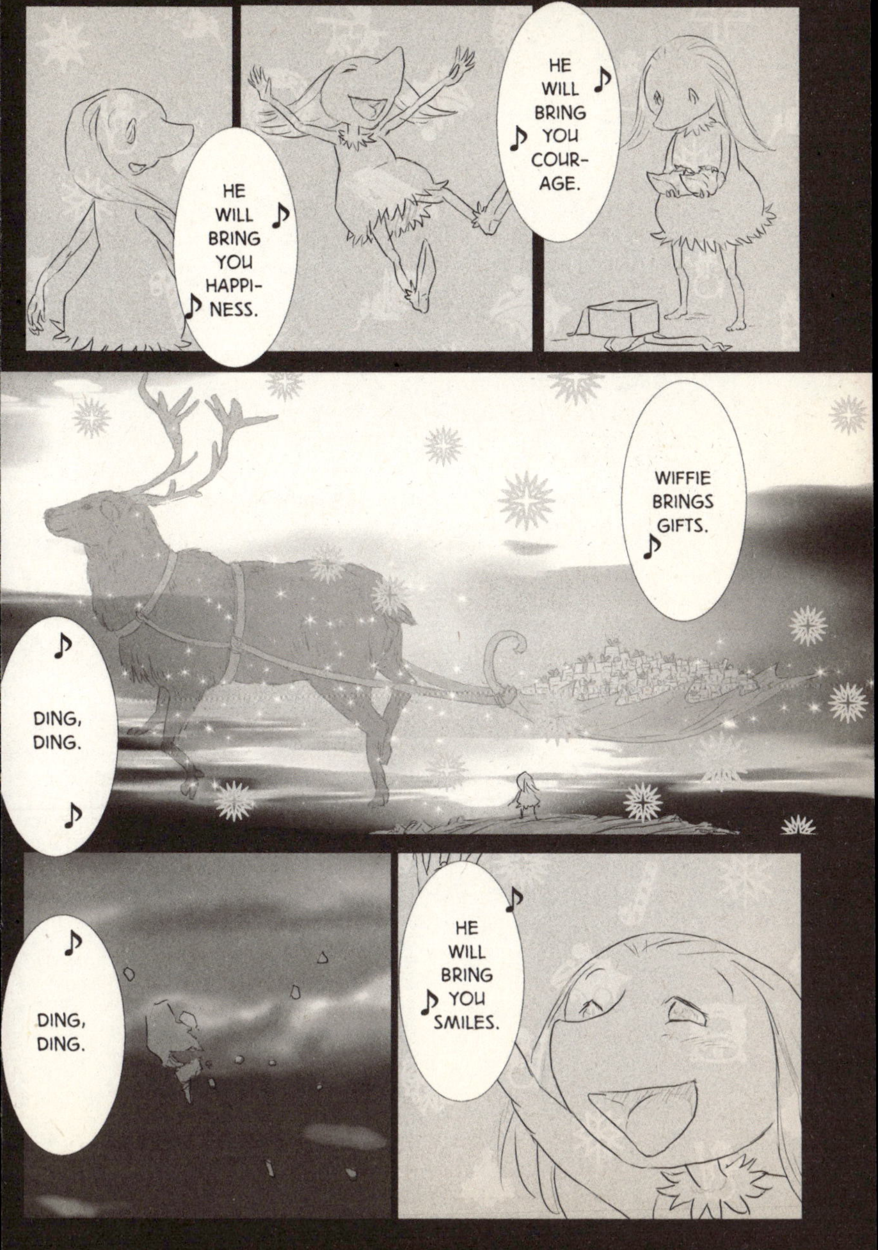
♪ HE WILL BRING ♪ YOU COURAGE.
HE WILL ♪ BRING YOU HAPPI- ♪ NESS.
WIFFIE BRINGS GIFTS. ♪
♪ DING, DING. ♪
♪ HE WILL BRING ♪ YOU SMILES.
♪ DING, DING.

DING, DING.
THERE'LL BE NO MORE GIFTS FROM WIFFIE NOW, HUH?
WE'RE SORRY, WIFFIE. WE'RE SORRY.

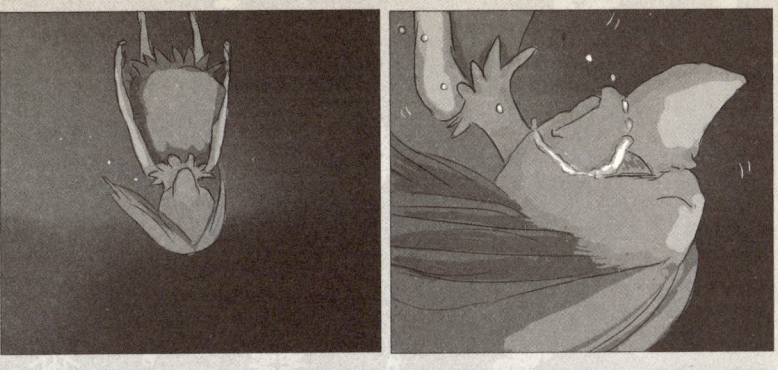

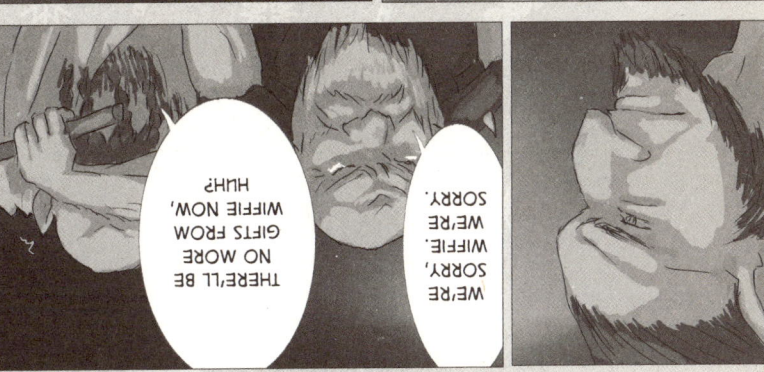

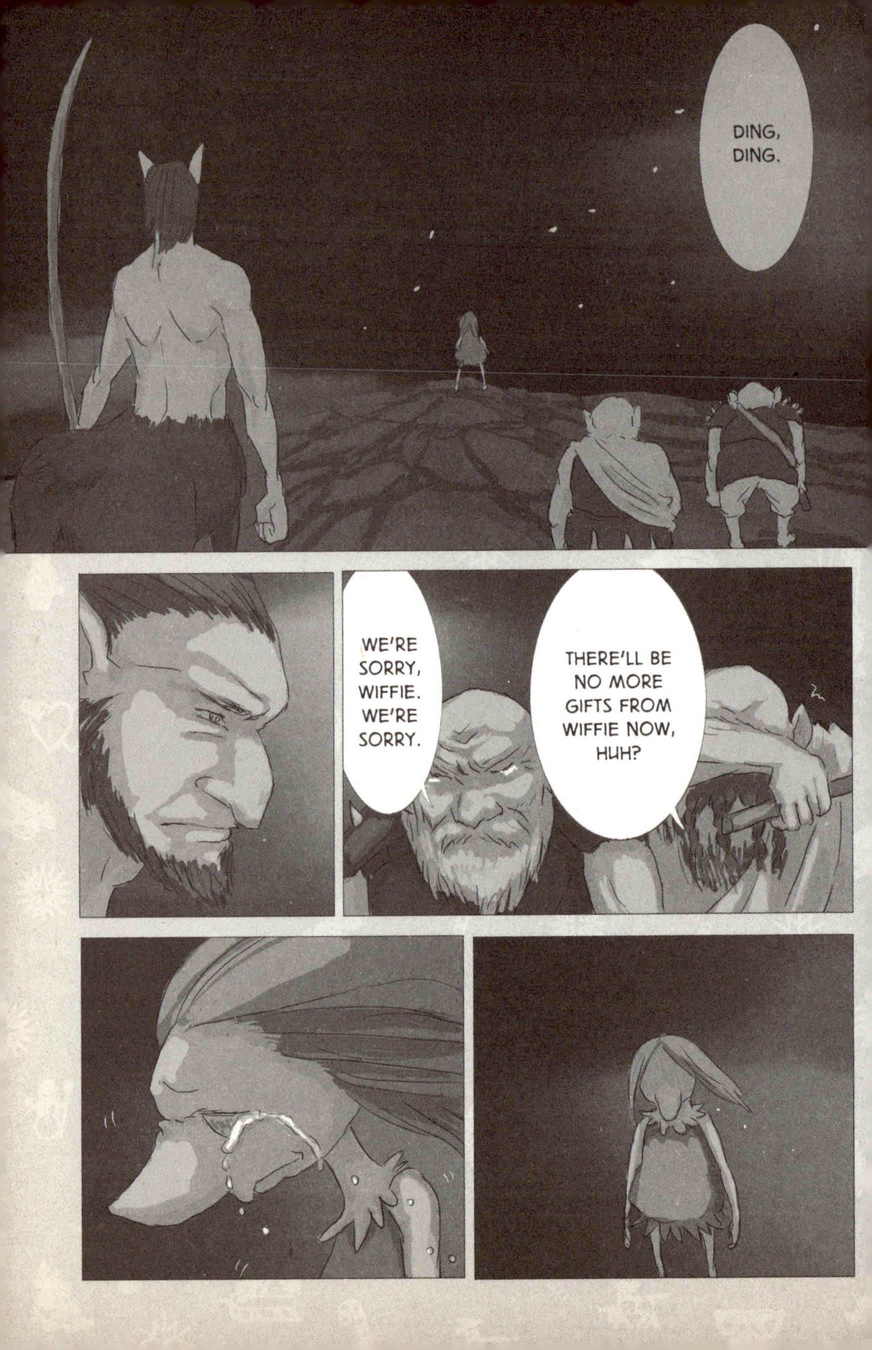

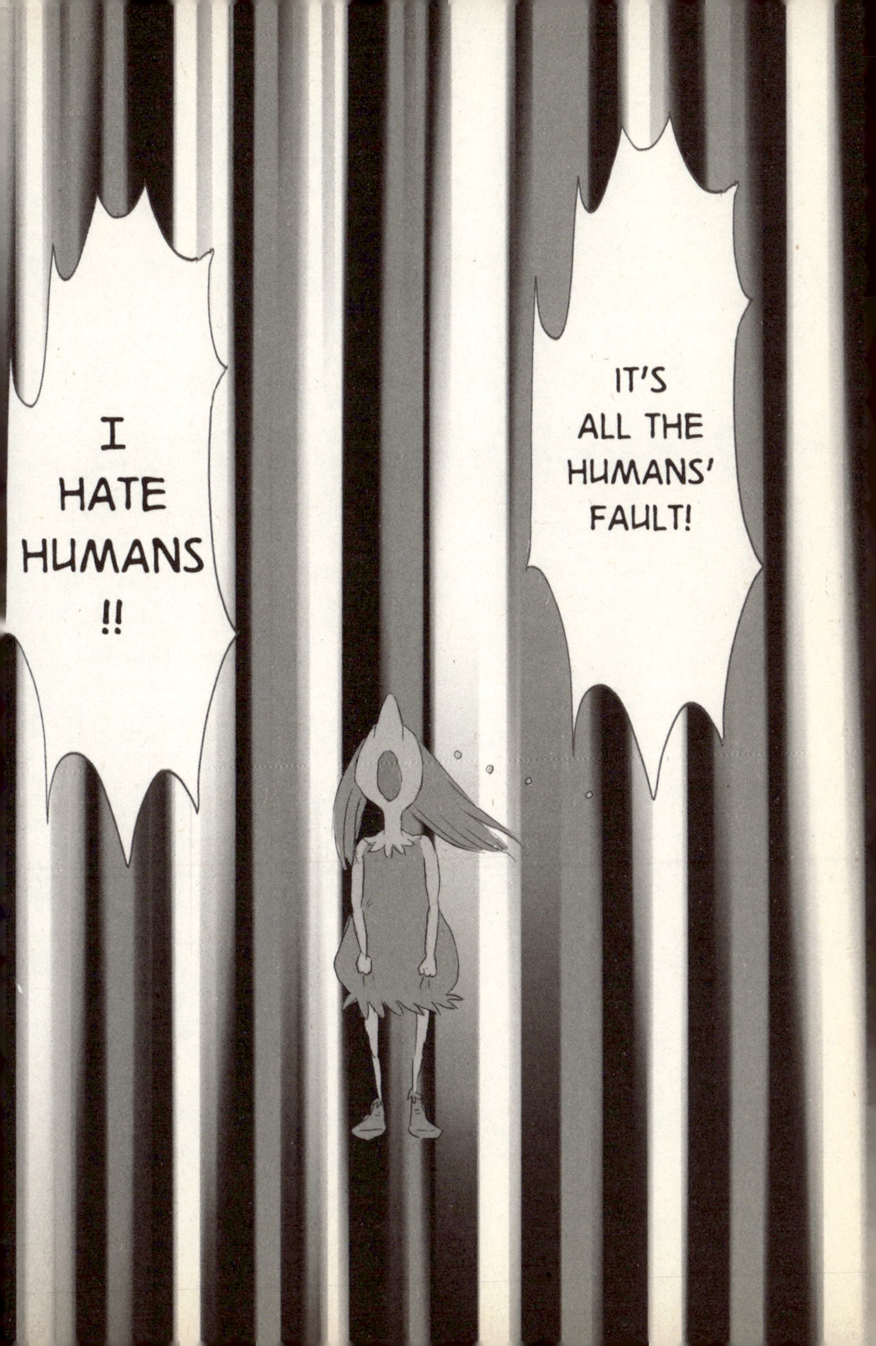
IT'S ALL THE HUMANS' FAULT!
I HATE HUMANS!!

ジャキ
O3!
LONG AGO, THE HUMANS COMMITTED SIN AND POLLUTED THE WORLD WITH TRAGEDY. BECAUSE OF THEM, EVEN PEACEFUL SOULS ARE BESET BY DEATH, SICKNESS, AND MALICE, AND EVENTUALLY ARE LOST.
WHEN OUR KING LEFT EDEN, HE CREATED AN UNDER-WORLD.
IT IS A PLACE FOR SOULS IN DISTRESS TO GO.

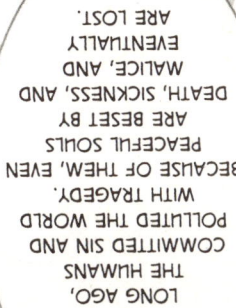

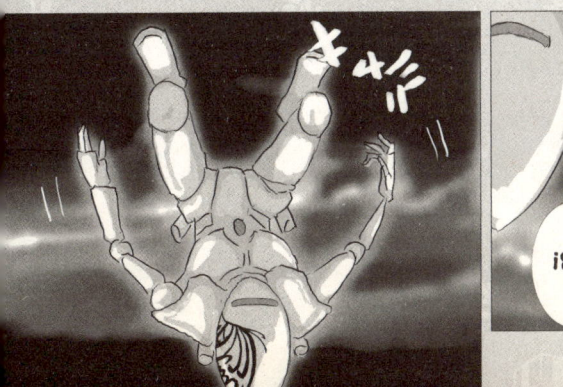

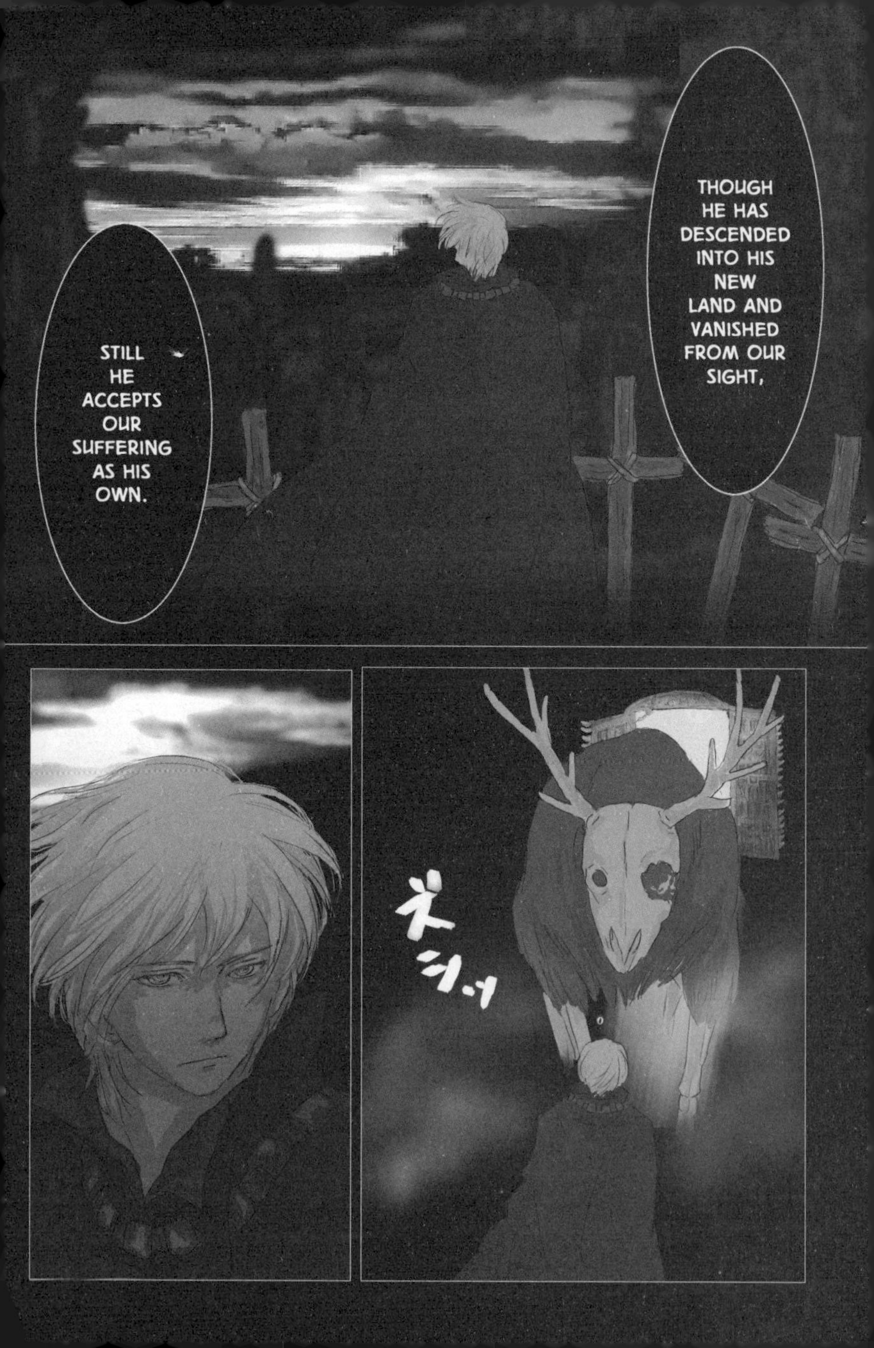
THOUGH HE HAS DESCENDED INTO HIS NEW LAND AND VANISHED FROM OUR SIGHT,
STILL HE ACCEPTS OUR SUFFERING AS HIS OWN.

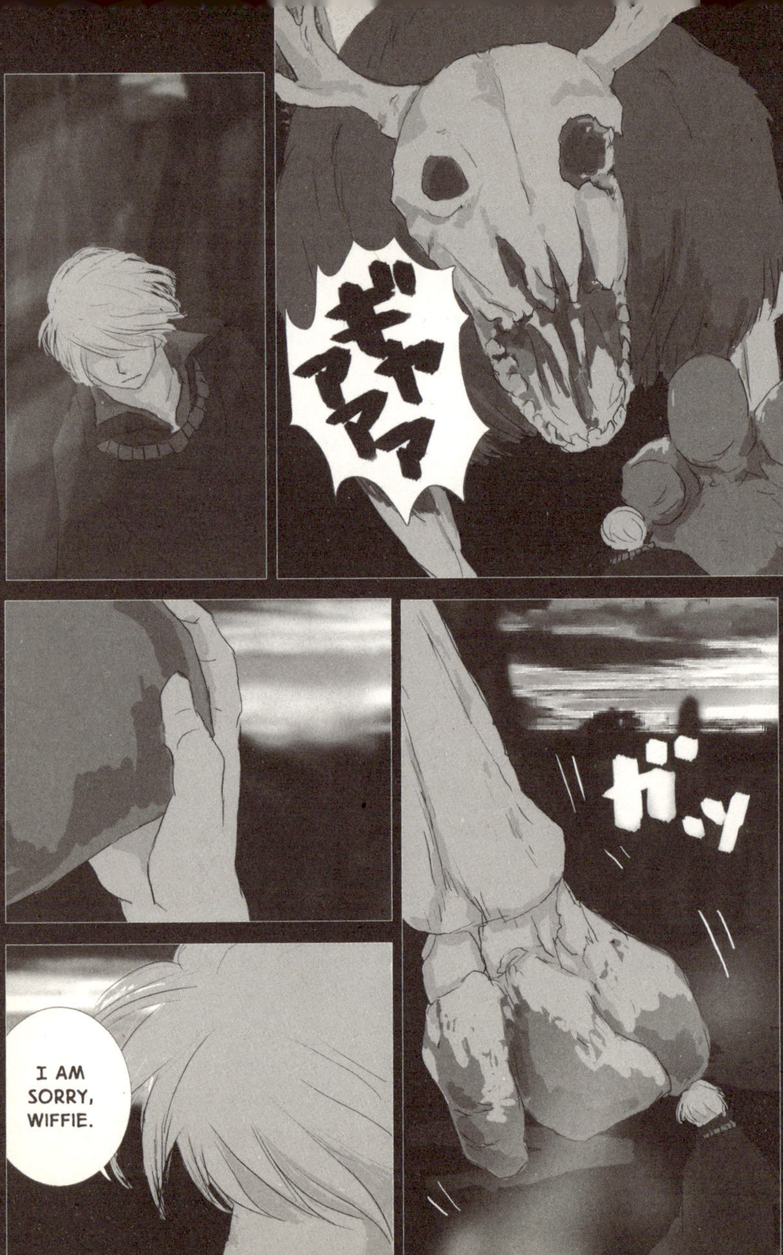
ギャアア
ガッ
I AM SORRY, WIFFIE.

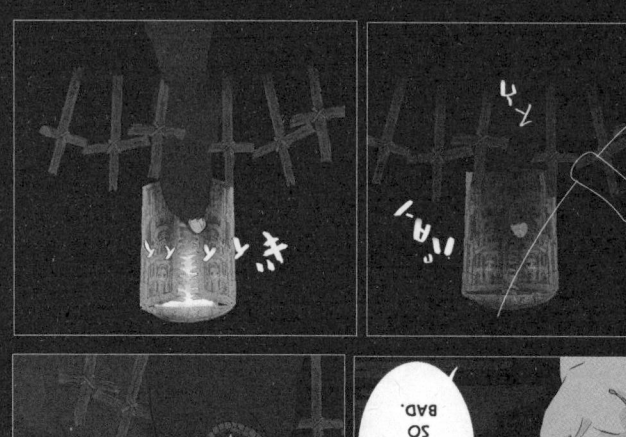

AND YET,
TO BECOME A MONSTER ...
...MIGHT NOT BE SO BAD.
HOW MISERABLE.

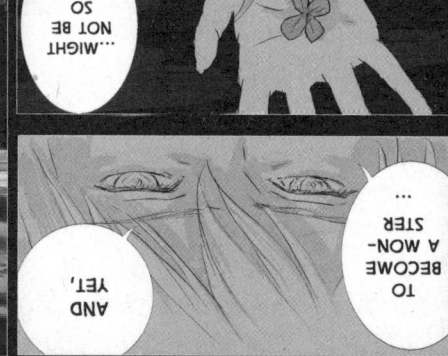

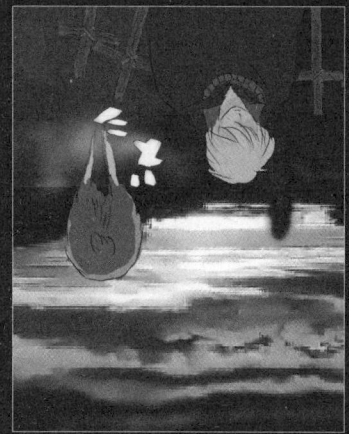

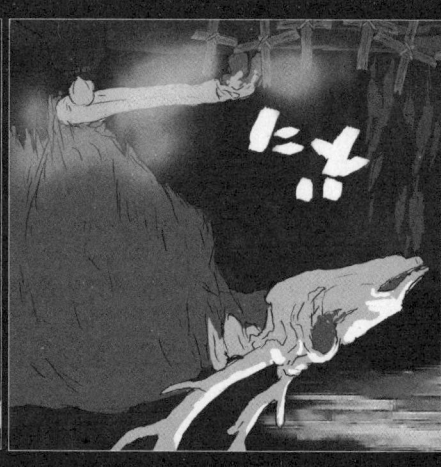

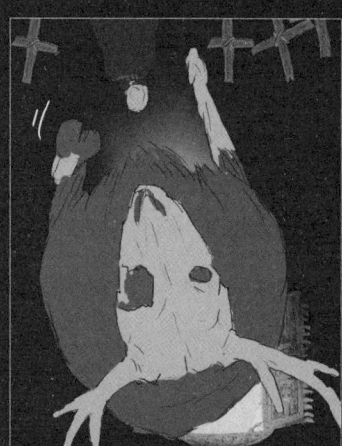

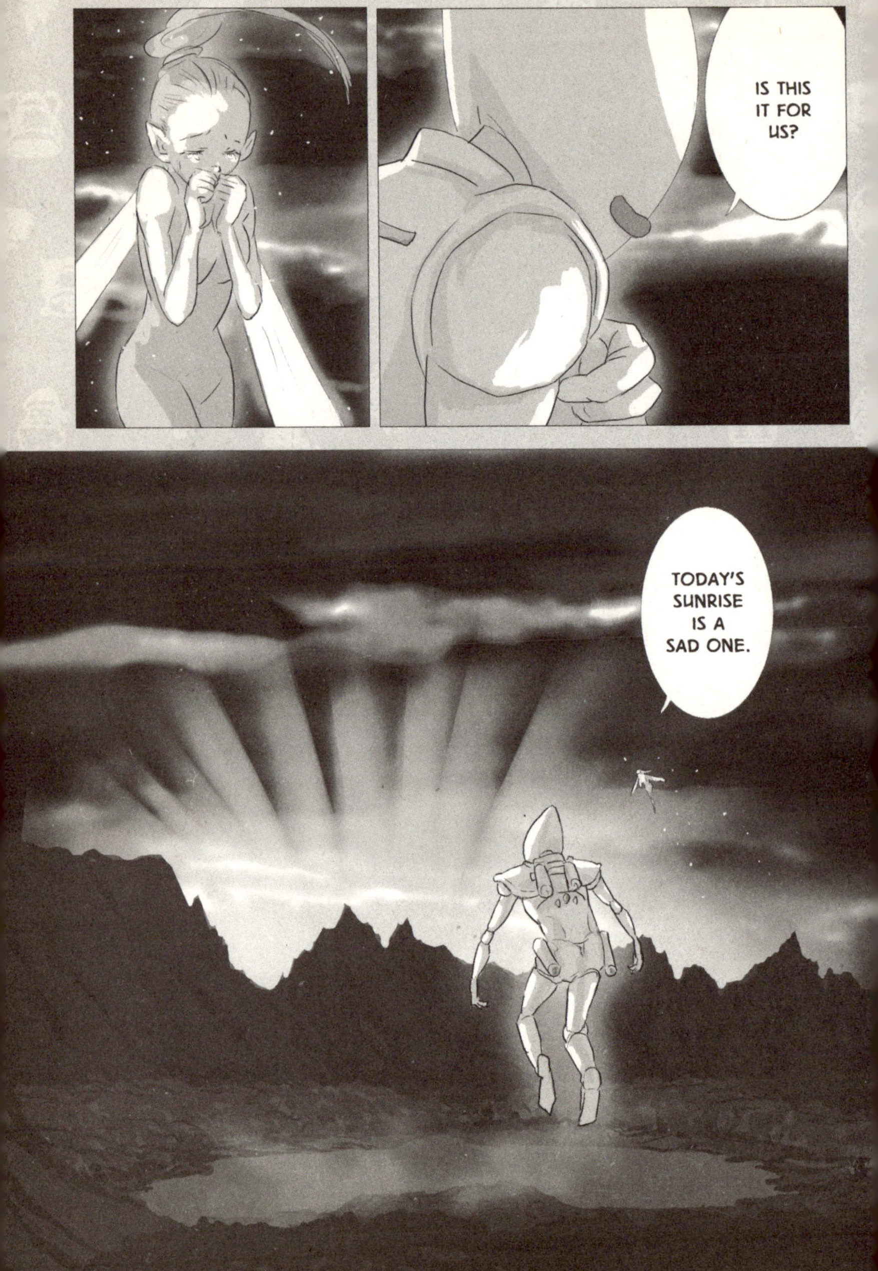
IS THIS IT FOR US?
TODAY'S SUNRISE IS A SAD ONE.

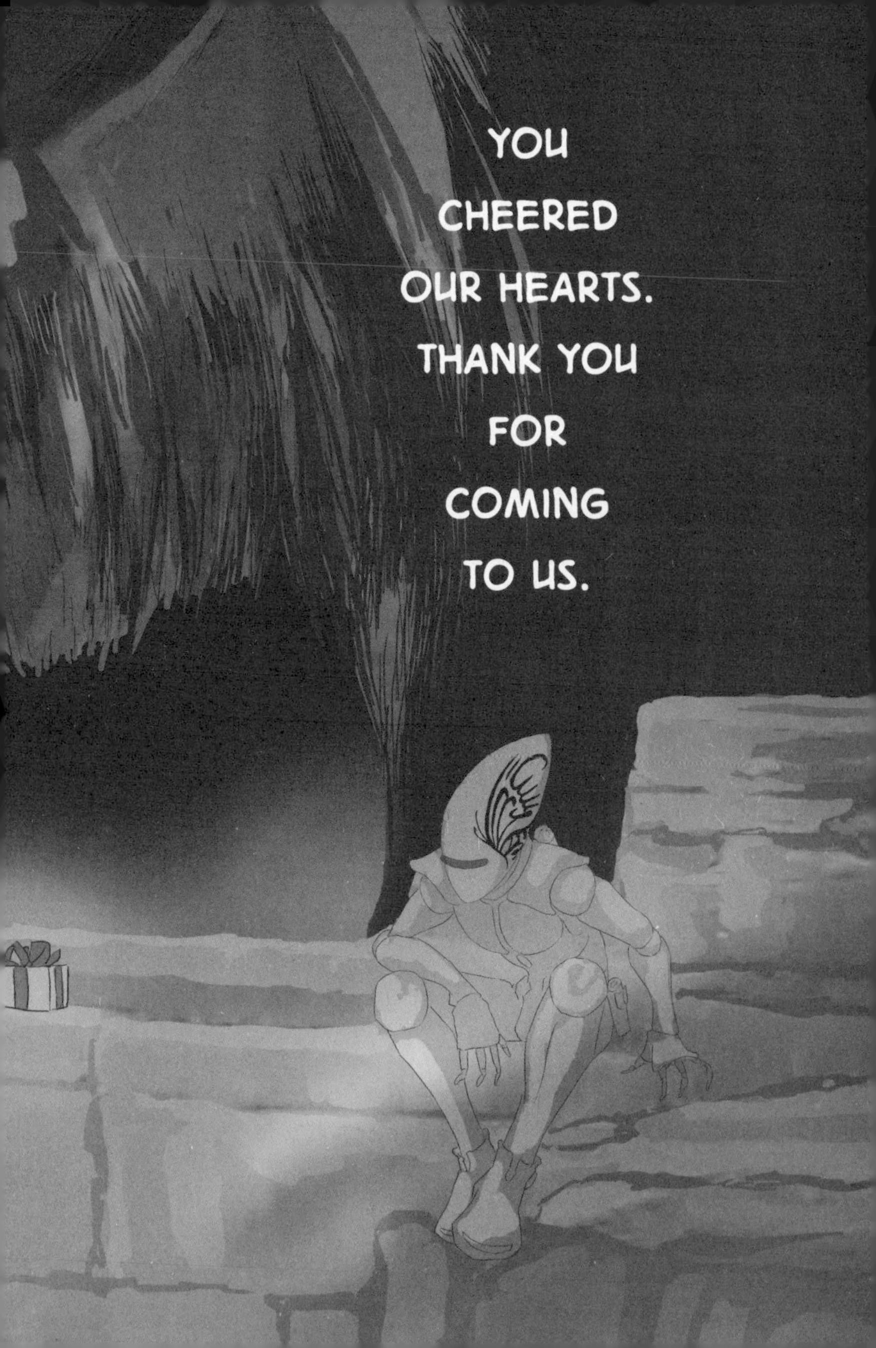
YOU CHEERED OUR HEARTS. THANK YOU FOR COMING TO US.

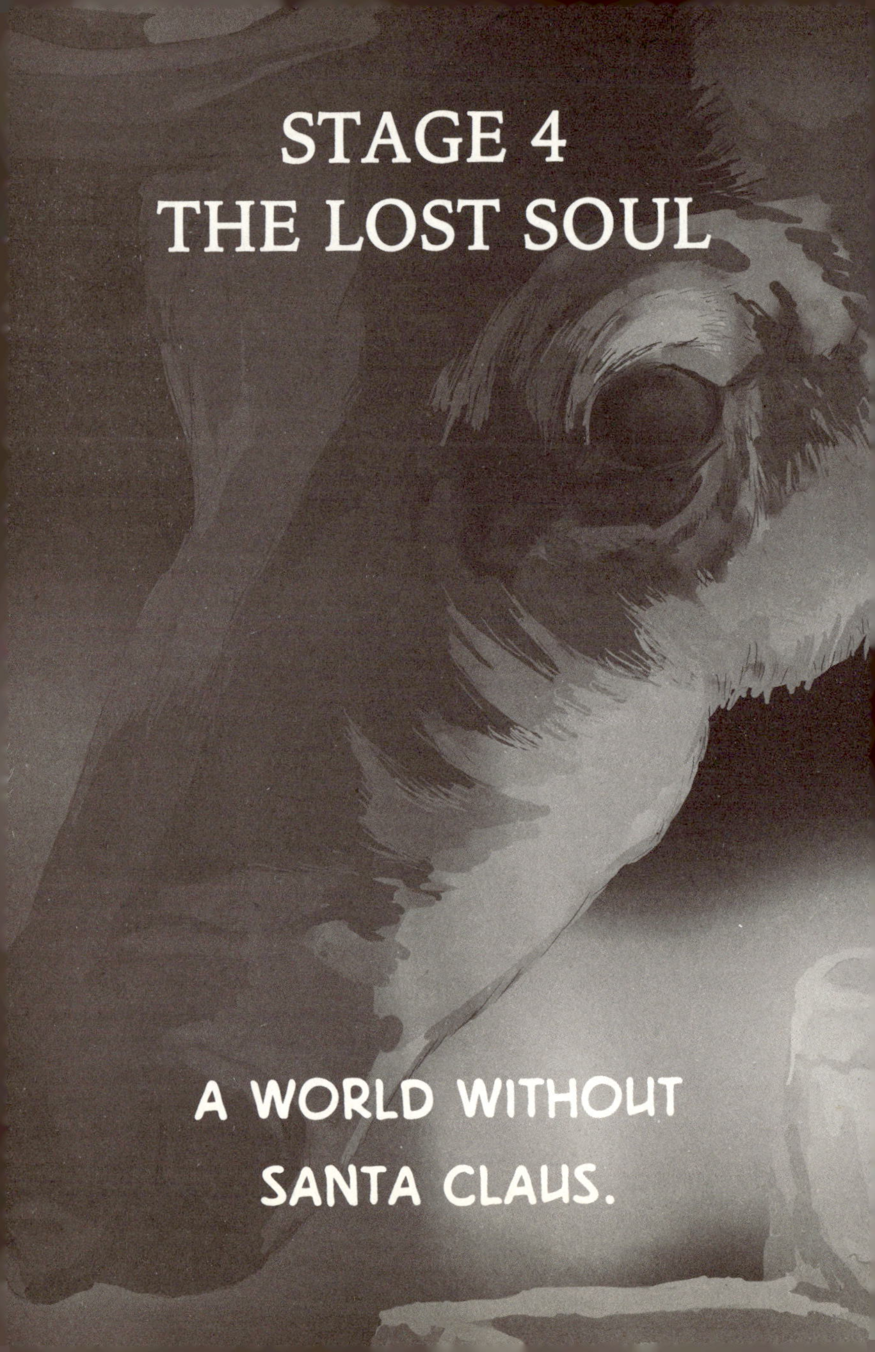
STAGE 4
THE LOST SOUL
A WORLD WITHOUT
SANTA CLAUS.

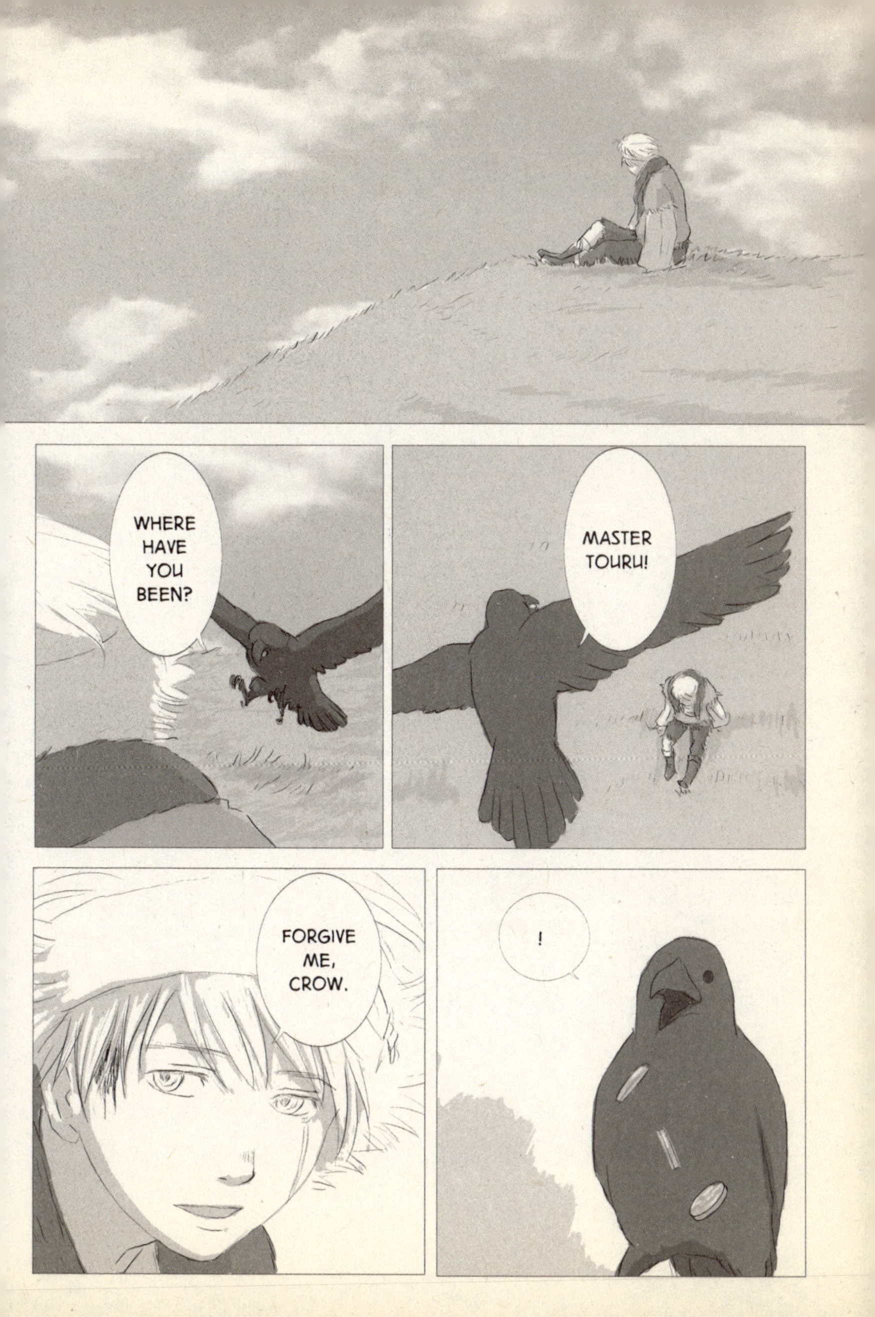
MASTER TOURU!
WHERE HAVE YOU BEEN?
!
FORGIVE ME, CROW.

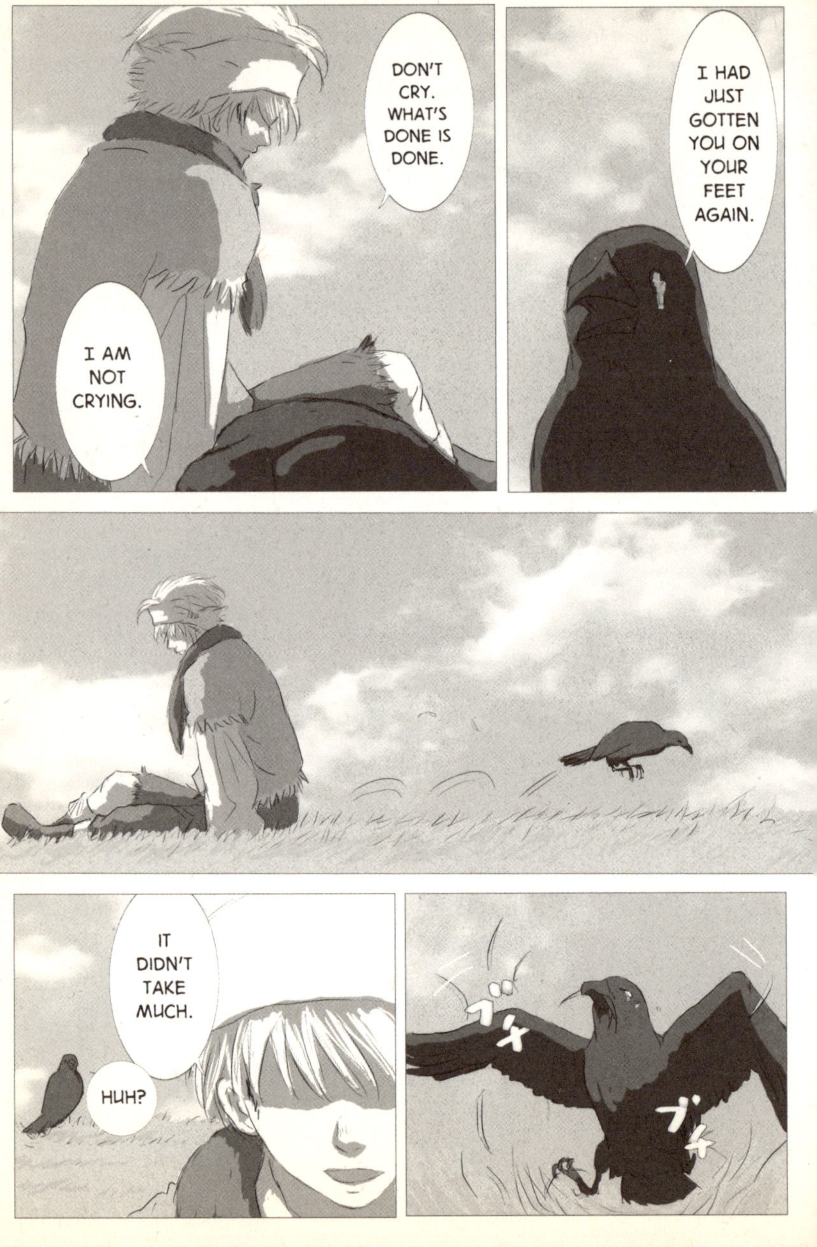
I HAD JUST GOTTEN YOU ON YOUR FEET AGAIN.
DON'T CRY. WHAT'S DONE IS DONE.
I AM NOT CRYING.
ブチ
ブチ
IT DIDN'T TAKE MUCH.
HUH?

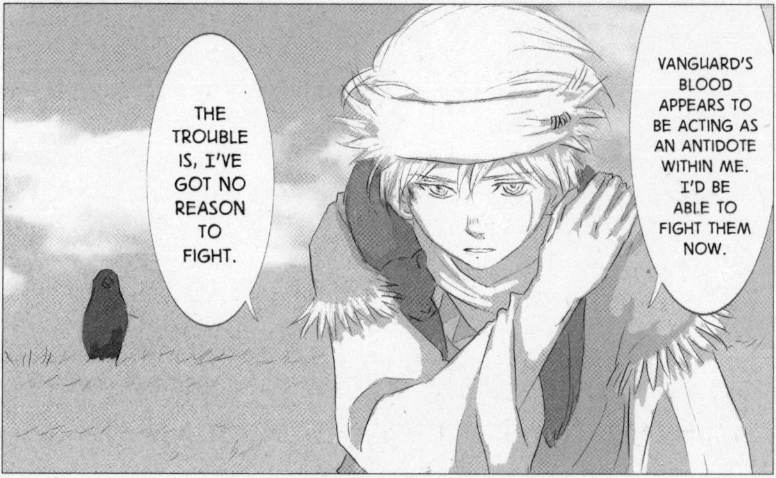
VANGUARD'S BLOOD APPEARS TO BE ACTING AS AN ANTIDOTE WITHIN ME. I'D BE ABLE TO FIGHT THEM NOW.
THE TROUBLE IS, I'VE GOT NO REASON TO FIGHT.

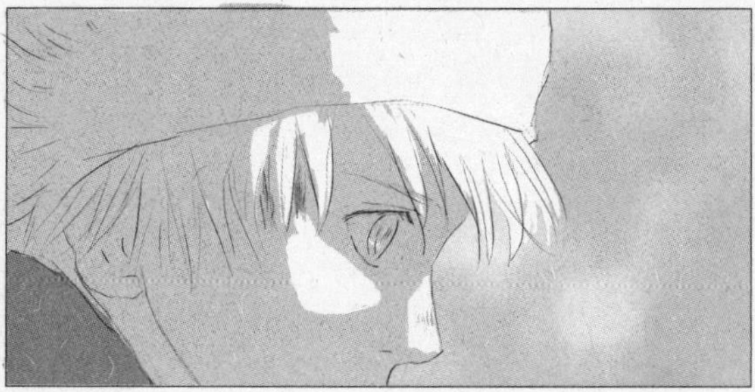

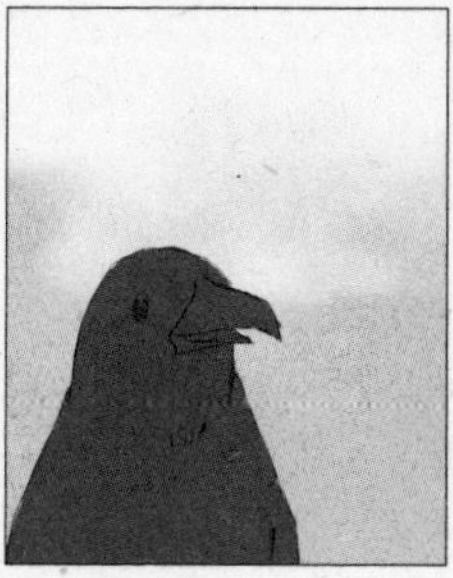

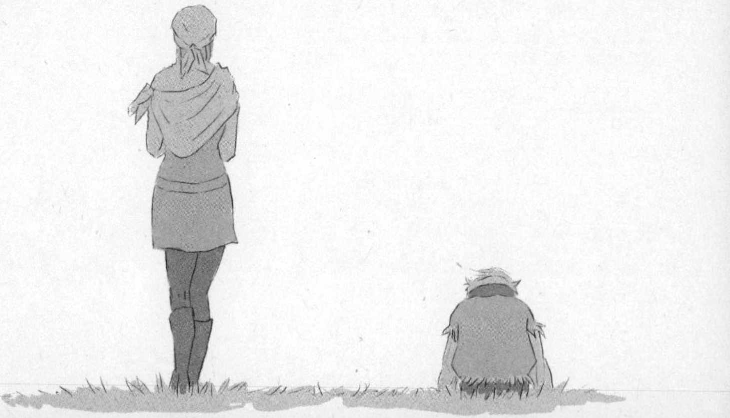

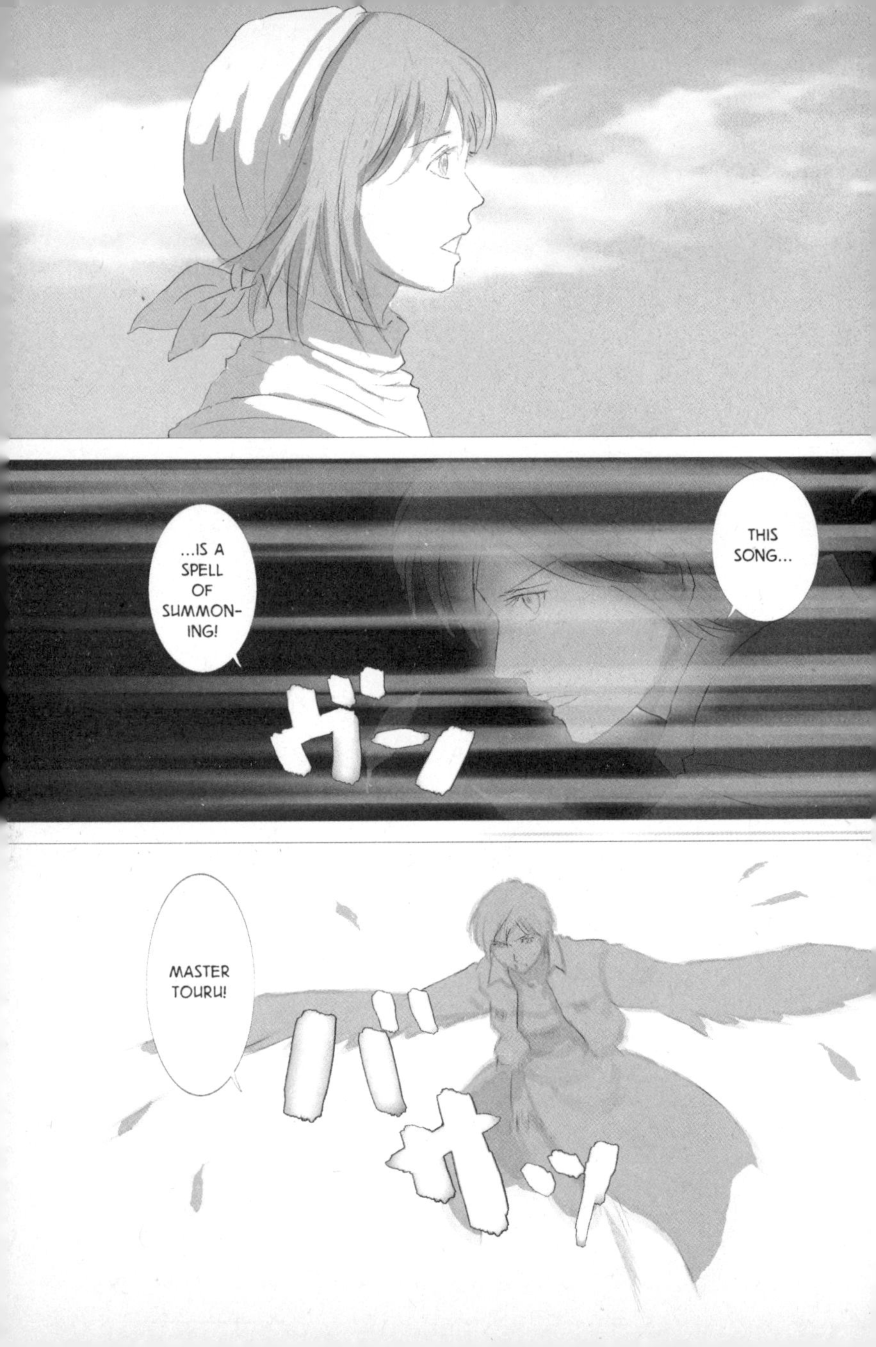
THIS SONG...
...IS A SPELL OF SUMMON-ING!
MASTER TOURU!

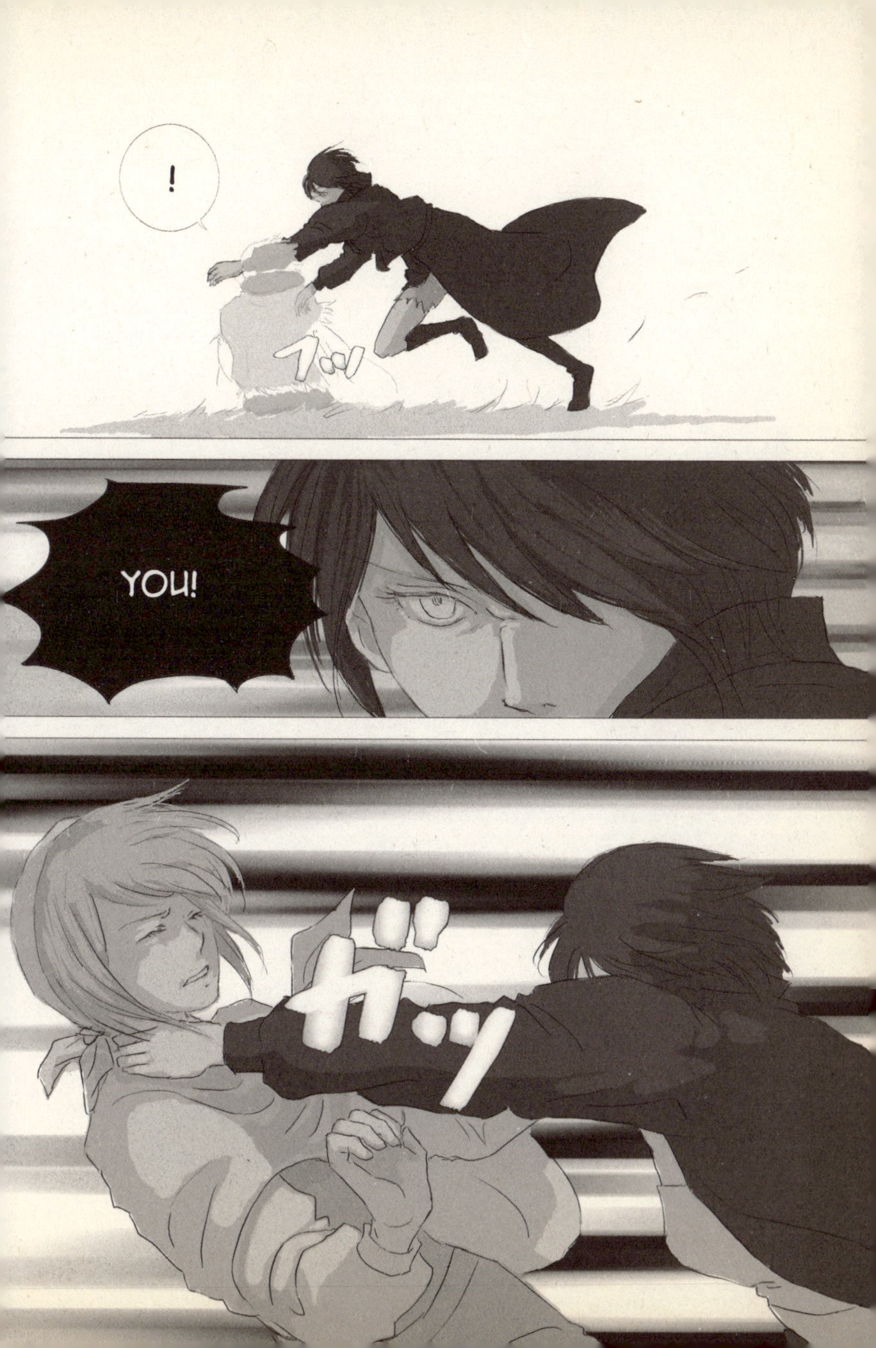
!
YOU!
ガッ

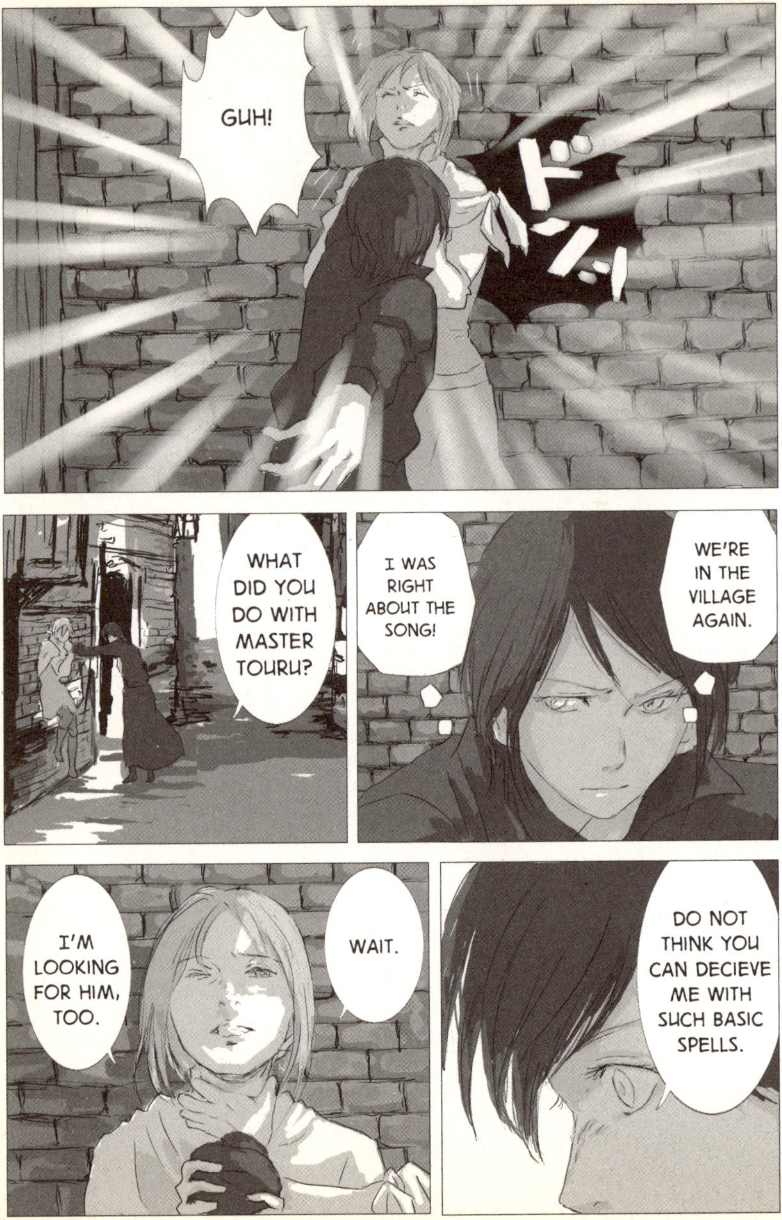
GUH!
WE'RE IN THE VILLAGE AGAIN.
I WAS RIGHT ABOUT THE SONG!
WHAT DID YOU DO WITH MASTER TOURU?
DO NOT THINK YOU CAN DECIEVE ME WITH SUCH BASIC SPELLS.
WAIT.
I'M LOOKING FOR HIM, TOO.

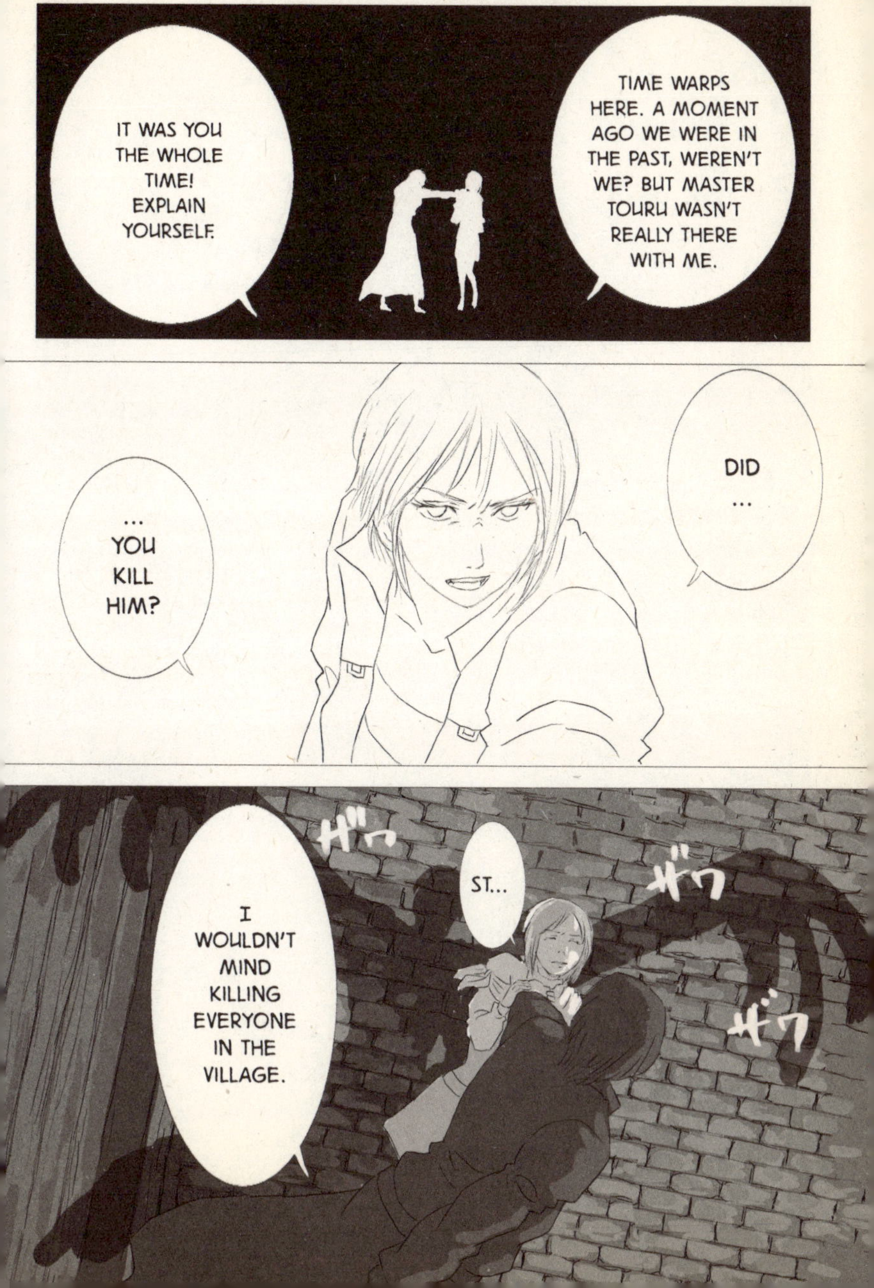
TIME WARPS HERE. A MOMENT AGO WE WERE IN THE PAST, WEREN'T WE? BUT MASTER TOURU WASN'T REALLY THERE WITH ME.
IT WAS YOU THE WHOLE TIME! EXPLAIN YOURSELF.
DID ...
... YOU KILL HIM?
ザワ
ザワ
ST...
ザワ
I WOULDN'T MIND KILLING EVERYONE IN THE VILLAGE.

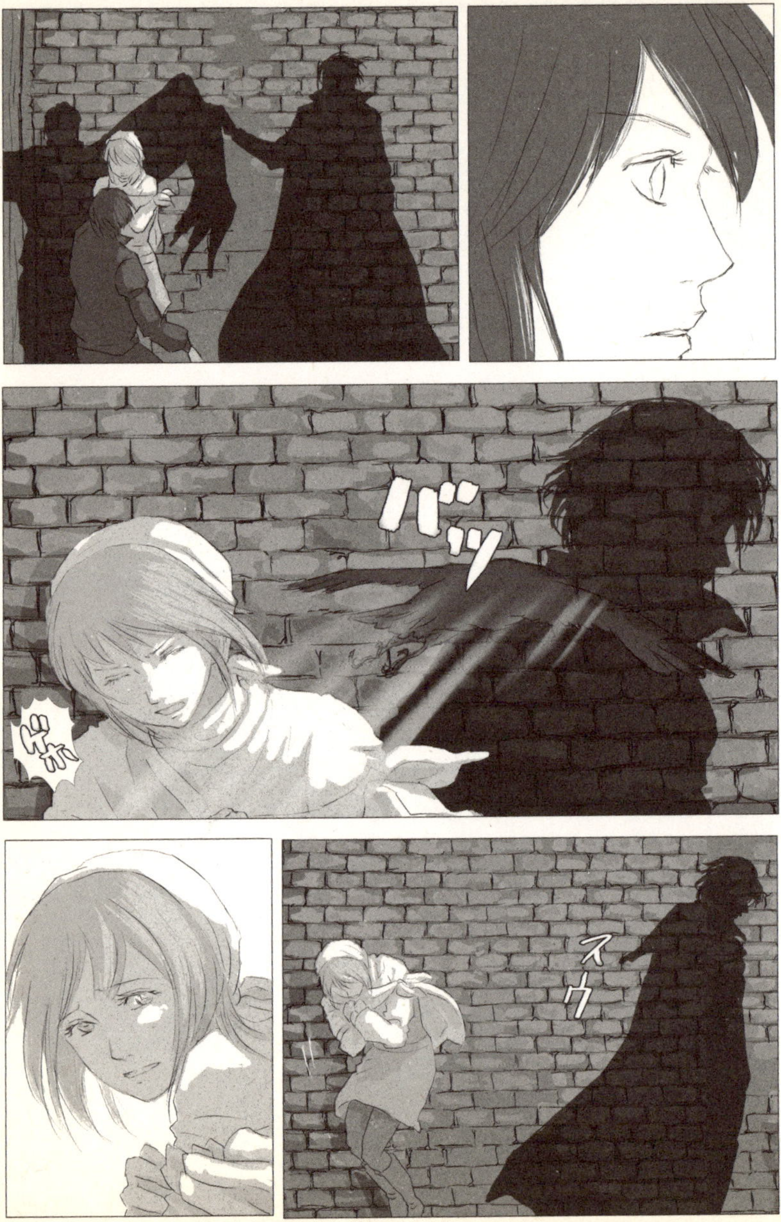
バッ
ドサ
スゥ

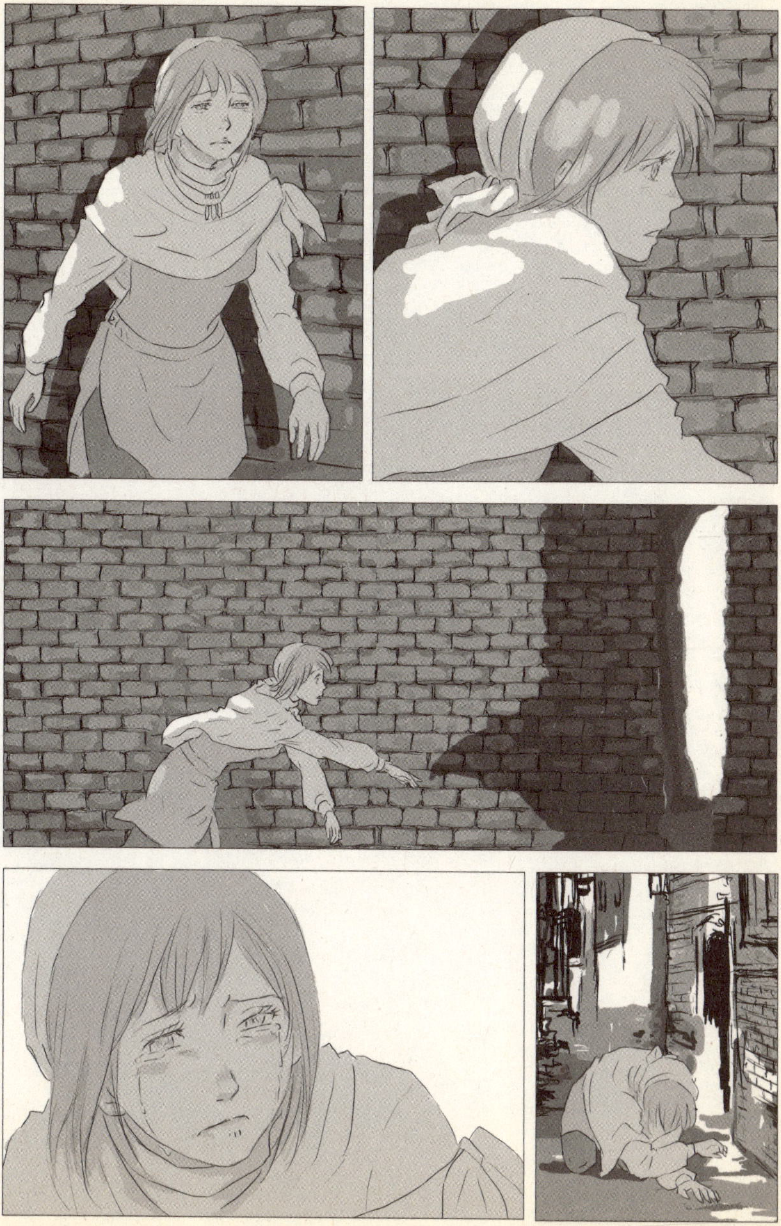

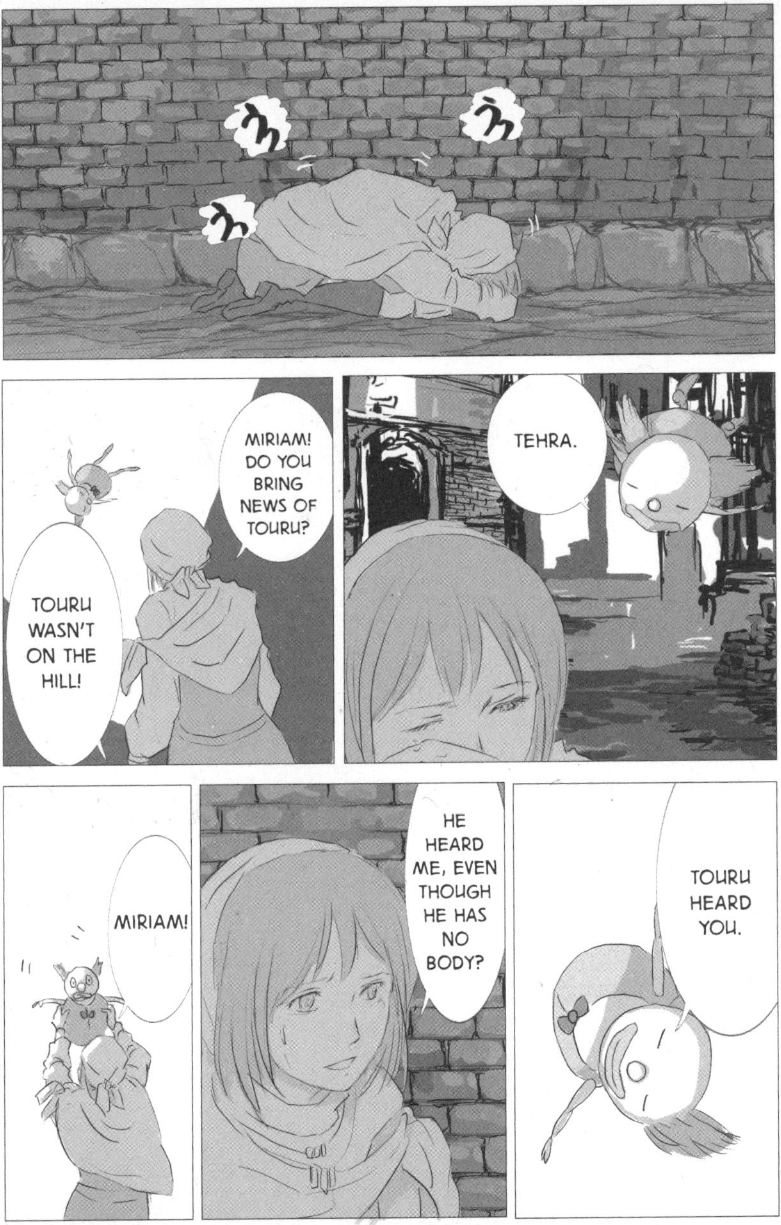
う
う
う
TEHRA.
MIRIAM! DO YOU BRING NEWS OF TOURU?
TOURU WASN'T ON THE HILL!
TOURU HEARD YOU.
HE HEARD ME, EVEN THOUGH HE HAS NO BODY?
MIRIAM!

YES, ONCE HE'S LEFT THE VILLAGE, MAYBE TOHRU CAN BE HAPPY.

IF THE FOG DOESN'T COME, TOMORROW WILL NEVER COME FOR THE VILLAGE. THE ANGELS' PLANS ARE IN MOTION. WE CAN'T TURN BACK.

TOHRU CAN.

THE FOG ISN'T COMING.

LOOK.

NO ONE COULD HAVE TAKEN HIS PLACE.

NO ONE ELSE COULD HAVE DONE IT.

TOHRU TOOK THE DISASTER WITH HIM.

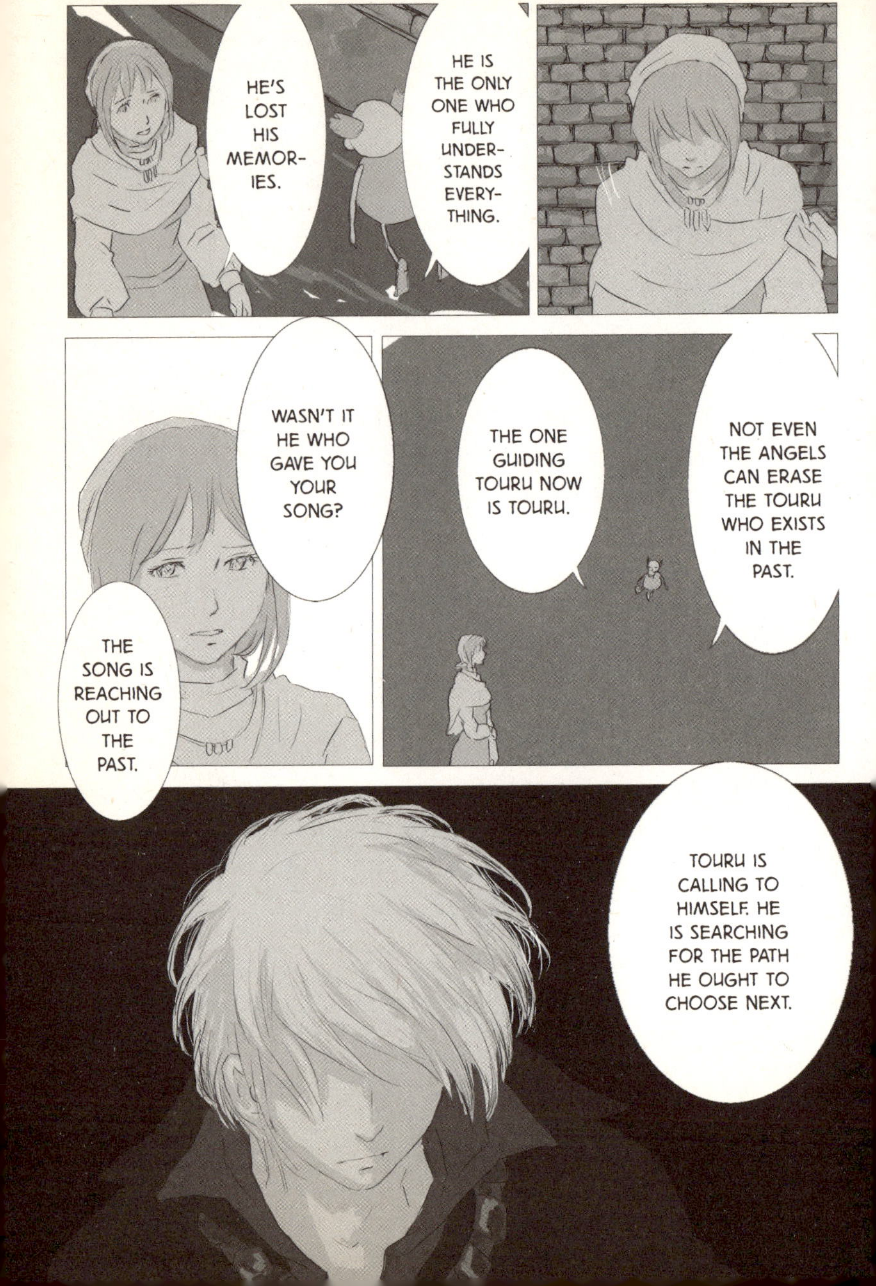
HE IS THE ONLY ONE WHO FULLY UNDER-STANDS EVERY-THING.
HE'S LOST HIS MEMOR-IES.
NOT EVEN THE ANGELS CAN ERASE THE TOURU WHO EXISTS IN THE PAST.
THE ONE GUIDING TOURU NOW IS TOURU.
WASN'T IT HE WHO GAVE YOU YOUR SONG?
THE SONG IS REACHING OUT TO THE PAST.
TOURU IS CALLING TO HIMSELF. HE IS SEARCHING FOR THE PATH HE OUGHT TO CHOOSE NEXT.

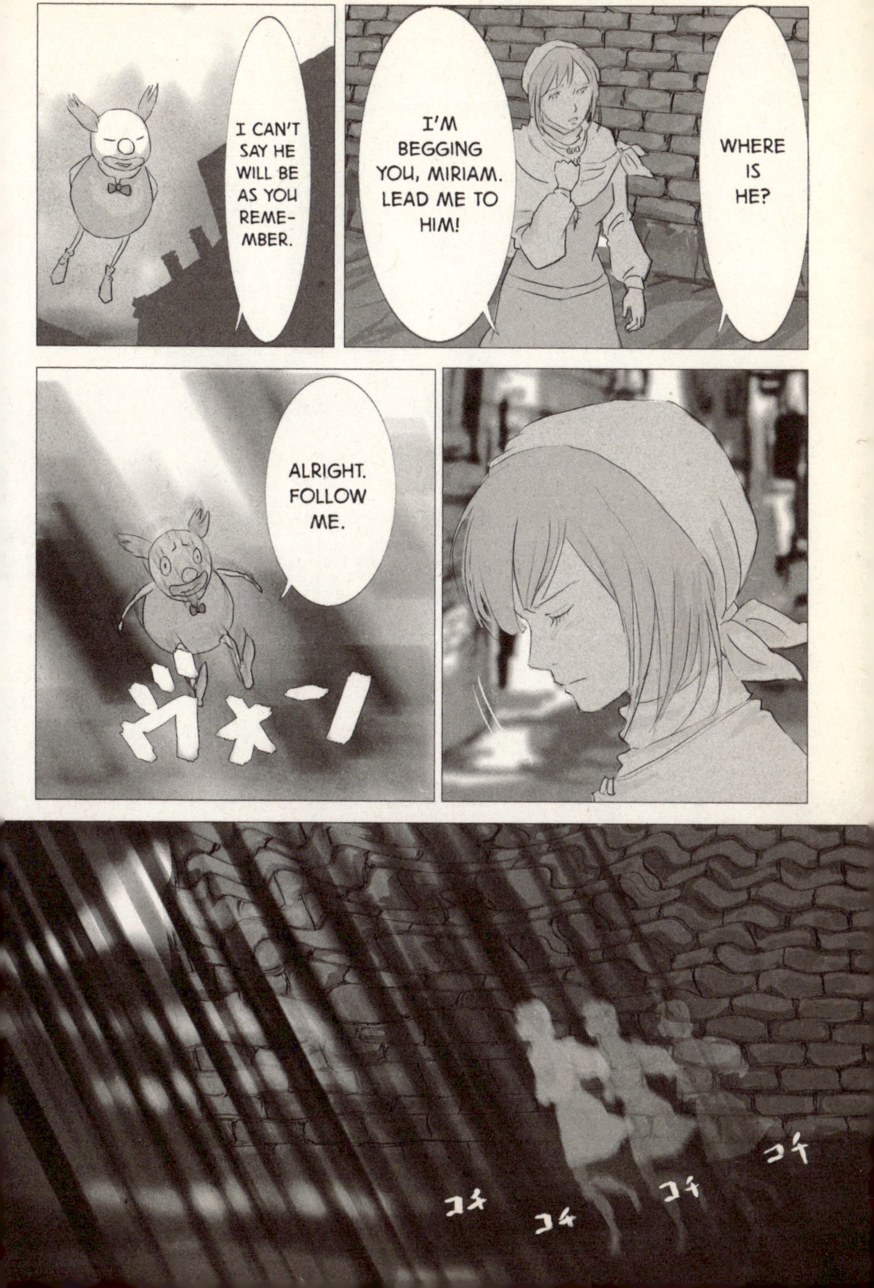
WHERE IS HE?
I'M BEGGING YOU, MIRIAM. LEAD ME TO HIM!
I CAN'T SAY HE WILL BE AS YOU REME-MBER.
ALRIGHT. FOLLOW ME.
コチ
コチ
コチ
コチ

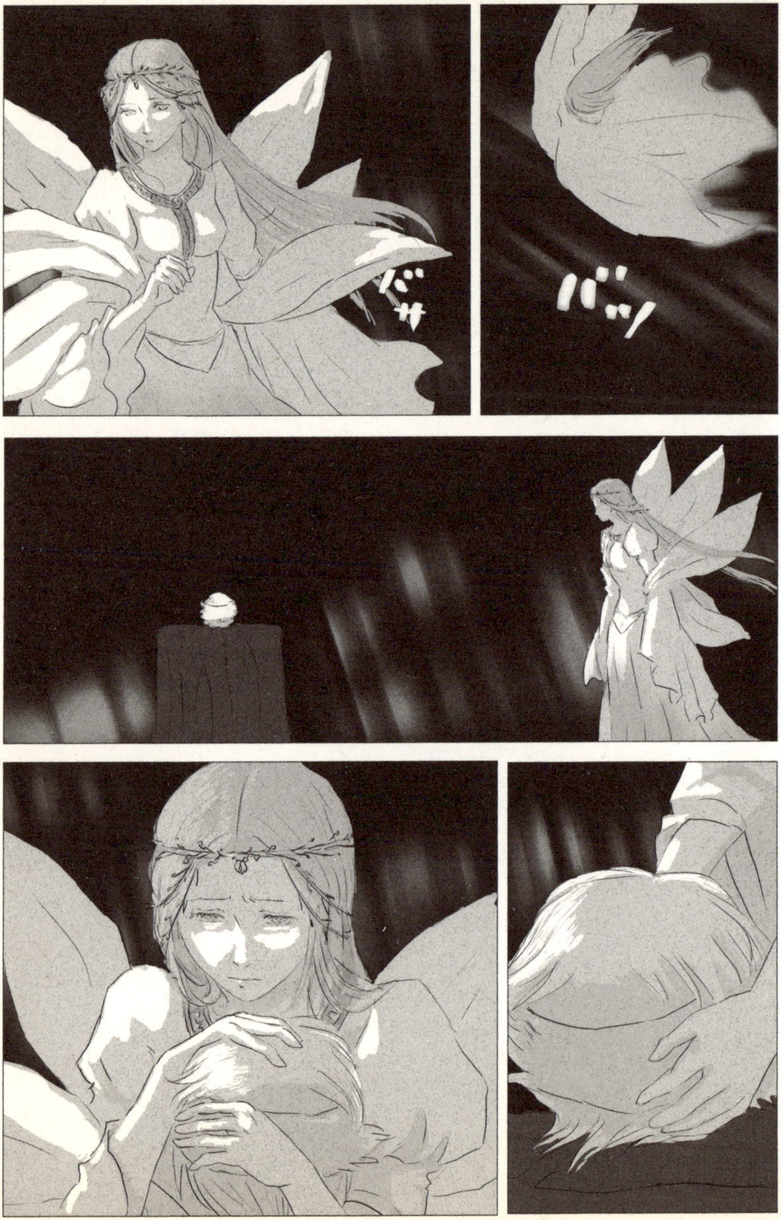
バッ!
バサ

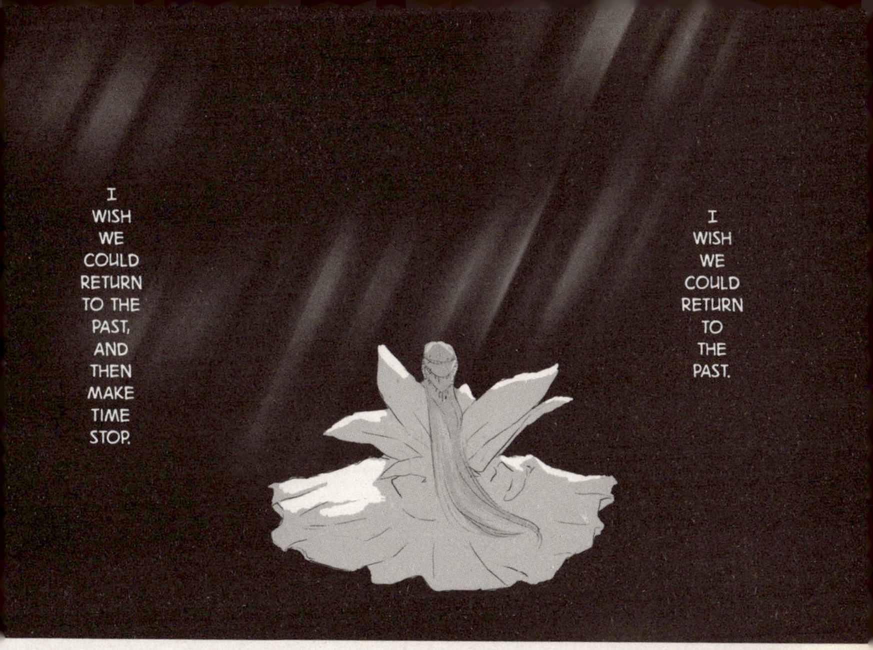
I WISH WE COULD RETURN TO THE PAST.
I WISH WE COULD RETURN TO THE PAST, AND THEN MAKE TIME STOP.
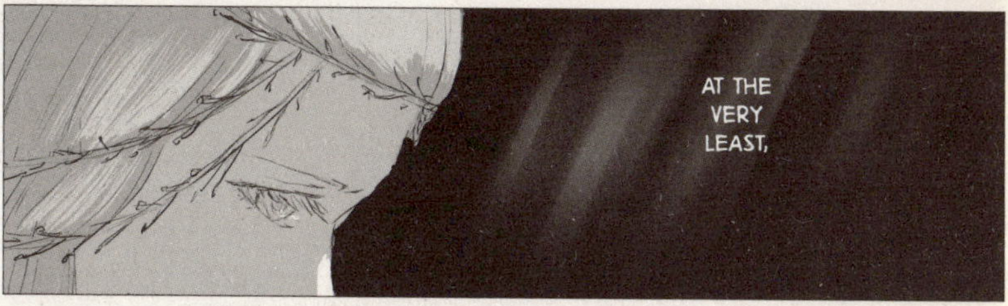
AT THE VERY LEAST,
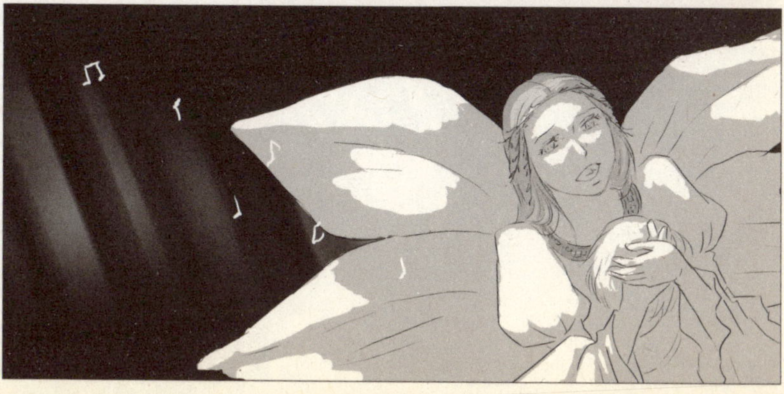

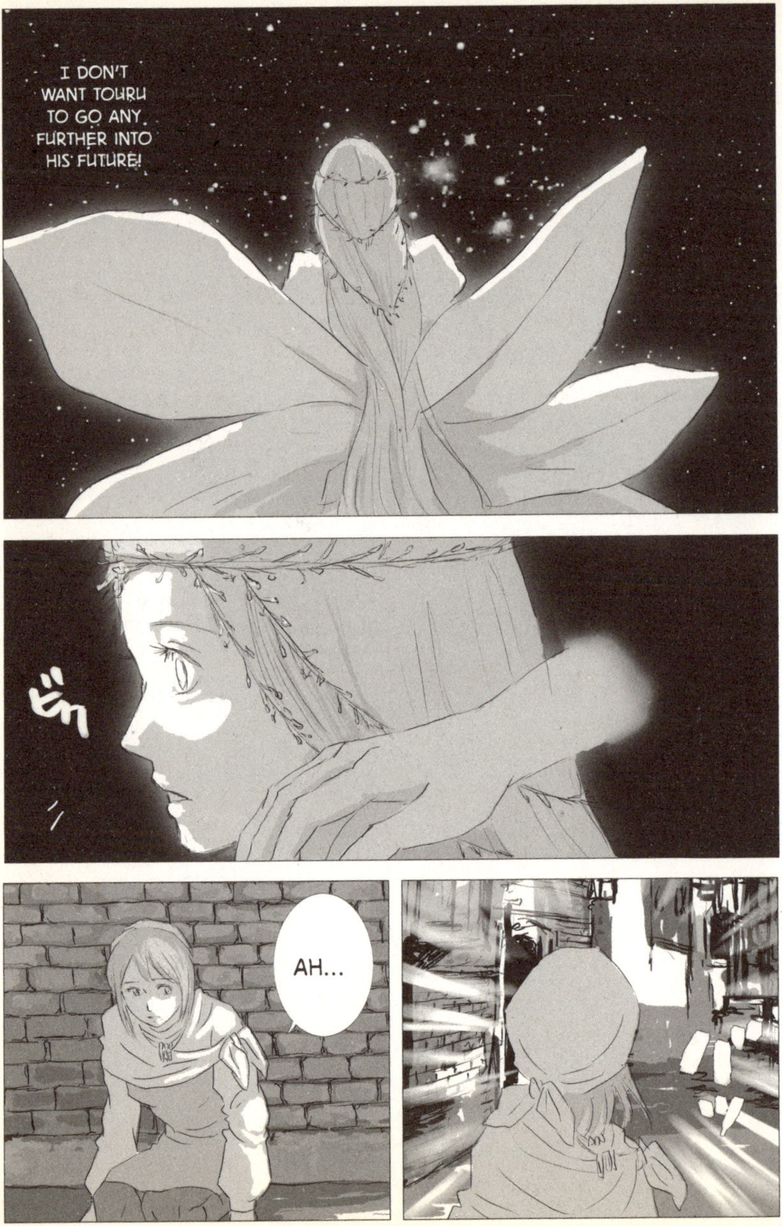
I DON'T WANT TOURU TO GO ANY FURTHER INTO HIS FUTURE!
AH...

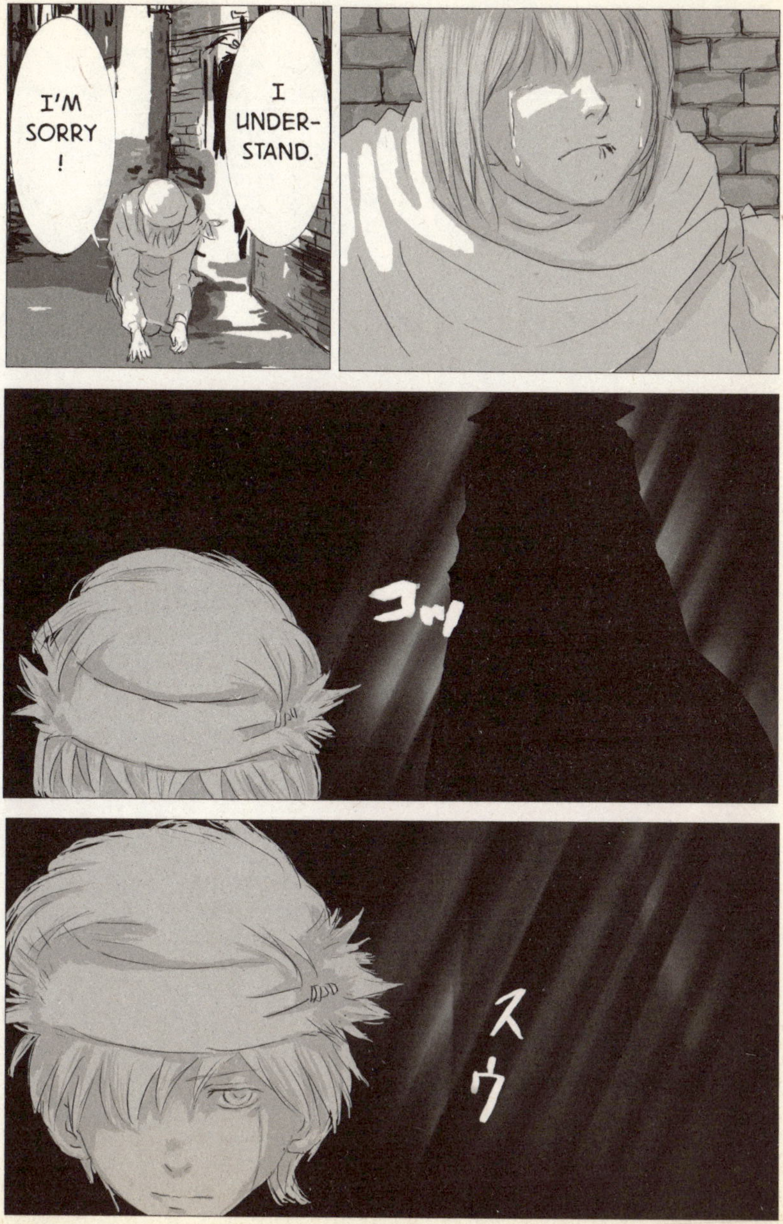
I UNDER-STAND.
I'M SORRY!
ゴッ
スウ

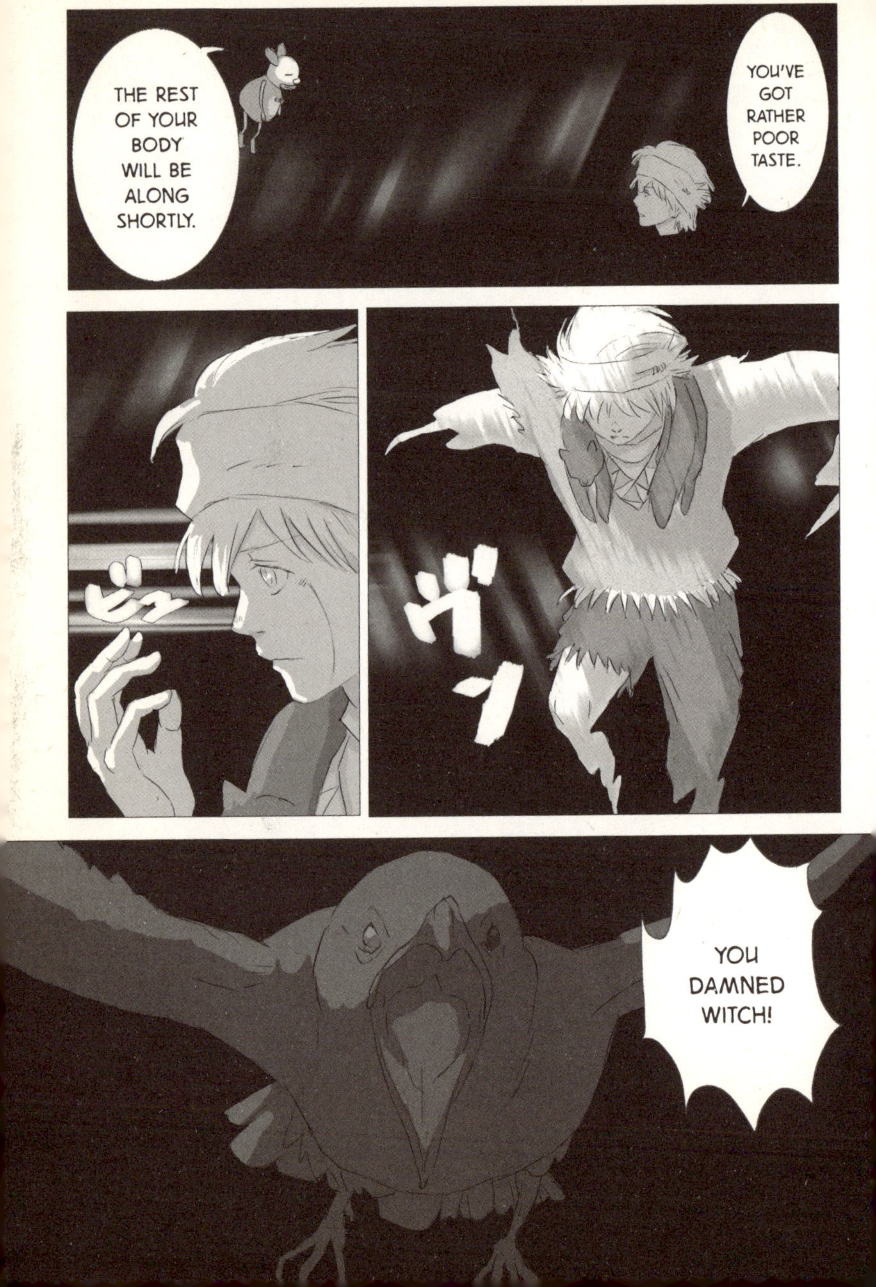
YOU'VE GOT RATHER POOR TASTE.
THE REST OF YOUR BODY WILL BE ALONG SHORTLY.
YOU DAMNED WITCH!

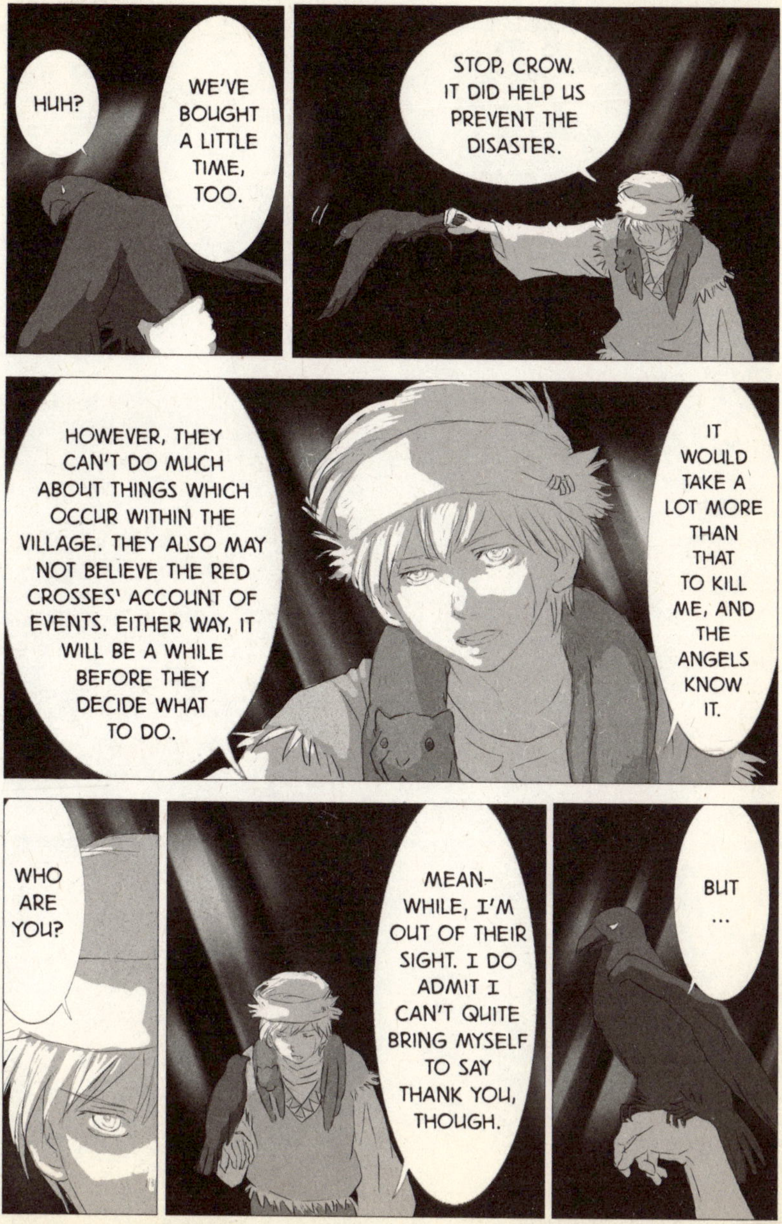
STOP, CROW. IT DID HELP US PREVENT THE DISASTER.
WE'VE BOUGHT A LITTLE TIME, TOO.
HUH?
IT WOULD TAKE A LOT MORE THAN THAT TO KILL ME, AND THE ANGELS KNOW IT.
HOWEVER, THEY CAN'T DO MUCH ABOUT THINGS WHICH OCCUR WITHIN THE VILLAGE. THEY ALSO MAY NOT BELIEVE THE RED CROSSES' ACCOUNT OF EVENTS. EITHER WAY, IT WILL BE A WHILE BEFORE THEY DECIDE WHAT TO DO.
BUT ...
MEAN-WHILE, I'M OUT OF THEIR SIGHT. I DO ADMIT I CAN'T QUITE BRING MYSELF TO SAY THANK YOU, THOUGH.
WHO ARE YOU?

I'M MIRIAM. MORE ACCURATELY, I'M ONE-SEVENTH OF MIRIAM.
YOU SHOULD REST UNTIL THE REMAINDER OF ME REJOINS YOU.
キイ

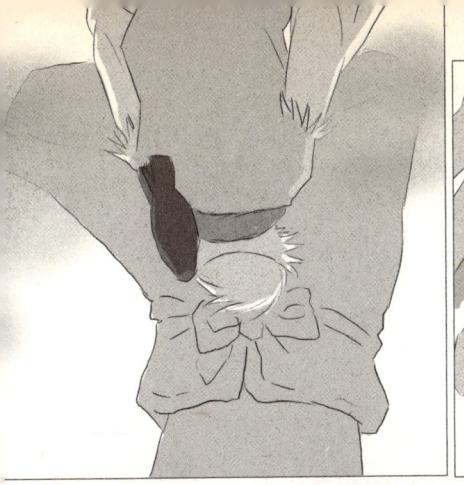

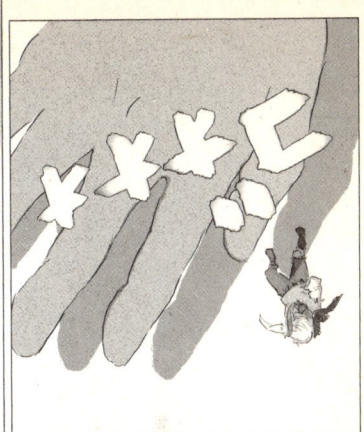

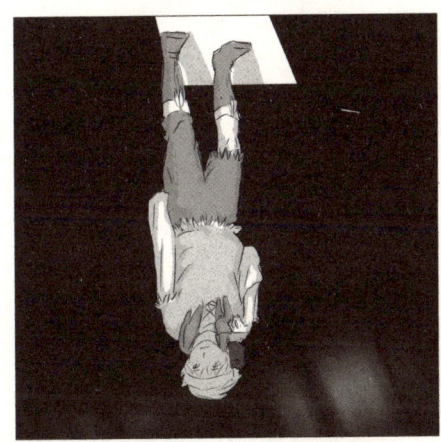

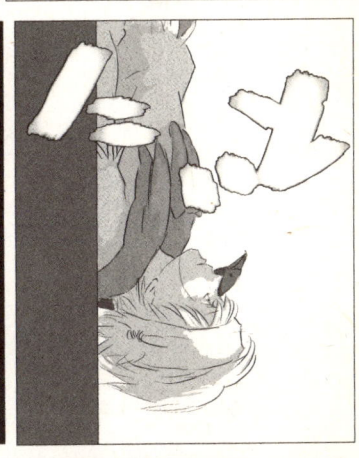

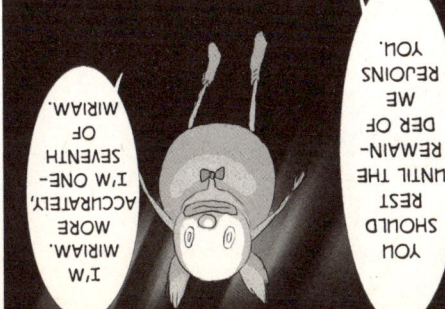

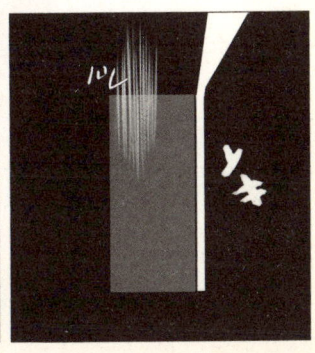

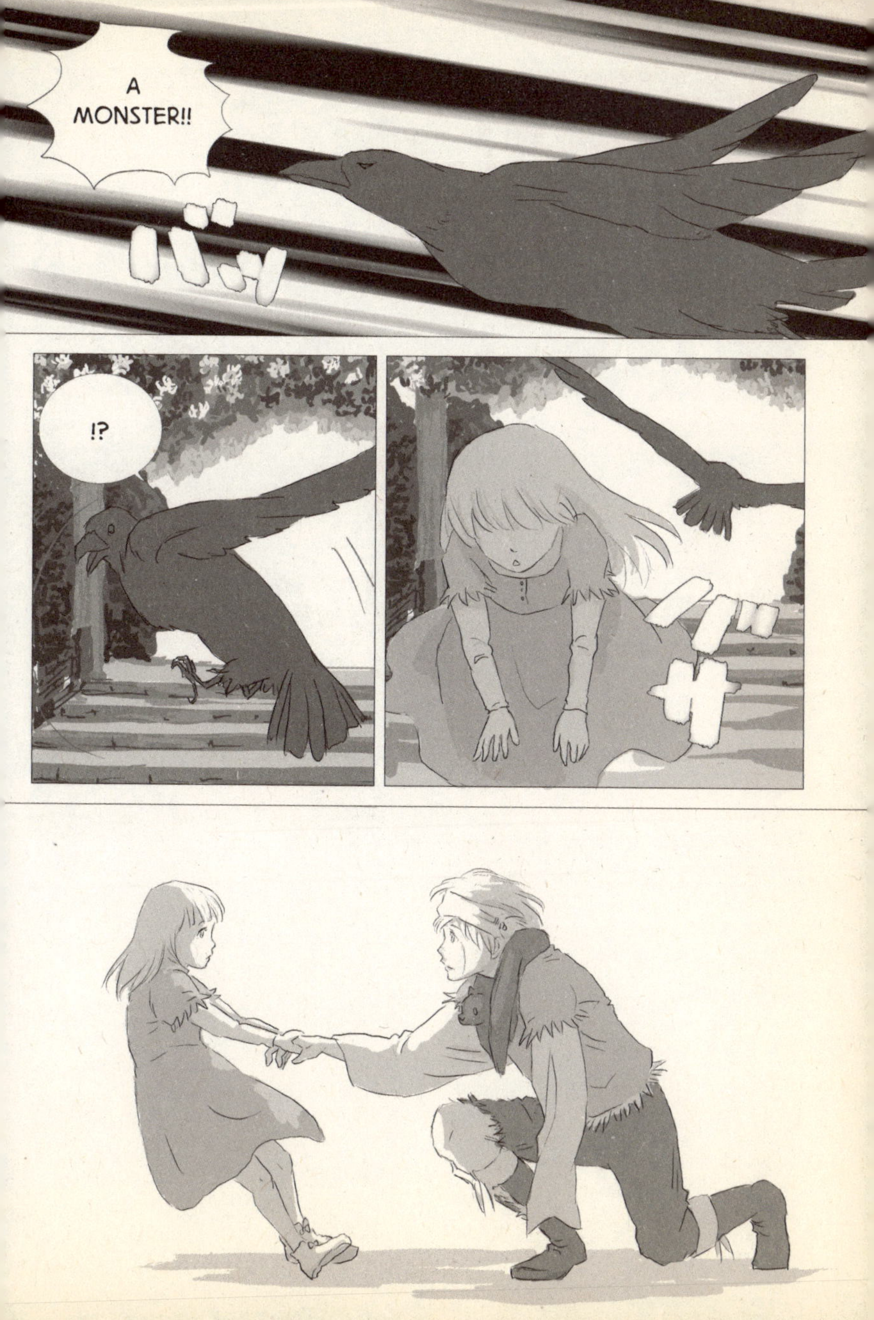
A MONSTER!!
!?

IT TRICKED US WITH MAGIC!

SO IT SEEMS.

WE'RE AT A LONE HOUSE APART FROM THE VILLAGE.

……

?

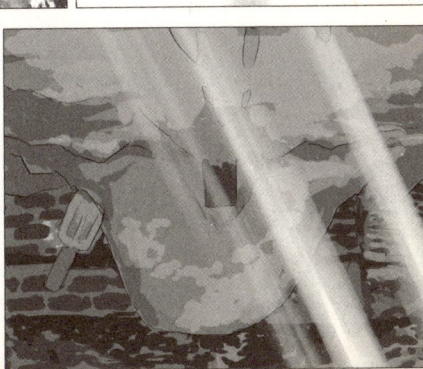

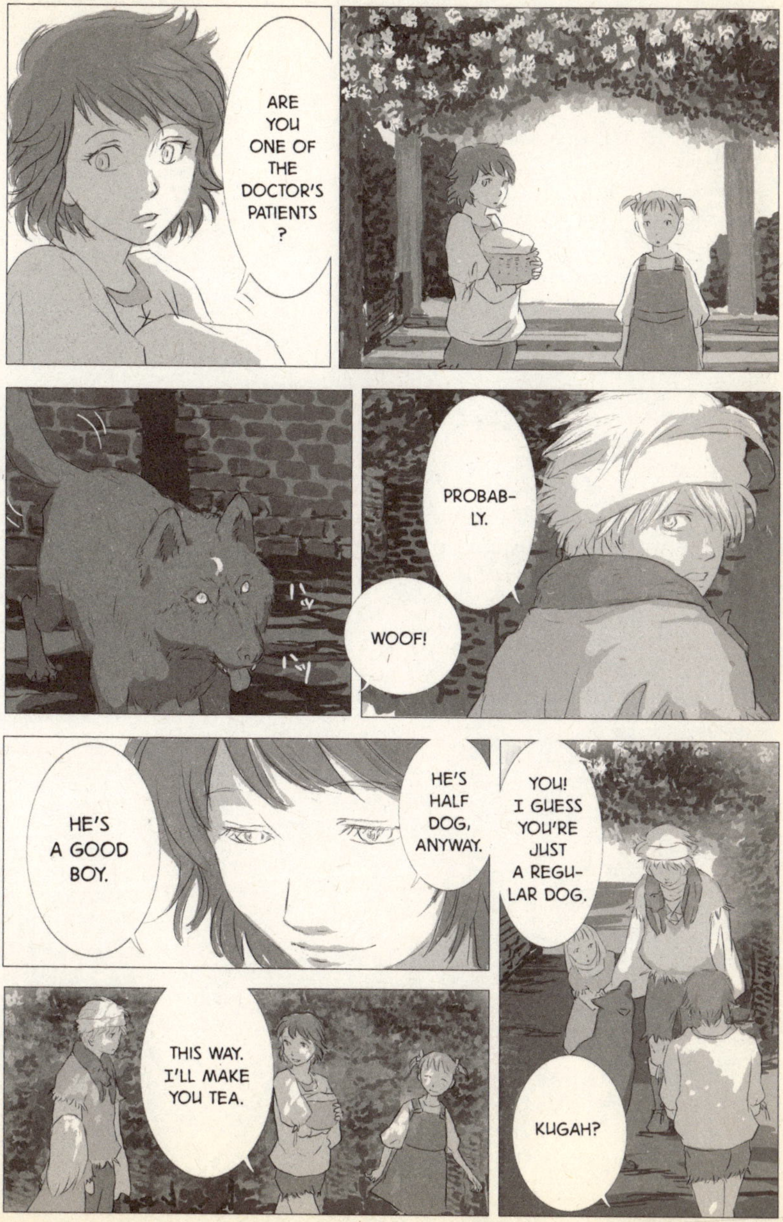
ARE YOU ONE OF THE DOCTOR'S PATIENTS ?
PROBAB-LY.
WOOF!
YOU! I GUESS YOU'RE JUST A REGU-LAR DOG.
KUGAH?
HE'S HALF DOG, ANYWAY.
HE'S A GOOD BOY.
THIS WAY. I'LL MAKE YOU TEA.

ESTEL!

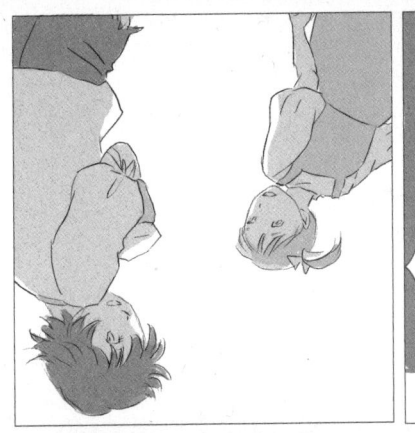

ARE WE IN AN ORPHAN-AGE?

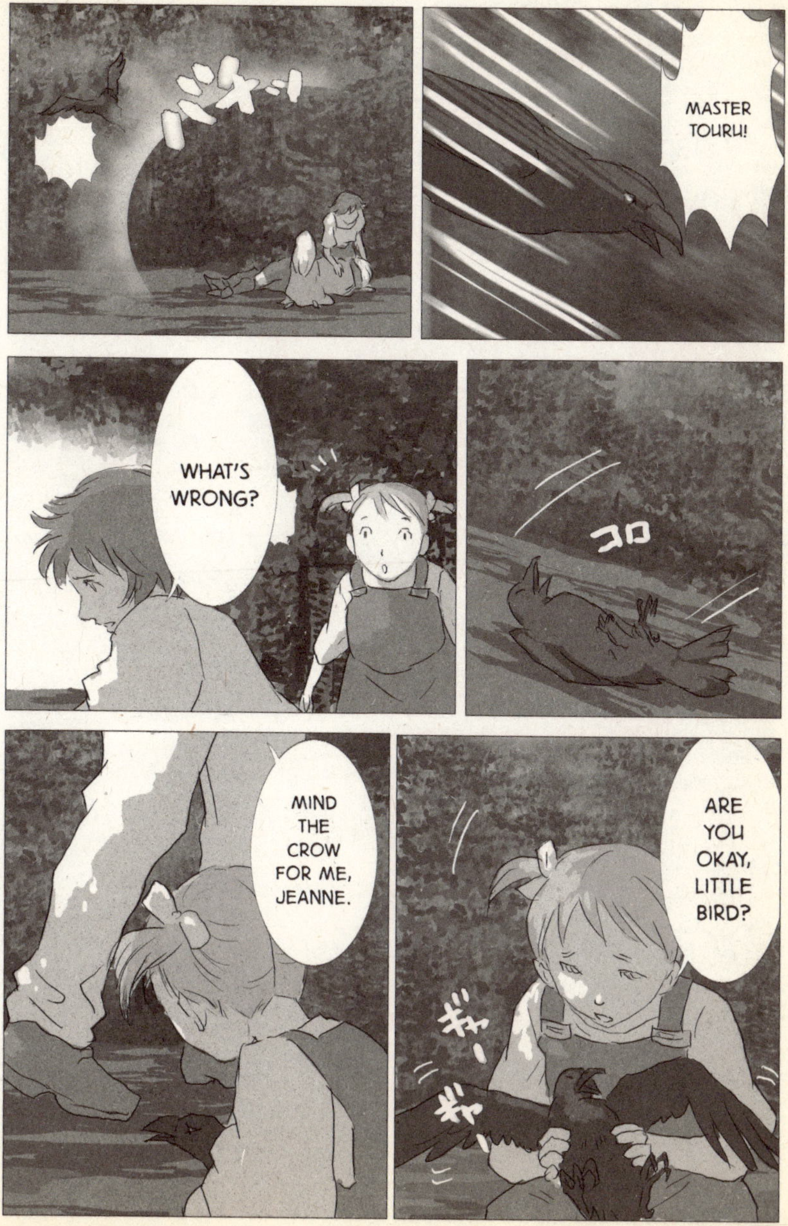
MASTER TOURU!
コロ
WHAT'S WRONG?
ARE YOU OKAY, LITTLE BIRD?
ギャ
ギャ
MIND THE CROW FOR ME, JEANNE.

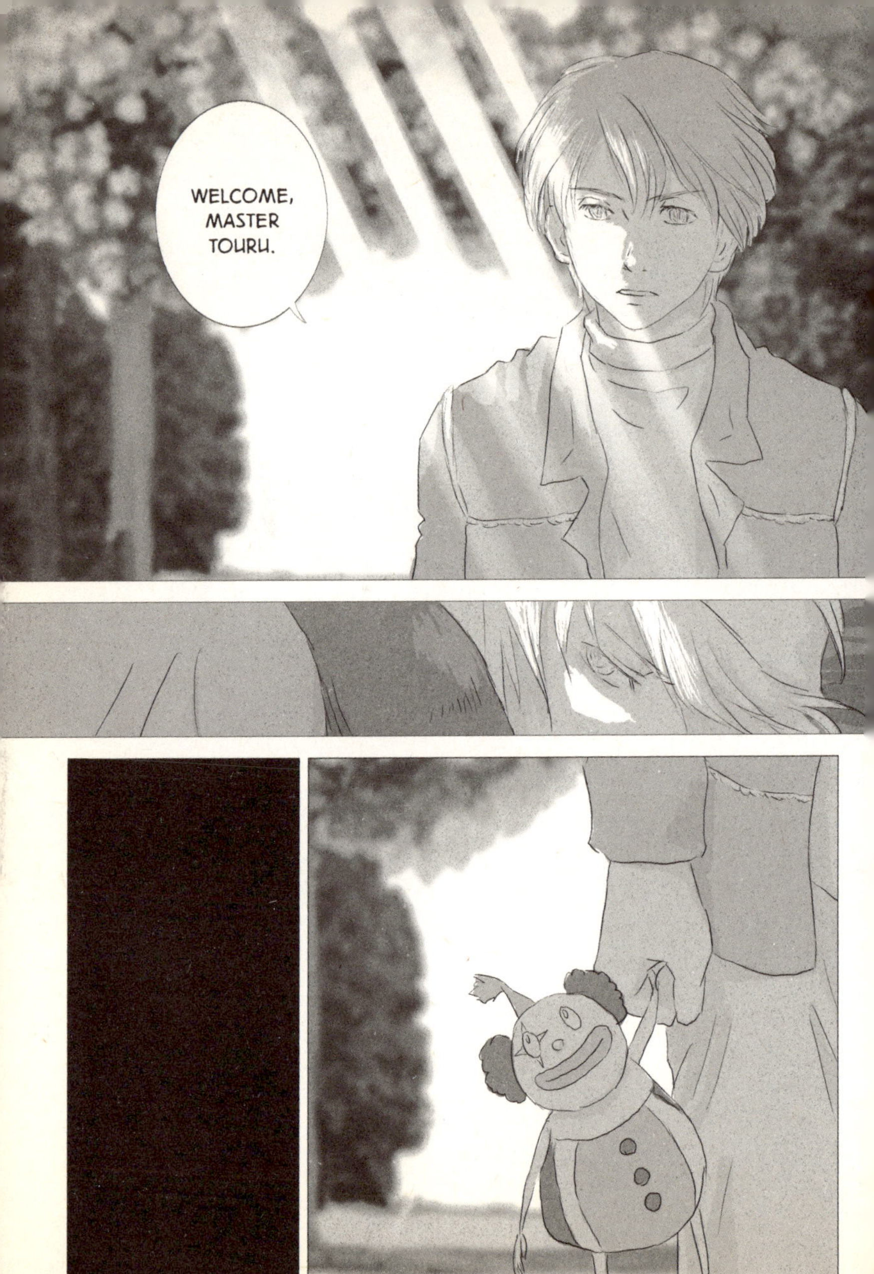
WELCOME, MASTER TOURU.

GEN
MANGA

INDIE MANGA FROM THE TOKYO UNDERGROUND

GEN STORIES ARE PUBLISHED NOWHERE ELSE IN THE WORLD. THEY COME STRAIGHT FROM THE ARTISTS IN JAPAN TO YOU. WE TRANSLATE THE STORIES AND PUT THEM OUT AS THEY ARE CREATED.